Secret of Ekaterinburg: The Hour-Glass

BY

Robert Spirko

Olive Grove Books, New York

Secret of Ekaterinburg: The Hour-Glass

Sale of this book without a front cover may be unauthorized. If this book has no cover, it may have been reported to the publisher as not sold or destroyed and neither the author nor the publisher may have received payment for the book.

All rights reserved under International and Pan-American Copyright Conventions. Published in the United States by Olive Grove Publishers, Medina, Ohio.

www.atlasbooks.com

Secret of Ekaterinburg: The Hour-Glass
ISBN: 978-0-9752508-3-9
Copyright, 1992, 1997, 2013 by Robert Spirko
Olive Grove Books is an imprint of Olive Grove Publishers, Medina, Ohio.

First Edition
Printed & Distributed by Bookmasters, Inc., Mansfield, Ohio www.bookmasters.com
1-800-BOOKLOG for book orders.

Secret of Ekaterinburg: The Hour-Glass

This is a work of fiction. The events described here are imaginary; the settings and characters are fictitious and not intended to represent specific places or living persons. All characters in this book have no existence outside the imagination of the author and have no relation whatsoever to anyone bearing the same name or names. None of the characters are distantly inspired by any individual known or unknown to the author, and all incidents are pure fiction.

The Central Intelligence Agency and the NSA have not approved, endorsed, or authorized this production or the use of the C.I.A. or NSA name, initials, or seal.

Cover design by Jason Alexander of ExpertSubjects.com

Secret of Ekaterinburg: The Hour-Glass

Books by Robert Spirko

The Palestine Conspiracy

Secret of Ekaterinburg: The Hour-Glass

Secret of Ekaterinburg: The Hour-Glass

SYNOPSIS

From the best-selling author of The Palestine Conspiracy who predicted the Intifada, the Persian Gulf War, and the liberation of Libya, Robert Spirko's new novel, the Secret of Ekaterinburg: The Hour-Glass, reveals a tale of intrigue, love, hope and historical consequence when justice meant revolution and freedom meant escape.

Starting with the brutal murder of Czar Nicholas II and his family in Ekaterinburg ordered by Lenin's Bolsheviks, suddenly, out of Russia, comes a family that holds deep and ordained secrets that can unlock the shackles of misery for millions.

In remembrance of this historic carnage, one person escaped to tell the truth of that fateful night after a Lenin death squad executed the Romanov family in cold blood without trial. Then, as now, only a few knew the real truth behind the Bolshevik motives that led to the untold thousands who would succumb to Trotsky's and Stalin's deadly purges. Relax, if

Secret of Ekaterinburg: The Hour-Glass

you can, as you begin a veiled journey into the evil depths of red terror, of secret murderous deals by Beria and his Cheka and NKVD killers.

Sergei Boscov and Andre Kirov, two boyhood friends, raised on a dacha in the Urals, kindle a lifelong brotherhood, even as they go their separate ways – Andre to a political career; Sergei to a military one – do they finally discover who their sister "Ana" really was. In a stunning conclusion, they become interlocked in a saga of espionage and deception which holds the lives of millions in the balance.

From the Urals to Moscow, from Langley to London, and from Tehran to Jerusalem, Spirko weaves a spy-thriller that will ensnare the world in a crisis of colossal proportion as CIA analyst Alex Ayers discovers that nuclear missiles are headed for Iran in exchange for this "miracle" of Ana. When you realize what is happening, it's too late. The Secret of Ekaterinburg has the power to restore everything.

Remember, 1918 is now.

And, the future may never come.

Secret of Ekaterinburg: The Hour-Glass

Photo courtesy of About.com

Secret of Ekaterinburg: The Hour-Glass

ACKNOWLEDGEMENTS:

To the people of the Free World, the United States and Russia who finally made peace for the betterment of mankind.

Israel and Palestine should make peace. If two cold war nations - the Soviet Union and the United States - can do it, then why not the Israelis and the Palestinians?

Neither are an invented people.

They have lived together for thousands of years and must do so in whatever future they have. Only they can determine that.

Robert Spirko, author

Secret of Ekaterinburg: The Hour-Glass

Forward

On July 17, 1918, the family of Czar Nicholas II of Russia was brutally murdered in a basement of the Ipatiev House, a local official's residence, in Ekaterinburg, a Ural Mountain mining town of a half-million inhabitants. The brutal executions took place viciously and without warning.

A number of factors were later cited for the swiftness and cruelty of this dreadful historic episode. No other Russian Royal Family had ever been subjected to the kind of dehumanizing disgrace as a result of the 1917 Russian Revolution orchestrated by Vladimir Ilich Lenin and his band of revolutionaries who successfully faced-off the Czar and his loyalist subjects - referred to as the White Russians.

The revolutionaries, who later became known as "Reds" or Bolsheviks-working class, stood-off the proletariats (White Russians or monarchists) for months and even years afterward, but so many were fed up with their lives, they soon joined the masses and overthrew the Czar's officials eventually installing a provisional revolutionary government to carry out the philosophies of Lenin and his allies. It has now been learned

Secret of Ekaterinburg: The Hour-Glass

from old KGB archives uncovered in 1991 that the actual order to execute the Romanov family was made by a personal written order from Vladimir Lenin himself. Unknown to the Romanov's, just prior to the murders, the White Army were only hours away from a rescue attempt involving the help of a Czech brigade of volunteers which had linked up with locals. Unbelievably and horrifically, before they could reach them, the entire Romanov family was murdered that night - Czar Nicholas II, his wife Empress Alexandra; daughters-duchesses Olga, Marie, Tatiana and Anastasia; and, a son and true heir to the throne, Tsaravich Alexi. Also murdered were the Romanov family's personal physician Dr. Evgenii Botkin; Aleksei Trupp, valet; Anna Demidova, housemaid; and Ivan Kharitonov, cook – eleven in all. A kitchen boy, Leonid Sednev, was called from the house earlier and escaped the killings. The bodies were later transported and buried in a local abandoned mineshaft of the Four Brothers Mine. The murders were kept secret for weeks, but eventually the execution squad had to return to the scene to re-bury the remains of the Romanov family once the secret was learned by local villagers. Fearing revenge, the bodies were moved to a new secret location, when

Secret of Ekaterinburg: The Hour-Glass

their truck broke down and they had to re-bury the remains in makeshift graves, the bodies once again burned with gasoline and then soaked with sulfuric acid rendering them unrecognizable. Now, uncovered from secret KGB archives in the old Soviet Union, actual KGB historians reveal the entire account and the many unknown details as to why the Romanov's were brutally executed. With the cooperation of the United States Central Intelligence Agency and identification made possible by elaborate DNA testing by forensic scientists from Great Britain and the Bethesda Naval Hospital, in Maryland, it was established that the remains of the Czar and the members of the family were indeed authentic from DNA samples from the British Royal family, German Kaiser Wilhelm and Czar Nicholas II. Autopsies and exhaustive forensic examinations were performed on the remains in 1991 when the burial locations were found by former KGB and Red Army officers. In 1992, then Secretary of State James Baker of the Bush Administration traveled to Saint-Petersburg and Ekaterinburg and witnessed actual autopsy proceedings where Russian forensic examiners made tentative identification of the remains and autopsy

Secret of Ekaterinburg: The Hour-Glass

samples available to western technicians which eventually proved beyond-a-shadow-of-a-doubt that the remains indeed were those of the Romanov family. Each of the family members were identified with the exception of one - that one individual remains unaccounted for and is still missing. That lone unaccounted person is Princess Anastasia Nicholaevna Romanov.

Both the first and second burial sites were searched and re-searched extensively then excavated again, but no trace of Anastasia was ever found.

Did she survive the terrible murders as the rumors suggested over the years?

Rumors persist to this day.

But, beyond that, this is the real story of the nearly 100-year-old mystery of what actually may have happened to Princess Anastasia Nicholaevna Romanov.

Mr. Spirko completed the first draft of THE SECRET OF EKATERINBURG: THE HOUR-GLASS, in 1992. Because of uncertain events in Russia, the manuscript was held until such time as threats to the democratic reforms by Mikhail Gorbachev and Boris Yeltsin became a thing of the past. But, the threats are there anew and worries about the future of Russia persist to this day.

Secret of Ekaterinburg: The Hour-Glass

Perhaps, **Sir Winston Churchill** said it best.
"Russia is a riddle, wrapped in a mystery, inside an enigma."

Secret of Ekaterinburg: The Hour-Glass

CHAPTER 1

The Ural Mountains, Peregrebnoye, After the revolution.

Ignoring the sting of the Siberian chill on their faces, the seven-year-olds scampered after each other in the autumn shadows of the Urals. The wind chilled the air dropping down over the mountain peaks twenty miles to the east, but already at this young age they were immune to the cold.

Snow-capped and exhibiting a ravaged tree-line where life begins and life ends, the Urals were a majestic tribute to a rugged way of existence. The mountains were magnificent and mystical in nature. To the average Russian, the Urals were the embodiment of what was held spiritually important. Somehow, the Urals brought a sense of control to those living within their shadows.

Through the centuries, the Russians survived, and in the process, they learned to outlast their enemies during the cruel Siberian

Secret of Ekaterinburg: The Hour-Glass

winters.

Andre and the other boy, who at one time lived a few miles away, were running around the field in circles mimicking a make-believe vengeance.

"Andre! Andre!" called Tanya. "You must come now at once. Supper is ready. Everyone is at the table."

They wheeled around from their game and ran full-tilt toward the farmhouse where heavy white smoke was billowing from the stone chimney of the dacha's ornate, bulbous Byzantine roof.

Hemlocks dwarfed the main house, its carpentry an artistic expression of an earlier time, even though the dacha had been built a mere twenty-five years earlier by Andre's father who had carefully crafted a beautiful cottage-farmhouse, numerous sheds and two barns on 500 acres of land somehow forgotten by the Bolsheviks. Andre's friend, Sergei Boscov, hadn't been so lucky. They had taken over his small dacha following the death of his parents and turned it into one of hundreds of collective farms in the area.

The hemlocks swirled in the wind. The boys were now in a breakneck race to the back porch when they clambered to a stop in front of

Secret of Ekaterinburg: The Hour-Glass

Tanya, the family matriarch.

Dressed in her usual yellow babushka and white apron, she was the one they knew who meant business, giving them an unsympathetic look while inspecting their hands.

"Da. You must wash before you touch the food," she reprimanded.

The others were waiting at the table for Andre and Sergei to join them. Three older sons, Anatoly, Alexander, and Mikhail; sister, Kasha; and Sergei's foster sister, Ana, giggled as the boys were marched into the kitchen.

They washed up in embarrassed silence without any conversation except the sound of Kasha's and Ana's occasional taunts, then reluctantly took their places at the huge oak supper table. Oiled serving plates were already piled with steaming food, harvested from the summer and preserved from an underground food crypt. But no one would dare touch any of the food until after the prayers were spoken.

Andre's father acknowledged the two at the table with a welcoming gesture to be seated, and with heads bowed, he gave thanks for Sergei's and Ana's comradeship. Russian families took special care of each other in this rural land like no other families in the world. Coupled with a strong belief in Deity and

Secret of Ekaterinburg: The Hour-Glass

country, everyone was linked as part of this centuries-old shared tradition.

No one dared move until the patriarch had spoken the thanksgiving prayers with a roteness which only Andre's father could impart while keeping the holy sanctity.

"We thank you for the good weather which has allowed us to harvest our crops early this year," said Dimitri Kirov, the 35-year-old patriarch.

Gratefully, they anticipated his ending remarks with a brisk "amen" as the nine pair of clasped hands dropped the instant he was finished and began the dispensing of meat and potatoes, the buttered barley, and without delay, started talking about the day's events. Black bread was at the center of the table for all to snatch.

"Tell me, Andre and Sergei," Dimitri asked. "What have you two been up to while the rest of us have been toiling in the fields today?"

The question caught Andre by surprise.

"Papa, we, too, have been working hard all day," he replied in a solemn tenor.

Everyone laughed mockingly at the quick response.

But, it was an honest answer and a thoughtful attempt to be like his older brothers.

Secret of Ekaterinburg: The Hour-Glass

Sergei interjected, "Yes, Master Kirov. It is true. We have been busy in the fields searching for the enemy."

"And what enemy is this that you have been searching for? There are no enemies here," Kirov laughed winking at the others.

"But, it's true. There are many. But, you cannot see them," Sergei said. "`Only Andre and I can see them. So only we can fight them. They are very dangerous."

"You may be more correct than you know," Dimitri assessed.

His comment suitably summed up the current situation in Russia. It was easier to see an enemy from without than one from within. And, it was harder to see your neighbors as communists, but some of them were nevertheless, Dimitri ascertained.

Everyone ate.

Elderberry pie was served and everyone sipped coffee from an old iron pot at the center of the table, handed-down from two generations of Kirov's.

The smell of fresh-brewed coffee hung in the air, and even though they were only seven, the boys, too, participated.

"Father," asked Andre. "`What will become of Sergei and Ana?"

Secret of Ekaterinburg: The Hour-Glass

"That has not yet been decided, my son," Dimitri directed his remarks to everyone at the table. "God, has not given us his answer yet. But, he will, in a short time."

The patriarch paused for a moment and looked at Sergei.

Tears welled-up in Sergei when he heard Andre ask the question. Most of the time, especially during the daylight hours, he could keep it away from his thoughts. But the question haunted him and everyone knew it. Andre sensed it, and his father sensed it, too.

A hush fell over the entire table, but Andre broke the silence.

"But, if he doesn't come to live with us, they will send him away," Andre spoke in protest.

"And who are they?" the elder Kirov asked.

"Why the Bolsheviks," Andre blurted out with anger. "I've heard all about them from Anatoly," he continued, then realized his mistake by putting his hand over his mouth.

The eldest brother glared at Andre.

"So, Anatoly," the patriarch asked. "Since when have you become chief politburo member at this dacha, eh?"

"Father, forgive me. I was talking to Mikhail in the cowshed this morning about the Bolsheviks and Andre overheard me. It will

Secret of Ekaterinburg: The Hour-Glass

not happen again."

"Nevermind," Kirov scolded. "No Bolsheviks will get their hands on Sergei or his sister. I promised their mother and father a long time ago that if anything happened to them, I would take care of Sergei and Ana. So, there is nothing to worry about. But, be careful how you speak . . . the walls have ears."

Everyone nodded.

"You see, Sergei, God has already given you an answer," the elder Kirov continued.

Sergei was comforted by the closeness of the family and the security of knowing that he would not be sent-off to Moscow or Kiev or to one of the many children's' camps built for war orphans.

He could barely remember his parents.

Friends of the family had told Ana and he that they had gone off to Moscow to work for the government and that they wouldn't return for a long time. In actuality, they had been executed by the communists as enemies of the state like so many other compatriots of the time. But, no one had the heart to tell them, yet. That would have to wait until they were older.

"Thank you, Master Kirov," Sergei responded to the gesture. "I will try to be like

Secret of Ekaterinburg: The Hour-Glass

another son. I will work hard, and I will not disappoint you. And, neither will Ana."

Andre smiled at Sergei and put his arm on his shoulder.

"Then, I have a new brother."

"Yes. Indeed, you have a new brother," laughed Dimitri. "And, another sister as well. So, perhaps God has not been so kind to you after all?"

Everyone laughed.

Secret of Ekaterinburg: The Hour-Glass

CHAPTER 2

Vladivostok, Russia, Oct. 20, 1989

Kirov squinted into the early sun as the submarine pen keeper waved to him while lowering the huge iron gate blocking the entrance to the subterranean opening.

Hidden in an obscure, craggy inlet along the northwest Pacific coast, 520 miles north of the large Soviet city of Vladivostok, the Krazcoff submarine base was a secret installation which few Soviet citizens knew about or ever dreamed existed.

Among the few elites who did was professional military officer, Sergei Boscov. Sergei was amazed at how quickly the massive 200-ton doors could move, gear-driven by huge underwater wheels turning slowly against the prevailing current.

The gates swung down under tons of pressure to cover the wake of the Russian nuclear attack submarine, the Saint-Petersburg,

Secret of Ekaterinburg: The Hour-Glass

a ballistic-missile launching craft capable of hurling two-dozen ICBMs each armed with 12 MIRV hydrogen warheads at an unseen enemy halfway across the globe.

The 83-year-old coughed and sucked in a quick breath, then lit an American black-marketed Marlboro.

He took several long, slow puffs and blew the smoke into the wind managing a slight satisfaction as the nicotine reached his lungs. He pulled up at his hooded parka to protect his neck from the icy chill blowing in from the bay. The backwash from the sub lapped against the sides of the sea pens and splashed against the bottoms of his boots, but he paid it no mind.

The silence was broken by a familiar voice, echoing along the sub pens.

"Andre, you old bastard," the voice rang out, "it's too early for a meeting."

Shouting at him was a naval commander walking briskly toward him as the Saint-Petersburg now effortlessly glided into its sub berth alongside six others docked for refurbishing.

"If the KGB has sent you here to spy on us, it's too late," he joked. "The American CIA has already learned everything there is to know

Secret of Ekaterinburg: The Hour-Glass

about us. They know more about us than we do ourselves, comrade?"

"Don't call me comrade, comrade," the voice shot back.

It was Sergei alright.

From a distance, he had not changed much. Of course, like himself, he was much older, but not necessarily wiser. He had chosen the red navy instead to further his career and it had not made him happy.

Despite that, they had both offered their families much in the way of a better lifestyle. As a submarine base commander, Sergei had not yet retired, even though he was eligible long-ago, and so he still got more than just his monthly ruble allowance and food allotment. The extras were more than enough for quality food, clothing, a few luxuries, and a small dacha west of the Urals. It had also secured a decent education for his children.

"Stop where you are and identify yourself, or I will shoot," Andre nodded acknowledgment. "Of course, maybe you're too old to shoot. Maybe we can just pension you off to the Kremlin to wash the limousines. But, don't worry. I won't shoot because they don't allow senior officers to carry guns anymore. And, besides the gun might not

Secret of Ekaterinburg: The Hour-Glass

work."

Andre grunted as he approached. Sergei was at his best when he used self-deprecating humor. The Russians practiced it a lot in their everyday joke-telling because little if anything ever worked in the old Soviet Union, and even now that everything had changed, things were improving at a snail's pace.

"Andre, my brother," Sergei fired back as he approached to within fifteen feet, "It is good to see you again, but whenever you come calling, I suspect there is trouble. I have learned to expect that from you. Do I have to ask why they have sent you here?"

Kirov smiled and drew in again on his cigarette. Sergei knew him well, he thought. He flicked down the cigarette and squashed it out with his high, black leather boot.

His eyes pierced the careful study of Sergei's stare.

"You won't like it," Andre's face stiffened as he quickly shuffled toward the more private area of the sea pen.

"Fool! You cannot be sure I won't like it until you tell me!" Sergei said turning to face him squarely. "Tell me, my brother . . . what is it?"

Lowering his voice to a near inaudible level,

Secret of Ekaterinburg: The Hour-Glass

Andre spoke, "KGB sent me. Counter-intelligence needs your experience as a former sub-pack commander. It's something so important; it could shape Russo-American relations for decades to come."

Andre's gray hair, matted with perspiration from an earlier-than-usual morning hike, made him look older than he was. The creases on his forehead were hard evidence of the years of frustration connected to his work as an intelligence agent for the FSS, the Federal Security Service, which had replaced the old KGB after Russians had renounced the communist experiment of some eighty years. He was a retired Soviet Air Force Commander who had helped fight the dirty police action in Korea with the same flying precision he had learned during World War II.

Kirov's meteoric rise in the hierarchy of the Russian Air Force had not prepared him to train as a spy in the KGB. Indeed, he knew the technology of electronic warfare and knew how to calculate its devastating effects on an unseen enemy, and he knew how to counter the western intelligence apparatus by using the many disguised techniques of electronic deception. He had learned his lessons well as an officer-pilot, and later, as a schooled KGB

Secret of Ekaterinburg: The Hour-Glass

officer in the use of counter-intelligence.

But, no one could tell by his outward appearance that he was an expert in geopolitical affairs because he never talked about it when he socialized with the others. Then, he was called upon to serve again as a jet fighter pilot and train the North Koreans in aerial combat in the skies over the Yalu River. As a crack fighter pilot at thirty-six, Andre had come to respect the Americans in Korea who had mastered the dogfight. They were good. And their equipment was even better giving them the edge.

He remembered how he was nearly blown out of the sky by the first-of-its-kind heat-seeking missile, fired from an F-86 Sabre jet when he dallied too long with a young American flyer. The error was nearly fatal as he saw the missile fly right by his exhaust. By luck, by skill, or by both, he had instinctively rolled left and put his Mig-15 into a steep dive as the missile passed. It had been a narrow escape.

His peers referred to him as, "old man" and "father wings" because of his age. Despite the good-natured joking, it had given him the opportunity to become friends with dozens of admiring Soviet pilots in their mid-twenties

Secret of Ekaterinburg: The Hour-Glass

who idolized him as a beloved flight commander.

The sun, now an orangish fireball, blazed through the subterranean entrance as it rose to the east. Andre squinted at Sergei and motioned for him to follow.

The two moved past the Saint-Petersburg, whose engines were now shut down, toward the end of the dock to a maintenance shanty alongside one of the huge repair cranes.

"No one must know of this," Andre cautioned him as they entered a small room. "You must tell no one what I tell you this morning. Not even your wife and family. Especially not them. It would put them in extreme danger. You, yourself, will be in even more dreadful danger."

Sergei's smile began to disappear as he positioned two chairs at a small table like chess players across from each other.

"Maybe you were correct after all, Andre. Maybe, I do not wish to know anything," he answered. "But, I suppose I have no choice, and I suppose neither do you.

Andre reached into his jacket pocket and took out a tiny transmitter, laid it atop the desk and pressed a tiny button to activate it. It emitted a high frequency that would obliterate

Secret of Ekaterinburg: The Hour-Glass

any chance of someone trying to eavesdrop on their conversation either through microwave scanning or electronic micro-bugs planted inside the shack.

"It is a gift from the KGB," laughed Andre of the transmitter. "It not only interrupts radio signals, but it scrambles our voices, just in case they can pick up our voices. I hope it does not scramble our brains."

He reached inside another pocket and took out a piece of paper and pushed it across the table.

Sergei picked it up, reached inside his coat and took out a small plastic viewer with a small screen comprised of liquid crystals, and moved it back-and-forth over the note. He carefully adjusted a pair of dials at the top and bottom and began reading the encrypted message.

"My God, are they serious?" he reacted with a start.

"Yes," Andre responded. "They are very serious."

"But, they cannot possibly mean this. We have come so far in such a short time," Sergei looked at Andre incredulously.

"Oh, they mean it all right," Andre said. "There are many against this, but those are my orders. And, now they are yours, too. Unless,

Secret of Ekaterinburg: The Hour-Glass

of course, we disobey those orders."

"I can hardly imagine a project of the scope and dimension of this?" Sergei said. "Has it ever been done before? I think it must not be possible."

"No. . . No . . . .actually, it has been done before, but, only on a small scale," Andre informed him. "For the time being, I cannot tell you where. But, it did succeed and it caught the enemy completely by surprise."

Sergei handed the secret communique back to Andre. He opened his coat and took out a small flask from one of the inside pockets, unscrewed the lid and took a swallow of vodka.

He handed Andre the flask.

Both used vodka sparingly, but when they did, it was not only to quench their thirst for alcohol, but to honor the serious occasions where the threat of life or death was imminent.

Andre took a long drink and gestured in a silent toast to his brother, then sat back and said nothing.

As boyhood friends, they had come to respect each other's strengths in critical situations. Both knew they could rely on each other in any situation and under any circumstances.

Sitting alone now for the first time in ten

Secret of Ekaterinburg: The Hour-Glass

years, they both sensed it would be no different this time.

"What do you mean disobey, Andre?"

"When we were children and we used to have our political discussions, did you ever question under whose authority we managed to live our everyday lives, Sergei?"

"Many times. And, I wondered if papa really would have killed that stranger when he rode up on his horse to take me away."

"And, what were you wishing for at that moment?"

"I wanted to yell, `Kill him, Mr. Kirov. Kill him. Do not let him take me away.' "

"But, that would have jeopardized the entire family, eh, Sergei."

"Yes. And, they still would have taken me. So, this is your point?"

"My point is there are other ways to resist, Sergei. There are other ways to realize a goal, ways in which there is much more satisfaction than just the killing of one evil person," Andre mused. "I have been thinking about these orders, and they must not be carried out by us nor by anyone else. If they are, then all of Russia is finished. Does that make sense to you, Sergei?"

Sergei took another drink from the flask and

Secret of Ekaterinburg: The Hour-Glass

let the vodka bite at his throat.

"Da, you are right, Andre. As usual, you are right. Do you have some kind of plan for this?"

"I must think about it more. I will need time. But, when that time comes, I know I will able to count on you, Sergei. Be watchful, and wary. Old KGB are still about. They do not forget. And, that is part of the problem with our new democratic system. The communist bastards are waiting in the wings for such an opportunity. Believe me, Sergei, if given the chance, they will seize it."

Their meeting was interrupted by the sound of a nearby work whistle signaling everything to a halt. The gates were being lifted as another sub backed away from its berth, slowly making its way out into the bay where it would begin a month-long shakedown cruise with its crew.

Although, he was now a base commander assigned to land duty, Sergei wished he could go with them.

"You were right," Sergei said wistfully. "Maybe, I didn't want to know."

Secret of Ekaterinburg: The Hour-Glass

CHAPTER 3

Peregrebnoye, After the revolution.

Andre and Sergei romped in the upper reaches of the old weather-beaten barn. It was one of their favorite rendezvous where they could look down and spy on others below.

The breeze blew in through the cavernous hay mound, quickly evaporating the moisture on the newly mown hay laid-in by the Kirov's. It was stifling hot from the humidity of the squashed-in hay stuffed nearly to the top of the old barn roof. The outer doors were forced open at both ends to allow the air to flow. The wrong combination of heat and humidity from green hay could cause an instant kindling known as spontaneous combustion. Such fires were not uncommon in the late days of summer before the prevailing autumn temperatures could cool the mounds. Through centuries of experience, the farmers knew to harvest the hay in the fields when it was almost dry.

Secret of Ekaterinburg: The Hour-Glass

Sergei and Andre stretched-out across the piles of hay and looked out beyond the outer doors where a massive iron tong hung from a cable track swinging above them in the gentle breeze like an enormous bird about to swoop down on them as if to pluck them up and dangle them over the edge threatening to release them forty feet to the ground.

"Does it remind you of a reptile-bird, too?" Andre said.

"Da," said Sergei. "My mother used to tell me when I was born, a giant bird carried me to our house and dropped me down the chimney of our dacha. But, of course, now I know that is not true. My friends told me that this giant bird actually was my father. I can hardly remember either of them now."

"I remember them some. I can see their faces when I look at you," Andre said. "We have much growing up to do and very much to learn. Soon, we will go to work in the fields with our brothers."

Sergei instinctively got up on his hands and knees and looked toward the horizon which stretched for a half-mile to one of the golden-brown, wheat fields.

He blinked.

"Andre," he said hesitantly. "There is some

Secret of Ekaterinburg: The Hour-Glass

movement by the creek."

Andre rose from his comfortable spot and peered into the setting sun.

"Where?" he asked.

"Over there, next to the row of trees," Sergei responded quickly.

"I don't see anything," Andre answered.

"Yes, you do. A rider and a horse, moving below the branches . . . it looks like they're resting near the creek."

Andre squinted into the sun.

"Yes, you are right! Now, I can see them."

"I wonder who it is?" Sergei said. "It must be someone from Peregrebnoye. Could it be the postman this late in the day?"

"I don't know, but now he is coming this way in a hurry. We must tell papa at once," Andre said from his vantage point. A fitful expression crossed his face.

"Hurry! Our brothers must be in the south field. It will take us fifteen minutes to run and alert them," Sergei yelled to Andre as they scrambled down the ladder to the floor below.

Andre hit the ground running with Sergei jumping from three rungs above.

"Wait," Sergei said stopping in his tracks.

"This way will take too long. The rider will be upon us in a few minutes. We must ring the

Secret of Ekaterinburg: The Hour-Glass

big bell on top of the grain silo."

"Yes, that is very good. We must hurry!"

With that, they ran to one of the huge twin silos and clambered up to a second-floor platform where they could reach the long rope. Atop one of the cone-shaped silos was a large cast-iron bell salvaged from one of the hundreds of Volga riverboats which had plied the interior of Russia during the early 1800s. Most of them were destroyed in the serf revolt of the 1870s when the serfs rebelled against the Czar for their own land. The only remnants of the old boats were the iron bells which had once beckoned workers to the docks.

The Kirov's had managed to get their hands on one and place it atop the silo. You could hear it for miles and they used it to signal danger or fire.

Both boys grabbed the rope at the same time and heaved up and down.

The bell pierced the air with a loud, long peal, tolling its signal as a warning to the men mowing in the fields.

The breeze cushioned the sound of the bell, but when it reached Dimitri and the brothers, they immediately stopped and looked in the direction of the dacha, then frantically tied the horses to a makeshift iron bolt in the field, and

Secret of Ekaterinburg: The Hour-Glass

began running in a formation resembling a militia charge.

"Andre! Andre! The rider is almost here! Where are our brothers?"

Andre ran to the other side of the platform and looked toward the south field. They were about a quarter of a mile away and coming in a hurry.

"They are coming, Sergei. They are coming fast!"

Sergei let go of the swinging rope and was first to scramble down the ladder and dash toward the courtyard where the rider was approaching.

Galloping at a speedy gait, the rider entered the courtyard and pulled-back hard on the reins of the black stallion causing it to recoil abruptly.

"Whoa! Whoa!" the rider shouted whipping at the horse. With nostrils flaring and froth oozing from its mouth, the stallion steadied itself and rested.

"Dobriy den, comrades," the rider said to them. "Is the master of this dacha about today?"

The boys stared at the dusty rider.

Andre was instantly on his guard. The rider was unshaven, heavy in the face, and looked awkward in the saddle, as though he had just

Secret of Ekaterinburg: The Hour-Glass

gotten on the animal for the first time. Even young Andre figured he was a better horseman than him.

"I know what you're thinking," the rider shouted. "But, you have never faced a full cavalry charge and lived to tell about it?"

Getting no response from the boys, the rider ordered, "I need to rest my horse?"

The boys motioned him to the hitching post where the spent horse immediately began to drink. The interloper wore a four-sided cap stitched to the top finished off with a blue button and a single red star sewn onto the front letting everyone know he was a Bolshevik.

"Comrades! Did you hear me? I asked if your father was about?" the rider asked again.

"Yes. Our father is coming up from the field, with the others, just now," Andre said hoping to reinforce the point of strength in numbers.

"That is good," he growled. "How many men are you here?"

"Six," Sergei, shouted back, "including us."

"I see. Then, you've got a good, hardworking farm crew," he said. "This dacha looks to be fairly productive."

They ignored the comment as he dismounted and carefully scrutinized his

Secret of Ekaterinburg: The Hour-Glass

surroundings.

"What do you want with my father?" Andre interrupted.

"It need not concern you nor your brother," he said. "You will learn soon enough."

Valerya and Ana peeked through the curtains, daring not to show their faces.

The rider turned to see the elder Kirov approaching with three other young men.

"Indeed, comrades. This must be your father and brothers."

"Yes," Dimitri yelled to the disheveled figure standing beside the horse. "I am the patriarch of this dacha. And, who might I be addressing?"

The rider was about thirty, brash, of average height with a muscular build; he had two scars, one near his upper lip and another alongside his nose.

"The name is Comrade Yakov Grachev. I am the minister of the local communist party for this district. I have come looking for a Sergei Boscov, age seven, who used to live at the dacha five miles to the west of here. That dacha is now a collective-farm owned and run by the state. I understand the boy stays with you and your family. Perhaps he is one of these two here."

Secret of Ekaterinburg: The Hour-Glass

Sergei backed away.

"Yes, he is here. We have taken him in with us. His parents are in Moscow working for the government. Is there a crime in that?" Dimitri questioned.

"None that I can think of, comrade," Grachev snapped back scowling . . . "only . . ."

"What is it you want with him?"

"I have come to take him with me. He is to travel with me to Kiev where he will be placed in a youth camp to be educated by the state," Grachev spoke as if he were reading from a document.

"You mean brainwashed?" Dimitri shot back. "Why is Sergei so important to the party apparatus, anyway? What if I say that you cannot have him, and that he is ours and that he wants to remain here with us?" Dimitri said angrily as he moved closer to him.

"It is not for you to decide. I have my orders from the party, comrade, to see that he accompanies me to Kiev by train. We leave from Peregrebnoye tomorrow morning at eight o'clock."

"And, if I do not agree?" Dimitri added.

"If you resist the order, you will be shot. Then your entire family, next. Believe me, I have seen this before, comrade. They will kill

Secret of Ekaterinburg: The Hour-Glass

you all on orders from the party. Do not doubt that."

"I do not doubt it for a minute, fool comrade. I only wonder if perhaps it would be worth it to save him from the likes of you."

"For you, perhaps. But, for the rest of your family, I think not?"

Sergei broke and ran to the house.

"That will do you no good," Grachev yelled to the boy. "I mean you no harm. I have my orders. So, I will come for him tomorrow at seven o'clock. Be ready. Keep your goodbyes' short, do you hear?"

"You filthy bastard," Dimitri said as he reached for his waist-knife and grabbed Grachev by the shirt.

Two of the older sons quickly intervened.

"Papa, don't."

"It does not matter what you think of me or the party, comrade? You'll be better off giving him up without a fight. Believe me, your family will be better off for it. I don't believe the party in this district knows that you are still operating this dacha for yourself. Everyone else's has been taken over. If you cooperate, they will probably overlook it. I am stating a plain fact."

Andre interrupted, "And what about

Secret of Ekaterinburg: The Hour-Glass

Sergei's, Ana? Will you take her, too?"

Stunned at Andre's mistake, Dimitri turned and yelled, "Silence, Andre."

"What?" Grachev answered. "What's this about a girl? "We have no record of a sister. Where is she?"

"Never mind. She is with us. But, you will not take her," Dimitri resisted. "She is of no use to the so-called p.a.r.t.y. apparatus anyway."

Grachev shifted nervously as Dimitri challenged him.

"The party will decide what is necessary. Enough. . . . anyway, I have no orders to bring back a so-called sister. Only the boy. I tell you now, comrade, I am doing you a good deed. I will forget what I have heard from your lips of this girl, Ana," Grachev said angrily. "She is of no use to us anyway. But remember, there may come a day when I will collect on this favor. Do you understand?"

The sons held Dimitri back.

Sergei watched from the porch as the men concluded their business. Grachev mounted his horse and settled comfortably into the well-worn saddle.

"Do zavtra. Good day, comrades. I will see you in the morning," he said swinging his

Secret of Ekaterinburg: The Hour-Glass

mount around abruptly while holding onto his cap. "Have another horse ready. The party cannot afford to buy horses it cannot feed these days."

Dimitri knew the rider would be true to his word and return the next morning to carry out his mission. He could tell he was a true party member. All his kind were dedicated and lethal.

"Sergei, I am very sorry," Andre said placing a hand on his shoulder. "I wish I could go in your place."

"No, Andre. It is better this way. Your family is in grave danger. The Bolsheviks, they are vengeful, putting to death those who oppose them."

"Yes," interrupted Dimitri, "It is true enough what you say. You know much for a young boy. But, we will talk of it no more," the patriarch ordered as he tried to comfort the two.

"I am sorry about this predicament. It means I must break my promise to your parents as well as to you."

"It is all right, sir. It is not your fault," Sergei's voice broke in mid-sentence. "You would have kept your word. The Bolsheviks have not kept theirs. Someday, the people will open their eyes . . . . "

Secret of Ekaterinburg: The Hour-Glass

"Indeed," said Andre. "Someday, we will open their eyes for them. Someday . . . "

"Come inside," Dimitri said. "Alexander . . . Anatoly . . . Mikhail. . . go back to the fields and get the horses. We are finished today. We will go back to work tomorrow after that centurion Grachev comes for Sergei."

Dispassionate time together, Sergei thought.

Yes. That would be appropriate. There would be more than enough time to cry alone.

Ana came running from the house and grabbed him, hugging him with all her strength. Then, she spontaneously kissed him on the cheek. And, he kissed her back, for the first time.

Andre just stood there because he hadn't expected that. He knew their roles as playmates, but he hadn't suspected they had such deep feelings for each other.

"Do not worry, Ana," Andre finally said. "We will write to him every week while he is gone."

Even as he spoke, Andre wasn't sure if it was enough to console her, but he spoke the words anyway.

Deep inside, Andre knew each had already learned something about life. That it had a beginning and that it had an end, but

Secret of Ekaterinburg: The Hour-Glass

somewhere in-between, there could be many beginnings and many endings before the final one.

When the revolution began, it had brought with it many uncertainties, and eventually these uncertainties had become permanent. Even basic freedoms could no longer be trusted. Andre had already learned that at a very young age, and he wondered if Ana and Sergei already knew that as well.

One thing was for certain, their lives had suddenly changed.

Dimitri and his family went inside to contemplate Sergei's fate. Later, while everyone slept, Sergei found it impossible to close his eyes. He wanted every waking moment to last.

He prayed in a whisper, "Please, God, by some miracle, lift this burden from me."

After a fretful hour, he fell into a restless sleep.

Secret of Ekaterinburg: The Hour-Glass

CHAPTER 4

Ekaterinburg, The Ipatiev House, Ural Mountains, July 16, 1918.

Czar Nicholas II walked from the antechamber wearing his favorite smoking jacket decorated with medals awarded to him by current European kings and heads of state.

Europe was in the throes of world war, and its old nemesis, jealousy and territorial gain linked to a sense of overpowering nationalism, had triggered old ethnic fires from within which had enabled military leaders to organize the masses into huge armies that plundered their way across the western European plains on into France and Belgium.

Nicholas stroked his smoking pipe and squashed a clump of Havana tobacco into the round end and struck a match against the white marble mantel. He could still feel the embers giving off a subtle warmth filling the entire library with comfort. He puffed on the

Secret of Ekaterinburg: The Hour-Glass

mouthpiece, drawing the aromatic smoke into his lungs, forcing a cough as he eased into his favorite chair letting his thoughts drift backward to a different time, a much happier time, twelve years earlier at their palace in St. Petersburg . . . it was 1906.

He heard the light footsteps beside him and turned to see his youngest daughter, five-year-old, Anastasia, beside him.

"Papa," she called out. "Read to me, papa, please."

"Good evening, my little one. Isn't it late for you to be up and about the palace?" Nicholas responded gently scooping her up onto his lap.

"Please, papa Niki, please?"

"All right, my dear. Since no one knows we're both here, I suppose it will be all right, just this once."

"And, what will you read to me, papa?"

"Well . . . let me see. For someone who is barely five years old, it must be something new and interesting. Perhaps, something from the newspaper, something you can't understand," he laughed.

"But, I don't like newspapers, papa?"

"Ha! Neither do I. They say such terrible things about me these days. Most of them untrue. Do you know there is a new newspaper

Secret of Ekaterinburg: The Hour-Glass

in Moscow and St. Petersburg called Pravda? It is supposed to mean truth. But, it is, in fact, far from the truth. These revolutionaries say that I have ordered thousands killed, but that is a lie. They are fighting among themselves politically, and the soldiers are only trying to keep civil order."

"Why do they lie about you, papa?"

"That is something you will understand as you become older. But, I suppose it is like this. Let me try and explain. Do you know what an hour-glass is?"

"No, papa."

"It is a glass where sand falls through. The sand is time that is passing."

"Does everyone know that, papa?"

"Not everyone my child, but that is very good, Anastasia. You are very smart indeed. But what everyone does not realize, and what you do not know, is that life in Russia is very much like the hour-glass. We have been spending so much time watching life flow from the top of the hour-glass to the bottom, that we have been careless and now we have very little time left to change things for the better. The grains of sand are like people. Soon, there will be only a few grains left on the top half of the hour-glass. So we must always make sure that

Secret of Ekaterinburg: The Hour-Glass

there is enough sand in the top of the hour-glass so that time and events and people can remain linked forever. Then, when you turn the hour-glass over, the falling sand is not broken. You see, my daughter, that is precisely what the Bolsheviks want. They wish to break the connection between society and the working class. That is the real meaning of the hour-glass, little one. Remember it, and someday teach it to your children. Tell them how the Russian people are very much like the fine grains of sand in the hour-glass."

"Yes, papa, I will. Please, tell me some more."

"Oh, but there is not much more to explain, except that we must never let the sands run out. If the connection is broken, there will be no one left to tell the others how terrible the Bolsheviks really are."

"I will tell everyone for you, papa. I will tell them. I will be like Peter in the fairy tale, and go about telling everyone how dangerous the wolf really is," Anastasia cried.

"Yes. You must do that, because these evil people will say that everyone will be equal, and that things will be better than they are, but that will never be the case. I pray that you never live to see that kind of injustice. They will take

Secret of Ekaterinburg: The Hour-Glass

everything from us and from everyone else, too.

"Anastasia, my child. I wish they could understand that I only want what is good for all of Russia. But, they do not listen anymore. Perhaps, it is this modern age. Young people are so impatient and restless. They want their dreams fulfilled immediately, and they are willing to pay any price for it."

Nicholas reached for a book from the tea stand; it was one of Anastasia's favorites, "Peter and The Wolf," and began reading.

" . . . and, when Peter cried . . . `Wolf! Wolf!' . . . from the nearby woods, the woodsmen came running with their axes, to save him. But, as they approached, Peter laughed at them and said, `You stupid woodsmen, there is no wolf, I have tricked you again.'"

"Why does Peter trick the woodsmen that way, papa?"

"Because, my dear, he is living in a fairy tale world and he is poking fun at them because they must work as slaves," the Czar said. "It is much the same way in the real world. They are taunting me in the same way, and when I send the soldiers to protect the people, I am the one who receives the blame."

Secret of Ekaterinburg: The Hour-Glass

"But, why does Peter keep crying wolf?" Anastasia asked. "The woodsmen will stop coming to help him. What if there is a real wolf?"

Nicholas smiled and kissed the top of her head.

"In that case, he will get eaten alive. Just as I am getting eaten alive because nobody understands that there is indeed a real wolf at the door - in the name of the Bolsheviks. But, that is another story, for another morning," he said lowering her from his lap.

"Now off with you. Go wake your brother and sisters, and see how they like that?"

Nicholas' thoughts drifted slowly back to the present.

* * *

Soon, sleep overtook him. And, Anastasia, the 17-year-old auburn-haired princess, stood motionless in the study observing his labored breathing. He looked older than his years, and his health was beginning to fail. She loved her father so much. She smiled and moved toward him . . . when suddenly and without warning, an explosion shattered the silence jolting Nicholas awake. Anastasia froze momentarily,

Secret of Ekaterinburg: The Hour-Glass

then ran frantically toward the czar.

"Papa! What is it?" she cried out. "What is happening?"

Nicholas moved to protect her, but before he could reach out to her, two men armed with rifles and bayonets entered the room pushing the valet violently in front of them causing him to tumble to the floor. The valet's shoulder was nearly torn away from a gunshot wound, and still the ragged Bolshevik soldier shoved him down hard onto a sofa sharply bringing his cavalry boot to rest on the top of his chest. Blood oozed through his shirt from the pressure of his boot.

"Attention, Czar Nicholas. Under the orders of the Socialist Red Army, you are being placed under military arrest. As a point-in-fact, your entire family at this moment is now under military arrest."

"By whose authority do you break in here and make such claims?" the Czar shouted pushing Anastasia safely behind him. "Where are my children . . . my wife . . . and the servants?"

"You idiot fool! This is not your palace. It is the place we have kept you captive for seventy-eight days. You will be put on trial for crimes against the people of Russia."

Secret of Ekaterinburg: The Hour-Glass

"Why, this is an unbelievable outrage. You will be shot as traitors to the crown of Russia."

"For someone looking down the point of a rifle barrel, Czar Nicholas, you speak bravely. But, you are naive. Do not miscalculate our intentions your excellency. The Ipatiev House has been surrounded by an army of revolutionary guards comprised of the people. The revolution has been won. Your white army cannot save you. They have been defeated and have joined us. Russia is under Czarist rule no more. Vladimir Ilich Lenin now rules Russia."

"This cannot be. I have not betrayed the masses. I have tried only to serve in their best interests."

Anastasia interrupted the disheveled Bolshevik as he moved toward Nicholas. She recognized him immediately. She knew him from hours of discussion in the Tsarkeo Selo palace gardens in St. Petersburg.

"Leave my father alone, Yakov. Do not harm him. He is a good man. All of Russia loves him. Leave him alone, do you hear me?" she screamed at him.

The Bolshevik commander brushed her aside with his rifle, and strode past her, grabbing the Czar by the shoulder. Nicholas was helpless as the other man put a pistol to the

Secret of Ekaterinburg: The Hour-Glass

back of Anastasia's head.

"I will kill her now, where she stands, if you resist any further," the brash Yakov shouted with a malignant hatred.

In the hallway, Nicholas could see his wife, Empress Alexandra, and the children, huddled together, having been suddenly awakened by the armed intruders. The young prince and princesses were wearing their bed clothing and specially fitted corsets made of ivory, rubies, sapphires and diamonds with jackets worn over top, the jewels secretly sewn and concealed within their clothing. The tightly fitted corsets were adorned with jewels all the way to their necks. Anastasia was dressed in a fine-jeweled corset and night robe hand-sewn by her Aunt. Hundreds of precious gems had been hand-sewn into the lining. Maria, trembled while Olga, the eldest, tried to console her whimpering. Alexis stood straight and seemed to sense the unquestionable danger to them. Like his father, he was of true aristocracy and performed like the prince he was. He showed his captors that he was not afraid and stood in front of his sisters and mother, trying to shield them from the Bolshevik soldiers.

Yakov waved his pistol at the squad of men encircling the family, and they were quickly

Secret of Ekaterinburg: The Hour-Glass

shoved down a flight of stairs to a room hidden beneath the Ipatiev House where they were forced to stand for an interminably long time. Nicholas was ordered to sit on a wooden chair and was repeatedly questioned by the man who called himself, Yakov.

"Czar Nicholas. In the presence of your entire family, you must answer truthfully to the following question."

"I don't understand," the Czar replied. "What further do you want of me?"

"Silence, you fool! You will listen and answer my questions. Your answers will be written as a record for us to judge, and for posterity to observe. You have been charged with the crime of murder and treason to the motherland of Russia. How do you plead? Guilty or not guilty to the people's court?"

"Where is this people's court?"

The ten armed militiamen held their leather slung rifles at waist level pointed constantly at the royal family members.

"You are looking at them. These are your judges, jury . . . and perhaps your executioners," Yakov said nervously fingering the handle of his black Nag ant pistol.

"But, who have I murdered?" the Czar added.

Secret of Ekaterinburg: The Hour-Glass

"Fool, you have murdered people you do not even know or ever cared to know. The revolution has been waged for three years, and your soldiers have murdered our people by the thousands."

"I have not been aware of any of this. I have not been informed of any of these murders. I have only seen what is printed in the newspaper."

"You really are a stupid fool. You have been reading your own newspapers. They print only the lies that you wish them to print. They listen to your henchmen, not to the real patriots of Russia. Ilich Lenin has been right all along. You are all bourgeois pigs. And, you must pay a penalty for your crimes against the people. You have been taking the wealth from the people and we are left to die. Now, we will take what is rightfully ours and re-distribute the wealth to the masses."

"And, who is to decide all of this? You are speaking of anarchy. Who is to decide these questions, Vladimir Ilich Lenin?"

"If he says so. Then, yes. But, it will be done by a committee of the people. They will decide everything. Who works where and who does what. And, what amount of wages they receive. We will get what is finally due us.

Secret of Ekaterinburg: The Hour-Glass

Lenin and his followers have promised us that."

For the first time, the Czar was clearly upset as he observed his beautiful family. He knew these men were experienced killers. He could see it in their eyes. They were accustomed to it. They had done so only a few hours before. He had seen their kind before, in the attack trenches on the Serbian front, and he could tell they were very well prepared in these matters, and that they went about their business with a steady, cold precision that made even Yakov himself uneasy. They were an experienced death squad and butchers of their own calling. And, it made Nicholas fearful for his beloved family. He knew that no one could enter the Ipatiev House to rescue them if his own army had capitulated in St. Petersburg. And, he sensed, it had. Now, his family was doomed.

"Answer the question, you idiot," Yakov prompted.

"Do not call me an idiot. I have only done what is right for Russia. My family had nothing whatsoever to do with my decisions. These decisions were mine alone, and I am solely responsible. Do with me as you wish, but I beg of you do no harm to them."

"You are in no position to beg or bargain. You have done what your bourgeois swine

Secret of Ekaterinburg: The Hour-Glass

advisors have told you to do. You have swindled the people out of what is rightfully theirs. Russian land," Yakov howled. "Do not harm them? If they are found guilty, they will be put to death for crimes against the Russian people."

The children, the cook, wounded valet, maid, physician, and Alexandra were all quickly alarmed by Yakov's ranting. Maria and Olga again began to weep.

"But, why? Why must they have to account for my sins?" Nicholas pleaded.

"Why? Because they are heirs to your throne. And, there must be no one left to ascend to that throne."

"But, what is the evidence to convict us of these alleged crimes against the people."

"You are indeed the naive idiot they say you are. I am the commander of this death squad as ordered by Beria and Lenin. You do not think I will shoot you? Lenin has ordered me personally to carry out this assignment."

"So, why does not Lenin or Comrade Beria do it themselves?"

The question caught Yakov by surprise in an awkward silence of embarrassment.

He recovered, "They are too busy with the revolution and designing the future. They have

Secret of Ekaterinburg: The Hour-Glass

left such small details to me and my men."

"Small details? You refer to our impending murders as a small detail? God will condemn you to hell."

"Well, you above all, Your Excellency, should know how large the details of murder are. You have ordered enough of them. You have indeed, trivialized the deed. As for God, I will wait to ask him myself. As for now, I am the judge of this tribunal."

"You make a mockery of Russian justice."

Nicholas kept Yakov off-guard with his constant counter-questioning, but the effect was making Yakov more angry and weary of the whole thing.

"Anyway," Yakov countered, tired of the continuing banal, "enough of this. You cannot win philosophically what you have lost on the battlefield. How do you plead?"

Nicholas stared at his family and the servants standing behind him at the far end of the room.

"If I confess to these crimes against the people, will you release them?" Nicholas asked as he rose from his chair looking squarely into Yakov's eyes.

"I make no promises. I do not presume to have the authority to do so. My orders are to

Secret of Ekaterinburg: The Hour-Glass

prosecute and punish the royal family. Those are my only orders. But, I could consider it on humanitarian grounds," Yakov groused, puffing on the butt of a loosely rolled cigarette, then nervously flicking it to the floor.

"Enough of this. How do you plead? That is the only question you must answer now?"

Nicholas stood isolated from the others in dreadful reserve. His face was ashen and disturbed as he looked at Alexandra huddled with Alexis and Anastasia, and the other four princesses.

He would not betray them. He would confess and die for his own indiscretions and misjudgments if it was God's will.

He turned to Yakov, and in a frank, loud voice so that everyone could hear, pronounced . . . "I am guilty!"

The ten executioners and Yakov shuffled nervously in place tightening their grips on their weapons.

"You will sign this paper stating that fact in front of my men as witnesses."

Yakov handed Nicholas a fountain pen and led him to a small desk in the same room at which Nicholas leaned over while another guard held a small oil lamp to light the area. "That will suffice, Your Excellency," Yakov

Secret of Ekaterinburg: The Hour-Glass

scowled feigning respect for the title of the Czar. "I will now carry out the punishment of the people's court."

"And, what punishment is that?" asked Nicholas.

"By the power vested to me in this people's court, you will be executed at sunset today with the members of your entire family and servants to atone for those who have died at the hands of your militia and political henchmen."

"Why, this is an outrage. You must not harm the children or the servants. My wife has done nothing. She has never uttered a word in anger. They are all innocent. If you must do it, then shoot me, and do it quickly. But, let them go, and return them to St. Petersburg - to prison if need be. I tell you they are entirely innocent of all this," Nicholas beseeched Yakov.

"Silence, you fool! This may be an outrage to you, but your betrayal of your own people is a far bigger outrage. We will do as we see fit."

"You mean you will do as you see fit?"

"Shut up! Keep silent. It is my business, and my business alone to pass judgment. You will all be taken away from here in the morning. But, first we must take official photographs of all of you in the next room for historical purposes. That is the only promise I

Secret of Ekaterinburg: The Hour-Glass

can keep to you. It is out of my hands."

Nicholas' head sunk to his chest.

One-by-one in single file, the guards led the children and Alexandra to an adjacent room. Nicholas and the servants were the last to be taken. Then, the Czar turned, and gestured with his hand as though to say it was finished, and walked from the room a few paces in front of the Bolshevik guards.

Then, suddenly, instead of escorting them out of the basement, they turned and ordered them to halt. The guards inexplicitly lined them up in front of a long basement wall, shoving them roughly, then abruptly stepping back about six feet from them, waiting for Yakov to re-enter the room.

When he entered, he barely looked at the family members, still wearing their finest bedclothes. When he did, he saw they still wore their breakfast jewelry, and the youngest, Anastasia, was covered head-to-toe in a sleeping suit ladened with jewels. It glistened and sparkled from a speck of sunlight entering the tiny room from a side window darting about the room like a tiny firefly when Anastasia moved. It was a ghostly sight. In spite of that, Yakov saw the people's money in that.

"Attention!" Yakov summoned-up the

Secret of Ekaterinburg: The Hour-Glass

courage to gain the focus of his ten men armed with 10.66mm Berdan rifles and Nagant 7.62mm gas-sealed pistols.

"Ready!"

Maria nearly fainted at the sound of the order. Olga let out an uncontrollable guttural squeal that unnerved the militia now aiming at point-blank range. Alexis stood transfixed with his father staring at the men. Nicholas kissed Alexandra on the cheek, and the children, in turn, all kissed each other one last time. They stood cowering in their fear like animals, shivering in their bedclothes, holding hands and praying at the same time. Alexandra, the empress and spiritual leader, led them in prayer, asking for forgiveness in unison, expecting to die as a holy family of the Holy Church of Russia. They appealed to each other with fear and love, and then let out sudden wails of terror.

"No! No! You mustn't. Please, no," Czarina Alexandra shouted. "Not the children!"

Nicholas put his hands up in front of his son to shield him from the bullets. He moved his body in front of him and desperately shoved Anastasia behind him, but he could offer no more protection.

Secret of Ekaterinburg: The Hour-Glass

Alexandra gathered the remaining children and knelt down onto the wooden floor praying to the Holy Mother begging the soldiers not to shoot. Maria, Olga and Tatiana, started to weep again trembling in each other's arms. Dr. Botkin fainted, falling to the floor. The wounded valet, Aleksei Trupp, tried to prop-up the Czar's physician, and stood before the execution squad helpless. Anna Demidova, the maid, nearly passed out from primordial fear and shrieked at the men as she frantically tried to get past them to another room. But, they literally beat her back into the small basement room with their rifle butts.

All of a sudden and without warning, Yakov issued the deadly order.

"FIRE!"

Eleven shots rang out in unison during the first volley. It was too late for anyone to stop them now.

It had begun.

Nicholas began to speak, and took the first shot directly into his open mouth. Blood spurted from the back of his neck and throat. He fell backward against Anastasia and Alexis who already was dead from a shot directly to the forehead. The prince died instantly. Nicholas struggled to regain his balance and

Secret of Ekaterinburg: The Hour-Glass

was struck again in the chest. Anastasia tried to hold him up but his weight was too much for her and she crumpled beneath him. She was hit twice, in the side and arm, and then a third time as a bullet grazed her forehead. The fusillade knocked her to the floor and she struggled underneath the weight of her brother and father. Blood spilled onto the wooden floor and it soon became a slippery tangle of bodies like animals in a slaughter-house. Another volley exploded from close quarters ripping into the Romanov's again. Anastasia slipped into unconsciousness, while the others flailed about in each other's arms desperately trying to escape the onslaught of bullets ricocheting off their corsets and against the basement walls. The execution squad itself was out-of-control, trying to reload their weapons while incredulous at seeing that most of the children were still alive and moving about the room. They repeated the volleys and reloaded twice more. The bullets struck the children with a muzzle velocity of 1500 feet-per-second with no apparent effect. Demidova was hit and fell onto her knees. Trupp was mortally wounded during the first volley, and Dr. Botkin died of two bullets to the head. The first shots had struck the children in their torsos, wrenching them from each other and

Secret of Ekaterinburg: The Hour-Glass

knocking them to the floor. The second and third volley had been directed at them at point blank range. And, after it had failed to kill them, the militia thought itself cursed or that something supernatural was occurring in the room. A few of the Bolshevik guards made the sign-of-the-cross, reloaded and fired yet a fourth and fifth volley at the children.

Was the invisible hand of God protecting them one of the soldiers shouted?

"We are cursed. The Holy Mother is protecting them," another shouted. "They will not die by our hands."

"Shut up, you fools," Yakov screamed at them and re-directed his charge of the execution.

"Keep firing. They are not immortal. Their corsets are protecting them, not God. Strike them with your bayonets!"

The maid somehow managed to get up off the floor and ran from the room screaming. She was chased down and bayoneted by two men, dying like a terrified, wild animal.

With that, the Bolsheviks finished them off, one-by-one, their bodies still quivering and writhing on the floor in a futile struggle to escape their horror. Their executioners thrust at them repeatedly with bayonet stabs to the

Secret of Ekaterinburg: The Hour-Glass

neck, backs, and sides. Another fusillade of shots followed, the sixth, now numbering as high as seventy shots erupting in small bursts of single individual bursts, staccato-like and at random. The sound was earsplitting.

Finally, after twenty-five minutes of this murderous spectacle, when the militiamen knew they had all been killed, the onslaught was halted by Yakov.

Anastasia lay wounded beneath her father and brother, Alexis. Maria and Olga lay draped in each other's arms facing their mother, who was lying straddled across Tatiana in a protective pose. Tatiana had been shot three times and bayoneted twice in the back. Alexandra had been shot through the heart and once in the head then bayoneted twice. The valet was still breathing until a guard grimly walked over to him and ended his personal misery by shooting him in the back of the head. Demidova lay dead in another room. Dr. Botkin and Ivan Kharitonov, the cook, lay beside each other. Kharitonov had not uttered a single sound during the entire event having been shot through the throat and neck.

They were all dead now. It had not been an execution, but instead a bloody and botched brutal murder of monumental proportion. The

Secret of Ekaterinburg: The Hour-Glass

Romanov's were all dead. Comrade Yakov Grachev had personally put an end to the royal dynasty of more than three hundred years.

Now Russia could breathe again. Now, the communists could get on with their social reforms for everyone unimpeded.

Yakov emptied the cartridges from his steel-black Nagant and nervously reloaded its six chambers saying nothing else of consequence to the guards. They, in turn, said nothing to him, only the occasional grumblings of unintelligible utterings among themselves broke the extraordinary silence. Yakov holstered his pistol in his side belt, and stared at the bodies for a few moments. Then, he turned, and instructed one of the revolutionary guards to make sure that their bodies were buried in a flooded, abandoned mine some ten kilometers on the outskirts of Ekaterinburg.

It would be done the guards obeyed. They all obeyed now that they had royal blood on their hands, because they knew if they were captured by the white army, they would be executed on sight without hesitation. They were marked men for the rest of their natural lives. So they would obey all orders from now on. Yakov knew that as well.

Inside the basement where the bodies lay

Secret of Ekaterinburg: The Hour-Glass

strewn across the floor swamped with blood, near Nicholas, near his son, lay the still body of Anastasia.

For several moments, every detail remained etched under Yakov's trained scrutiny.

Then, suddenly, as quickly as he had ordered the executions, he ordered everyone to leave the room. As the blood coagulated on the wooden floor, Yakov's eyes focused solely upon Anastasia; he saw a finger move, a fraction-of-an-inch, trembling and hanging onto life. At first, he thought he hadn't seen it, but after a closer look, he saw her hand move again, with a certainty. He bent down and pulled her out from underneath her father and brother, and analyzed the situation carefully. Was she still breathing? Was she still alive? His hand reached for his bayonet at his side, but then he studied her and lowered her head back to the floor, then got up and went to the doorway.

"Leave me here. I will call you when I need you. Go find yourselves something to eat in the village. Take your time, these bodies are not going anywhere. Talk to no one about this. In a few hours, bury them all at the location we discussed. I will bury Anastasia myself personally. I will meet you at the burial site

Secret of Ekaterinburg: The Hour-Glass

later."

The men did not question his orders. They knew better than to do that. And, so they left the scene immediately as they were told. Yakov returned to Anastasia and picked her up, and when nobody could see them, he hurriedly carried her to his car and sped away to an unknown destination, and an unfinished assignment of his own. For the sake of his own soul and well-being, this unfinished business had to be taken care of at once or she would die. But, why his change of heart? He realized in his exhaustion, that even he had had enough of the ordeal and was himself sickened by it all. He couldn't bring himself to personally kill her. He, at one time had loved her as a child, but later came to love the Communist Party more. Now, as a marked man God would surely make him pay for this act in hell when his time came.

The bodies would not be moved for another six hours, and then they would be dumped down a deserted, old mineshaft and covered with sulfuric acid in the Four Brothers Mine. A week later, rumors ran rampant and it soon became common knowledge that something horrific and evil had occurred at the Ipatiev House. Yakov and his men were forced to

Secret of Ekaterinburg: The Hour-Glass

return to the mineshaft and recover the remains. This time, the Bolsheviks tried every conceivable means to make it impossible to identify the Romanov's by dousing gasoline over the bodies and burning them and again pouring sulfuric acid over them. Yakov's men then transported the remains to a new location several miles away from the original site and because the old, war-ravaged truck broke down in the middle of the road, the soldiers resorted to digging a makeshift shallow mass grave off the roadside and reburied the bodies. This was done in an attempt to mislead villagers who might search for the bodies. Regrettably, this impromptu plan would work for seventy-five years.

Indeed, there was a parallel horror of irony at work in the brutal deaths of the Romanov's, related to the method that it was brought about.

The inefficiency of socialism was apparent right from the very beginning. It was not perfection, this murder. That was for certain. But, another thing was for certain.

Russia would be no better off without the royal family than with it.

Secret of Ekaterinburg: The Hour-Glass

CHAPTER 5

Kiev, The Ukraine, June 5, 1927

Sergei had been at the youth camp for more than four years after Comrade Grachev and the communists had taken him away. The time had passed slowly without much contact from his adopted family, but he was able to keep his own fears in check by keeping in touch with them by letter. At the camp, the communists held indoctrination classes on a daily basis, and if you didn't attend, you were sent to the nearby coal fields to labor until you dropped or to one of the Stalin collective farms to toil in the fields. The boredom alone could kill you, but if you were young and strong enough, it was not so bad unless you were emotionally and physically exhausted. If that was the case, they just shot you.

He had seen his adopted brother, Andre, and his stepfather only once during those years since his departure, at a brief meeting when Dimitri and Andre journeyed to Kiev for a

Secret of Ekaterinburg: The Hour-Glass

collective farm federation conference to discuss new goals for the never-ending five-year plans set by the Soviet agricultural committee.

That year, however, Sergei had managed to get a furlough from the Borispol billet near Kiev, and because he was now sixteen he would be allowed frequent weekend passes. He traveled by train to meet them.

When he arrived, he almost hadn't recognized them. Andre had grown much taller and his hair had darkened. Sergei's had remained blonde but straw-straight, and he was a good two inches taller than Andre, a fact he joked about by calling him "little brother." Andre didn't let it bother him. He figured it was the price of being a good brother.

"My God, I cannot believe how time has passed," Sergei blurted out jumping down from the passenger car as the train steamed to a halt. "I wouldn't have recognized you, Andre except for your being with Dimitri. He has not changed as much as you have."

Andre seem pleased by the remark, and shook Sergei's hand then gave him a bear hug. Amidst the bustling crowd at the station, hundreds of Soviet soldiers mixed into the sounds of hot, rising steam and the high-pitched train whistles. The noise was

Secret of Ekaterinburg: The Hour-Glass

deafening. And, the flow of travelers to other parts of the Soviet Union created a pulse-like urgency to get somewhere quickly. It invigorated Sergei as he paused to take it all in. Living in the camp had not been pleasant, and during their visit together all they could talk about was the family dacha, Andre's own adventures and, of course, Ana, the one girl he could not forget.

He had missed her more than he imagined. His eyes flashed brightly whenever Andre mentioned her name, and Andre long suspected that something more than just a friendship was between them. So, he kept his opinion to himself, but always found it curious that Sergei would always manage to write regularly to Ana, and only infrequently to the other family members. Andre told Sergei that Ana was now an apprentice learning to become a seamstress. His other two older sisters had both finished secondary school and had already married nearby villagers who worked on nearby collective farms.

"I cannot believe I am here talking with you. Have you heard? We have invented our first multi-engine airplane," Sergei said eagerly. "Our scientists are the best in the world."

Secret of Ekaterinburg: The Hour-Glass

"Yes," Andre laughed. "But, they are still starving."

"Why, of course. You are here for the agricultural meetings called by Comrade Stalin. I hear this meeting is the most important one ever."

"Nyet." Dimitri scowled. "Over and over again, that's all we hear. Only because we are private farmers have we managed to keep our heads above water. They are ruining the land everywhere."

"Shhh, quiet. You must not talk like that in public. There are NKVD agents everywhere. These comrades do not tolerate criticism of any kind, and especially not that kind of bourgeoisie remark. You put yourself in great danger by expressing those feelings in public," Sergei cautioned putting his finger to his lips and looking around to make sure that no one was nearby to hear his boasts.

"Oh, I don't really give a damn. It's all true and anyone who denies it, denies himself. But, come; let us find a private place to visit," Dimitri groused trying to put an end to the exchange.

"Yes. . . let us go. There is a small outdoor café along one of the boulevards near the station," Sergei offered. "I only have a few

Secret of Ekaterinburg: The Hour-Glass

hours to visit, then I must return to my official chaperon on the train. They keep me under constant surveillance, but I do not know the reason why."

"I know the reason," Dimitri scowled, his brow stiffening as he turned around and looked behind him in the direction of the train. "The NKVD bastards don't trust anyone. Not even themselves."

The trio wrestled with the suitcases and strode from the crowded train ports and out into the bright sunlight. It was already early summer and Kiev was simply magnificent. The fresh, warm air hinted at the promise of life which lay ahead for them.

The war had been over now for ten years, and the Russian people were the most optimistic ever, even under the strict constraints of Josef Stalin, their new ruthless dictator.

Strolling down one of the sidestreets, Sergei guided them to a small cafe he had frequented during his previous visits to the city. Everyone ordered coffee and sweet rolls which was what they could afford to spend. At twenty-three the boys already looked beyond their years physically. Their intellect and political knowledge was equally as imposing and quite remarkable. This new generation was

Secret of Ekaterinburg: The Hour-Glass

aggressive and inquisitive by nature.

Sergei had developed into a large, muscular youth, blue-eyed and clean shaven, almost a full-grown man. His hair glistened golden in the sunlight as he walked with a slight limp from an ankle injury he had suffered while jumping from a hay rake. Andre, the "little brother," sported a shock of tousled dark brown hair, draped across his forehead. He toasted their reunion by lifting his hot, steaming coffee mug toward the others and uttered the characteristic, "Za zdorovja!" from his lips.

"To our health," everyone rejoined.

"Da," Sergei and Dimitri responded with smiles.

Dimitri stiffened again. "They have you under constant surveillance?"

"Yes, that is so," Sergei answered. "I don't understand why?"

"I know the reason," Dimitri answered, "I have known it for years, but I would not think you would be a threat to them since you were only a child when your parents were killed."

"Why would I be a threat to Soviet state security?"

"Listen. I must tell you something you do not know. Brace yourself for this, Andre, because what I have to say will not be pleasant,

Secret of Ekaterinburg: The Hour-Glass

and you will not believe it, but try to understand my motives for keeping it secret from you. You were told that your parents were killed in the first war. But, they were not killed like you were told; they were killed by Stalin's NKVD agents. They came in the middle of the night, like angels of death arriving in a black sedan. These angels of death were the elements of the Cheka, the secret police organized by Lavrenty Beria. Poisonous. He and his henchmen took away thousands like your parents and killed them all in desolate, isolated areas in-and-around Moscow, in woods, in bogs, in out-of-the-way back-alleys, or anywhere else they could conveniently kill them without any witnesses present."

"Beria's men," Dimitri continued, turning his face away from Sergei's and spitting on the sidewalk. "Murderous swine."

"Impossible!" Sergei interjected. His face froze with the startling revelation from Dimitri. "It's true," Dimitri continued. "This was kept from you to protect you. The NKVD accused your parents of being German spies. But, everyone who knew your parents, knew the lie was created by the communists to cover up. Whenever someone failed to cooperate with their plans, they were suddenly and

Secret of Ekaterinburg: The Hour-Glass

systematically liquidated by Beria's men. This state genocide was an efficient method to do away with thousands of political dissidents by creating false circumstances and blaming it on the war. Stalin's henchmen declared your father and mother enemies of the state, and then came for them without warning. They were shot then buried in a trench along with scores of other alleged enemies of the state. That is why they are watching you. Because, the stupid bastards believe, like all our fearful comrades believe, that dissidence is hereditary. Ha! What fools they are! So, they will watch you for signs of disobedience. Be wary, and be careful whom you trust."

"I cannot believe it. It is unthinkable. Is there proof of this?" Sergei asked looking straight into the eyes of his old friend, and father-figure. "Yes. These things are all true. I am distressed to have to tell you these facts, but you had to know sooner or later. We waited because we knew when you found out, you might one day attempt revenge against them and ruin your future. I know for a fact that the charges against your parents were fabricated. But, I do not know the exact reason why. In time, you may discover the final truth. But, no matter what anyone tells you, your parents

Secret of Ekaterinburg: The Hour-Glass

were never traitors to the Russian people. They hated the Germans with a passion and fought in their own way for their motherland. That is a fact I know for sure. I swear to it as God is my witness."

Sergei stared at Dimitri.

"And, you are certain of all this?" he asked.

"I have spoken the truth. Take my word for it now," he said. "There will be ample time to investigate this on your own someday. Perhaps, when we see each other again. But, for now, we will speak of it no more, but rather talk of more pleasant things. . . "

Dimitri let his words trail off into nothingness as they sat quietly around the cafe table. Sergei reached over and poured more coffee from the porcelain carafe.

After a brief silence, Dimitri asked, "Where will they send you after our visit is ended?"

The question now somehow seemed out of place as Sergei grappled with the reality of what Dimitri had just told him. He could feel his anger building, and he knew he must control his urge for revenge at all costs. Someday, somewhere, he told himself, these same comrades would pay, every last one of them. Somehow, he would manage it, in his own lifetime. Even if it meant ending his own

Secret of Ekaterinburg: The Hour-Glass

life in the process of carrying it out. But for now, this would have to wait, until he was ready and in a position to do something about it. Then, he would arrange it.

Dimitri and Andre could also be in danger. He had to protect them, too, as they had protected him all these years.

"I am supposed to return to the young men's billet to work alongside others my age," Sergei finally answered Dimitri's question. "Then, I am supposed to continue my Education at nearby Brovary, a small village just east of Kiev."

"And what are they training you to be?" Dimitri questioned him like a father would his own son.

"I am serving an apprenticeship in electrical engineering. Following graduation, I will attend the University of Moscow where I will earn a degree there. And, after that, I don't know. Maybe, I will be a farmer and return to the dacha," he laughed letting go of his anger.

The others doubted that.

Dimitri knew the communists already had plans for Sergei. He was extremely intelligent, just like his father and mother, and they knew how to exploit that in an individual. Just like the thousands of war refugees who would become the icons of party dogma to be later devoured by the inhumane system which propelled them toward everything material for the state and away from individual thought and expression.

And when they were finished, the state would leave them nothing but the regrets of a wasted lifetime, the remains of spent geniuses spewed out like garbage on a landscape of intellectual skeletons - nothing left but the bones of stolen identity and creativity. They would become the modern robots and the human drones of the communist gulag. Nothing material would be passed along to this new generation of Russians, not even families, but none of them knew that yet. They thought they were inventing a better way of life. Their children would be raised without religion, without a belief in God, without material possessions, without loyalties to families or each other, and without the freedom of political thought.

This creation of a dysfunctional society would leave its mark not only on the immediate generation, but even the later ones who would decide the outcome of eventual world order.

It was a frightening contemplation for Sergei. As a good Russian, he knew only too

Secret of Ekaterinburg: The Hour-Glass

well that by stripping families of every proud possession they owned, including their children, it would leave them devoid of any meaningful reason to live. It would mean an unknowing and slow strangulation of the human spirit for millions. And, sooner or later, society itself would falter.

Why couldn't Comrades Lenin and Stalin see all this. Or had some of his colleagues already seen it and decided for themselves it was not for them anymore. Leon Trotsky was probably one of those who had come to this inescapable conclusion. All of them eventually would come to the same inescapable conclusion, one-by-one, until over the years, they were all gone. Like Hitler's armies, Russia would devour them all. Except, most of these men were murdered by Stalin and the men who were closest to him. Did they really know what they were doing?

Time would deliver the ultimate truth, Sergei figured, as he watched Andre and Dimitri sip their coffee. The truth would always be known in the end. Even the Bolsheviks themselves understood that. That was why they named their first communist newspaper Pravda. It meant truth. What hypocrisy.

Secret of Ekaterinburg: The Hour-Glass

"I must leave now," Sergei interrupted his own thoughts. "My train leaves in fifteen minutes. If I miss it, they will reprimand me severely. Will you see me off?"

"Will we see you off?" Andre and Dimitri said at the same time.

Sergei laughed and said, "You are such good friends, it is difficult for me to thank you after all you have done for me. I am sorry to hear the dacha is no more and now a collective farm. I would have liked to return someday. I don't know if I could bear to see it divided into equal parts. One thousand acres gone. I cannot imagine it divided."

"Neither can we," Dimitri added. "We must still work there under state orders, and we have given up the main house for everyone to share. It has been turned into a dormitory for waywards of the state. It turns my stomach."

"Before I go, please tell me about Ana. Is she married yet," Sergei asked. He remembered when he had first come to visit the Kirov's at six years of age and meeting her. He had liked her from the start, even though she was a year older. Somehow, even at that early age, he felt something special about her. Maybe it was her auburn hair, her light blue eyes, or her laugh, but he knew there would be no one

Secret of Ekaterinburg: The Hour-Glass

else in the world for him. He still felt the same way about her five years later, even though he had only seen pictures of her she sent every year.

But, he could tell she had developed into a lovely young woman who would marry soon, perhaps someone else. And, that possibility caused him desire and ache in his heart.

"She is fine and sends her love," Andre told him feeling embarrassed at the thought of Sergei having so strong emotions for his sister. It hardly seemed natural, but he understood and accepted it. "She told me to give you this parcel, and you are not to open it until after we leave."

Andre thrust the package into Sergei's hands, and laughed, but Sergei, unable to control his excitement didn't hear the words, and opened it anyway. It was a woolen scarf, hand-knitted by Ana's own hands. It was exactly what he needed, and somehow she knew exactly that. It was also a signal to him that she would wait for him to return. It really was what he had needed to survive their separation. But, Andre still hadn't answered Sergei's question, and he could see the anxiety drawn over his face, too embarrassed to ask again.

Secret of Ekaterinburg: The Hour-Glass

"Of course, she is still unmarried," he added. "And you know, come to think of it, she never mentions marriage to any of us. And she never speaks of any other men from the village. Do you think perhaps she is not the marrying type, Sergei?"

The teasing was good-natured as they walked the quarter-mile back to the train station. Unknown to them, a diminutive man standing near a street vendor, lit a cigarette, shifted to a more natural stance leaning against a lamp post, and watched them re-enter the train station. He signaled to another man with a touch of his hat, near the entrance ramp to follow them as they walked toward the trains.

Soot and fly ash, from the smoldering locomotives made it difficult to see. But, the three, arms linked together walked past the station guards unchallenged and careful not to be separated by the surging crowds rushing forward. Sergei pushed his way through the crowd towards the correct railcar, and with a quick leap, his chaperon pulled him up onto the passenger deck with a firm grip and a reassuring nod.

As the locomotive lurched forward in a cloud of rising steam and belching black smoke, the mob backed away from the dirt and

Secret of Ekaterinburg: The Hour-Glass

grime waving good-bye to their friends. Dimitri shoved himself forward and handed Sergei his luggage as the train began to pull away. Sergei waved to them as the train picked up speed and the framework of girders gave way to the blue skies outside the terminal.

Andre and his father were shoved out of the way by the massive crowd and yelled to Sergei that they see him soon.

Sergei called out, "Tell Ana that I will write to her every month. Tell her I will not forget her."

"She will not forget either," Andre yelled back. "No one will forget about you."

CHAPTER 6

Kiev, Aug. 14, 1943

Sergei sat alone in the building which housed the students designated to follow a vocational path in electrical engineering. He was bored with city life, although Kiev had a certain amount of excitement to it unlike Moscow before World War II had begun.

Under the massive control of the German army, Kiev took on an almost fatalistic relationship with its people. The German war machine and the commanders who took their oath-of-allegiance were now under the strain of diminishing food and weapon supplies. Moreover, the Third Reich's inside command structure was beginning to falter, like the rest of the Waffen SS. This same command structure dictated that all of Ukraine's food and perishable commodities were to be confiscated by the German army for its own consumption, leaving little of anything for the people themselves.

Sergei penned a letter to Ana back in

Secret of Ekaterinburg: The Hour-Glass

Peregrebnoye. "My love, there is nothing more left here, and if I am to succeed in a career in electrical engineering, it will have to be after this terrible war is over. If I stay in Kiev any longer, I will have to adapt to the political will of either the German Army or the Russian Army, whichever succeeds first. I have learned from several of my classmates who are spies in the Ukrainian underground that the German army is weakening, and is now subject to increasing desertions.

"Of course, what the Nazis don't realize is once they divulge to the Russians any or all information they have life does not get easier for them. They are shot at once simply because there is no extra food to feed them. The Germans devour everything in their path. We hear reports they have even turned to shooting prisoners. And, they are conscripting Ukrainian national militiamen to fight their brother Russians in an attempt to save the dwindling food supply. In any case, I am fed up with living a meager, subsistence of a life. I must leave here soon before the entire Ukraine is destroyed. I know it is much worse where you are but still my conscience dictates that I must either return to you soon or die here. With much affection, Sergei."

Secret of Ekaterinburg: The Hour-Glass

He addressed the envelope, moistened it with his lips, and sealed the letter to post later in the day. His roommate entered the room and observed Sergei sitting astride a window seat overlooking the third floor of an abandoned munitions storehouse. Sergei watched the rain soak the dead leaves on the pavement outside his apartment. The droplets captured them in a lifeless damp coating.

"What are you going to do, Sergei," asked his roommate.

"What do you mean?"

"I know you are depressed. We are all miserable here. We all want to leave and go home. But, the Germans will kill us if we try. Our only hope is to wait for rescue from either the American or the Russian army, whichever can break through first."

"Da. But, the wait is unbearable. And, what is the guarantee that any of us will come out alive. The Germans are taking prisoners for forced labor at hundreds of camps in Germany and those that surround Kiev. The real purpose, I am told, is to dispose of Jews while they build roads. I don't know if that is true. But, once they leave here, nobody ever sees them again. I hear that if you are not strong enough to work or if you refuse, they shoot you on the spot."

Secret of Ekaterinburg: The Hour-Glass

"Be thankful you are not a Jew," his roommate said.

"Does it make any difference? We Catholics are next on their list. Then, whom after that?"

"Yes. I have heard these same stories, Sergei. But, we must not listen to such talk, even if it is true. You cannot imagine what horrors I have dreamed about such thoughts. The SS took my mother and father from Shuleveska two months ago. They are Jews and I have not been able to locate them since. I've searched everywhere. My younger brother, I was told, died of pneumonia, before he reached the camp. He received no medical attention from either the Ukrainian army or German army because he was of no use to them. It is a barbaric situation, I tell you. And, it will get worse. I must escape. If they knew I was a Jew, I wouldn't last long. Would you consider fleeing with me?"

"If I knew there was a good chance to survive behind the Russian lines . . . yes . . . I would."

"Then, there is a way, and we must do it before it's too late."

"But, how can we?"

"I have been devising a plan, but you must

Secret of Ekaterinburg: The Hour-Glass

tell no one, not even your best friends where we are going. If you do, it will jeopardize us. Do you understand?"

"Da," Sergei replied, listening fervently to the plan unraveling before him.

"Here is what I have done so far. We can make our way to the train station at night pretending to be going home in a drunken stupor after partying with friends from the university. The German soldiers will believe that, and I think we can walk past the train station for a bit, and into the rail yards where they load the trains with ammunition for the German front. Once inside the rail pens, we can climb aboard one of the hundreds of boxcars and hide among the munitions until the train departs."

"But, how soon would that be?" Sergei questioned Josef Prachek.

"I have timed the trains from when they are loaded to until they leave. Once loaded, the trains leave within two days to a week maximum. Of course, it will be dangerous because there are guards assigned to each train, but not so many that they can detect us. Once we get close to the Russian lines, we leap from the train and hide until we make our way back to the Dnepr River."

Secret of Ekaterinburg: The Hour-Glass

"Da. But, what about food?"

"We will need at least a week's supply to keep us alive. If all goes well the train will pull out in a couple of days. It's a two-day ride to the front, and a two-day walk after that. If the train does not pull out of the station on time, the SS will be searching for us everywhere as soon as we are reported missing. . ." Sergei's voice trailed off into stony silence. Both knew they would be rounded up as deserters or as members of the Ukrainian partisans. The penalty for attempting to escape was death by firing squad.

"But, what if the Russian army captures us before we can cut through their lines to safety? What if they decide we are deserters, too?"

"Then we are either dead Germans or dead Russians. It makes no difference, we will still be dead. But, we are dead men anyway if we stay here any longer. We have no choice. The Germans will almost certainly put us into conscript camps. Eventually, they will kill us. Trust me, Sergei, when I say we are already dead."

"Stop! You have convinced me. All I need to do is look around and see the others who also want to go home, perhaps to fight against the enemy. We have all stayed too long for our own good and for the good of Russia. We will do it."

"All right then. We will gather enough food for one week, and we must do it now. The sooner the better," Sergei repeated without taking his eyes off Josef.

Sergei knew his fate was in the hands of a roommate he hardly knew but who was a Russian like himself. He trusted he was not a spy who would turn him over to the Third Reich bastards.

"It's a pact between us," Josef said in an oath like response and shook Sergei's hand. "God, help us if they capture us."

"They won't," Sergei said solemnly clutching his letter to Ana. He extinguished the flame flickering in the oil lamp on the window ledge with a quick breath.

"As God is my witness, they will all remember us for what we are about to do, Prachek. The Germans will pay for all they have done. For every Russian they have killed, for every Ukrainian child they have murdered, for every Jew and Slavic family they have massacred, they will pay dearly in the end. I promise that in a vow to God."

Secret of Ekaterinburg: The Hour-Glass

CHAPTER 7

Kiev, Aug. 15, 1943

The pair planned their escape as soon as possible. If the plan went perfect Sergei and Josef would be out on a drunken excursion in the midst of the patrolling Wehrmacht units along the city's restaurants and pubs.

One-by-one, students living in the dormitories would leave their rooms between seven and nine o'clock to go into town for a bout of drinking with their classmates. Sergei and Josef would leave their barracks at precisely eight-fifteen careful not to arouse suspicion among their peers or the campus guards.

They dressed inauspiciously, but warmly enough to suit their traveling aboard the local freight trains running between Kiev and Moscow, especially if the weather turned sour and they had to hide in the freight cars several days before the train pulled out for the front. Munitions trains were usually longer than

Secret of Ekaterinburg: The Hour-Glass

regular supply trains because the German Army commanders deemed it necessary to keep the trains running as infrequently as possible and only when necessary so as to keep saboteurs and Russian dive-bombers guessing when the resupply runs were being made.

"Hurry, Sergei," called Josef. "We must make it to the rail yard by eleven o'clock. That will give us a few hours to be seen among our friends, then we will drift away during the commotion to the back streets then on to the freight yards."

"I know, I know," Sergei answered impatiently while locking the door to their sleeping quarters in the barracks. "We must be extra careful tonight. There are spies everywhere, even among our own kind."

"Yes, but it is a risk worth taking if we are ever to see our families again and to do something for mother Russia," Josef spoke carefully choosing his words.

The pair moved out into the facade called "the quadrangle" located inside the perimeter of dormitories which housed some 500 of the most promising engineering students in all of the Soviet Union. The elite students had been the privileged few, from the beginning, chosen from among the millions of Russian school

Secret of Ekaterinburg: The Hour-Glass

children for their I.Q. and performance scores as measured against all the rest.

These select five hundred would then be educated and indoctrinated into the communist system, an educational kind of gulag, to eventually become model citizens and faithful party members among the hierarchy of intelligentsia and party apparatus. They knew they were a privileged lot, but they also never forgot their backgrounds as cogs in a despotic communist system which had exploited the masses in favor of a bureaucratic minority.

"Josef. Quickly. Move down the side street. Over there. Do you see them?"

"Da. Two of them. Coming this way. If they stop us, remember what we have to do."

The two moved silently along the sidewalk with the two German sentries approaching them with rifles slung over their shoulders.

Josef and Sergei kept their eyes averted as the two soldiers approached looking them over routinely. Sergei kept his glance lowered but nodded as the two guards passed by. They were five steps beyond them now and walking quickly away, when abruptly one of the guards turned, and yelled out a command.

"Achtung! You there."

The pair stood transfixed in their tracks, and

Secret of Ekaterinburg: The Hour-Glass

turned to face the soldiers.

"Why are you both in such a hurry, tonight?" one of the guards asked as he approached them while the other remained a short distance away.

Josef looked cautiously at Sergei and gave his rehearsed reply.

"I did not think we were walking so fast as you were. Perhaps, it was you walking past us faster than you thought? Believe me, we are in no hurry to join our already drunken bastard classmates at the beer halls."

"Da." Sergei chimed in. "They are indeed a drunken lot, even though they are still our friends. Sometimes you have to associate with pigs if you wish to dine, eh?"

The soldiers laughed sharing the humor with them.

"Yabol. You are seemingly better boys than most of the vermin we encounter here. Enjoy your drunken binge the rest of the night while it is early. You won't remember any of it by morning," the soldier joked and let them pass moving away into the darkness of another alley.

"Auvetersein," the boys responded in German. The Germans liked it when Russians spoke to them in their native tongue. It made

Secret of Ekaterinburg: The Hour-Glass

them feel as though they were being accepted in a part of the world where everyone despised them.

Josef whispered to Sergei.

"Be careful. Don't say too much. The less said the better. Let them do the talking. Be respectful."

"Of course," Sergei answered nervously. "The swine didn't even realize I was talking about them?"

Both could contain themselves no longer and laughed as they distanced themselves out of earshot of the two guards.

The target of their evening excursion was the local pub, situated along one of the back alleys along the main corridors of Kiev. It was a ghastly pub, known for terrible liquor and equally bad food. It was inappropriately expensive but the companionship was excellent. Josef and Sergei knew several of the other boys from their farm region, and a handful of others. The rest they hardly knew and could not trust. To pass time into the early hours of the morning, mostly everyone played darts or a peculiar Russian type of card game called Fools Hand.

The game was played by four persons, but with only enough winning cards for three.

Secret of Ekaterinburg: The Hour-Glass

After several hours of this diversion, and two or three pints of beer, Josef and Sergei glanced at the clock as it neared the eleven o'clock hour. A cursory glance at each other assured everything was going according to the plan and that it would be time to leave as inauspiciously as possible. How would they manage to do that without arousing any unusual attention?

Josef told Sergei that he would excuse himself to take a long piss in the men's room. He would delay his return, long enough, so that Sergei could complain once or twice as to what was keeping him away from the card game. Josef could then appear to become drunker and drunker, drinking himself into a stupor. When he didn't return from the urinals, Sergei would go to retrieve him, and he would position himself across his shoulders as if he was on the verge of passing out barely able to walk and remain upright.

Like a good friend, Sergei would announce he must take pity on the poor bastard, and return him to the barracks. After all, it was the only decent thing to do with a good "buddy."

Sergei went into the men's room to retrieve Josef after much boisterous complaining . . . "Where in the hell is my drunken roommate?"

The two stumbled from the men's room,

Secret of Ekaterinburg: The Hour-Glass

with Josef's arm slung across Sergei's shoulder and dragging one leg.

"He is shit-eyed," announced Sergei proudly. "My friend here is drunken through to the bone. I cannot leave him here in the urinals all night even though he deserves it. He will be impossible by morning. My apologies to you all, but I'm afraid we must end the evening. We will continue our card game some other night my friends!"

The remaining pals at the table howled hilariously at the sight of them hanging over each other in a carefully choreographed balancing act. It was nothing new for a classmate to drink himself into mental and physical oblivion. The pair departed to a wild, cheering standing ovation.

As soon as Sergei and Josef had cleared the doorway, waving good-bye to their remaining partyers, they slid off to one of the side streets they knew would take them to the freight yards virtually undetected.

"Shhh. We must be extremely careful to avoid attention from passersby. We cannot take any chances now. Our goal is nearly in our grasp." Josef said soberly in a whisper.

The two moved deliberately toward the freight yards walking along the darkened,

Secret of Ekaterinburg: The Hour-Glass

deserted alleyways, detouring for an occasional trash can placed in their path by some unknown citizen to trip a wayward drunkard unaware of the pitfall. Just one more alley to negotiate, and the rail yard would be in sight. I would be an extremely dangerous place for them to be after curfew.

Without warning, the blackness gave way to a well-lighted corridor of fence and track that looked impenetrable and impossible to cross. It was guarded by several German soldiers.

"My God, Josef. I thought you said most of the trains were unguarded."

Sergei abruptly pulled up and stopped at the corner of one of the buildings.

"They usually are. Something important must be happening tonight. It's a tough break for us, but we still must try or lose the advantage in a few days."

There were two trains pointed in the same direction on parallel tracks.

One, a regular-looking engine with about twenty cars ready to roll; the other, a much longer and heavily camouflaged one, that bore no insignias or any markings. Which train would they choose? They both agreed without discussion, the longer train. It was the munitions train without a doubt. They would

Secret of Ekaterinburg: The Hour-Glass

have to make their move now or do this all again some other night, and by then, it might be too late.

They wished each other good luck, and walked slowly through the shadows, down the corridor when the guards moved to the other side of the line of railcars.

Swiftly and silently, they climbed inside one of the open boxcars and disappeared among the crates of shell casings.

They prayed that no one had seen them and that in the morning after their departure no Russian dive-bombers would find them in their bombsights.

Secret of Ekaterinburg: The Hour-Glass

CHAPTER 8

The Dnepr River, Ukraine, Jan. 30, 1944

The German army had been shredded and worn into exhaustion by the Russian counter-offensive. Entire whole platoons and several small army units had frozen to death while encamped along the lakes and rivers during one of the worst winters in Russian history. Thousands of German soldiers lay dead in the fields, frozen to their machine guns with thousands more dying of hunger because field kitchens would not operate in the extreme Siberian cold which crept in from the north. Thousands more had simply given in to the brutal elements and were surrendering to the Russians in an effort to stay alive for a few more months, a form of self-preservation evoking a strong natural instinct hoping they would see their families again. Most of them wouldn't.

As this great drama unfolded, the once-proud German juggernaut ground to a slow but

Secret of Ekaterinburg: The Hour-Glass

determinant halt.

Essentially, the Waffen had already been stopped by the winter of 1941 but the generals hadn't realized it, Now, after three grueling years, the Wehrmacht was now on the verge of collapse, and an ever increasingly stronger Russian army lay in wait just a few miles across the vast frontier poised and armed for a massive counterattack which would finish them off forever. The Wermacht high command knew nothing of this doomsday force poised to launch a counter-campaign of death and destruction.

They had miscalculated badly. This time the miscalculation would cost them the war and put to an end Hitler's dream of the conquest of Russia. In a few hours, the Russian's surprise counter-offensive, formulated by the capable Field Commander Gen. Marshall Georgi Zhukov would be launched.

No one in the German high command would fathom how nine new Russian divisions supposedly destroyed earlier in battle, could appear out of thin air mobilized at full strength, and begin a surprise attack across the Dnepr.

A lone German garrison on the river the morning of the attack remained oblivious to the threat. It was a dark and quiet usual winter

Secret of Ekaterinburg: The Hour-Glass

night with nothing moving in the early dawn at 5:17 a.m.

All was quiet on the eastern front.

Then, suddenly and without warning, an artillery barrage began.

Hans, a young German SS sentry peered through the fog to see movement on the opposite shoreline. He wasn't sure what was happening. Instead of alerting anyone, he continued to observe what appeared to be Russian T-54 tanks, about twelve, moving into new positions some half-mile away across the river. He could barely hear their engines, but he could feel the vibrations of the heavy machines as they rolled across the shoreline opposite him. Were they pulling out or newly arriving? The sound traveled inharmoniously through the heavy, damp air as he awakened another sentry sleeping inside the bunker.

"Dieter. Dieter. You dunkoff! Get up at once. Hurry! Something is happening across the river."

Dieter bolted upright from his sleep sack, rubbed his hands together, stood up and looked through his field binoculars to see what had alarmed Hans so much.

"What is it? What do you see?"

"Look. Over to your right. That's it. Do

Secret of Ekaterinburg: The Hour-Glass

you see them? About a dozen of them. Tanks! What in God's name are they going to do with them?" Hans uttered out loud.

"We must alert, headquarters?" Dieter responded, huddling against the wall of sandbags, blocking the icy wind from his shoulders.

"Perhaps. But, I don't see any movement at all now. Do you think they are grouping for an attack? Where would they attack? There is no bridgehead. Why would they be organizing them there?" Hans said.

"Yabol," Dieter echoed. "Yes, they have stopped their movement."

Both soldiers peered through their binoculars, then suddenly the roar of the tank engines became louder, and more aggressive.

"My God, Dieter!" Hans spoke excitedly. "`It is impossible. But, I see it with my own eyes. They are coming across! They are coming across! It cannot be possible? They cannot do that? No tank can do that."

The Russian T-54s had moved in a precise and orderly line to the edge of the river bank, then swiftly and without hesitation, one-by-one, followed each other across, toward the German side.

"Quickly, call up central command and tell

Secret of Ekaterinburg: The Hour-Glass

them what is happening," Hans called out to Dieter.

Hans knew the river was thirty feet deep in some spots, with an average depth of twelve feet, and a current-flow of fifteen kilometers, much too swift for tanks to merely float.

What was happening here was some kind of Russian miracle. The Russians were doing the impossible. They were moving massive mechanized units across a river that could only be crossed with a bridge. But, there was no bridge.

Physically impossible, but they were doing it anyway. Dieter was on the field telephone to German headquarters screaming into the mouthpiece.

"Achtung. Achtung. This is SS unit 3. The enemy is counterattacking! The Russians are counterattacking us at the 346 command post!

"No, I am not out of my mind. I am telling you they are sending tanks across the river where there is no bridge."

Hans was frozen in fear. He knew the high command must think he had been drinking. But, he and Dieter were as sober as fish out of water, and they were witnessing it with their own disbelieving eyes. They could now see more tanks massing on the other side, poised to

Secret of Ekaterinburg: The Hour-Glass

travel the same route that the others had initiated. A long, thin tank line, now formed across the river, firing their guns forward as they rolled across the water.

It was beginning to get light, and they could see more clearly now.

"My God," Hans said aloud, "there must be 100 of them coming across. Tell central command they will be upon us in only minutes. Mobilize! Mobilize everyone! At once!"

But, it was too late. Suddenly, and without warning, a T54 fired a 120mm shell squarely into the bunker with devastating force. The explosion killed Hans and Dieter instantly cutting communications between the bunker and German headquarters. Two brave soldiers fighting impossible odds joined the thousands of dead Germans who had tried to invade an impenetrable homeland facing a determined people now seeking everlasting revenge for the slaughter of millions of innocent families in Russia, the Ukraine, Poland, Czechoslovakia, and the other allied countries on Russia's borders. Both Hans and Dieter were now among the casualties of war who had followed a flawed German high command allowing Hitler to manipulate his way into power with a hateful philosophy and corrupt ideology. They

Secret of Ekaterinburg: The Hour-Glass

had been like the rest of the German people who had followed an insane leader into an unwinnable war.

What Hitler hadn't counted on was the stubbornness of the Russian army. They could be ferocious when cornered and they had indeed been cornered. And, on this particular morning, what the Germans didn't know was that the Russian commanders had ordered the construction of an underwater bridge twenty-four inches below the surface across the Dnepr, one that could not be seen in the muddy waters by day or night. It had been built by frogmen and construction engineers a half-mile in length, close enough to the German side so that the T-54s could point their tanks in a straight line toward a particular visual target, and cross over to the other side, performing a battlefield miracle before the Germans very eyes. Indeed, in their first attempt, the German units were caught completely by surprise.

Tank upon tank advanced to shore, crossing unimpeded by the lack of organized return artillery fire. It was too late. The spearhead had succeeded magnificently along a five-mile front, including a diversionary artillery barrage of incredible magnitude. Some 600,000 rocket and artillery rounds were fired along the five-

Secret of Ekaterinburg: The Hour-Glass

mile front as the counterattack was simultaneously launched in a devastating fashion that only the Russians could appreciate and the Germans could only experience.

It was massive followed by advanced infantry units crossing at several other points on pontoon bridges along the River, and simultaneous air strikes by hundreds of Russian dive-bombers and fighter planes which now dominated the skies over Russia. The Luftwaffe would not or could not fly. There simply were no more German planes left. With that, the Russians overran and easily pulverized the remaining Germans into oblivion. After only four days, the entire German army had surrendered, some 250,000 Hans' and Dieters' lay dead or wounded in the Russian snow with their blood becoming the symbol of the new Red army. The siege had ended at last.

Death and defeat would soon envelope the entire German army, its machinery, its high command, all the way back to Berlin where it all started.

It would take another six months to achieve, but the Russians and their allies would complete it in a devastating finale that would take no prisoners.

The collapse of the great juggernaut was at

Secret of Ekaterinburg: The Hour-Glass

hand.

A bridge beneath the turbulent waters.

An invisible bridge.

Placed under the very noses of the German army.

Even Helen of Troy would have been proud that day.

Secret of Ekaterinburg: The Hour-Glass

CHAPTER 9

Vladivostok, Krazcoff Naval Base, Oct. 20, 1989

Andre grasped Sergei's hand as they prepared to depart. They hugged for what they knew might be the last time without emotion knowing deep inside what the other was thinking. Time and a trusted brotherhood enabled the two pals to do that.

That same closeness had served Andre after Sergei was taken by the Bolsheviks so the genuine concern was still there. This time, it would not be quite the same they sensed, but again, they had little choice.

"My brother," Andre said. "You know what we are facing. This must be done. And you know I as a former military man and you still one of them, we are sworn to each other not to obey these orders even if it means death to the both of us.

"I realize this, Andre. No one knows this better than I do," he said solemnly and without

Secret of Ekaterinburg: The Hour-Glass

hesitation.

Sergei released his grip on Andre's hand as they stood there for a brief moment then left the tiny shanty.

"Tell, me. Is there any precedent for this kind of thing?" Sergei asked.

Andre paused. "Yes. I will tell you about it when we next meet," Andre answered. "In the meantime, you will not hear from me again until I contact you at this phone number on November 14 at precisely 1500 hours. Understood?"

"Perfectly," Sergei answered. "But, where is this telephone and is it secure?"

"I have checked it myself. It is at a place of your liking."

Andre slipped him a folded piece of paper.

"Memorize it and then burn it," he cautioned.

Sergei read the contents then reached into his pocket and struck a match and watched the flames consume the piece of paper. The ashes fell from the palm of his hand, the wind carrying them into the bay.

"Now my friend you will give me a tour of your great naval base and all the important equipment you have here which you are not supposed to show me," Andre nagged. "Come .

Secret of Ekaterinburg: The Hour-Glass

. . if only they knew we are brothers."

Sergei grinned, but as they left the shanty doorway, they wiped the expressions from their faces hiding all traces of emotion relating to the clandestine meeting. Both men strode quickly past the submarine pens where refurbishing work was already beginning aboard the Saint-Petersburg.

"It is a behemoth of a war craft is it not?" proclaimed Sergei.

"Indeed," replied Andre. "But, I am more interested in the other pieces of equipment you have at the other end of the yard. Can we take a closer look without anyone noticing?"

"Oh, they will notice. How can they not? But, I am the base commander, and I can go anywhere I please and with whom I please," Sergei said. "There will be nothing suspicious about us. It will look normal. Anyway, there's nothing especially secret about them anyway. But, you are still the curious one, aren't you?"

The two swung past a circle of submariners playing cards at a makeshift table. Startled by their sudden appearance, the crew quickly rose to salute Sergei, but he immediately waved them off with a hand gesture signaling them to remain seated. They nodded in appreciation and continued playing.

Secret of Ekaterinburg: The Hour-Glass

Sergei had a distinct leadership style. It was one of common sense and decency. When the men were relaxed or off-duty, he showed them the simple courtesy of leaving them alone to their thoughts or private time. But, once aboard a ship, he demanded their total obedience and complete respect, especially when giving orders.

The men liked and admired him in return. He had once commanded the Saint-Petersburg and other ships. Men and machine worked efficiently as a unit, so precise that other naval officers were often envious of Sergei's command presence.

As commander of the sub base, he was in charge of 15,000 personnel including an additional 3,000 "spetznatz" troops used to infiltrate enemy lines, sabotage infrastructure and destroy civil targets during wartime. "Spetznatz" were the mirror image of the elite "special forces" teams the Americans had in place around the world.

Now because of several peace initiatives with the United States, the danger of war seemed very distant, but old habits die hard and it still remained in the back of everyone's mind. It had been five years since the new missile treaties had been signed and both countries had

Secret of Ekaterinburg: The Hour-Glass

into effect a "stand-down" order re-targeting their nuclear missiles away from each other's major cities. They were no longer each other's enemies. Who would have thought such a thing possible merely a decade ago? Sergei and Andre used to talk about such things when they were young, but in reality they never believed it could happen in their lifetime.

Nonetheless, the agreements had never been really tested in a crisis involving both countries except during the Persian Gulf War, just prior to the great cooperation between the two superpowers.

Andre wondered if there would ever come a time when that agreement might be put to a stronger test – a direct test. He hoped it never would, and he was sure that Sergei felt the same way, too. No real Russian ever wanted a war with America, or any of its allies especially after their Afghanistan experience. Much of the same held true for thousands of other Soviet families and the daily toll that war had taken on their lives. Their self-esteem was damaged irreparably in the losing effort, and they were in essence held directly answerable by the world for the mass-killing of Afghan peasants who offered fierce resistance to the invasion. The Soviet families had by default become part of

Secret of Ekaterinburg: The Hour-Glass

an efficient killing machine of people in a foreign land with whom they had no real quarrel.

"Look over there," Sergei motioned as the two men left the protected subterranean entrance and stepped out directly into the bright sunlight. "What do you think of that?"

"My God," Andre said with surprise. "It is massive. How can it possibly move? It must weigh an enormous amount. How much can it really lift?" he asked.

"It can lift a light cruiser or one end of a heavy cruiser. We have twelve of them here at this base alone and we can perform emergency repair work below the waterline in one or two days."

Andre was amazed. His eyes moved toward the far end of the naval yard and kept searching until he caught a glimpse of what he had come to see. Yes, they were there.

"But, that is much more impressive," Andre said without a smile. "Do you know what I mean?"

Sergei did.

They were now approaching the most sensitive area of the naval base, yet no one dared challenge Sergei's authority, even with the presence of a stranger walking about with

Secret of Ekaterinburg: The Hour-Glass

him.

Sergei looked around. "My brother, once these are launched for the secret mission and when the rest of the world learns what we have done the earth will stand still for a moment, eh?"

Andre drew in a deep breath and shuddered slightly.

"The earth already had stood still for a day. Remember, Andre?"

"Yes, I remember. The murders. July 17, 1918. A terrible day. And, now we have come to this."

"Yes, and to think what the possible reaction of the Americans and British will be when they discover these ships cannot be denied," he said. "They will be convinced."

"Twenty-five of them here," Sergei said as he admired the neat vertical rows facing the inlet, "and twenty-five more at Beringovsky that will be ready in the next few weeks."

The men stood silent flanking each other while observing the work being performed on the sleek new vessels. Each ship appeared to be near operational readiness and were the size of small fishing trawlers. But, these were a lot different. The trawlers regularly plied the oceans of the world as part of the Soviet array

Secret of Ekaterinburg: The Hour-Glass

of electronic spy vessels parked off the coast of the United States and other western countries to gather information on military bases, or eavesdrop on secret missile launches. The only fish on board were highly sophisticated electronic surveillance equipment to observe what the Americans, British and other NATO nations were up to.

These more modern, similar-looking vessels were arrayed for another purpose, one unannounced and still kept secret known only to the KGB and to the inner-most, trusted officials working in the newly formed government of the Commonwealth of Independent States (CIS).

"Come, now we must visit base operations. Our orders are awaiting even though we already know them. I believe I must go to Kiev, and you will travel to Moscow, my brother," Sergei whispered. "You will have a better time than I will. The Ukrainian women are prettier than the Muscovites, but don't tell them I said that, O.K. It is a matter of personal preference?"

"Nyet. I will tell only the ones who ask about you," Andre laughed grabbing Sergei by the shoulder slowly walking off in the direction of Red Navy Headquarters.

Secret of Ekaterinburg: The Hour-Glass

There was still time to be cheerful but in the back of their minds they feared future events could still betray them.

The refitting of the Saint-Petersburg continued on schedule.

Secret of Ekaterinburg: The Hour-Glass

CHAPTER 10

London, The Times, Oct. 20, 1989

Rick glanced briefly at the memo he found on the heap of journalistic rubble he called his desk. The note had been put there by Pete Driscoll, his editor but he could not quite believe his eyes.

"Assignment: Moscow. Determine if emerging Russian leader is a threat to new capitalism."

"Damn it," he muttered to himself.

He and Adrienne had just returned from the middle east and were set for a two week, well deserved honeymoon after being married in Riyadh. He sucked in a deep breath.

"I guess a job's a job," he said to himself and began shuffling papers around pitching his unfinished assignments into a nearby trash can. There were always plenty of trash cans around a newsroom. You could count on that to rid yourself of the daily frustrations you couldn't deal with. But, that was the only thing you

Secret of Ekaterinburg: The Hour-Glass

could count on in the news business. That's where most of the assignments ended up anyway - unwritten, unfinished or newsworthy journalism. He hated it with a passion because it was an afterthought sort-of-career that had nearly impoverished him. It was the only profession he knew where a person could graduate with a degree from college and still make less than a starting janitor. Why couldn't newspaper people catch up with the real world and offer a premium pay scale like doctors, lawyers and stockbrokers. After all, he figured reporters were supposed to be regarded as professionals. That's what they called themselves. Consummate professionals. But hell, those inflated feelings of self-worth didn't pay the bills and neither did the editors. Only hard cash did and that was scarce in the journalism trade. Not only did you have to be masochistic to work for nearly free, but you had to have a pathetic view of yourself as a voyeur.

Rick knew journalists were good at deceiving themselves and dedicating themselves to a lifetime of poverty and low self-esteem. That's why most of them were liberal socialists. They all knew they would be poor for the rest of their lives and he knew he

Secret of Ekaterinburg: The Hour-Glass

had become one of them. He was a graduate of news journalism from Kent State University, but his degree didn't automatically make him the consummate professional he purported to be. He had under his belt, long lean years of hard work ranging from dull public affairs reporting to exhilarating foreign correspondent work which had eventually earned him his spurs as a seasoned and savvy reporter.

But, Waite didn't look at his job as lifetime work. Few journalists did. If they admitted so everyone knew they were lying. Most joined the profession because they could do little or nothing else. The profession was an asylum for all the other professional misfits who had somehow wandered into the vocation. Everyone was working for that one successful story which would enable them to buy themselves out of the profession and into something more decent. It's not because they loved the profession. Most of them moved on into the more stable, lucrative corporate PR field. It was just a matter of time for most. But what's worse, the corporate executive types never really trusted any of them. They needed their skills and journalism connections, but they couldn't trust them or their ideology. They just used them for their own ends.

Secret of Ekaterinburg: The Hour-Glass

Eventually, if Waite had the balls he would dump journalism and get into a more productive career, one that would pay well on a regular basis. But, in the event he did get stuck in the news field, his plan was to freelance his way to fame and fortune. And, that wasn't easy. First, he had to get through the next 10 years or so in one piece. Some of his previous assignments, had nearly got him killed or ruined his career. His first real international assignment had been in Brazil trying to track down a Nazi war criminal rumored to be living there. He never did find him. Then, he spent five years mired in the middle east on the UPI assignment in Beirut where he had met Adrienne and subsequently discovered the plot to involve the region in a nuclear war. That had been the story of a lifetime, and he had won the Pulitzer for it, but he didn't make any money from it even though his breaking story had caught the entire world off-guard. He had been forgotten after that once again. The prize money was meager, but it was nicer getting the respect he finally deserved from his colleagues. He would use the money up fast. And, he would use up the respect he got from it just as quickly. Someday, he had to get a real job. But, for now, he and Adrienne would be off to

Secret of Ekaterinburg: The Hour-Glass

Russia. She would not like that. She had longed for an assignment in Rome or Paris or to some other exotic place.

But, this?

Gray, dreary Moscow.

The thought of it made him wince. He finished clearing off his desk and poured an old cup of coffee into the same trash can with his papers letting the brown liquid soak into the news copy. He watched it for a few seconds then set off in the direction of Pete's office. As he rounded the corner, he nearly bumped into another reporter meekly exiting the same office. Rick was in no mood for being passive. He despised those who were.

He barged straight into Pete's office.

Pete was a large, imposing, one-dimensional man, who could be counted on to be sitting in his usual spot scowling at a piece of news copy or at a computer screen ready to edit-to-death a rookie reporter's badly written story.

Rick sensed that he was not pleased with the piece he was reading. That probably explained the quick exit by the neophyte reporter. So, he started in first hoping to catch him off-guard.

"Moscow, Pete?" Rick said getting his attention quickly. "Why in the hell are you sending us to Moscow. The capitalism story is

Secret of Ekaterinburg: The Hour-Glass

old news. It's been almost six years now. There's nothing happening there that hasn't been hashed or rehashed."

"That's what you and your other bullshit friends out in the newsroom would like to think," Pete countered.

After a short pause, he added, "And who is WE. You're the one who is going, not Adrienne."

Pete motioned for Rick to sit down on the old couch near the end of his desk handing him a map of the former Soviet Union.

"Shut up and listen to what I have to say," Pete said.

Pete Driscoll was a crusty old bastard, but he was a time-tested editor who wrote news stories from the gut and he had an instinct for a damned good news story. A lot of reporters didn't like him but most respected his ability to smell out a good news story. You had to give him that much.

"We need someone over there with experience. Our bureau chief is having a hell-of-a-time digging out good, solid news stories. To make things worse, he's saddled with a bunch of rookie reporters fresh out of school who don't know shit about international reporting. Those damned useless schools of

Secret of Ekaterinburg: The Hour-Glass

journalism back in the states taught them to be experts in nothing. Hell, half of them can't even spell and the others hardly know how to write a lead-in. And, besides, he wants out of there and he's been giving me the same old crap, you know just like you did when you were with UPI for us in Beirut. Look, I know the capitalism angle is an old one, but there's just got to be something more happening over there. It's been too fucking quiet for too long. I can't explain it. It's just a hunch. Nothing can be that quiet for that long, especially in Russia. You know, transition and all. Murphy's Law says something's in the wind. I just want to make sure there's someone there who knows what he's doing when Murphy shows up."

"Well, what exactly are you looking for?" Rick asked feigning interest. "Believe me, everything's been written, rewritten and reworked over and over again."

Pete countered, "Nothing is ever all written. That's why we hire all of you bastards. I want you there. You know the ropes better than anybody and you're the best God-damned reporter I've got for this," Pete said buttering him up for the kill.

"Christ, Pete, you don't have to do that," Rick rubbed the back of his neck feeling

Secret of Ekaterinburg: The Hour-Glass

uneasy.

"Adrienne's not going to like this one damned bit, and I don't either. Especially after I baited her with the possibility of the Rome assignment a few weeks ago. She's gonna . . . you know what."

"Hold it, Pete interjected. "Remember, five minutes ago, I said who said we? I didn't say anything about your wife going along on this assignment?"

"But, I thought . . . "

"Well, you thought wrong," Pete countered.

"Wait a minute. How long do you expect me to be over there?" Rick asked.

"I was thinking of making you permanent bureau chief," Pete tested.

"Goddammit!" Rick shouted and stood up from the couch. "You expect us to be apart all that time? Christ, we just got married! We've hardly gotten to know each other, no less attempted some sort of damned honeymoon!"

"Easy. Don't get pissed off," Pete thundered. "Here's the way I figure it. Because we're short-handed in eastern Europe, I'm assigning Adrienne to Stockholm. It's just a short flight from Moscow. You two can work all week, then rendezvous on the weekends either in Moscow or Stockholm - all on the company.

Secret of Ekaterinburg: The Hour-Glass

Does that sound better?"

Rick had to admit it did with the Stockholm part thrown-in. Even if they couldn't be together during the week, they could stay in touch by phone or computer, and it was only a two-hour flight between Stockholm and Moscow aboard Aeroflot.

He paused for a minute to rethink things.

"O.K. I'll run it by Adrienne tonight. But, you owe me, goddammit. By the way, how much is the raise going to be if I take it?"

"Well, that's another thing I wanted to talk to you about," Pete started apologetically. "You see, the thing is, salaries have been frozen for about three months now, and with the economy the way it is over here, and with nothing bringing in additional revenues, there's not going to be much of a raise.

But, look at it this way, it's a chance to make a name for yourself again, and see Russia to boot," he said hoping to entice Rick into the deal.

"No deal," Rick countered. "I've already seen Russia. I want a $200 a month raise for both of us, or the deal is off and I'll start free-lancing tomorrow. And damn it, Pete, I'm serious. We'll be gone this weekend and you'll lose two damned good reporters. And, you can

Secret of Ekaterinburg: The Hour-Glass

take that to the bank."

Pete knew Rick wasn't a bluffer especially when he was angry and he was too smart to lose two dependable reporters.

Pete folded his cards quickly.

"O.K. You win," Pete lamented.

"Get your bags packed. I want you in place by Sunday. Your tickets will be at Heathrow waiting for you."

Rick turned to leave.

"And, one more thing," Pete interjected before Rick could reach the door.

"This here piece stinks," he looked up from the paper he had been reading when Rick entered his office. It was his latest article. Pete crumpled the paper in his palm and casually tossed it straight into a nearby trash can.

Rick just smiled and walked out the door, "That's O.K. I already beat you to it. Check my trash can for the rewrite. I only write to the level you pay me, anyhow."

Pete's face turned red. Rick had gotten the best of him again and he knew Pete would probably dig his work out of the trash can to re-read it because Pete knew his work was damned good.

In the meantime, Rick returned to his desk and finished cleaning up then he quickly left

Secret of Ekaterinburg: The Hour-Glass

for the London flat the pair had recently leased.

That was another problem he had to deal with right away to see if he could get the advance on his apartment back. Damn, he had forgot to mention that to Pete. He wanted The Times to spring for that, too. They were the cheapest of cheap bastards.

Exiting the front steps, he called for a taxi and set off for his apartment. He would meet Adrienne there in a few hours when she came home from work.

A light rain began to fall as the taxi pulled up to the curb. Rick got inside and gave instructions to the driver.

CHAPTER 11

CIA Headquarters, Langley, VA., Oct. 20, 1989

Alex Ayers hit the outskirts of the D.C. city limits at a high rate of speed, drove west along Interstate 66, then north onto the Washington beltway. It was early and there was not much traffic in the way. The beltway led to the George Washington Memorial Parkway, a long stretch of urban road where mother nature and the chamber of commerce tried to co-exist just inside the Virginia state line a few miles northwest of Arlington.

His destination was one of the many suburbs which ringed the nation's strategic capitol.

Langley.

It was an impressive, affluent bedroom community where many of the nation's policy-makers and analysts connected with the Central Intelligence Agency raised their families.

Langley was located just far enough away from the Washington pressure-cooker where gridlock was a way-of-life not only on the roadways, but inside the same mentality that

Secret of Ekaterinburg: The Hour-Glass

could be found in big-government bureaucrats whose daily lethargy hypnotized the public as they endeavored to perform their own brand of political magic in the halls of Congress. This same frustration expressed itself in the scores of suburbs ringing the tiny, politically scarred capitol. D.C. even frazzled the nerves of the old politicos, the wily longstanding veterans of past campaigns and the confident freshmen newcomers who wanted to get things done fast.

Thus, Langley gave Washingtonians an escape from the nerve wracking charged political insider hustle. God, how the escapades could be comic relief at times - real life snapshots of themselves. And, Langley was one of the many suburbs which offered a safe retreat into the gentle foothills of idyllic Virginia.

Alex pressed the accelerator harder and watched the speedometer glide toward 75 mph. He knew he was over the limit, but what the hell, he felt important enough not to worry about it. All he had to do was flash his CIA credentials to a police officer and he would be let go without any further explanation. Those were the perks of special agents on "Company" business.

Catching and passing car-after-car, Alex

Secret of Ekaterinburg: The Hour-Glass

figured it was a 25-minute drive to CIA headquarters this time of day but at this rate, it would take him fifteen.

The CIA had come a long way since its inception during World War II, known then to only a handful of Washington insiders as the Office of Strategic Services or OSS. It had fast become the official secret spy agency of the U.S. government under presidents Franklin Roosevelt and Harry Truman. Eventually in the early 50s, its name was changed to the Central Intelligence Agency and suddenly it no longer was a mere group of rogue agents embarking on various daring secret missions during wartime. The agency or the "Company" as it became known by its nickname, was organized by the elite and powerful in Washington and it soon had become fashionable to regard the CIA as the agency that could get things done.

People familiar with Washington's inner workings involving issues of national and international importance, knew the organization had become an invaluable, efficient network of spies and intelligence gathering operatives around the world - literally the eyes and ears of the U.S. government policy-makers.

No matter what the threat in any part of the

Secret of Ekaterinburg: The Hour-Glass

world, the CIA was the master spy organization of deception and disinformation. It got the job done when others couldn't and became the best intelligence data-gathering and analytical coterie devised by any government anywhere.

It had uniquely served as an early warning center monitoring foreign government operations that might affect the national security, often before critical decisions were made by those same foreign governments.

Even in the early years, radio transmissions and special couriers delivered information about the perceived threat of communism to Americans long before the actual crises would occur. Repeatedly, when going into strategic negotiations, U.S. presidents knew more about the enemy's ability than the enemy knew about itself.

Tied-in with the intelligence and spy-gathering groups were military technicians from various military branches who used highly specialized, sensitive equipment in sophisticated spy planes like the U-2 and the SR-71 Blackbird, a high-altitude spy plane which could cruise at nearly 2,300 mph at an invisible altitude of 100,000 ft.

In 1959, a now obsolete U-2, an effective but less capable lower-flying spy plane, had

Secret of Ekaterinburg: The Hour-Glass

been shot down by the Russians with spy-pilot Lt. Col. Gary Powers at the controls.

The Soviets knew he was up there somewhere, but they couldn't reach him with their low altitude jet fighters or missiles. This infuriated Premier Nikita Khrushchev to the point of irrational and idiotic behavior. Powers was captured during a final mission when he experienced engine failure at 80,000 ft., and forced to a lower altitude where a Soviet missile finally blew him out of the sky. His luck had run out. And, so had America's.

Powers was catapulted out of the spy plane by his ejection system and parachuted to safety on Russian soil. He was captured by Russian farmers and soldiers then paraded before Khrushchev while the entire world watched on television. It wasn't in living color, but it didn't have to be. The Ruskies had a field day with the world news media blaming President Dwight D. Eisenhower for the fiasco. Ike later had to eat crow and admit the Russians had caught the U.S. literally "red-handed."

Alex was in a hurry now, the speedometer shooting past 80 mph. An aerospace design engineer by education, he had worked on the design of the new Blackbird, and then moved on to another even more important eventual

Secret of Ekaterinburg: The Hour-Glass

replacement, the top-secret Stealth F-117A reconnaissance fighter-bomber.

In 1992, the government had secretly launched an even more powerful replacement for the 1990s and beyond, a hypersonic spy plane, dubbed the "Aurora," which could fly 50 miles to the edge of space and cruise at speeds of over 6,000 mph, and an even faster space plane was already on the drawing boards – Pegasus – which could cruise at 12,000 mph. Still, Pegasus was an apt name from the Lockheed's infamous and clandestine skunkworks because the plane could fly to the edge of space and beam down laser lights similar to the Aurora Borealis reflecting from Alaska to the northern hemisphere below, but in this case, no one would see the laser light show. The beams were invisible to the naked eye and could only be seen at the precise angle they were being aimed toward their target.

Things were changing so fast, it was difficult for even him to keep track of the new technology. No wonder the Russians had lost the space race with their competitive edge in technological warfare crippled. Reagan had made sure that Russians wouldn't be able to keep up. Their economic system simply couldn't keep pace with U.S. production and

Secret of Ekaterinburg: The Hour-Glass

economic flexibility.

Today, fresh, younger agents were required to perform quickly what he and other CIA agents took years to learn through trial-and-error logic, raw and gut-felt experience in the field.

Such field work was often tedious and dangerous rewarded with low paying bonuses in return for taking high risks which often culminated in botched assignments or agents unnecessary deaths, courtesy of the world's counterspy organizations always on the prowl against an enemy of the people. Worse, because some liberal news agency blew an agent's cover, many U.S. spies were unwittingly led to their deaths because of a leaky unreliable press When that happened, and an agent lost his life because of it, the CIA made them pay for that, sometimes with an accident.

During the 1960s, the CIA had played a critical but unheralded role in the Cuban Missile Crisis. Some say, that severe misjudgments were made by the agency and blame was charged by then President John Kennedy, who summarily threatened in a public speech at Annapolis to disband the CIA in its entirety. That miscalculation probably

Secret of Ekaterinburg: The Hour-Glass

cost him his life. And then there was the momentous decision made by President Nixon to end the Vietnam War, prompted by startling new assessments handed to him by the CIA concluding that the war was an unwinnable one. The change in direction was a feather in the Company's cap which it wore well into the 70s and 80s. Solid analysis and evidence provided to President Reagan culminated in the demise of the Soviet Union which collapsed on itself ending 70 plus years of communist governments.

The National Security Agency (NSA) was then formed as an adjunct intelligence eavesdropping gathering center which fed thousands of bits of intelligence data to the CIA for analysis. That agency was nicknamed No Such Agency (NSA). So, the agency was broken down into two main components – an intelligence data gathering operation using spies in foreign countries; and the NSA, a super-secret analysis and strategic planning center under the wing of the CIA where analysts pored over countless reports sent in from American spies, space satellites and spy planes from every corner of the globe. That operation continues to this day.

Secret of Ekaterinburg: The Hour-Glass

* * *   * * *

Now, well into Virginia, Alex turned off and headed south along the parkway, an interesting but relaxing stretch of highway. He leaned forward and flipped on the morning news.

WVAB – AM - his favorite station. The format was all news during peak drive time until 10 a.m.

Alex's wife couldn't stand it, though. She didn't like his compulsive listening to every facet of the world news because it always seemed to interfere with their private time together. She could tolerate his preoccupation with national and international news, but not with the seemingly endless trivial stuff.

Alex would laugh at her impatience. He loved detail, an analyst's curse, which she couldn't understand. It had always been part of his very nature. He was destined to become a CIA analyst because of it. Anyway, that's what his dad had always said he was suited for.

Alex adjusted his rear-view mirror, and nonchalantly gave it a quick glance. He checked it twice before catching sight of the white Buick Reatta about a quarter-of-a-mile back.

He had a habit of looking over his shoulder,

Secret of Ekaterinburg: The Hour-Glass

even when he was enjoying a drive. It was his training as an agent, an ever-watchful habit that had saved his life a few times spanning a 20-year period. It was like a built-in radar or early warning. He seemed to sense when something unusual could happen. And, like many other agents, who possessed the same foxlike habits, he had developed an uncanny sixth sense through hard training and by reliving those close calls in his nightmares often waking up in cold sweats only to be awakened out of his fear by his startled wife who called to him "wake up. It's all right. You're home, now."

He wasn't worried too much about the white sports coupe edging closer to him because there were two other cars in-between and three more in front of him. But, none-the-same, he had spotted it and kept tabs on it. It was the only car in the mix which hadn't turned off in the last five miles. The other cars had done so at various points and had been replaced by others at irregular intervals, so the nagging wariness remained with him. The white Reatta definitely bothered him. It remained fixed in the back of his mind as it continued to keep its distance while he kept checking on it.

That's what was wrong, Alex thought.

The driver was keeping his distance a bit too

Secret of Ekaterinburg: The Hour-Glass

regular.

"Probably a coincidence," Alex mumbled to himself. "The damned guy's hanging in there though. Let's see what he does when I do this."

Alex made a hard right at the next intersection, downshifted quickly and pulled over to the berm.

Checking the intersection in his rear-view mirror, he watched as the white Reatta swept by with two men in blue uniforms looking straight ahead.

Alex turned around in his seat to get a better look at the car, then chuckled out loud to himself. Maybe, he was becoming a bit too paranoid in his late 40s.

But, old habits die hard, he rationalized. Better to be safe than sorry. But, he knew he really didn't need to apologize to himself.

He put the car in gear again, made a quick U-turn back and made a beeline quick right in the direction of CIA for the next five minutes.

This time there would be no more delays.

The radio station he was listening to went silent for a few seconds, a station identification tone pinged on, and a news announcer cut into the regular broadcast.

"We interrupt this program to bring you a special bulletin. A Pentagon spokesman has

Secret of Ekaterinburg: The Hour-Glass

just confirmed to the Associated Press that Peter Jenkins, a special agent with the Central Intelligence Agency, has just been gunned down by two unidentified men outside his Arlington home about 20 minutes ago. State police and FBI units are on the scene and have begun an intense search for the two gunmen who fled the scene.

Witnesses said the two men drove away from the Jenkins home heading west from Arlington. Witnesses were unable to identify the license plates or make of the car. Mr. Jenkins was apparently watering his front lawn, when the two men pulled up to the curb and called him over to their car. The two men then got out and opened fire with automatic weapons hitting Jenkins at least eight times. The gunmen were described as having dark hair and dark complexions, and wearing sunglasses. No further statements are being issued by the FBI or CIA related to Mr. Jenkins' role at the CIA, but it is believed that Mr. Jenkins was an international weapons analyst at the Langley facility. We will bring you additional information as the story develops. We now return you to your regular broadcast."

"Son-of-a-bitch!" Alex muttered to himself. "What the hell is going on?"

Secret of Ekaterinburg: The Hour-Glass

He pressed the accelerator to the floor as the turbo-charged Mustang lurched into passing gear and roared past several other cars just ahead of him.

Careful, he reminded himself. Better to get there in one piece.

Damn it! Jenks had been a special friend to him for years. But, why in the hell would anyone want to take him out?

He was a brilliant analyst for the CIA, and was the first analyst to "see" the buildup of the Iraqi war machine just prior to the invasion of Kuwait.

But, what the hell was he working on that was so damned important that someone or some terrorists would want to kill him.

The Middle East. Eastern Europe. South American drug lords? He didn't know. But, he would find out soon.

Just a few more miles to go and he would have some answers. The Company already knew Jenks was dead. He wondered what else they knew about it?

Maybe they didn't know anything?

Why had Jenks telephoned him last week and asked him to check out some old file photographs taken from a spy satellite a couple of years ago? Was it related to his impending

Secret of Ekaterinburg: The Hour-Glass

visit today?

Where was that white Reatta, now? Alex automatically looked ahead and in his rear-view mirror. No white car. And, no one was following him.

At 75 mph, it was as fast as he dared go as he caught sight of the main gate. He let up the pressure on the accelerator and eased the car toward the four-lane entrance, a quarter-mile to the guard gate. In a few more seconds he would be inside and find out what was going on.

He slowed to wait his turn in line at the main gate. As he approached the guard post, a steady line of cars idled forward ahead of him. He watched impatiently as the two marine guards waved everyone through.

"Strange," he muttered to himself, "Why-in-the-hell are they in a such hurry. They're not asking for the blue cards." He reached down and flipped open the middle console to make sure his 9mm Beretta semi-automatic was there. Reassured at the sight of it, he reached inside his suit pocket for his blue I.D. card.

Two marine guards in blue jackets waved car-after-car through the checkpoint. It didn't look right?

As he approached, one of the marines stiffly

Secret of Ekaterinburg: The Hour-Glass

crossed over in front of him to the other side and signaled him to pull over.

"Now, that's definitely not routine," he said out loud.

His hand instinctively reached for the 9mm just as he saw the first marine draw his weapon from a side holster and point it at his windshield.

No reflection from their sunglasses.

Non-issue sunglasses.

Civilian wear.

"God-damnit," Alex reacted. "It's a set-up."

"Fuck!"

He slammed his foot down hard on the brake pedal, and turned the steering wheel hard right fumbling inside the console for his Beretta.

The second marine aimed his gun at the windshield right at Alex's head and fired once at point-blank range.

Then again in rapid succession.

The shots would have been deadly if not for the bullet-proof glass Alex had installed a few weeks earlier.

He aimed the car at the guard and jammed the accelerator to the floor. The car roared to life and caught the marine in the midsection throwing him back and underneath the car.

Secret of Ekaterinburg: The Hour-Glass

Alex felt the car crunch over the marine's body as it caught and dragged him underneath the car's spinning frame. By this time, Alex had found the 9mm.

The second guard, taken by surprise, opened fire from behind but the bullets ricocheted off the rear window.

Alex slammed on the brakes again and skidded to a halt. He kicked open the door and rolled out through the passenger side flattening himself on the concrete, and mechanically clicked off the safety of the steel-jacketed Beretta.

Steadying himself against the side of the car, he stared into the smashed, bloodied face of the dead man laying crushed beneath the car's frame. So far he had killed one of the two guards without firing a single shot, but he knew that was about to change. His predicament was getting worse as he observed the second marine move toward him with his rifle aimed at the open driver's window.

Did the marine think that Alex was still inside? It was all the opening he needed. Alex crouched as low as he could as the gunman approached some 50 feet away. He positioned quickly, and squeezed-off a round aiming high to the chest, his gun steadied by the car's trunk

Secret of Ekaterinburg: The Hour-Glass

deck.

The shot from the Beretta hit the guard in the left shoulder, to the right. The high impact round stopped him in his tracks, but the rifle wielding gunman still managed to open fire.

Alex reflexed in a controlled and steady motion, returning deadly fire striking the marine twice more in the chest, this time squarely in the middle.

The bullets ripped through his heart and knocked the marine backward, up and off his feet. Blood gushed from the mortal wound, yet the dying man still tried to get off another shot. He swung his gun wildly in the air firing off two more rounds.

Alex fired a fourth and final time, taking a headshot.

Kaposh!

The marine's forehead exploded into a ball of red.

Alex blew out a whoosh of air and quickly looked around for any anyone else.

Drivers entering the compound had careened to a halt and dived beneath their car seats for cover.

Alex carefully checked behind him and scanned the sentry post.

"Son-of-a-bitch," he sighed to himself.

Secret of Ekaterinburg: The Hour-Glass

"This is connected to Jenks. No IFS, ANDS or BUTS."

He walked toward the dead marine. His blue uniform was drenched in blood. Alex didn't recognize him. And, he hadn't recognized the other dead one either.

These were no marines.

They were imposters. Terrorists.

But, who in the hell were they?

Alex pulled back the slide of his 9mm clearing the weapon.

His peripheral vision picked up the white sports car hidden behind the guard booth - the same white Reatta that had tailed him earlier. They were coming from the Jenks hit. And, they were coming to hit him.

"Son-of-a-bitch," he reckoned to himself. "This is as close as it gets."

How could he be so careful and still damned near get himself killed. He wiped the perspiration off his forehead and looked behind him at all the people.

They were still sprawled all over the pavement gawking at him in disbelief.

He walked past the guard shack and looked over toward the bushes when he saw the bodics of the two regular guards. They were both dead each shot through the back of the head,

Secret of Ekaterinburg: The Hour-Glass

execution style.

Satisfied there were no other terrorists, he removed the magazine from his weapon, reached into his car, took out another fully loaded one, and slammed it into place. He had fired only four times, but had made four good body hits. He coolly slid the Beretta into its side holster, got back inside his car, turned, and roared past the main gate toward CIA.

Others arriving at the scene, raced by him in military jeeps but he didn't stop. He figured he had to get inside and find out just what the hell was going on.

He had two scores to settle now.

Jenks' death, and his own personal battle with whoever it was who had just tried to kill him.

Working for the Company.

That's the way it was.

You made sure your life insurance was paid up.

Secret of Ekaterinburg: The Hour-Glass

CHAPTER 12

CIA Headquarters, Langley, Va., Oct 20, 1989

CIA chief Ben Kasim walked over to the computer terminal when he heard the printer switch on. A hard copy was coming in from one of his London operatives. Kasim picked up the sheet from the laser printer as it slipped from the rolls and up onto the plastic bin then nonchalantly walked back over to his coffee mug cooling off perched on the edge of his desk. He began reading the message and leaned back into his cushioned, roller-ball high-back chair carefully propping his feet up on his meticulous mahogany desk.

The message read: Reporter Rick Waite: assigned to Moscow as London Times bureau chief beginning immediately. Wife: Adrienne assigned to Stockholm as news correspondent. Both to commute and rendezvous on weekends. Both under 24-hour surveillance per company orders. Teams in position. Confirm message.

Secret of Ekaterinburg: The Hour-Glass

STOP.

Kasim reached down and pressed a tiny button on the printer and watched the light blink once to confirm receipt of the message back in London. A smile formed on his face as one of his team agents entered the briefing room. Perfect. Alex was just who he needed to talk to.

"I'm glad you're here," Kasim said to him. "You must know what happened at the front gate ten minutes was a designed attempt to kill you specifically."

"Know, hell! I was in the line of fire for a reason. They already killed Jenkins!" Alex thundered back slamming his fist down on Kasim's desk. "Just what the hell is going on? Where in the hell is our security. Everything's way too Goddam lax. Christ, they could've gotten ten or twenty agents at the gate!"

"No, they were only after two. Jenks wasn't so lucky," Kasim replied. "Nice work, Alex. You are one lucky bastard though. You always were. And, so was everyone else. It doesn't always work out that way. Jenks didn't have much of a chance in front of his home earlier this morning?"

"Yeah, I know. I heard about it on the radio driving in. That's what tipped me off to

Secret of Ekaterinburg: The Hour-Glass

watch for something unusual. Christ, doesn't the agency make phone calls to us anymore? They could've reached me on my cellphone. I mean, it was pure instinct, reaction and training . . . . and, like you say, . . . and a lot of luck."

"Well, that's why we train all of you first. It tends to add a little longevity to your career."

"And, just who in the hell were those guys?"

"We don't know, but thanks to you, they sure as hell aren't going to volunteer any information."

"Excuse, me? I was trying to stay alive out there."

"Easy, Alex. We'll know soon enough who they are." he quipped. "Look, after, you've settled down and had a cup of coffee, I just got something in from London which should interest you."

"Is it connected to what happened here this morning?"

"Maybe."

"Don't bullshit me. What the hell is really going on?" Alex demanded to know more.

"Honest to God. We really don't know yet. Maybe it's minor. Maybe it's something big. There's been some movement at the Times. They're jockeying some reporters around again. Only, this time, they're moving a couple of them to Moscow and Stockholm. Rick and Adrienne Waite. They're the pair who uncovered the Palestine conspiracy five years back."

"That doesn't sound like anything minor, does it? Yeah, I remember them. Real crackerjack journalists. Straight-up reporters. Very good at covert work. But, didn't you say a month ago they had married and were out of the undercover business?" Alex prodded.

"Yeah. But, we've been kinda keeping tabs on them off-and-on over the years. You know, nothing constant. Just a routine check every now and again. The moral thing to do you know. They always seem to be near something before it happens. In Beirut, they were on to it big before we knew what hit us. Maybe they're on to something big again. Anyway something going on inside the old Soviet Union would definitely interest me. Wouldn't it you?"

"Well now, what-in-the-hell do you think is so damned special about a move to Moscow or Stockholm? There are droves of international reporting staff over there and they've been there for some time. Nothing much going on over there since the wall came tumbling down?" Alex kept pushing Kasim.

"Well, that's just it. A lot of times, these

Secret of Ekaterinburg: The Hour-Glass

asshole reporters know more than we think they do. As much as I detest the bastards, they do have a kind of sixth-sense about this stuff. You know kind of like you do. I mean we're good. But, sometimes they're better at it than we are. Maybe it's pure luck. I don't really know. Know what I mean?"

"I guess sometimes it works that way," Alex said casually pulling up a nearby chair and pouring himself a cup of coffee using someone else's mug from the day before. He nudged himself closer to the far side of Kasim's desk not wanting to get too close yet not wanting to miss any detail in Kasim's facial expressions. He could read people really well. Always could. He wondered why he was so curious about two hotshot reporters being sent to two different and separate destinations.

"Anything going on in Moscow or Stockholm that we don't know about?"

Kasim's reply was quick and to the point.

"No. I checked with our intelligence units late yesterday and with our counterparts, British ICE. Nothing new to report from them, either."

"Then, why are you still so damned concerned?" Alex pressed him.

"Well . . . it's just a hunch. You know, like I

said, you kind of get a feel for this. It's like a burning in your gut. After 25 years in this business, you just know it's not heartburn."

"You mean the same kind of feeling one of those reporter's gets?" Alex replied.

"Yeah, it must be," Kasim said staring at the ceiling. "Just like one of those good-for-nothing wire reporters. Nothing's going on as far as they know or we know. And, nothing's going on as far as the London Times is concerned. So, just what the fuck is going on? They're sending their two best reporters to that part of the world just to waste money?

Maybe? Maybe not? Maybe it's just coincidence. All very routine. But, what if it isn't? And, then I get this burning sensation in the pit of my stomach. . . "

"Relax, Kase. You've been watching too many of those damned CIA movies from Hollywood. Besides, you're getting too old for this kind of worry. You'd better start thinking about your retirement instead and leave this espionage stuff to us younger guys," Alex laughed.

God, Kasim hated it when his field agents called him "Kase." It smacked of letting your subordinates get too close to you and that wasn't good for security at the CIA. But

Secret of Ekaterinburg: The Hour-Glass

sometimes he had to go with it, especially if it came from Alex Ayers. He could put up with it from him because when he needed to get something done, Alex could do it.

"I'm too young to retire. Hell, I'm only 64. When you catch up to me, give me a call, I'll give you a few pointers on the counter-terrorism trade. Retirement. Who in the hell wants that?"

"Easy Kase, I was only kidding. Don't take everything so Goddamned seriously."

Kase smiled and handed Alex the message.

"Don't call me Kase . . . Alexander."

Alex hated nicknames, too.

He studied the message, then laid it back down on the desk and took another swig of coffee.

"Say, if you don't mind, while I'm over at operations, I'd like to check out something that came in last week about the Russians. Any objections?"

"What is it?"

"Oh, nothing much. I haven't had time to get over there yet to check it out. This will get me there. I'm curious about a set of intelligence photos north of Vladivostok. Satellite photos picked up some sort of shadow extending out from Krazcoff. But, it stayed the same. It

Secret of Ekaterinburg: The Hour-Glass

didn't move, and didn't look like a sub track or anything. But, our photo analysts asked me to take a look at it."

"Well, what's it look like from the enhanced photos," Kasim asked him.

"Well, that's just it. It should be a sub track from one of their secret bases, but it's not. I don't quite know what to make of it. I want to take another look at it. But, I'll need more time to analyze it and that'll take more time away from what you want me to do. Is that O.K. with you?"

"No problem here. You're caught up with everything else anyway?"

"Yeah, I'm clear." Alex answered.

"Just, don't let it take all your time. You're supposed to be a read-analyst, not a photo analyst. But, knowing your unique approach to just about everything, they probably feel you might be able to come up with a more creative interpretation."

"Look. I'll try to keep it as short as possible. Anyway we owe those guys a favor for their work on the Persian Gulf."

Kasim knew he was right.

"O.K. Give it your best shot, but don't let them monopolize your time. Know what I mean?"

Secret of Ekaterinburg: The Hour-Glass

"Sure . . . look, I'll swing over there now and spend a couple of hours. I'll enjoy the ride. Hell, after this morning's trouble it'll be a relief. It's beginning to get hot already and it's only May."

Alex swung his chair around stood up and drained the rest of his coffee out of the dirty mug into the sink. He spotted a mucky stain at the bottom of the mug.

"Christ. Doesn't anybody ever wash these damned things out," he said annoyed.

"Wouldn't do any good anyhow," Kasim added.

"Why's that?"

"Everybody's so damned paranoid around here, they might think something's wrong with the coffee if it tasted good."

Alex broke up.

"You know, you're right. But, who would try to kill any of us that way? This morning's way is more direct. From Russia With Love. The Ruskies are our friends, right?"

"As far as I know they are . . . but, . . . "

"Yeah . . . I know. Trust, but verify."

"Vintage Reagan?"

"Yeah. Wasn't he great?" Alex said as he left the briefing room.

"Oh, one more thing. Keep me posted if you

Secret of Ekaterinburg: The Hour-Glass

find something those guys miss," Kasim yelled to him as he left. "I like to keep score on who's doing what around here. And, I like to give credit where credit is due if you know what I mean."

"Sure do. Thanks for the extra time. I appreciate it. Nothing like keeping the photo skills honed."

Kasim waved him off with his coffee mug. Others were beginning to arrive and it was just as well they had kept their conversation shorter than usual. He didn't want anyone else to know what they were discussing.

He was a stickler for the intelligence credo "need-to-know." The doctrine simply meant, if you don't have a need to know don't ask. It's none of your business. And, don't volunteer any information either. It was that simple. The KISS technique. Keep It Simple Stupid.

Kasim turned to the computer keyboard and typed in a message to London CIA and encoded it before transmitting.

"Received message re: Moscow and Stockholm. Surveillance as usual. Keep me informed. STOP. A.B. Kasim." He waited for the confirm light to blink back. It did.

Secret of Ekaterinburg: The Hour-Glass

CHAPTER 13

CIA Langley, Oct. 22, 1989

It was nearly dark before Alex returned to the CIA office after his visit to the top secret intelligence photo room where he and a colleague had scrutinized a batch of satellite photos relating to something in Russia which he had been curious about for some time.

On the drive back, he thought about what his friend had said

"Alex, take a look at this one," Keitel had told him pushing a color transparency toward him over a smooth, lighted glass about the size of a card table.

Alex deftly slid it beneath a small eyepiece and peered through the magnifier. Good Lord. What the hell was that?

"What in God's name do you make of it?" Alex asked him.

Keitel leaned over the eyepiece and took another look.

"I don't know. I've never seen anything quite like it since I've been at recon. You tell me,"

Secret of Ekaterinburg: The Hour-Glass

Keitel replied.

"I don't know what to make of it, either," Alex remarked renewing his analysis of the photograph taken from synchronous orbit some 25,000 miles above the earth by Air Force Intel II. "It sure is interesting though. What the hell could the Russians be up to with all that equipment near Krazcoff?"

"I don't know. Never gave the photos much thought, you know with all those offshore drilling rigs and fishing trawlers they're always moving around. The photos never puzzled me until you asked me about them. I don't understand why they're arrayed at Krazcoff. I remembered this batch about a year ago and pulled them up on the computer again for re-analysis. We had nothing like this on file now or ever before. We don't know what the equipment is for, what it's to be used for or where it's going?"

Wiping his brow with his shirt sleeve, Alex abruptly raised up from the eyepiece, and looked at Keitel.

"Are you telling me because we don't know what it is or because we haven't seen it before that it might pose some kind of threat to us?"

"I didn't say that," Keitel retorted always on the defensive with Alex.

Secret of Ekaterinburg: The Hour-Glass

"No, you didn't say it," Alex shot back. "But, Goddam it, you didn't have to. I've been around long enough to draw my own conclusions about what it might mean, right?"

Keitel nodded to him and took another look for himself. He just didn't like what he was looking at, even though he didn't know what it was.

"I'll tell you what," Keitel whispered to Alex. "Just for the record, to make sure we do this right, what do you say if I make a routine inspection of all the unusual photographs during the past two years where we uncovered something unexplainable and try and see if any of them relate to this?"

"That's a damned good idea, Artie," Alex answered reaching for his coffee mug. "I wish I'd thought of that?"

"I get paid more than you double agent guys. And, besides, you're a little out of practice."

"O.K.," Alex interrupted, "but don't say anything to Kasim about this until we can verify something on it? O.K.?"

"Agreed."

Alex pushed the maps of the old Soviet Union aside and drank down the rest of his coffee swallowing the black liquid quickly.

Secret of Ekaterinburg: The Hour-Glass

God, the stuff was absolutely poison, but he drank it anyway. He hated those damned coffee machines which promised you good brew but dispensed nothing but foul-tasting stuff instead.

"Look, I've got to get back to headquarters. Let me know when you come up with something? One other thing. What did you make of the hit on Jenkins this morning?"

"I dunno. I haven't had time to think much about it with everything that's been going on around here. I feel really bad for his wife and kids. Jenks was one of the good guys. Great to work around. He was a brilliant analyst. It's really a damned shame."

"I know I'm not supposed to ask but do you know what he was working on?"

"You're right, you're not supposed to ask, but what the hell, who knows when you might get into some sort of accident these days," Keitel whispered leaning up on his elbows from the glass table. "`If this gets back to the top, it's all over for me. We've been friends a long time, Alex, so I'm going to trust you on this. Jenks was working with another double agent inside the old Soviet Union, on something big that was in progress there, but he didn't discuss it much. It was too far up the intelligence circle

Secret of Ekaterinburg: The Hour-Glass

for the likes of me. So, he wasn't dropping any of the information on me. But, he did mention one thing. It was strange and not like him. I think he mentioned the other agent by name, you know like in an afterthought as though he was thinking out loud. It was a rare faux pas for Jenks; it was like he was going over something in his head while he was looking at some old reconnaissance photos. He might have been re-thinking an old conversation when he spoke a name like he was talking to someone. I pretended not to hear him, but I remembered it just the same. Maybe it was some kind of code-word."

"What did he say?"

"Hour-Glass."

"Hour-Glass?" Alex repeated it.

"Yeah, at least that's what I thought he said. In Russian . . . pesochnye chasy."

"It didn't mean anything to me, and I never asked him about it. You know the old need to know habit taking over?"

"Anything else that might be important?"

"Uh, uh. Except that Jenks was always intrigued about the fact that the Russians were able to beat the German army with 12 army reserve divisions which had been supposedly decimated earlier by those same German troops

Secret of Ekaterinburg: The Hour-Glass

in the middle of 1943."

"Why would he be fascinated by that piece of history?"

"I never asked him about it specifically, but he talked about it in general terms all the time. I'm not much of a historian on World War II, but, his fascination had something to do with the counterattack at the Dnepr River."

"The Dnepr?"

"Yeah, ever heard of it?"

"Oh, sure. Everyone who knows anything about the Russian spring offensive against the Germans, knows about the Dnepr River," Alex said lying through his teeth.

"Doesn't mean anything to me, either," Keitel said.

"Yeah," Alex said changing his stance, "Look, I've got to get the hell out of here or Nelson will wonder where I disappeared to. I owe you for this. I really appreciate it. Keep me posted if anything else on this comes up. I'll let you know what I get on my end."

"Bullshit, you will," Keitel grinned as he left. Keitel knew better than to ask a field agent for information. Keitel's job was to facilitate information for processing to the agents, but not vice-versa. It just didn't work that way. At the CIA, communication was a

Secret of Ekaterinburg: The Hour-Glass

one-way street coming from the direction of the agent who controlled it. It was an understood thing.

Alex moved through the doorway with a backhanded shove and turned the corner toward the elevator taking a glance at a ginger-haired assistant wearing a tight dress. It was nice to know that at 48, they still smiled at him. He turned and looked squarely at her butt as she maneuvered by him. God, he sucked in a quick breath. Maybe, he'd have to visit more often. The elevator door opened and he got in without a word watching her disappear around the corner.

In the car, he saw traffic ahead of him was heavy and directed his attention to the more pressing things at hand. The Mustang moved smoothly across two lanes to the right.

Krazcoff. Vladivostok. What the hell was he looking at? Hourglass? Russia? Did those things make any sense? He drew a blank as his car rolled to a stop on the crowded beltway just outside Langley.

He turned on the car radio for some music but found a traffic report instead. He already knew where the traffic jam was. He was part of it. He wiped the perspiration from his forehead, and rolled down the window to wait.

Secret of Ekaterinburg: The Hour-Glass

He would wait for a while.

Secret of Ekaterinburg: The Hour-Glass

CHAPTER 14

Peregrebnoye, The Urals, Sept. 10, 1944

The Wehrmacht juggernaut had rolled rapidly to the outskirts of Leningrad and Moscow in the spring of 1941 but remained stalled there for two years during the two horrible winters of 1941 and 1942.

If Hitler had been able to grasp the kind of weather he would encounter, he might have postponed his decision and avoided the impending disaster which beset his generals – perhaps by not even opening the campaign "Operation Barbarossa" while elements of the war were yet unresolved in Western Europe.

In spite of Hitler's military genius, his decision to invade Russia was executed over the objections of his generals and it became his own personal command decision. It was both brilliant and risky at the same time, at first going smoothly but then faltering badly. His insistence to open a second front would cost thousands of lives and thousands more captured by the Russians sent to prisoner of war camps

Secret of Ekaterinburg: The Hour-Glass

where they were neither fed well nor treated well for the remainder of the war.

Those who managed to survive the war returned home as miserable wrecks of their former selves, pitiful reminders to their families of the ill-conceived policies of the Nazis hierarchy. By the spring of 1941, General Zhukov, commander of the entire Red Army, was ready to launch a massive counter-attack against the remnants of the barely-capable SS units operating with the Wermacht.

The Russians had spent nearly two years building up their forces with help from America supplying them with steel and armaments. They were able to manufacture everything from airplanes, to massive new tanks which could withstand the threat of the great German Tiger tanks and the munitions necessary to sustain a heavy all-out offensive that would last nearly a year and defeat the Germans in a bitter protracted fight. These weapons were planned and designed, well-away from the industrial cities of Leningrad, Kiev, and Moscow. The actual manufacturing facilities were disbursed and tucked away in small industrial cauldrons thousands of miles to the east, well-beyond the range of German dive bombers, east of the Ural Mountains in the

Secret of Ekaterinburg: The Hour-Glass

small villages scattered in the Tundra region where thousands of laborers toiled by day and night to produce an immense quantity of weaponry for eventual retaliation, a final retribution that the Germans would find unimaginable.

Now, as Sergei trudged through the fields toward Peregrebnoye, he hoped his family would recognize him or that they hadn't all been dispersed like so many other thousands of families due to the inescapable horrors of the war. It was important to him. He had promised them he would return alive from Kiev, especially he had promised to Ana.

He and Josef had been on the run for six months and the pair had managed to evade both the German and Russian armies traveling to Toletska on the western edge of the Urals. They then had worked their way closer to Petrivoska aboard other trains and when they could no longer make progress that way anymore, they climbed aboard peasant farm wagons which would take them to within fifty kilometers of their respective villages.

On the way, they could see that wherever the Germans had marched they had destroyed the infrastructure of Russia. Wherever they had laid a boot to the ground there was nothing left

Secret of Ekaterinburg: The Hour-Glass

standing. They were witness to what a losing army could do to the land. And, worse, what their own army in an earlier hasty retreat could do to render the land almost unusable. Russians got used to looking at the barren land and burnt-out ruins eventually dislocating the thoughts of family life from their souls and minds. Neither Sergei nor Josef had seen their family for three years but still, somehow, had managed to correspond up until the day they had made good their escape.

Alone now - Josef had separated from him some 500 kilometers ago heading for Sovinsk, Czechoslovakia – Sergei walked the last three kilometers along the familiar winding road that had been cratered by German aircraft. They had bombed everything that resembled war production in an effort to purge the countryside of weapons manufacturing. But, the gigantic effort by the Luftwaffe had failed to stop it, just as it had failed to stop the Londoners with its thousands of sorties. The bombs, however, did destroy the thousands of dachas and livestock either hit accidentally or on purpose in an effort to destroy the morale of the people. Sergei rested against a fence-post which marked the beginning of his father's property. Wiping perspiration from his forehead, he craned

Secret of Ekaterinburg: The Hour-Glass

forward his gaze piercing the morning mist straining for a glimpse of the old dacha nearly a mile away.

He knew in September, when the dew evaporated rapidly from the heat of the morning sun creating a thick haze which hung low over the pastures, that he would have to get closer to see the farmhouse. Actually, it was a blessing, he thought. No one on patrol would be able to spot him unless they stumbled upon him accidentally. The thought was reassuring to him. He would be able to hear them long before they could see him and he could hide somewhere quickly. After resting for awhile, Sergei gathered his knapsack, slung it over his shoulder and continued his trek toward the dacha. Aided by the familiarity of the landscape he knew so well, he noticed the earth had a strange crustiness to it, one he recognized as being frequented by no animals or earthen plow. It disturbed him to think his father was unable to work the farm anymore or worse, that the Bolsheviks had taken the dacha during his long absence.

Krunch! Krunch! The sounds reverberated under his boots as he plodded across the frozen ground. Krunch! Krunch! The sound crackled as his boots pressed through crusty Siberian

Secret of Ekaterinburg: The Hour-Glass

frost and then as quickly as the sound was unleashed, there followed an instant silence as each boot lifted off the ground. It was a brisk twenty degrees even though the sunlight was quickly warming the air and melting what was left of the protective frost.

He was now within shouting distance of the dacha, but he had heard nothing or seen no one about. And, just as suddenly as the sounds of silence enveloped him, the sudden appearance of the familiar dacha cascaded toward him as if he was seeing a sudden panorama frozen in time.

"Hello . . . Hello . . . Is anyone here?" Sergei called out in an attempt to rouse anyone who might still be sleeping.

Where was everyone this morning?

As the mist parted, he took in the big, main house, standing there almost exactly as he had left it, except for the twin silos a few hundred yards away. They had taken a direct hit by bombs and had been virtually destroyed. Only a single, partial silo stood crookedly erect as a silent grave marker of death and destruction yielded by the Stukas' efficiency.

"Hello . . . Hello . . . Das vidonya! Sergei shouted loudly as he could. He was upon it. He heard a shriek then saw a movement. Was

Secret of Ekaterinburg: The Hour-Glass

it Ana? One of the sisters? Or a German?

Quickly, he crouched behind the old stone well, carefully removing his winter cap peering over the edge toward the house. It was Yendel, the old Russian wolfhound moving slowly toward him in a low growl. The old farm dog was still doing his job and when he got near enough to catch Sergei's scent, he evoked an instant burst of recognition that took Sergei's by surprise.

"Yendel, you old hound. You are still alive you mangy thing. It is good to see you again. You must be close to fifteen now. I can't believe you are still here," Sergei exclaimed his happiness at seeing an old friend even if that old friend wasn't a person.

The wolfhound sprung up wanting to get a lick at Sergei's face, but the old dog could no longer manage it. The best he could do was to nip at his belt and nuzzle into the palms of Sergei's hands. Finally, Sergei stooped down to let him lick his chin and his cheeks.

"Good old Yendel," Sergei stroked the dog's head and neck. "Good old boy. It is good to see you again. And, you remembered me, too?"

When his excitement subsided, Sergei looked around searching for still more signs of

Secret of Ekaterinburg: The Hour-Glass

life but there didn't seem to be any.

"What's happened to everyone?" Sergei looked at the dog. "Isn't there anyone here anymore?"

Sergei rose from his crouching position, and moved toward the farmhouse observing everything to be in its place. He walked slowly onto the back steps near the kitchen door, then paused and turned. He listened, then cried out.

"Ana . . . . Ana . . . . Are you there?"

His shouts echoed across the barnyard.

"Ana . . . Valerya . . . Dimitri . . . Is anyone here?"

Silence followed.

Then, he heard the unmistakable metallic clank of a bolt sliding across one of the wooden doors of the barn. He stood motionless and turned slowly toward the sound.

Rapuch! Rapuch! Another sound echoed twice.

Sergei knew it as the unmistakable bolt of a Kalashnikov being unlocked and slammed into its firing position. He knew he was in the gun sight of an unknown intruder on the farm and dared not make a sudden move.

Someone was watching his every move. Facing the barn, he saw the lower door swing halfway open, but he could not see anyone

Secret of Ekaterinburg: The Hour-Glass

moving it, only the long barrel of a rifle slide through a narrow slit, barely visible.

Should he speak now? Before he could muster the courage, a voice commanded.

"Who are you? Why do you come here?"

Sergei gathered the strength to identify himself.

"I am Sergei Boscov. I live here. This is my home. My father and mother are Dimitri and Tanya; my brothers and my sisters all live here."

With that the bottom door swung wide open, the old creaking hinges shattering the silence.

"Da. Is it really you?" a familiar voice answered.

Sergei recognized the voice instantly and threw his hands into the air.

"It is I, Sergei. I have returned from Kiev. Please do not shoot me dead. I have walked too long and too far for that. Please . . . point the Kalashnikov away from me."

Shrieks of laughter suddenly erupted from inside the barn and two new distinctive voices were heard.

"My God, Sergei," Ana bolted down from the hayloft swinging open the hay mound door. "It's a miracle. You have come home. I cannot believe it. You are a grown man."

Secret of Ekaterinburg: The Hour-Glass

Also climbing down from the hayloft was Valerya a dark skinned brunette more tomboyish than Ana who only occasionally managed a girlish giggle when excited.

Ana hadn't changed much. The last time they had seen each other was more than five years ago. Ana was now forty-three and more beautiful than he had remembered. She, too was a mature woman with a natural beauty and long auburn hair. It was a magic formula for romance. She was the talk of the men in her region and they all spun tales of how unattainable she was. Their hopes had been dashed over and over again by Ana their dreams transfixed on a goal they could not conquer. Ana was someone they could only dream about. All who had tried to gain her favor had failed. They performed amazing feats of chivalry and back-breaking duties for her parents in an attempt to win her over. Ana tried not to take advantage of them gently letting them know where they stood in relation to the almost-forgot Sergei. She thanked them for their kindness invoking a charm so effective that they could hardly take offense to the polite refusal to let herself be courted by any of them. It was a gesture of good will. And, so these men could not help but embrace her kindness and her spirit, and still they would endlessly return for more of the same velvet punishment at the beginning of each month when more work needed to be done.

Sergei fixed his eyes on hers for a full minute before he could bring himself to speak to her. Then they embraced, for what seemed like an eternity and kissed passionately, she still in her work clothes and Sergei badly disheveled from his many months on the road. It would not make any difference to them as he softly stroked her dark hair and silently wept.

"It is good to see you. It has been so long without you, I thought I would go mad. I cannot believe that I am here at last," he whispered.

"I cannot believe it either," Ana replied, looking at Sergei while caressing his hair and straightening his dusty cap. "But, it is true. When we looked up through the courtyard and saw you approaching, we were afraid and hid. We didn't know who it was. Then, we couldn't believe our own eyes. I still can't believe it is really you. You look like a ghost."

"I am no ghost. I am real. Where is Dimitri and Tanya?" Sergei asked her. "And, what has happened to the barn?"

"Mother is inside the dacha but she is not in

Secret of Ekaterinburg: The Hour-Glass

good health. She is resting. Father is in the fields probably sleeping under a large tree somewhere but he will tell us he has worked all day when he returns," Ana giggled with a glint in her eye. "He will be home soon. Stay here with us until he returns. We will make you something to eat. You must be famished and you must tell us everything about that has happened since you left us. What is happening throughout Russia? Have the Germans been defeated? They cannot defeat us. They cannot defeat our people."

Her questions rambled forth, coming in quick spasms that even Sergei, quick-witted as he was, could hardly fathom. He could not quell her enthusiasm.

"All right, Ana. I must collect my thoughts. I cannot even begin to answer such questions with ease. I need to rest. First, eat, then sleep. I am very tired. I have walked for so long. Wait until father comes from the field and when I see mother, then I will tell you all of you together even if it takes all night."

"Yes, it probably will," Ana leaned over and whispered to him. "If it does, you may sneak into my room. I will kick Valerya out and we will finish the story there."

Sergei gave her a peck like kiss on the cheek

Secret of Ekaterinburg: The Hour-Glass

so as not to arouse suspicion by Valerya who might talk too much later. Valerya gawked at them, blushed, but said nothing, even though she knew what they were thinking. It was none of her business. Indeed, everything had been private for Ana and Sergei while they were growing up, and in the absence of each other's presence, they had managed to stay in love by letter. Now, they could share their feelings with each other at last. They both sensed a future together now as they entered the farmhouse to greet Tanya.

It would be quite a reunion. Sergei was home at last. And, Dimitri would be home soon from the fields.

Everyone would celebrate.

Except for the brothers.

Sergei assumed they were in the fields with Dimitri.

But, they were not.

Ana hadn't told Sergei about them.

CHAPTER 15

Peregrebnoye, Sept. 11, 1944

Sergei gently held her in his arms at the window bench in the front room of the old farmhouse while they watched the unforgiving winds blow in from the Urals, eastward toward Onsk.

There was much to catch up on.

Sergei had been away for five years, and he was nearly thirty-three now and solidly built. The years of engineering school and military training had seen him grow into a man who now seemed twice his former size as a farm youth. Everything had changed about him including a fresh and confident look.

He still had his thick blonde hair; neatly combed; a square, powerful jaw; sturdy shoulders, and a long stride when he stepped across the courtyard. He had slung over his shoulder a backpack with all his earthly belongings in it, including the scarf she had knitted for him. When she saw him in the courtyard, she recognized it and knew it was

Secret of Ekaterinburg: The Hour-Glass

him immediately. It had come in handy during the long walk from Kiev that nearly froze him to the bone. He was now a full six-foot, two inches in height, and weighed 210 pounds; and, his rugged appearance nearly took Ana's breath away. Even her sisters were now envious of what she would possess.

Ana was also thirty-three with dark, long brown hair that unraveled when she didn't have it pulled back of with her babushka.

"Why haven't you married?" Sergei asked something he had never posed in his letters.

"You must know the reason?" she replied.

"I don't," he played with her feelings.

"Foolish . . . boy . . . . " she responded on cue.

He protested, "But, I am no longer a boy. Perhaps, a naive young man, but nonetheless, still a grown, Russian man."

Ana sighed.

"But, you still look as though you have been chasing Andre in the fields," she teased him turning slightly away.

"What is it?" Sergei took her by the shoulders and gently turned her toward him.

"What is it? You expect me to stand in front of you and give you the reason for my not marrying?" she said scolding him like a child.

Secret of Ekaterinburg: The Hour-Glass

"I have no idea?"

"Then you have no real feelings for me."

"But, I love you very much."

"Are all men the same the world over. Can't you see who is precisely in front of you?"

Finally, seeing that she was at her wits ends with him, he said, "Yes. I do know the reason. It is that you've been waiting for me to return all this time."

"Da," she replied. "I have spurned all the others in hopes for you. They have offered marriage. Some of them simply a reason to stay out of the military," she pushed her finger into his stomach. "But, others were far more serious, and they really thought me even pretty. Do you?"

"Of course. You are beautiful. Pretty is less than you standing before me. It is also why I have waited. I want to marry you," he let his emotions spill forth.

Ana nodded, then kissed him on the cheek pushing his hair back from his forehead.

"I knew it all these years. There is no one but you and you for me. It is God's will, is it not?"

Looking out from the window bench they traced the moisture beads with their fingers as they had done as children wondering if anyone

Secret of Ekaterinburg: The Hour-Glass

knew how they felt about each other. Ana placed her fingers to his lips in an unspoken bond of suppression like a pact between beloveds who would remain together until the end of time. Outside, the winds swirled to the sides of the old barn rocking the nearly fallen silo leaning against the remnants of the other. Except for its strong stone foundation, it barely remained upright.

Breaking the spell, from the kitchen, Tanya called them to supper. The familiar sounds of the dacha were beginning to return to him again and life filled the air. It was a sound which he had longed to hear again, not heard since the Russian army had come to take his brothers into conscription.

What had become of them? What had become of his much-loved brothers? Sergei had to find out the answers to these distressing questions when Dimitri returned home from the fields. It would be an illuminating reunion.

But, Sergei knew that aside from telling him of their marriage plans, his unaccounted for brothers would be the most important subject that evening at the dinner table.

Secret of Ekaterinburg: The Hour-Glass

CHAPTER 16

Langley, CIA Headquarters, OCT. 29, 1989

Keitel leaned over the lighted glass table and zoomed in on the intelligence photo with a precision-guided hand that moved ever so slightly in a circular motion. He was machine-like and he instinctively had a knack for finding tiny important pieces of intelligence information that no one else could. His uncanny ability uncovered things even the most advanced computers couldn't detect. It was his 35 years of experience with the agency which made Keitel a most invaluable commodity and a dangerous man to the unseen enemies on other continents. Keitel was indeed a company legend, one who offered his unashamed loyalty to the CIA, the United States and his family, in reverse order.

There was never a hint of scandal about him. If he discovered something he thought was related to a case you were working on, it was impossible to discredit him if he could

Secret of Ekaterinburg: The Hour-Glass

connect it to national security. He could be like a bulldog about it and this persona could erupt into a defiant anger if he had to defend his position. Normally, his aloofness, was kept hidden under his rough, sandy-colored hair, his thick, heavy eyebrows which made him appear younger than his 55-year-old frame would belie. He bent over the table for hours at a time peering at the images he had dredged up from the old files.

But, these he was perplexed about. These photos were closed from the curiosity of agency "insiders" out of the loop or to those who had no business peering into the "old" Soviet Union. But Keitel was authorized by top secret clearance to do so whenever he felt it was necessary to update himself on any new satellite images in that part of the world. A stickler for detail, he knew every quarter-inch of the photographs. He had studied them for hours on end, even entire weekends once leaving his wife and kids on the outskirts of a Virginia mall to fend for themselves while he obsessively forgot about them. But, here, he didn't quite know what his MIT cultivated brain was looking at.

He had seen nothing unusual or comparable them. What was it that Jenks had said to him

Secret of Ekaterinburg: The Hour-Glass

under his breath. Troika? What did that mean? Troika? In Russian meant three. A threesome, he chuckled to himself.. But, what did it really mean? Keitel studied the Krazcoff photo like never before. God, the hidden harbor was huge in geographical scope. The Russians could hide anything there for years before anyone discovered it. Was there something he and the others simply couldn't see?

What was it that the CIA was looking for during the commercial Korean Air Line 747 spy plane over Kamchatka in 1983 before a Soviet fighter pilot in a MIG-23 Flogger cruelly shot it down without warning. Aboard was a U.S. congressman and 268 innocent civilians who all perished on the shoot-down. At first, the Russians denied any knowledge of the incident, then claimed it was an intentional shoot-down and an intrusion over Russian territory, defending their action. It clearly was no accident on both sides. The flight was clearly intentional but was never publicly acknowledged and the Soviets had to concoct a quick but unconvincing "threatening over flight" of Soviet airspace" which violated their security in order to justify the whole affair to the world. What was the CIA trying to film. Were they on to something that only a few in

Secret of Ekaterinburg: The Hour-Glass

the top echelons of the CIA and NSC knew something about? If so, then the shoot-down was indeed no accident. And, the Russians, indeed, had been waiting for the plane. The U.S. had made similar over flights before, but were undetected through an elaborate setup of a similar Navy Reconnaissance plane flying in concentric circles as a diversion in close proximity to Flight 007 as it neared the Kamchatka Peninsula. Of course, the flight was meant to cover the spying by the EC-1 electronics intelligence plane flown by the Navy. It was simply a diversionary plan gone awry.

What the hell was all that equipment for in those shipyards? Keitel was now running on adrenaline high, pondering, studying, peering, wondering and squinting through the pale-blue glass-lit background slowly moving his magnifier across the negatives.

Point. K-5, coordinate 4.9. Point K-6, coordinate 4.10.

Click. Click. The counter in his left hand moved in a sequence checking-off the quadrants he had already covered. It was a tedious time-consuming business but you had to go over something again and again to produce results. Ever so patiently, he pointed

Secret of Ekaterinburg: The Hour-Glass

the magnifier near the entrance to Krazcoff, then slowly covered again the four miles to where it harbored the equipment. Five hundred pieces of equipment he didn't recognize. All ocean-going. All-climate. They appeared to be flat on top, with squared-out afts, almost like miniature aircraft carriers, but only 200 feet in total length. Judging by the satellite angle and the shadow they cast, they stood about 30 feet high, which means they drafted in the water about 12 feet, a deliberate low profile compared to other vessels. What the hell could they be? He zoomed further down along the sides of the hulls. Curious-looking devices he thought. Along the right side were rows of vent-like panels similar to vents along the sides of submarines which allowed water to be sucked into the ship to give it weight for submerging. The procedure could be reversed to allow the water to be blown out from its ballast tanks for the sub to lighten itself and surface.

Why would these vehicles need such devices? They sure as hell didn't look anything like subs, Keitel wondered.

Peculiar. He kept the thought in the back of his mind and continued to study the photos calibrating the glass back-and-forth across the

Secret of Ekaterinburg: The Hour-Glass

ships. He wondered why Flight OO7 was so important to the U.S., and why we had vehemently defended the over flight as innocent, like an over-protestation of the fact. Yet, everyone in CIA and NSC knew differently. Hell, anyone with any basic Air Force knowledge knew that you didn't mis-program a computer on a flight toward the South Korean peninsula knowing that you're passing right by one of the most top-secret Soviet navy bases in the world. For a pilot to program one mistake into a pre-flight calculation was one thing, but to make two such mistakes was pure undeniable bullshit. Everybody, including the Soviets, knew better. Even the old Air Force intelligence guys who used to make the pre-flight checks and figure the flight plan for the military knew better. It had to be deliberate, alright. And, even when the U.S. began its line of disinformation to the public, everyone suspected otherwise. You just didn't screw-up the pre-flight coordinates on in-putting it into the computer. It could cost lives. And, it did. It was no mistake. Keitel could count that as a given.

Still, there was something not factored in here. Something unknown to him – hidden about Flight 007.

Secret of Ekaterinburg: The Hour-Glass

Keitel looked away from the glass for a few seconds. Something had distracted him. Something. A shadow. One. Maybe, two. Christ, his eyes were burning. He looked away from the negative again and rubbed his eyes, then buried his face into the magnifier again.

Good, God! He saw it. What the hell is that? Jesus. . . . two of them. He began to perspire profusely. . . Keitel quickly looked around to make sure he was alone, and instinctively reached down to push a button that activated the security locks on all doors leading to the small, glass-caged room he was in. He heard the electric locks arm themselves.

"Whew!" He drew in a quick breath. "I don't believe it. It can't be. No wonder he had missed it. They were inside another shadow behind the sub pens. A shadow within a shadow.

If you jiggled the instrument just a little to catch more of the reflected light, it changed the density enough so that you could barely see it . . . it was a technique he had practiced years ago while analyzing reconnaissance photos during the Cuban Missile Crisis. There was no doubt it was there whatever it was. Everyone knew if Keitel said it was there, then it was. The CIA could now count on that. Because Keitel said so.

Secret of Ekaterinburg: The Hour-Glass

"Son-of-a-bitch," it quickly dawned on him. "They're going to attack somebody.

"There is no mistake being made here," Keitel said out loud and reached under the table to press a button that would record his words. "Two medium-sized bridgeheads, floatable, transportable, stacked alongside the main deck barely exposed. Two of them. There must be more to go with the rest of this ghost fleet. Where were they? Stored somewhere? Underground? Probably? If these two exist, there must be many more to match up with the rest of the fleet at Krazcoff." He switched off the recording device. Keitel didn't know the answer to that question, but he knew they had to be somewhere close by. That would make logistical sense. If not, how were they bringing them onto the base?

There were a lot more questions he wanted to dictate into the microphone hidden inside a clock radio near his viewing desk. But he wanted to do one thing first. He had a promise to keep.

It was one that could get him fired - even prosecuted for violating the United States Secrecy Act. But, he knew he had to do it or he wouldn't be able to live with himself. Anyway, he owed Alex this one. When anyone saves

Secret of Ekaterinburg: The Hour-Glass

your skin, not once, but twice and you get a chance to live to see your kids grow up, you owe him big time. Keitel knew Alex would understand if he didn't share this information with him but he wouldn't understand a man who gave his word and then violated that principle.

Keitel drew in a deep breath. He loved the United States. He loved the government he worked for. And, he loved Alex as a brother. He would do nothing to jeopardize national security. That was a given, but at the same time if he could fulfill a promise to a friend, then it was a risk that became part of the territory. And Alex would understand both principles as applied to field agent work. There were some risks that you just had to take if it didn't compromise anyone or anything at the agency. A slight delay reporting-in wouldn't hurt.

He checked the perimeter outside the room, pushed down the speed-dial button on the telephone and dialed Alex's special phone number they used on such occasions. It was untraceable.

Alex's voice mail responded on the second ring with the usual "The number you have dialed is not a working number" message recorded to throw off any would-be callers to

Secret of Ekaterinburg: The Hour-Glass

that number. After he heard the tone, Keitel punched in a special three digit code and the phone rang again. This time Alex answered on the other end from a cellular phone at an unknown location armed with an RF inhibitor which would block any possible listening device or trace.

"Alex."

"Keitel here."

"What's up?"

"I found it. Unmistakably hot! Something you'll sure as hell be interested in."

"For instance?"

"Study up on your Russian history near the end of World War II then meet me in eight hours at the usual rendezvous."

"Are you sure you got something?"

Keitel was not one to make jokes at a time like this but he had to let him know he was serious.

"Do you remember the Cuban Missile Crisis?"

Alex grimaced on the other end of the cell phone.

"That big?"

"That big."

"One o'clock?"

"One o'clock," Alex repeated.

Secret of Ekaterinburg: The Hour-Glass

Keitel hung up the digitalized receiver and disconnected the call. The scrambler indicated that no one had intercepted or tried to intercept the phone frequency they had just chatted on. The light blinked twice and blinked off. In twenty-four hours, the top levels of the CIA and NSC would all be surprised, Keitel thought letting out a pent-up gasp from his lungs. God, he hated moments like this even though he relished the challenge.

He turned off the lighted desk, secured the negatives in a safe beneath the desk, and let himself out of the work station. It was a bit past midnight. He walked down the long semi-lit hallway which connected row-upon-row of work stations the same as his.

There was only one difference. Keitel was the best at satellite map imaging, and tonight he was the only one working.

That's why he was so good at what he did.

He could run that extra mile.

Secret of Ekaterinburg: The Hour-Glass

CHAPTER 17

Langley, Oct. 29, 1989

Keitel sped to the rendezvous spot. It was fifteen minutes from CIA headquarters even if you drove it fast. He knew better than to keep Alex waiting after baiting him with important information he had just discovered. He sure as hell didn't want to irritate him.

His headlights pierced the night. It was just past midnight and pitch black. No moon. Only clouds obscuring everything absorbing the reflected light from the suburbs like a chamois soaking up water after a wash. Keitel headed north and made a quick right onto Belvedere Road for about a mile until he spotted the familiar boathouse nestled in a deserted spot off the Potomac.

Agents, CIA and otherwise, often used these isolated spots for clandestine meetings because they afforded the protection of the surrounding water plus they could easily observe foreign agents approaching them, how they had arrived and if they used the same direct approach the way Keitel had just come in. Headlights could

Secret of Ekaterinburg: The Hour-Glass

be seen from a greater distance, long and flat, and car engines and other approaching noises could be heard a long way off. Keitel pulled up alongside the dilapidated mooring and parked the car with its front wheels turned outward pointing its headlights in the direction where he had entered, just in case he had to light up the area quickly on his way out. He wouldn't want to back up the car first then have to swing it around in an emergency. Several agents had died that way. Getting caught with no way out.

Meanwhile inside, Alex peeked through the boarded up window making sure it was Keitel. He watched Keitel the entire time for anything unusual. He watched for anyone following Keitel just like he had done when he arrived earlier. Now, he made sure of Keitel's approach.

Keitel appeared to be alone.

Alex knew Keitel's old "beater" Chevy anywhere from the mere sound of it, and watched as Keitel got out of the car, leaving the door slightly ajar, not enough to cause the interior light to stay on. Keitel knew funny things happened. In a rush, doors might not open when you needed them to. He moved cautiously toward the boathouse. He was looking for Alex's car, but he couldn't spot it,

Secret of Ekaterinburg: The Hour-Glass

yet he knew it must be hidden somewhere nearby in a safe but easily accessible spot.

"It's about time you got here," Alex said matter-of-factly.

"Hell, I'm a full five minutes ahead of schedule. I've learned to drive like you. You must be on edge about this," Keitel replied deftly.

"You're damned right I am. When one of the best analysts at the CIA says to you over the phone that he's discovered something far more sinister than missiles in Cuba, the hair on the back of my neck stood-on-end about two inches . . . then turned grey."

"No shit?" Keitel grinned.

"No shit," Alex replied.

Both, sat down, along one of the benches fishermen used when it rained.

Keitel lit a cigarette; Alex followed suit.

"Well, what have you got?" Alex chimed-in.

"What I've got is the possibility that the Russians are going to launch an invasion somewhere in the world, but I haven't had time to think about when or where or any other aspect except to wonder just how they're going to use all that equipment."

"What equipment?" Alex asked.

"It's those reconnaissance photo we were

Secret of Ekaterinburg: The Hour-Glass

looking at a week ago? We couldn't figure out what we were looking at, you know the hundreds of boat-like vessels, ramped-in for several miles along Krazcoff Bay?" Keitel remarked. "Well, I found two items that will simply amaze you when you realize what they're for."

"What do you mean?"

"Well, I zoomed in as close as I could on them. I didn't see them at first. I had zoomed past them possibly a hundred times without seeing them. But, then . . . there they were . . . inside a shadow, just the kind of thing the KGB does to throw off our imaging satellites . . . so we can't see them. They get lost in the background radiation on the reflected infrared scans . . . and . . . the human eye just doesn't see them. Neither will the computer . . . unless."

"Go on . . . " Alex prodded.

"Well, I slipped in the special filters to cut through the shadows, and zoomed-in, I still didn't see them, until I accidentally re-angled the light across the negative, and all of a sudden there they were."

"What's they?"

"What I saw was that the items positioned inside the shadow were portable bridgeheads . .

Secret of Ekaterinburg: The Hour-Glass

. the kind of erector-set playthings that a unit of advanced engineering corps would use to build movable bridges. Or decks. All hinged, so that they can be swung down and snapped into placed on one of those two-hundred-foot-long beauties - all 500 of them. A gigantic floating bridge once you connect them

"Jesus! Yes! It's a water thing all right. But, five hundred of them. How can you be sure?"

"Well, my guess is there has to be that many to fit across the five hundred or so vessels parked along the shore. They sure as hell ain't going fishing in those damned things."

"How long are each of them?"

"Two hundred feet in length, with a slight arch and two pontoon floats on each end for stabilization. I estimate they could probably hold anything the Russians have mechanized or want to move across them," Keitel went on.

"Five hundred of them. Christ, that's a twenty mile bridge more or less depending on the spacing. What in the hell are they trying to cross? And, where?" Alex asked.

"Damned if I know at this point," Keitel answered, "but, we're going to have to try and figure that out and what their time-line is. That means we're going to have to report it at the tomorrow morning meeting."

Secret of Ekaterinburg: The Hour-Glass

"No, Keit. We can't do that," Alex said, coughing out the trapped cigarette smoke burning in his throat.

"What in-the-hell are you talking about?" Keitel responded tersely. "You said if I give you a few hours' notice on this there wouldn't be any problem with anything I turned up. Now, I don't have to be a genius to figure out what I've got here, and what it means. Right?"

"Yeah, you're right. But, you know and I know, they probably won't call me in on this. They'll give it to some other analyst," Alex remarked.

"Look. You are their top analyst, Alex. But, if they feel differently about it, there's a way I can fix that," Keitel reminded Alex.

"How?"

"I can say it was because of your insistence that I take a look at these old reconnaissance photos that jumped me onto this. Those guys appreciate that kind of creative insight. I'm sure they'll get you in on it because you're the one who originally found it. Am I right?"

Alex knew he was. It was finders keepers at the Company even when someone stumbled onto something unusual during a routine mission. The overseers liked that kind of creativity and they liked to develop and

Secret of Ekaterinburg: The Hour-Glass

continue the originator's insight because if a hunch proved out right the first time, it usually proved out a second time. That's how patterns were analyzed and established.

"O.K. I'm just a bit paranoid about this since Artie was killed. Christ, I'm even getting a bit jumpy about you, Keit."

"Relax, you know me too well."

Keitel ferreted-out another cigarette from his soft-pack and offered one to Alex. They puffed on them silently for a few minutes keeping their thoughts to themselves, trying to figure out where all that equipment might be headed for.

Alex, was good at this. He had done it most of his life. He flicked his cigarette to the floor and squashed it out, then kicked it into the black water inside the boathouse where no one would think it was a regular meeting spot.

"Keit, you asked me if I knew Russian history? How's yours?"

"Not so good. Hell, I had a rough time with our own without worrying about the Ruskies."

"No . . . don't go back that far. Go back to the end of World War II. Remember what Artie was muttering to himself? Troika. Do you remember what it meant in 1944. Remember the Manhattan Project . . . code-name for the

Secret of Ekaterinburg: The Hour-Glass

development of the atomic bomb? Troika was the code name for the massive counter-offensive against the Germans. It was the beginning of the end and the Russians knew it had to be executed flawlessly. That's it, damn-it. The United States, Great Britain and Russia, all knew it was coming. The Germans didn't. It was the secret counter-attack at the Dnepr River. Troika. The U.S., England and Russia. That's the troika. The Ruskies crossed the God-damned Dnepr right in front of the Germans eyes. And, they didn't see it coming. D-Day was the second horse in the troika; and the third and final horse was the dropping of the atomic bomb on Japan. The Ruskies had built a fucking underwater bridge using frogmen at night. And, then they crossed over right on top of the water, nearly rolling over top of the fucking Krauts. Those T-34s, towing artillery pieces, came streaming across that river like fucking salmon swimming up the Oregon River. That's what he was muttering about. Christ, I'd be muttering, too."

"The counter-attack at the Dnepr River."

"The Ruskies did that?" Keitel reacted incredulously. "You mean they built the fucking bridge under water?

"All of it. A mile long. two feet beneath the

Secret of Ekaterinburg: The Hour-Glass

surface of the water so it couldn't be seen by the naked eye during the day. The heavy flow of silt blocked enough light so it still couldn't be seen by German air patrols, either."

"Jesus H. Christ. The Ruskies are crazy aren't they? How in the hell did they think of that?"

"Hey, listen," Alex replied. "The fucking Russians are the best chess players and magicians in the world. What the eye doesn't see the mind doesn't comprehend. They think in riddles and puzzles. Fourteen steps ahead of anyone else when planning their strategic moves. Yep. It's just like the clever bastards. Really fucking ingenious."

"Yeah," Keitel chimed-in and was at a loss for more words.

"The only mistake they made was they didn't realize that somebody like me fifty-five years later would take the time to read a little bit about their history. General Zhukov. You know him? He was something else. It was his idea. One smart son-of-a-bitch. He shepherded that idea right down to the last frogman."

"Zhukov?" Keitel said.

"Yeah, General Georgi Zhukov. Field Marshall of the entire Red Army and spring counter-offensive of 1944. He planned every

Secret of Ekaterinburg: The Hour-Glass

minor and major detail. He wanted to make the Germans pay right down to the last, god-damned storm-trooper. Biggest thing of all, he wanted to surprise the hell-out-of-them, you know . . . scare-the-living-shit-out-of-them, demoralizing them. It made the attack that much more effective."

"Can you imagine those damned Krauts all huddled-up in their fortified bunkers suddenly seeing dozens of Russian tanks skimming along the top of the Dnepr coming their way," Keitel said in wonderment. "Christ. They were probably pissing in their trousers while they were talking to their field commanders."

"Yeah. What a piece of warfare," Alex said.

"What should I do next?" Keit asked. "You're the strategist?"

"Look. Give me forty-eight hours to make sure on this. On your end, find those 500 bridgeheads? If they aren't in sight, I'm not sure two of them are going to convince Nelson or any of the other honchos. Plus, you need to come up with some solid visuals if you can? I'll try to come up with the where and why and some other bullshit, O.K.?"

"O.K. That's it, isn't it?" Keitel said.

"Not quite," Alex retorted. "Just one more thing. I appreciate all you did for me on this.

Secret of Ekaterinburg: The Hour-Glass

It's going to be hard to repay you."

"You already did when you saved my life," Keitel told him waving off the thank you. Alex appreciated the comment.

Indeed, Alex had been a close friend all these years. Even before his life saving act, they had grown close working on various missions during the Kennedy Era. Both had worked on the Bay of Pigs and then finally the Cuban Missile Crisis before Oswald's bullet ended the life of the young president.

As Alex left the boathouse, he shook free the thoughts and headed back toward his car. Suddenly, he caught the sound of something unusual, a slight rustling of leaves near the dirt road where he had hidden his car. He looked over his left shoulder, then focused his sight back toward the boathouse where he saw Keitel walking slowly toward his own car. He caught his attention and signaled him to stop. Looking down at the ground, he saw another pair of footprints leading from the boathouse toward his car.

His mind whirled as he shouted a warning to Keitel . . . "Keit . . . don't open the car-door! Get down!"

The sounds were staccato-like as they pierced the night air. They had been set-up.

Secret of Ekaterinburg: The Hour-Glass

Keitel's forward motion stopped as he spun around when the first round struck him in the right shoulder. He instinctively tried to drop to the ground and it was that act alone that probably saved his life because the next round struck the left support post of his car and ricocheted harmlessly into the Potomac somewhere.

The third round was directed at Alex. But, he was already on the ground rolling toward tree cover and a patchwork of brush near his car. He reached for his Beretta, and flicked the safety off and let the blue-steel slide slam against the breech. Fully armed and ready for anything they would throw at him, he scoured the wooded area for configurations on all sides of him, guarding his back inching his way on his stomach toward Keitel's position.

Whoever it was, was using night-vision equipment. Whoever it was, was real good at this. He knew Keitel had been hit, but the sniper had missed him again when he had turned his body back toward the boathouse. After catching his breath, Alex decided he couldn't wait any longer. Keitel might be bleeding to death and he had to take a calculated risk to get closer to him. He knew the sniper would anticipate that and open fire

Secret of Ekaterinburg: The Hour-Glass

on him when he made his move. Alex quickly prepared to deceive the sniper. He knew the shots had come from his left. The sniper would figure him to move away from the shots. Instead, he would move toward him then around to Keitel's right, to a sparse tree-line along the dirt road from the boathouse, and finally to Keitel's car - if he was one hundred percent lucky.

Alex crouched, then took off with lightning speed toward the attacker's position. It must have rattled him for he opened up erratically firing toward the sudden sound missing his target badly. Several more shots punctured the air, the last one echoing a distinctive "ping" as Alex heard the magazine being ejected from the sniper's handgun. He was reloading.

"Hang on, Keit," Alex yelled and changed direction as he ran as hard as he could toward the tree-line. Knowing the assassin would not be expecting him to give away his position away while on a dead run toward the car, Alex heard another magazine slam into the breech of the sniper's gun, but it was too late. Alex was now running at full speed and made a desperate headlong dive toward the left front tire of Keitel's car and the relative safety that it provided. Karrump! Alex slid about two yards

Secret of Ekaterinburg: The Hour-Glass

as sand and dirt rolled up inside his shirtsleeves. Not enough time for the gunman to aim and fire again. He landed in front of Keitel laying face-down in a pool of blood with his arms stretched over his head.

Alex heard more movement in the trees. The sound was heading away from them. The assassin had decided to cut his losses and get out while he could. Now, the assassin was on the defensive. Alex peeked toward the sound from behind the car, and aimed at his last-known position.

"Keit! Damn-it. Talk to me," Alex yelled and rolled him over on his back.

"Jesus. He really got you good, didn't he?" Alex said checking to see if he was still alive. He was. But, he was losing blood real fast and having difficulty breathing. They both had to get out of there, and he figured he couldn't get out by car because whoever was out there was still waiting for them.

"C'mon, Keit. Stay with me, now. Don't die on me. I saved you twice, and God-damn-it, I'm going to do it again. You'll owe me big time for this." Alex dragged his lifeless body toward the boathouse his heels dragging in the dirt holding Keitel up under his arms. Alex backed through the door with adrenaline

Secret of Ekaterinburg: The Hour-Glass

strength. Toward the back was an old rowboat rigged with a small outboard motor. He hauled Keitel's limp body onto it and rolled him into the boat's bottom. Then, he climbed in carefully aiming his 9mm at the entrance to the boathouse so that whoever might come in uninvited, would face a good chance of ending up dead at the hands of a marksman. He grabbed at the pull starter and gave it a tug. Nothing . . . the motor turned over and quickly chugged to a stop. He tried again. Nothing. Maybe the gas tank was empty. No time to check.

"Come on . . . you bastard . . . fire up. He pulled the choke handle and tried once more and suddenly the old motor sprang to life. He pushed the throttle to full forward, knocked off the choke and let the boat leap through the weathered double doors and out onto the black waters of the Potomac. He ducked just in time to clear the beam as the boat revved to its maximum 10 mph.

God, it was a helluva maneuver but he didn't have A chance to appreciate it. It was their only chance to survive this. He stabilized Keitel as best he could as the boathouse receded slowly but steadily into the distance. Alex pointed the bow toward the nearest buoy lights he could

Secret of Ekaterinburg: The Hour-Glass

see on the opposite shore about a half-mile away. He knew this part of the Potomac well having fished near there and knew he was looking at Brighton's Pointe. Once he reached it, they both would be safe. At least for a while.

He had to get Keitel to a hospital fast. He looked down at him in the darkness and could barely see him breathing, his chest slowly moving up-and-down in a struggle to capture the cool night air.

"Keit. Can you hear me? Hang on. Christ, hang on."

There was no response. He was unconscious from the loss of blood and losing more. Alex had to stop the bleeding if Keitel was going to live, but he couldn't do that until he reached shore. The boat's tiny motor droned on breaking the eerie silence as the waves lapped-up against the sides of the boat nosing its way against the river's flow.

Like the Russians at the Dnepr, Alex and Keitel were attacking a river. And, like the Russians, they would reach the other side in only minutes.

Secret of Ekaterinburg: The Hour-Glass

CHAPTER 18

Krazcoff Naval Base, Nov. 13, 1989

Inside the dingy quarters of Russian Naval Intelligence, Andre casually picked up the telephone that linked him to the outside world. He was being careful in his movements, his everyday thoughts expressing his ideas to no one - to no one who counted in the navy hierarchy anyway.

Andre couldn't even trust his wife, especially her, because if he told her anything and the Russian Federal Security Service (FSS) found out anything that might compromise her, they would squeeze it out of her through her social acquaintances. No one fully trusted anyone in Russia these days even though the glasnost reforms had been in place for several years.

That way, he rationalized, there was nothing to tell, because if his wife didn't know anything there would be no repercussions. And because he truly loved his family, he didn't want to involve any of them in anything as

Secret of Ekaterinburg: The Hour-Glass

consequential as state government secrets. Certainly, at least in Russia, it worked that way and most probably it worked the same way in the United States. Except, he had heard of some cases where CIA agents were ordered to marry someone to use as deep cover for any covert actions necessary to carry out an assignment.

Andre dialed the rotary telephone.

The Russians still used them while they were converting over to the newer more modern touch-tone, digitalized system – a system that would be more difficult for foreign intelligence operatives to either listen in on or for spy satellites to run surveillance overhead. The digitalized process and the subsequent scrambling devices that were being used were far more sophisticated than those used in the past where agents either "bugged" the system using tiny diodes secretly installed into the mouthpiece which could then be intercepted electronically. Or, they used tiny transmitters hidden somewhere inside the room, buried in the walls, or attached to phone lines outside the target structure. Even these transmitters could be foiled by simultaneously transmitting over several other changing frequencies using a randomized oscillator to transmit harmonics, impeding the receivers of even the most

Secret of Ekaterinburg: The Hour-Glass

sophisticated cyphers. But, even if successful intercepts were made deciphering was another much more difficult matter. Most spies would make a statement and if it made sense in normal conversation, a pre-programed set of matching counter-statements would give it a different meaning for the authorized person meant to hear it. That authorized person would then "match" the statement to a set of pre-programed codes to decode it.

Andre completed the dial and activated the scrambler. Even though he knew it would protect him from U.S. counter-intelligence eavesdropping, he knew the Russians had a counter-measure installed by internal security enabling them to spy on their own people. He couldn't counter that. So, the phone call would have to sound as business as usual.

"Hello. Sergei? It is Andre. How is the old silver-haired fox, this morning? I've got some extra time, and I want to talk to you about that little "babushka" you were interested in. You still are interested in her aren't you? Good. Let's have coffee in about 30 minutes unless you are already fucking her?"

Andre laughed to make it sound normal.

On the other end, Sergei feigned his side of the conversation to convince whoever else

Secret of Ekaterinburg: The Hour-Glass

might be listening.

"Dos vidaniya," Andre hung up without looking at the phone cradle. Eager to get started for his secret meeting with Sergei, Andre turned off the computer terminal which showed this morning's deployment of Russian nuclear submarines and signaled to his aide to prepare his departure from the operations room.

The aide obeyed nodding his head from the other side of the glass partition and snapped to attention as Andre opened the locked door at the same time reaching for his thick, woolen gray winter cap. It was already unusually cold for this time of year. The weather had turned bitter from the early Siberian fronts that had swept down from the arctic across thousands of miles of barren tundra to suck life out of everything it touched as it edged deeper inland then eastward and outward toward the Pacific.

Only the southerly coastal flows from Asia and the South Pacific currents made Vladivostok and Krazcoff a seaport from where winter operations could take place, in terms of launching and maintaining their fleet of nuclear submarines and other large warships. They had not one single warm-water seaport anywhere in Russia, and it had been that way since Peter the Great ruled. Geography and land mass had its

Secret of Ekaterinburg: The Hour-Glass

price. Murmansk, high up on the rim of the arctic circle, above Sweden, was already frozen-up since September, and sometimes it could be blocked by thick ice in late June. It was impossible to keep a shipping lane open very long without a fleet of ice-breakers operating routinely every day that far north, and even that didn't work if the cold spell lasted a long time.

"Comrade, Lieutenant," Andre spoke, "please inform my superiors, if they inquire, that I am inspecting the sub pens this morning. I shall not be back until noon."

"Of course, Colonel Kirov. They are not on base this morning but if they telephone-in, I will tell them what you have told me."

Andre smiled. Russian officers were still referred to as Comrades even though communism had now been officially dead for nearly a decade. It still made them believe in the power of the military and the usefulness of how the military ran things. Old habits were hard to break and there was no purpose in changing tradition as long as tradition made things work. And, it worked to perfection. Fear always worked best in the military. Young Russian officers were afraid of anything that might jeopardize their careers. If they

Secret of Ekaterinburg: The Hour-Glass

made serious mistakes in the line of duty or if they made several of them often enough, they could get booted out of the military establishment and their lives would revert to being miserable, forced to work like ordinary citizens; their wives, in return, would then make them even more miserable in repayment.

"Sir, Comrade," the young lieutenant snapped-off taking a step backward while executing a flawless salute.

"Your overcoat and gloves."

"Thank you," the ever so-correct Colonial replied, returning the salute and finished snapping on his holster carrying his Russian-made semi-automatic pistol. "You have served me well this week, Lieutenant. You may have tomorrow off. Please shut down all security equipment here. Is that understood?"

The Lieutenant tried to contain his excitement but a slight smile curled in his lower lip and he thanked the colonel profusely.

"A question sir, if I may ask?"

"Yes, of course."

"Is there a special answer to be given if headquarters calls and neither of us are here to make decisions?"

Kirov smiled. "You are indeed a thorough officer, in the unique tradition of the great

Secret of Ekaterinburg: The Hour-Glass

Russian Navy. Yes, the special answer for the dispatcher is that we have closed down the intelligence operations for tomorrow because of proprietary briefings?"

"But, what does that mean?"

"Headquarters will know what it means. It is not for junior officers to know every reason or what kind of orders are given here. Am I clear on that point?"

Kirov was a little perturbed at the question, but he understood the anxiety of the young officer to simply cover himself in the event that something went wrong in their absence.

"Da," the young officer saluted stiffly, dropping the smile from his clean-shaven face. "I will inform dispatch."

"In any event if the duty officer calls while you are here that is the message you will give him. If he calls while we are both gone, he will be given the same message via the dispatcher. The message will be the same. Only the messenger will be different."

The young officer, named Ivan, nodded.

"Just be sure when you leave to tell the dispatcher, or we'll both be court-martialed for dereliction-of-duty," Andre said with a sober face.

Kirov put on his overcoat, fastened the

Secret of Ekaterinburg: The Hour-Glass

snaps on the long woolen coat which hung down to his ankles, and pulled on his cap. He exited the building quickly and in a few seconds was out in the cold Russian air. The winds were brutal and he could see the gale warnings posted at the far end of the base. Soon, it would be blowing snow-squalls.

"Good God!" Kirov muttered under his breath. "Does the world know what bitter conditions we Russians constantly live under?"

He swore in Russian and continued his long strides toward the gray military command car which would take him to his self-appointed rendezvous with Sergei.

As he climbed into the old car and turned the key, the engine slowly groaned to a start. He drove from the naval base to the outskirts of the peninsula, past Krazcoff Sound miles away from the naval base where he and Sergei would meet. It was a small, out-of-the-way place where they could talk in private while people could still see them.

They must be extra careful now. The NKVD staff roamed all over the navy base and they trusted no one. He knew if he was to be successful, he had to make sure they weren't being monitored.

Now, he was about to tell Sergei, a lifelong

Secret of Ekaterinburg: The Hour-Glass

boyhood friend, that they were about to betray their "mother Russia" with a plan so diabolical and infinitely perfect, that once begun, no one, would understand what was happening until it had happened.

"I must find a way to reassure him," Andre said to himself as he drove along the coastal two-lane road, which would take him to the restaurant not frequented by naval officers or other military personnel.

The old car growled under the strain climbing a small hill then slid around a bend in the road, and finally coasted down a gentle slope where Kirov spotted the familiar eating establishment.

The winds blew sheets of snow across the roadway and soon it would be impassable for local traffic if the storm kept up. Only a few Red Navy personnel had access to autos, and so it probably didn't matter much. Those who did, didn't even want them because they were more trouble than worth, unless you had a military mechanic at your disposal who could constantly care for it. They were too expensive for private citizens. Even in the days of perestroika, success and wealth had been slow to come to Russians. Most villagers still preferred their reliable horses or public

Secret of Ekaterinburg: The Hour-Glass

transportation for getting to-and-from work or for holiday travel. Trains or buses worked fine for most. But, they ran so infrequently, it made travel unpleasant, impersonal and inconvenient.

The unpaved road ended at the weather-worn entrance to the restaurant. Andre knew Sergei would already be inside, eagerly waiting for the new information he was about to learn.

Andre stepped from the car, the wind roiling up against Him nearly knocking him to the ground as he fought for his balance. It was indeed appropriate. Soon, the entire world would be off-balance in the same roil.

He covered his face with his coat collar and went inside to meet Sergei.

Secret of Ekaterinburg: The Hour-Glass

CHAPTER 19

Brighton's Pointe, Va., On The Potomac, Oct. 30, 1989

Keitel was dying, but Alex had to prevent that from happening. As soon as he reached shore he had to get him to a hospital.

Pointing the bow of the old motorboat toward the nearest buoy marker he could see, Alex steered the boat through the dark swift current to within a few yards of the shoreline where there was a boat ramp and walkway leading to a house some fifty yards from shore.

He throttled-back the outboard to idle and let the vessel coast up onto home-produced beach near the weathered beach house. As he jumped over the side of the boat, a porch light blinked on at the house. Alex could see some people on the back porch gathering to see what was going on.

"Down here! Over here, quickly! Help me!"

Two men tumbled from the porch and began running breakneck toward Alex's rowboat.

Secret of Ekaterinburg: The Hour-Glass

"What happened?" one of them yelled seeing Keitel's body lying face-down in the bottom of the boat. Blood trickled from his mouth.

"He's been shot. We've got to get him to a hospital. How close is the nearest one?" Alex asked with staccato-like urgency.

"About three miles," one of the two men answered, "but, my friend here is a doctor."

"A doctor?"

"I'm a vascular surgeon," one of the men responded. "Not that it makes any difference here. This man's almost dead. Get him inside quickly."

The three men carried Keitel's lifeless body uphill across the backyard and inside where they laid him across a kitchen table propping up his legs with one of the pulled out table extensions.

"He's in pretty bad shape," the doctor said triaging Keitel's condition. His friend was already on the phone calling for an ambulance. "He's lost a lot of blood, still losing it internally, probably in the left lung."

He pressed an index finger into the wound to stop the bleeding as best he could and felt for the slug. Then, he tore a piece of kitchen towel, packing it into the flesh to stem the flow

Secret of Ekaterinburg: The Hour-Glass

of blood. He wasn't worried about infection. He had to keep him alive right now.

"There's not much I can do for him here. I can only try to help him breathe and keep his heart going until the paramedics get here. It'll only be a few minutes. They're damned good out here," the young doc said monitoring Keitel's vital signs. He was used to this and didn't waste a lot of motion by asking dumb questions. It was part of his practical emergency training he had received during medical school. There was no time for small talk or unimportant questions in a crisis. There would be plenty of time afterward if there was an afterward for the victim.

He changed Keitel's position to a slight upward angle to help his breathing, cushioning his head with a pillow gathered from one of the chairs.

"It'll make his breathing a bit easier."

Keitel's eyes were starting to fixate at the ceiling when gazed down at Alex trying to figure out where he was. He tried to speak but blood leached from the side of his mouth. His face was stone gray. The young doc cleared his mouth with his fingers and instructed Keitel not to speak.

But, Keitel wouldn't have any of it.

Secret of Ekaterinburg: The Hour-Glass

"Alex ," he managed, "there's something I've got to tell you . . . something important."

"Don't talk now," Alex tried to reassure him. "You can tell me at the hospital."

"No I might not make it. There's something about troika you ought to know, something I didn't remember at first. Maybe, I didn't think it was important. But, it's about the code-word. Artie answered himself with another code-word. I didn't think it was important until I saw the negatives."

Keitel's voice caught in his throat, and he began spasming up blood and vomit. The physician, pretending not to listen, grabbed a salad bowl from a nearby countertop and let Keitel's stomach contents spill into it.

When he was finished, Alex asked, "What was the other code-word?"

"Hour-glass."

"Hour-glass?"

"Yes. That's it. Remember, when I asked you how well you knew the history of the Russian counter-offensive of World War II? Besides the bridgehead there was another reason for the offensive kicking off at that precise location on the Dnepr."

Alex respected Keitel's knowledge of the war. He had been a Soviet specialist in the

Secret of Ekaterinburg: The Hour-Glass

agency years before and only recently had become a photo intelligence analyst transferring over to special satellite reconnaissance. The doc looked at them incredulously knowing he wasn't supposed to be hearing any of their conversation, but he was there in the room and didn't have much choice nor could he excuse himself when a man's life hung in the balance.

"Hour-glass," Alex. It's another name for a secret operation to capture one of the Czar's descendants you know the Royal Family of Russia. Several of them had continued to live in Ekaterinburg, in exile after escaping the death squads of Beria, but they continued to hunt them down. Where they could they either assassinated them or brought them back for trial. Several were believed by the NKVD to be living in Czechoslovakia and Poland. Guess who they had a lead on during the spring offensive? In St. Petersburg, they had called her "hour-glass," a Russian NKVD code-name. That code name belonged to Anastasia. All the Romanov's had code names. It was Anastasia. Either Marie or Anastasia was rumored to have survived the murders that night. Which one, we don't know for sure, but my feeling is that someone inside the agency knows all this and is

Secret of Ekaterinburg: The Hour-Glass

now willing to discuss it with someone. Find out the real significance of "hour-glass" and you'll have the answer to that identity, and maybe some other answers you need."

"This Troika was one of the code-names for a simultaneous secret operation during the war?" Alex said.

"Yes. The Russians were always overly melodramatic about these covert things even back then. They liked to name them after something significant in their past history. Find out about "troika" and "hour-glass" . . . Keitel spoke in gasps now, his breath diminishing rapidly. He was almost gone.

"Easy, Keit. Hang on now. If you fucking die on me I'll kill you myself."

Alex leaned down to make sure Keitel could see his face Keit attempted a grin, but judging from his gray-like pallor, Alex knew death was at hand. Keitel closed his eyes.

The doctor checked him for a pulse. It was thready. Then, two paramedics burst into the room with a stretcher and began setting up their equipment.

An I.V. was started in one arm giving Keitel the much-needed blood-volume in order to live; another I.V. inserted into his other arm. The sudden jolt of glucose to his blood supply was

Secret of Ekaterinburg: The Hour-Glass

like a shot of adrenaline. Keit opened his eyes squinting at the kitchen light overhead.

"Nobody ever told me that God was fluorescent."

Alex and the young doctor laughed quietly at the remark stepping aside to let the paramedics take over the emergency procedures. Even though he was better trained, they did this all the time under adverse conditions. He now was there only in the event he had to cut open his chest and perform emergency heart massage or to open an air passage. With the I.V.'s in, Keitel now had a chance to make it to the hospital alive.

The two parameds lifted Keitel onto the stretcher, and as soon they belted him in, wheeled him to the waiting ambulance.

Alex hung back for a second and asked the doctor if he could use the phone.

"Sure, go ahead," the doc said knowing better than to refuse.

"Look, he's a personal friend of mine. I'm a member of a United States government agency one I can't identify and one you've probably had no experience with unless you're in the spy business. You'll have to trust me on this. But, please forget anything you heard here tonight. For the sake of you and your family, don't

Secret of Ekaterinburg: The Hour-Glass

identify yourself to the press and don't mention this to any of your friends. O.K.?"

The doctor glanced at Alex and shook his head. It was none of his business what had happened out there on the river. Nothing he wanted to be involved in and besides, he'd been around worse people ranging from gang-members bleeding to death in emergency rooms to Mafioso dying in shootouts. Alex could tell the doc wanted no part of this.

"I've got to go. I need your car. I'll leave it at the hospital. You'll be reimbursed for the use of it. Is that O.K.?"

The physician shrugged and handed him the keys.

"It's the blue sports car parked in the circle out front."

Alex thanked him and left.

He had to get to the hospital before the ambulance. There was no way he was going to let Keitel die. They had come too far together on this. Besides, he had promised his wife he'd look out for him. Keitel was too valuable to lose. He was his most trusted friend and there was nothing he wouldn't do for him. He had to make sure they did everything possible at the hospital.

The doctor was already on the phone,

Secret of Ekaterinburg: The Hour-Glass

calling ahead to notify the trauma team to be ready for a gunshot wound to the left thoracic area in case the ambulance radio wasn't working. Alex overheard him talking to the attending physician.

"Gunshot to the chest. Patient in shock. I.V.s already begun. Plasma in. Needs blood, he's wearing a blood I.D. tag. B-positive."

Alex knew that information would save them precious time. And, time was what Keitel needed.

Time.

Alex needed time, too.

Time was a precious commodity.

Time could save both of their lives.

Secret of Ekaterinburg: The Hour-Glass

CHAPTER 20

Peregrebnoye, The Urals, Nov 2, 1944

Dimitri hadn't returned from the fields like he was supposed to. Sergei had an ominous feeling that something was drastically wrong. His absence confirmed his growing fears that something had happened to him.

Seated beside Ana, he made mental observations, watching the family interact all-the-while keeping an ever-present eye on the window to the outside courtyard. The sisters readied the meager meal "provided" to them from the local communist apparatus. They no longer were allowed to grow their own crops or sell any privately. It was strictly prohibited by the party. The dacha had finally been taken over by the Bolsheviks and the district party.

Where it once was a beautiful, well-kept farm that grew a variety of profitable crops for market, it had been turned over to the state to produce whatever they "ordered" and in quantities the land could not support. The state used forced labor using primitive outdated

Secret of Ekaterinburg: The Hour-Glass

farming techniques the Soviet bureaucracy had mandated. No soybeans, no hay, no barley, and no alfalfa. Nothing except rye and wheat to make the Russian staple black bread. The dacha didn't even produce milk anymore. There was no milk because there were no more cows. They had all been slaughtered to feed the Red Army at the front. The war had taken care of a lot of problems for some, but it had created more problems for the others left behind. The beautiful dacha that Sergei knew from boyhood was withering before his very eyes and was on the brink of death like all of Russia.

Sergei broke his self-imposed silence.

"Tell me, what has become of Dimitri and my brothers? What has happened to Andre? Where are they? What is delaying Dimitri? You are hiding something from me."

The matriarch put a finger to her lips in an attempt to silence Sergei's questions.

"They have taken Dimitri, too. Your brothers were reported missing in the war two years ago in the service of the Red Army. We don't know if they were killed defending Mother Russia as were thousands of others like or if they are themselves prisoners of the Germans. They are young and strong. Perhaps they somehow survived. Andre is the only one

Secret of Ekaterinburg: The Hour-Glass

we know for sure who survived. He is in Moscow, serving as an attaché to Premier Stalin himself. It is quite an accomplishment is it not? But, if you remember, that was always his ambition was it not? To be politically important and to do something big. We have not heard from him in many months. We don't know if he is safe. I have never trusted that murdering Stalin. He calls himself a liberator but that label should be changed to murderer."

Sergei asked incredulously, "How did Andre obtain that kind of position? Did he join the communists voluntarily? It is unthinkable."

"Like any practical person these days. In order to have an opportunity in life or even the pursuit of an education, you must join them and pretend to be one of them. I cannot really believe that Andre is one of them, but he has to survive. We all have to survive on this farm. We will not abandon it even though they don't allow us any acres to grow for sale. If we leave here, what will become of us? I would just as soon perish here than to give in to them. If it were not for Valerya and Helenka, I would be lost. Ana is of marrying age now. She will find a man soon."

Ana and Sergei blushed with embarrassment.

Secret of Ekaterinburg: The Hour-Glass

"Aahhmm," Sergei stumbled to find the right words. "You see, mother, I have been meaning to talk to you for some time now and have not mentioned this in my letters because I did not know if Ana had been spoken for or promised to another. I . . . that is, we have discussed it for several months by letter and again just prior to dinner. We have decided to marry."

Squeals of delight came from Ana's sisters. The matriarch clasped her hands in obvious pleasure at the announcement. She had suspected as much but a Russian mother cannot assume to choose what her daughter must choose for herself. In Russia, life was difficult enough, and no Russian family made it more difficult by choosing for their children. There was a certain amount of pragmatism built into the existing society throughout the past centuries, especially in the Urals where there was a certain "family rule" Russians lived by and enforced steadfastly. Staying out of your children's affairs of the heart was one of those unwritten rules unless, of course, the marriage had been arranged for other purposes.

"Da. It is good. And, I am pleased for you both. But, Sergei what will you do now that you have left the Ukraine? The Red Army will

Secret of Ekaterinburg: The Hour-Glass

be looking for you, too."

"True . . . but I have a technical degree in electrical engineering from Kiev University, one that qualifies me to work on important sensitive weaponry in war production. It will be my passport to a civilized life and one that I can use to take care of all of you. First and foremost, of course, my priority will be Ana and eventually our own children but I will see to it that you will all be secure."

The Tanya and the girls conversed excitedly and listened carefully to Sergei's plans. For now, he was the new patriarch of the family and he would be important to their futures.

"One more thing. When was it you last heard from Dimitri? I must find him. If he is still alive, I vow to return with him. Let us pray that he is safe. The war cannot last much longer. It is nearly finished. We are attacking the Germans mercilessly west of the Dnepr. Have you heard? The Germans are in full flight. Their retreat is in disarray and it won't be much longer until we send them back to Berlin. We will defeat them."

Sergei and Ana squeezed hands underneath the table.

"I promise to find him . . . and my brothers, even if it is only to find out where they are

Secret of Ekaterinburg: The Hour-Glass

buried . . . if it's the last thing I do," Sergei recited in an oath.

"Do not consume too much of yourself in your duties to others," the matriarch cautioned. "Dimitri loved you like one of his own son's, and I know you did also in return, but you must attend to yourself first and your personal needs as a priority. If I know Dimitri, and I do, wherever he is, he has probably figured a safe way for himself. He will survive. If he is dead, then his soul is safe with God. In either case he is safe is he not? Be careful, Sergei, if you go to Moscow. It is a dangerous place politically, particularly if you dislike the communists. They rule everyone and Stalin trusts no one. He will murder anyone he suspects of betrayal."

Sergei respected Tanya's wisdom even though he hardly needed to be reminded of the realities of Russian life in the Stalin era. He, like millions of other Russians were already aware of the ruthless nature of the dictator as the legacy of Stalin had unfolded. Most were afraid of him, so afraid, that they refused to even consider rising up against him. During the Ukraine potato famine and genocide of the 1930's, Stalin conveniently purged more than 5,000 of his best military officers, just months

Secret of Ekaterinburg: The Hour-Glass

before the Germans invaded.. That barbaric act alone had confirmed everyone's worst fears – that not only was he insane, but he was psychopathically brutal. One day he would have to be ousted from power. But, who would be the one to perform this impossible deed? Like those who surrounded Hitler, all had become corrupt with power and frozen with fear, their thoughts devoid of action. So they did nothing.

Was Andre now one of his henchmen, one of the feared, whom everyone hated? He found it hard to believe, but he knew he must confront him and find the answer to that question in two weeks. For now, he could re-familiarize himself with his bride-to-be and enjoy the surroundings of the dacha while he had time. After his departure, there was no telling how long he would be away.

In the morning, they would be married by a local communist official in town then they could at least be intimate as a couple for the next few weeks. It was something they had both longed for.

He would spend at least three months in Moscow looking for a job, or perhaps even better, do what Andre had done, obtain a position in the "party." His disdain for the communists, after all, had its roots at that very dacha. And, it was appropriate that his mission to reunite the family should begin from there. He remembered the many conversations they all had at the dinner table.

Dimitri had told them how ruthless the Nazis were, but he had also warned them of the growing threat of the communists.

And, now, in a reversal of fate, Sergei would have to help them defeat the Nazis that the whole of Russia hated.

Secret of Ekaterinburg: The Hour-Glass

CHAPTER 21

Krazcoff, December 13, 1989

Andre entered the Russian eatery and brushed the snow from his overcoat. The place was dimly lit, and the dark gray skies with only a few windows, did little to brighten it. In the background on a speaker hidden somewhere gypsy violins played the shrill pitches of a Hungarian "chadas," a spirited gypsy folk dance.

The Russians enjoyed all kinds of ethnic folk music especially their own. Virtually all Russians knew how to dance the folk dances; the men could do the energy-sapping leg-kick atop any table or platform they could find when the mood presented itself which could be almost at any occasion.

There were only a few patrons in the café at this time of the day and the few who were there could no longer afford to eat a lavish meal. Russians were not eager to eat away from their homes because it was still horribly expensive for them. The military families, however, were

Secret of Ekaterinburg: The Hour-Glass

far different. They could afford to do it nearly every day, if they wished. Although few did. Most of the women still did the cooking in their tiny apartments and would rather hoard the money they saved for extras. Most lived in the rectangular, high-rise military-style apartments near the base. These stark facilities provided them with the bare frills they had come to expect in the service of their country and perhaps more aware of the privileges of belonging to a military family.

Andre spotted Sergei off at a corner table with a view toward the bay.

He walked over and greeted him with a bear hug and a slap on the back.

Now, Andre realized he not only was putting their unique friendship to a test but also their very lives.

Did he have the courage to see it through? What would Sergei's reaction be to the plan? Would he be a willing participant? Or, would he back out? Andre knew Sergei had never done anything like this before, and it would be new to him. Sergei had more to lose, but Sergei was the only one he could trust with his own life.

A bottle of Vodka sat on the table half-empty. Sergei poured two glasses and they

Secret of Ekaterinburg: The Hour-Glass

toasted each other.

"Tell me, Andre, why is this meeting so important, and so secret?"

"Because it must be. Remember when we were growing up, and we were the only two on the dacha with secrets kept from everyone else and we never betrayed those secrets?"

"Da. Those were wonderful days. But, things are a little different today. We are much older; we still share some personal secrets, but we are a lot wiser now, eh, Andre, and the enemies are real?"

"Perhaps ? But, this one thing I know for certain. The communists are on the move again, and they are fighting a crucial battle to reorganize from their disaster five years ago in the elections."

"Yes, I am aware of that. They are continuing to be bothersome and I cannot fathom any more of them at this point in our history. They are a determined bunch of old fools are they not?" Sergei said unsmilingly.

"Is this why you have asked me to meet with you to discuss even more politics?" Sergei chided Andre.

"Naturally, not. But, it is related very closely to it, my friend. In all the years I have known you, I have never known you to betray

Secret of Ekaterinburg: The Hour-Glass

me. I would trust you with my life, and the very life of my family and children. This is the reason we are here today. I am working with a group that will guarantee that Russia remains free from the clutches of communism. I know there are some who would say this is treasonous, but they are from the old school who want to return to the glory days of the Bolsheviks. Believe me, I personally repudiate those ideas and I abhor the thought of a bunch of old renegades taking over our lives once again. We must do something about this and the time is now before it is too late."

"So, you have decided to take the responsibility of directing Russia's future upon yourself?"

"Nyet. Not by myself. There are others involved, in secret like you and I. Most important we need your expertise on this."

"But, first you need me to promise you not to betray you. . . . " Sergei guessed correctly.

"That is quite right. Brother, I assume you would not betray as a family member and I don't feel I need to put such a damnable question to you, but the others have required it of me for their own protection. Believe me, I have reassured them that you are to be trusted," Andre apologized.

Secret of Ekaterinburg: The Hour-Glass

Sergei had always been the quiet, studious and cautious one. Andre, on-the-other-hand, had been the calculating, bold, impetuous one even brazen at times to his superiors.

"You don't need to apologize. I owe you my life and I made a promise to you that I would never let anything happen to you as a brother. I am married to your sister, am I not? Her blood runs through your veins and yours through hers, and now that same blood is mixed in my daughter's veins. I would not jeopardize our families even if they put a gun to my head. Now tell me, what is it that you wish of me?" Sergei asked his elbows set forward on the table and his hands clasped.

Before Andre could answer, a waiter came over and interrupted asking for their order. Both, already well-familiar with the menu quickly gave the waiter their order and went back to their conversation pouring more vodka into their empty glasses.

"Sergei, there are certain communist factions inside the Kremlin who will attempt to overthrow the present regime, topple him from power, and perhaps even kill the president and return the country to the previous Soviet empire it once was," Andre continued.

Sergei winced when he heard the words.

Secret of Ekaterinburg: The Hour-Glass

"But, they must do that through democratic elections. They do not have the ability to overthrow the present government, do they?

"According to our calculations, they cannot wrest power from the majority. They have a sizeable minority bloc throughout Russia, but the government is firmly entrenched in the hands of those who wish it to continue along the lines of capitalism. But, there are those inside the army, air force and navy, who wish to purge the president by forceful his overthrow even if it means death to our leader. And, believe me, Sergei, they have more than enough power through old political KGB cronies, some young hotheads, and the FSS to see it through if they cannot achieve it by other means." Andre explained.

"And, what military leader would do this to the leader of his own mother Russia?" Sergei asked.

Andre paused for a second and looked directly at Sergei.

"You," he replied solemnly.

Startled at his words, Sergei knocked his glass of vodka over spilling some of it on the red tablecloth.

"Are you mad? I have no reason to kill the President."

Secret of Ekaterinburg: The Hour-Glass

"I know that and you know that . . . but they don't know that."

"What do you mean . . . they?" Sergei nervously put the question back to Andre.

"They . . . are the real plotters against the president. They . . . the communist elite have been planning such a move for years and if they cannot remove him from power one way they will do it the other way. Therefore, we have decided that we need to place an operative inside the communist apparatus, you know a party apparatchik to become one of them, to spy on them for us from within and to convince them that you are the man to remove the president from his office one way or another."

"Andre, you have completely lost your mind. I've no experience in these kinds of things, not the least espionage. And you are talking about domestic espionage, a guaranteed death sentence by firing squad if I'm caught. I don't think I am capable of such a deed?"

"You don't really have to want to do it. You must do it. There is no alternative for us. But, you won't have to kill anybody. Believe me, there are plenty of communists who will jump at the chance . . . to be a hero of Russia at least in their own minds. Even without you, they are bound to carry out their plan anyway. At the

Secret of Ekaterinburg: The Hour-Glass

same time, while this is happening, you must point towards taking over the party and keep control of things until we can complete the rest of the plan."

"Comrade Andre," Sergei responded in a more formal tone than he normally used, "exactly what is the rest of this plan that you are talking about?"

"Listen, these idiots who want to return to the harsh days of confrontation against the western powers, cannot be trusted. I am afraid that this unbridled power will run wild unopposed and lead to something far worse than we could ever imagine."

"And, what is it that we cannot imagine?" Sergei asked.

"My brother, certain specific information has come into my possession that details what the old communist fools have in mind. Inside the old politburo and certain elements of the army, intelligence operatives have been smuggling nuclear missiles and certain fissionable material for the production of atomic weapons to an outside country known only to a few. I cannot provide you with the name of that country at the present time, but I can only tell you that it is somewhere in the middle east, and that this country is a sworn

Secret of Ekaterinburg: The Hour-Glass

enemy of the United States. In effect, because of that, they will become a mortal enemy of Russia as well. We both have the same interests now. The destruction of either one of us could lead to the destruction of the other very easily."

"Are the politicos in the U.S. aware of such a dissident movement inside our country?"

"Da. We have been in contact with certain members of the Central Intelligence Agency in Washington and have provided them with secret contacts and information. They have shown very great concern about the situation," Andre went on.

"What must we do now?"

"Trust me. You have already done it judging by your interest in this matter."

The two finished the bottle of Vodka then ordered another.

"What are they proposing?"

"It is the intention of the communists to provide these missiles and nuclear arsenals to this third country so they can launch an attack against either the United States military in Bahrain or use them to dominate the Euro-Asian region from Turkey to Persia and India well into the next century. Even we would be threatened by our own missiles. But, those

Secret of Ekaterinburg: The Hour-Glass

ideological bastards cannot see the mistake in that."

"So, we must make them see it for their own security?" Sergei surmised correctly.

"Another correct assumption," Andre praised. "You always were superb in analyzing political intrigue."

"What is the rest of the plan?"

"Once you are established inside the party apparatus, respected and trusted, then we will launch our plan to deliver these missiles to the United States instead."

"But, how can that be accomplished? And, how will we be able to hide that fact from the powers-that-be in the military who are involved with the communists in this?"

"Ahh! Sergei, perhaps I have misjudged you. We are not going to hide the fact that we will be delivering the missiles and warheads. While they are assuming they will be delivering these components to this third country, they will actually be ferried across a large body of water using the equipment you have already seen housed at Krazcoff."

"Incredible. Impossible. You mean those bridgeheads are going to be used in this plan?"

"Yes. They are the key to it. There are some two hundred missiles and nuclear

Secret of Ekaterinburg: The Hour-Glass

warheads that have been secretly sold to this country for a king's ransom. They are more than powerful enough to destroy the entire world if they get into the wrong hands. And, believe me, Sergei, those are the wrong hands wouldn't you agree?"

"Of course, I agree," Sergei drank the rest of his drink and shuffled his feet nervously on the floor.

"Careful. . . relax. . . do not look around . . . smile. . . " Andre's eyes quickly scanned the room without moving his head or position at the table. He observed the waiter casually standing near the television set watching the Russian news in black and white, the cook in the kitchen going about his culinary duties, and the owner sitting at the counter wiping away the dust that had collected or had not collected, in an effort to look busy. The five other patrons were seated at their respective tables and booths not wishing to be bothered by anyone.

"One never knows if there are FSS agents at hand, perhaps inside this very cafe while we are eating. O.K. . . It is safe . . . Calmly reserve yourself and take a few deep breaths because there is much more to learn. However, that must wait for another day, Sergei. The main point of this meeting is not so much the details

Secret of Ekaterinburg: The Hour-Glass

of the rest of the plan but refers to my original question. What I am asking you to do, would you do it for our families and will you do it to save Mother Russia?"

Sergei turned slowly in his chair, and picked up the glass of vodka, swallowed the rest of it, swilled down with a skill he had learned in the Ukraine.

"It is a shock to me. Even if I agree to it, I pray that you will spare me all of the details? If I disapprove, how can you still be sure that I won't turn you in to the authorities?"

"Sergei, to betray an associate is one thing, but to betray a member of your very own family is unpardonable . . . in this case, the death of your soul."

Andre repeated an old Russian saying**. "Предайте друга; Вы выдаете себя. Предайте семью; Вы предаете Бога."**

"Betray a friend; you betray yourself. Betray family; you betray God."

Sergei knew it by heart. It was in his heart. The lessons of rural Russian life had imprinted these values in him like a duckling's instinct to its mother. He had no other choice. To betray Mother Russia was one thing, punishable by physical death. But, betraying a member of your own family, was punishable by ostracism

Secret of Ekaterinburg: The Hour-Glass

from within the family and that was worse than any death sentence the FSS could impose. In fact, those who had gone through it, had prayed for death to relieve their guilt.

"Take your time Sergei, it is not an easy thing that I ask. A few more days or weeks will not make any difference," Andre rejoined.

"But, it would to me," Sergei retorted. "You could never be sure by my hesitancy that I could be trusted to the fullest. You would never be sure of me ever again. No my brother, I do not need more time. Whatever is in our future, we are in this together. My time has come now, this very minute. I will do it. Whatever more there is to learn, I will look forward to learning it and eager to fulfill my part of the bargain."

Andre was gratified with his decision. It was the one he had hoped he would make, and the one he had prepared himself for. He had spent no time planning an alternative he thought might be necessary. And, Sergei had not let him down. He would join the conspiracy to rid Russia of these unmentionables these traitors to the cause of freedom and democracy.

"But, there is one small thing I do ask in return. It is a small gesture, but one which I

Secret of Ekaterinburg: The Hour-Glass

will need to convince myself that the entire plan is worthwhile," Sergei asked.

"And . . . that is . . . ?"

"That is, I would like to be present in Moscow, alongside the President, when the final minutes of the plan are executed. I want to see on their very faces the leadership of the communist traitors . . . I want to confront him when he witnesses the final piece of the conspiracy as it falls into place. I want to see the expression on his face. I want to feel his rejection. I want to see his sense of revulsion just like he saw entire generations of despair and hopelessness created by the system they installed and then abandoned. And, then I want to see him arrested. And, there is one more thing. I have always wanted to know what the actual circumstances of my father and mother's death were. How they died during the war? Were they really killed during an air raid or were they murdered because they knew something sinister inside our government? I will want you to provide me with answers to the truth of this matter. It is what will motivate me to do this perfectly. Can you understand how important this is to me?

Andre nodded. "If it is that important, I will get you all the information. As for the other, it

Secret of Ekaterinburg: The Hour-Glass

won't make any difference where you are, but I promise you, you will be close-by when the time comes to spring the trap.

"All right, then. It is agreed upon. Upon my oath," Sergei recited and reached across the table to clasp Andre's hand.

One final toast to each other and they signaled to the waiter that they had finished their business. Andre paid the bill and both left the cafe together.

They stood along the shores of Krazcoff watching the fog rolling in toward them. Soon, they would be enveloped in the gray mist and soon their very lives would be enveloped in the same fog of uncertainty.

Both, turned-up their collars.

They hugged each other and slapped each other on the back then left to attend to their various duties leaving behind nothing as evidence except the empty vodka bottle while the waiter cleared away the crockery plates. The waiter moved with deftness, moving around the chairs and tables, picking up the unused food items and discarding them into a small trash container. He then refilled the napkin trays, folded new table cloths, and carefully lifting one of the napkin holders from the table where Sergei and Andre had been

Secret of Ekaterinburg: The Hour-Glass

sitting. He then reached underneath and removed a small, metallic disk the size of a small button.

He quickly slipped it inside his pocket along with the rest of the money left at the table as a gratuity. Inside his pocket, the disk was a tiny computer chip that had recorded everything the pair had said and secretly transmitted it to a small, nearby field station which housed two FSS agents. The two agents were away, but the tiny, sensitive, voice-activated disk had performed flawlessly and had automatically recorded everything that had been discussed.

There would be nothing left to the imagination of the FSS agents when they sat down together to listen to the electronic interception the following day.

Not much in Russia had changed. In many ways it was still the same country as the old Soviet Union.

Everything was supposed to have changed, but in reality nothing had changed.

Secret of Ekaterinburg: The Hour-Glass

CHAPTER 22

Langley, CIA Headquarters, Oct. 31, 1989

Alex returned from the hospital to find a message waiting for him at his CIA station in Langley.

He barely had time to pour himself a cup of coffee when his secure telephone rang. It was the chief. There was a meeting in thirty minutes sharp. He braced himself.

Do they already know about Keitel? If this was about something else, should he tell them now? No, perhaps it was still better to lay low for now, until he could collect his thoughts make some sense out of the attack and try to understand just what the hell he had gotten himself into.

"Yeah, I'll come down right away. Who's going to attend?"

"You, myself, the Russian analyst, Keitel, if we can raise him. You know where he is? His wife said he didn't come home last night. Something about working late on something."

Secret of Ekaterinburg: The Hour-Glass

"Uh . . . no, not really. That's not like him though. He usually lets everyone know where he can be reached."

"Let me try a few calls . . . and I'll see you at the meeting. Same place?"

The chief liked to move the meeting locations around inside the CIA to throw off anyone who might be a mole for a foreign operation. God only knows they had problems in the past on this and it had paid off.

"We'll be in the blue room. Be prompt."

"Right," Alex answered tersely knowing there was no such place as the blue room but he knew it was the code word for meeting room number five. Blue was the fifth color in the spectrum, Number 5. ROY G. BIV. Red. Orange. Yellow. Green. Blue. Indigo. Violet. They could reverse the order if necessary to light blue in which case it would become room number three.

He hung up the telephone and promptly called Johns Hopkins. The charge nurse in the intensive care room answered on the second ring.

Alex spoke immediately, "This is the friend of Art Keitel, a patient of yours who was shot in the boating incident last night. How's he doing?"

Secret of Ekaterinburg: The Hour-Glass

"Is this Mr. Ayers?"

"Yes . . . has his condition improved?"

"I just told you five minutes ago that his condition had improved from critical to serious since last night."

"Just a second. I didn't call you five minutes ago."

"Well . . . someone identifying himself as Mr. Ayers did wanted to know what Mr. Keitel's condition was. And, I gave that person the same information I just gave you.

Alarmed, Alex reprimanded himself for not giving the nurse a password to identify himself . . . "Look, from now on, don't give any information to anyone but my voice. Can you remember the sound of my voice? And, don't let anyone in to see him except his wife. She'll have proper identification. This man is a very important person in our government, and he needs to be protected. Someone is trying to kill him. I will arrange for a security team to stand guard around him twenty-four hours a day. You notify your hospital colleagues or whoever you have to that this is happening. Don't let anyone near him, understand?"

"Yes, sir. I'll take care of it right away. You don't have to worry. He's in good care."

"But, I will worry. I get paid to worry."

Secret of Ekaterinburg: The Hour-Glass

Alex hung up; he appreciated the no-nonsense approach of the nurse. She didn't bullshit around. She understood what was at stake and reacted to it. If her psychological self-control was as good as her job skills she might have possibilities for the CIA. But, that was for another time.

He redialed internal CIA security.

"Hello. Harry. Alex here. Look, I've got a big problem with one of our guys. He got hit last night while he was with me at a secret rendezvous which turned out not to be so secret. He's in real serious condition at Hopkins with a gunshot wound to the chest, but it looks as though he's going to pull through. I need him covered, round-the-clock for at least two weeks. Can you get a team over at Hopkins right away. It's got to be a team you can absolutely trust. No need to mention this to anyone else, including the chief. It's on my authority. Got it? O.K., thanks. Do it."

Alex knew that his status at the company entitled him to use the chief's authorization whenever he needed to in order to get something done pronto. He was one of the elite agents and had been for a long time. It was at times like this that he knew how to gauge and use that power. It's not that he really wanted to

Secret of Ekaterinburg: The Hour-Glass

keep this from the chief but he needed a few more hours and a lot more information before he would feel comfortable telling him what he thought was going on. The chief would give him that much.

Alex wheeled around in his chair, finished his coffee, and looked at his watch. The meeting was in ten minutes. No time to do anything else. But, he'd better think up something good for Keitel's not being there. He'd think of something on the way to Room 5.

Alex turned down one of the many long corridors weaving through the labyrinth of hallways and secret passageways that he and the other agents knew so well. It was their playground and each knew how the hallways interconnected, which corridor was the quickest way to get from here to there.

The place was unusually active for a weekday morning. Unusually busy but not alarming. Was something already up? Maybe something new on the guard shanty hit a few days ago? He passed a few people he'd worked with on several cases a few weeks ago, and nodded to them as he passed them in the hallway. The endless corridors were bright with fluorescent tubes making the tile walls look absolutely stark. He passed Room 2, and

Secret of Ekaterinburg: The Hour-Glass

proceeded further down another hallway, and found Room 5. Everyone was already inside when he opened the door.

"Mornin, chief. . . gentlemen?"

They responded with a "mornin", each seated behind the long narrow table with coffee mugs poured in front of them. At the long end of the table was a recorder and a viewing screen with some charts on it. Nothing unusual so far, Alex thought. Let's see what this is all about.

"So, gentleman. . . let's get down to business," the chief chimed in as Alex sat down. Everyone knows everyone else around the table so there's no need for niceties."

The chief reached inside his pocket, took out a cigarette lighter looking device and pressed a button. A bolt slammed through the steel door they were behind and a high-frequency scrambling device silenced their voices to any possible recording devices trying to penetrate inside or outside the room. It was business as usual.

"Gentleman. We have a serious problem. There has been a breach of security inside the organization and because of this two field agents have been killed. We think their killing is directly related to someone on the inside

Secret of Ekaterinburg: The Hour-Glass

whose identity we don't know. Jenkins was working on a super sensitive case involving the former Soviet Union and a country in the middle east on something we haven't been able to pin down yet. I gathered you all together here this morning because you are the top five analysts in the company, and the hierarchy has decided that it's most likely the potential mole is still active inside our organization and that he or she is extremely dangerous, or holds some information that is critical to the security of the United States. What's worse is that we have no clue on what that information might be? That's why you're all here. We need to shed some light on this, because gentlemen, if we fail, the security of the United States will have been compromised and will continue to be compromised. With the present state of world affairs, I don't need to tell you how important that is."

Alex started to turn uneasily but caught himself. Behind, a glass partition, which looked like a simple mirror, a camera was recording their every movement in reaction to the chief's opening remarks. Alex knew how the CIA worked from the inside and assumed he was being filmed with all the rest. He relaxed a bit in his chair.

Secret of Ekaterinburg: The Hour-Glass

"Anyone have any theories on this?"

Alex quickly chimed in.

"Chief a few of us haven't been here for a couple of days, bring us up to date on Jenkins. What about him and what was he involved in?"

"Well, both were working on a case involving the former Soviet Union and missile components scheduled for eradication over the next six months. They were working on it diligently with the Pentagon guys and Department of Defense to bring some semblance of control over an untenable situation involving nuclear warheads which might get into the wrong hands of some terrorist organization or terrorist country. What they and we didn't realize that the deal they struck with the Russians had been monitored for some time apparently by a middle eastern country which also had a deal with a rogue Russian radical politico to divert some 100 pounds of enriched plutonium and missile warheads including 200 SS-18 missiles scheduled to be destroyed to this country in exchange for $25 billion dollars in gold bullion."

So far, so good. None of the men seated around the table reacted to the disclosure by the CIA chief indicating to observers that nobody

Secret of Ekaterinburg: The Hour-Glass

had heard anything about the current mission or at least was too aware of it.

"What Jenks didn't know was that the origin of this plan came from inside the Oval Office and the double cross by the rogue Russians came from an unknown operative inside the KGB working with Jenks who had set up the plan with the Russian military. The part Jenks didn't know was that the KGB operative was being paid $5 million by the CIA, but this same operative was also being paid to deliver the components by these same middle eastern terrorists. In other words, this guy was making money twice off the same deal. Another $20 million. Gentlemen, we were simply being outspent for deliverance of these missile systems. The Russian government was being paid the sum of ten billion dollars by the U.S. to make these weapons inoperable as part of the Start treaty. Now, we knew the Russians were desperate for hard currency and this fit the bill perfectly for them. But, what the Russians didn't know and we don't know is who is the rogue KGB agent who set up the rogue deal? In exchange for the $10 billion from the United States, they were to supply us with those missiles and warheads for destruction. Instead, someone struck a double deal with this middle

Secret of Ekaterinburg: The Hour-Glass

eastern nation. The Russians are $10 billion better off and God knows what happened to the missiles."

Everyone at the table looked uneasily at each other, but no one said anything. Their apparent surprise of the plan pleased the CIA chief. He felt if there was a traitor in the group, it wouldn't be one of his close-held operatives or analysts. Especially any of these five agents. No, it had to be somebody else, somebody who had access to sensitive information yet who didn't know all the details.

Alex held up a pencil and got the attention of the chief.

"Go ahead, Alex."

"When I heard the news over the radio about Artie, it puzzled me and I couldn't make heads nor tails of it. What really rattled me was the attempt on my life at the main gate two weeks ago. It was a close call and I couldn't figure out why someone was trying to kill me, too. I have no connection with the case unless the rogue agent inside the Company thought that I did. And that brings me to Harry Keitel. You all know Keitel, right?"

The group nodded.

Alex continued.

"Well, I ran into him right after the incident

Secret of Ekaterinburg: The Hour-Glass

at the main gate and he said something that struck a chord in my head, something that I'd never heard before. I'm not going to divulge it here or what that is exactly yet, but in due time if there's any importance to it, I'll fill everyone in on it at the proper time. Anyway, when he mentioned this to me, and I know we aren't supposed to discuss cases outside these walls, but you know and I know it happens. Hell, as long as we're all loyal to each other, no breaches of security were lapsed, then no harm has been done. After he mentioned this to me, I asked him to check something out for me involving Russian history and we were in the process of discussing that matter last night about 1 a.m. at a secret rendezvous point that only he and I supposedly knew about. What happened was that someone else apparently knew about it and arranged a hit on both Keitel and me."

The group definitely reacted to this astonishing statement because they all knew a foreign hit team assigned to take Alex and Keitel out usually didn't fail.

"To continue. . . whoever it was, made the attempt and damned near got us both. They hit Keitel, but missed me. Keitel is barely hanging onto his life at Johns Hopkins, and chief, I've

Secret of Ekaterinburg: The Hour-Glass

already placed a cover on him just minutes ago. Keitel is the best, photo analyst we've got. And, he discovered something that'll make most of your hair turn gray. But, I can't tell anyone anything yet until I can verify that perhaps what you told us here this morning, chief, is connected. There's a good possibility it is. If that's the case, then I'll brief everyone here as soon as possible. Because of our long-standing rule of security I can't divulge what that is now."

Alex's update on the matter really got everyone's attention. They were on the edge of their seats listening to his carefully crafted words.

Like the cunning analyst he was, he was playing his cards close to his vest; indeed perhaps even on the inside of his vest to be sure, notwithstanding the chief's presence.

He even really didn't have to tell him anything until he was ready.

And the chief knew it and respected it. It was a protocol Alex could not waste.

Secret of Ekaterinburg: The Hour-Glass

CHAPTER 23

Johns Hopkins Medical Center, Nov. 1, 1989

Alex pushed through the elevator doors and pressed the UP button to the med/surgical floor on the fifth level.

As he exited the elevator, he faced a battery of specially-positioned federal agents assigned to guard Keitel. He recognized two of the four from when they had worked together on special security assignments for the Company. The other two were new, but since the other two were there with those he already knew he had no need to distrust them or their legitimacy. But, still his guard was up since the main gate shooting several days ago.

Alex flashed his CIA identification and the guards quickly waved him through the first tier of protection, and then past a second which got him to the nurse's station. There he met a more formidable resistance in the way of a charge nurse. He could tell by her demeanor that she was the no-nonsense type. She wasn't smiling.

Secret of Ekaterinburg: The Hour-Glass

She was meticulously uniformed and seemed to be prepared for anything as he approached.

Memorizing her hospital nametag, he asked, "I'd like to check on the condition of Arthur Keitel?"

The nurse deadpanned him, "Excuse me?"

He repeated it showing his I.D., "I'd like to check on the condition of Keitel, . . Artie Keitel. I'm with the Central Intelligence Agency. He's a close friend of mine."

"Oh . . . I see. I'm Sarah, the head nurse of this unit . . . these are all your friends, too?"

"Uh . . . yes . . . they're as you know with the CIA . . . here to guard the patient."

She looked into his concerned stare and reassured him that Keitel had responded well to treatment of the gunshot wound.

"Uh . . do you think I could see him. He is allowed visitors, isn't he?"

"Yes . . . but, you can't stay long . . . he's still weak from all the blood-loss," the nurse said glancing at Keitel's chart. "You know he's very lucky to be alive. I understand one of his pals hauled him across the Potomac in a boat. That guy must have been pretty gutsy, huh?"

Alex looked uncomfortably at the compliment and the nurse knew immediately that she was talking to Keitel's personal hero.

Secret of Ekaterinburg: The Hour-Glass

"Oh, you were that guy? O.K. You can go in and see him, but only for 10 minutes."

Sarah didn't have to explain the rules to him, she was just repeating standard hospital procedure. Anyone who had saved a man's life wouldn't do anything to jeopardize his medical treatment once he had made it all the way to the hospital.

"Thank you. Thank you very much. . . " and she directed him to Room 515. One more guard at the room's entrance stopped him and gave him a quick search. He took Alex's 9mm promising to return it to him when he left.

"Sorry, Alex. You know the routine?"

"Yeah . . . I know. It's all right. Feel a little naked though."

The guard laughed and shrugged his shoulders.

Alex entered the dimly lit room, glancing around its perimeter. Keitel was propped up in bed sleeping connected to several I.V. lines. In the corner sat a solitary female, petite and brunette, her head lowered in her hands as if she was praying. She hadn't heard him enter and didn't look up at first, but she knew his voice when he spoke to her.

"Sorry, Ellen. I didn't know you were here?"

Secret of Ekaterinburg: The Hour-Glass

Even though she recognized Alex as a friend, the break in the silence startled her for a second as he stepped in from the shadows or the doorway. She got up slowly from her chair, walked over to the doorway and hugged him.

"Thanks, Alex. Thank God you were there again."

Alex put a finger to her lips.

"He was there because of me. Not the other way around. I feel responsible for this."

"It's all right. He's going to pull through. It was touch-and-go during surgery, but he made it, and the doctors say he'll be as good as new in a few weeks. Whatever it was that got him there, I'm sure you thought it was terribly important to you and the country. Right?"

Alex shook his head. She had been married to Keitel for 25 years. She was hardly a beautiful woman, but she was beautiful in other ways. Her genteelness and quiet demeanor sparked a confidence in the man who had always wanted to take care of her and their three teenagers still at home. God, he was glad Keitel had made it. Hell, he was glad he was there with him. But, he felt terribly bad that it had happened because of something they both needed to share. Some piece of information that some foreign agent or someone inside the

Secret of Ekaterinburg: The Hour-Glass

CIA wanted to thwart.

"Uh . . . I didn't do as thorough of job as I usually do in making sure that no one was watching us," Alex apologized. "I almost blew it. Do you think I can try and talk to him now?"

"Yes, he's been sleeping for a while now. Go ahead and wake him. I'm sure he'll be glad to see you," she nodded gently touching his shoulder to reassure his request.

Alex walked over to Keitel wired to a myriad of sophisticated electronic equipment monitoring his vital signs, checking for respiration, cardiac rhythm, blood pressure and God only knew what else to evaluate his medical condition.

He stirred him gently. . . .

"Keit. It's me, Alex. Can you hear me?"

There was no noticeable movement in his arms and legs just the steady breathing through an oxygen mask. It would make it difficult for him to talk, but Keitel finally opened his eyes and attempted a slight smile.

"Son-of-a-bitch," his words choked through the oxygen mask after a brief effort . . . "What the hell happened? Where have you been? I've been here for hours. Uh. . . why is it that I always end up on the hospital side of the

Secret of Ekaterinburg: The Hour-Glass

equation whenever someone tries to off one of us?" Keitel said his eyes darting back-and-forth around the room.

"Because you're a big easy damned target. You've got to lose some of that weight, so they'll go after me instead," Alex chuckled patting him on the arm.

"Who in the hell do you think it was?" Keitel asked.

"I don't know yet. But, there's got to be a connection to Jenkins and the assassinations three weeks ago," Alex whispered to him. "Do you think it was anyone inside the company? Did you talk to anyone about this beside me?"

Keitel widened his eyes to signal Alex. No way. Alex had known better than to ask.

"Then, it's somebody in the Central Committee," Keit. "It's got to be someone inside - high and dry."

"And that can only be one of five people. Besides you and me, that leaves three others, not counting the director. Do you want to count him out, Keit?"

Keitel leaned a bit toward Alex, "Yeah . . . I suppose we can count the chief out, huh?"

"Maybe you can, Keit. But, I can't. Not now. Not after this. Anything's possible here. Anything."

Secret of Ekaterinburg: The Hour-Glass

"Look, I came over here to make sure you were all right. Is there anything I can do for you, for Ellen or the kids?"

"No . . . we'll be all right. I'm sending the kids to stay with Ellen's sister in Brownsville, Pennsylvania, a small town near Uniontown. Know it?"

"Yeah, I know it. Some friends of mine are from there. I'll check in with them every-so-often if that's what you want."

Alex knew exactly what Keit was thinking, and he didn't want to have to make him ask for the favor.

"You know damned-well it's what I want. Thanks."

"I'll take care of it, Keit. Don't worry about a

 thing. Consider it a privilege."

"What about Ellen?"

"She's fine. She'll be here with me most of the time . . . she'll have two agents from the company assigned to her full time. Don't worry about her?"

"O.K. Are they guys you're sure of?"

"Yeah, I've known them a long time. They're O.K. They've all been checked out thoroughly."

"Keit . . . just the same, I'll check in with her

Secret of Ekaterinburg: The Hour-Glass

every so often, too . . . in case. You know, if it's someone that high up in the agency, Christ who in the hell can you trust?"

"Look, I know you're right . . . but, try not to worry her. I think whoever it is will leave the family out of this, but you don't know how desperate they are to avoid detection. Try to play it low key for her sake, O.K.?"

"Right, Keit. Look, there was one thing I didn't get a chance to ask you at the boathouse if you're feeling up to it."

"What's that?"

"Well, I don't know quite how to put this . . . but, are you absolutely sure about the analysis of those photos? Hell, I'm embarrassed to even ask you that, but I don't have any choice. They're going to rake me over in the next CC meeting and my ass is going to be on the line. It'll probably mean my career if I'm wrong. You've never given me bad information before and we've been through the Bay of Pigs thing together, the Cuban Missile Crisis, Grenada, and God knows what all since the Persian Gulf. But, I need to hear it from you again . . . just to be sure when I walk into that room tomorrow."

Keit understood where Alex was coming from. He nodded to him with "his damned-sure look."

Secret of Ekaterinburg: The Hour-Glass

Alex patted him on the shoulder and told him not to worry. "Hell, we've already got our thirty years in. Why worry? We're covered by government pensions," Alex said with a quick wink as he turned and walked toward the doorway. He gestured with a fist-like wave, shrugged his shoulders at Ellen, and was out the door quickly and down the hall past the guards after he reassured her that the agency would look after her husband.

He turned the corner at the nurse's station and made eye contact with the head nurse. Then, he did something he normally didn't do because of the political incorrectness of it. He winked at her. To his surprise, she winked back at him. They both broke into relaxed smiles and went about their business. He had to figure out what to do with the rest of the evening. He didn't want to drive all the way back to the CIA station because he was dead tired. And, that was made worse by the lousy weather moving-in across the Chesapeake. A new front had come through that afternoon, and it was beginning to prove the weatherman right this time.

Rain. Lots of it on the way. And, that added up to flooding and traffic jams along the beltway and side streets. It happened all the

Secret of Ekaterinburg: The Hour-Glass

time in Baltimore and it could be even worse near the Capitol. He hadn't seen so much rain since he station chief in London. As much as he admired the English, he hated their lousy weather.

He put on his raincoat, hurried down the escalator, jostling past people who weren't in a hurry, and slipped through the lobby guards almost unnoticed, through the doorway quickly and out into the parking lot trying to locate his car.

He spotted it in no time remembering where he had parked. Two lanes over, ten cars down, on the left. Parked opposite a Reatta. A white Reatta.

The memory flashed to him in an instant. Could it be the same car that had followed him the morning of the assassinations? Not likely, but possible. What was the odds of that happening in a metropolitan area of 6 million people and 4 million cars? The Reatta wasn't that popular of a seller, perhaps 50,000 total for that model year. What was the odds on that, he thought. His instinct told him so it didn't look right. His hair bristled on the back of his neck, a familiar feeling that warned him that danger was present. His eyes flashed from left-to-right searching along the parking lot rows, looking

Secret of Ekaterinburg: The Hour-Glass

for unusual movement.

Shadows. Anything that looked out of the ordinary.

He slowed the pace a bit. He needed more time to analyze the situation. The rain was coming down harder. Then, he heard a car start its engine. It was the Reatta. The driver flipped its headlights on and up popped both lights in unison silhouetting the front of his own car. The parking space next to the Reatta was empty. And, he was approaching that space from the opposite direction and he would have to walk across its path to get to his driver's side door.

He slowly slid his hand down near where his vest would be and held it there as though he was buttoning his coat, then deftly slid the hand inside his suit coat lining, and felt the familiar grooved handle of the black 9mm holstered securely to his chest. His thumb methodically clicked off the safety as he approached within 20 feet of the empty parking space holding a newspaper over his head to distract the two passengers inside so they wouldn't pay attention to his gun-hand.

The rain was pelting down now. It was nearly impossible to see the two silhouettes inside the Reatta, but he could make out the

Secret of Ekaterinburg: The Hour-Glass

glowing motion of a lit cigarette moving to someone's mouth. The motion stopped. He must be inhaling now, Alex figured. The glow brightened and froze in midair. But, the car was idling a bit too fast for his liking. The driver was getting ready to lean on the accelerator.

Slowing his walk even more, he realized he didn't really have to go to the driver's side. He could confuse them by turning early toward another car and that would give him a greater angle to get behind them. They wouldn't expect that he thought. Boy, are they going to be surprised. He was so tense his breath caught in his throat.

Ten feet away, now. A few more feet. But, what the hell was he going to do when he got behind them, have a cigarette with them in the rain? He couldn't just turn around and retrace his steps to the hospital? They would know for sure, he had spotted them and they might try to do something really stupid. There were other people in the parking lot and someone could get shot in the confusion. And, he couldn't just walk up to two strangers in a car, point a pistol at them and order them out of the car. What if they were legitimate? Waiting for someone.

He had to think fast. Luck had to be with

Secret of Ekaterinburg: The Hour-Glass

him. Alex bent forward hiding his Beretta underneath the newspaper pretending to shield his head with it; then when he got within one parking row of the Reatta, he suddenly turned right, a parking space sooner, parallel to his own car and strode briskly past the pair in the parked car.

Both men's heads jerked around trying to locate him in the downpour. They weren't sure he was behind them.

Suddenly, the driver shifted the car into reverse and started backing out of the parking space. Alex crouched behind one of the adjacent cars, dropped the newspaper to the pavement and pointed the Beretta's barrel downward to protect it from the rain, holding it close to his knee in the classic, make-ready firing position he had been taught as a CIA field agent.

His senses were on adrenalin calibrating everything around him in almost slow-motion detail, his mind analyzing the situation as it unfolded.

His movements were quick, but methodical, his eyes moved back-and-forth across the parking lot in an attempt to make sure there would be no one in his line of fire.

The car backed out of the parking space, its

Secret of Ekaterinburg: The Hour-Glass

headlights piercing the night rain, then suddenly the car's backup lights silhouetted Alex standing near the rear fender.

The passenger-side door flung open and one of the men, a mustached, dark-haired bulky man of middle eastern appearance, stood up and aimed a revolver at Alex.

Alex's reaction was immediate and deadly.

Partly instinctive, partly training, his gun-hand snapped upward in a rigid motion while his left hand clasped his wrist, the Beretta set for firing, came up to eye level and before the dark-skinned man could re-focus on Alex, the decorated field agent fired two shots, hitting him twice in the chest, throwing him back against the car door down and back into his car seat.

"Karump! Karump!"

The shots echoed through the parking lot and were quickly muffled by the torrent of rain. Blood squirted to the inside of the windshield. The driver reacted with terror and vaulted from the other side of the car. He drew a gun and fired from behind another parked car while his car idled in reverse, backing out of the parking space on its own.

Alex yelled at the man, "Throw down your weapon. Step out into the open!"

Secret of Ekaterinburg: The Hour-Glass

The man acted as though he hadn't heard him, and opened fire again, nearly hitting Alex in the right arm. The bullet smashed into the side-mirror of an adjacent car.

"God-damn it. Enough of this," Alex muttered to himself and ducked below the terrorist's line of fire.

"Throw it down," Alex shouted at the blonde, fair-skinned terrorist.

The idling car slammed into a line of parked cars and jolted the gunman to panic. Alex could sense that the assassin wanted to get back inside the car. With both car-doors open, the gunman ran frantically toward the car and dove onto the car-seat, pushing the dead body out the driver's side door and onto the pavement. He reached across, pulled the door shut and jammed the gearshift lever into drive. Alex anticipating the move was already on the run toward the rear bumper of the car.

The assassin raced the engine as the car lurched forward with Alex jumping onto the bumper, struggling to hang on as the accelerating Reatta roared past the narrow row of parked cars. It was a perilous perch and he needed both hands to hold on as the gunman felt the car sway when Alex's body weight came down hard on the rear causing the

Secret of Ekaterinburg: The Hour-Glass

steering to become unstable for an instant. Desperately reaching at the rear windshield wiper blade with his left hand, Alex clung for dear life as the car careened toward the lot exit gate.

Desperate to be rid Alex, the driver pointed his gun over his shoulder and fired. Sweat pouring down his face, the terrorist fired again. Alex ducked behind the trunk as the car picked up momentum. The assassin had shot five times, and Alex was counting. That left the guy with one bullet, and an almost impossible shot to make. But, sure as hell Alex didn't want any part of that last one. More than one agent had gone to his grave trying to make a shooter miss by pushing his luck to the limit.

Alex peered through the fogged-up back window and aimed his Beretta at the silhouette driving the car. One shot toward the lower right side of the man's back should incapacitate him but not kill him. No vital organs there.

As the car sped toward the front gate, the ticket-taker stared incredulously at the careening car angling almost out-of-control toward him and the gate that stood at the entrance to Farber Avenue. Gripped by fear, the gateman finally dove out the doorway and onto a shrub-like knoll behind the ticket booth

Secret of Ekaterinburg: The Hour-Glass

as the car struck the black-and-yellow gate snapping it off and tossing it thirty feet up in the air.

"God, if he makes it to the beltway, I'm finished," Alex thought. "I've got to take him out now."

Alex took aim as the car whipped around the corner and onto the avenue quickly picking up speed toward the beltway ramp a quarter mile ahead. He squeezed off a first shot knowing that he would have to fire twice; once to shatter the glass for a clear shot at the driver; the second, to wound or kill the driver.

"Blam!" the gun exploded and the back window shattered into thousands of crystal-like pieces flying through the air. The same round took out the front part of the driver's side windshield and sprayed the driver's face with flying glass.

"Aghhh!" the driver yelped as glass fragments splattered onto his face. He raised his gun over his shoulder to fire again but Alex saw it and ducked below the trunk again, the bullet exploded harmlessly past. Alex raised his weapon to eye level and without hesitation fired the second time.

"Blam!"

Straight to its mark, just a bit high as the

Secret of Ekaterinburg: The Hour-Glass

driver slammed forward into the steering wheel. The car veered side-to-side with the man's foot wedged hard against the accelerator as the car headed toward a large tree. Alex saw it coming leaping from the car before they hit. He tumbled to the wet cushiony ground as the car slammed into the huge oak tree. It didn't budge as the car folded up like an accordion.

Alex was still holding his gun. Mud was stuck in the barrel. No use to him now as he got up from the grass. The assassin was out of ammunition, but, he was taking no chances. Cars honked their horns as he approached the driver's side. He approached the disabled vehicle, and saw the driver was unconscious, slumped over the steering wheel, blood running down his forehead and face. But, he was still breathing.

And, that's exactly what Alex had wanted.

A real, live honest-to-God terrorist. One that could be delivered for interrogation. One who could answer the many questions as to exactly who-in-the-hell he was working for. And, most importantly who had killed the other two agents and who had tried to kill him and Artie.

It was a beautiful piece of field work with a bit of "mother luck" to go with it.

Secret of Ekaterinburg: The Hour-Glass

But, what the hell. Who's to argue with luck.

In most cases, luck had a lot to do with success including narrow escapes like this. Alex reached into his pocket for his cell phone and dialed *7711*. He ordered a pickup car to retrieve him and the gunman.

The CIA would provide its own medical team and ambulance for this case. Even though Hopkins was a mere half-block away.

The CIA's field hospital in the D.C. area, would take care of this guy. He would receive the best medical treatment available and more for CIA purposes.

Besides they might want to question him once-or-twice under duress. Alex grinned with satisfaction, but hell, they could let him die as far as he was concerned.

After they got all the information they could.

Secret of Ekaterinburg: The Hour-Glass

CHAPTER 24

Johns Hopkins, Baker Street Entrance, Nov. 1, 1989

Alex was on a dead run.

People seeking cover behind trees and bushes gawked at him. The acrid smell of gun smoke hung in the dampness.

He was running as hard as he could back to the hospital parking lot where he had left his car but that wasn't his main objective. He needed to get back to Artie's room in a hurry. He realized what was happening. The hit team was planning to finish him off there. His matted hair pushed down over his forehead as he reached inside his pocket for the cell-phone he always carried pressing the speed-dialer to connect him to agents guarding Artie's room. He felt the soles of his shoes slipping slightly on the wet parking lot surface as he tried to dial the keypad while on the run. He couldn't stop now for he was in a race against death now, and death was winning.

He had been a fool to chase the pair he had

Secret of Ekaterinburg: The Hour-Glass

just killed. They were a diversion. A deadly diversion, but an effective way to get to the real target.

"God-damnit," he yelled to himself. "Stupid move."

"Jesus," he muttered again as he ran the four blocks past the petrified gate guard who cowered as soon as he saw Alex approaching him from the opposite direction with a gun in one hand and a phone in the other.

Alex ran right past him his eyes fixed on the front steps of the hospital.

Inside, on the fifth floor a lone nurse moved into position near Artie's room.

Rain pelted Alex as he raced past his car.

"Just a few more steps to the front door," he muttered to himself. "Almost there, now."

He ran up the steps and catapulted himself through the revolving door, shoving people aside in a desperate attempt to reach the main elevators. Reacting quickly, he pressed the call button and eyed the lighted dial above the elevator door telling him which floor the elevator was on.

A woman back away when she saw the gun, and the hospital guards abruptly reacted and moved toward Alex. He held up his CIA I.D. The guard backed off slowly hand still on his

Secret of Ekaterinburg: The Hour-Glass

gun. Another, recognizing Alex lowered his own weapon, motioning an all-clear signal to the others. Alex asked him for his security phone. He pressed the talk button.

"This is Alex . . . Secure the patient. Secure the patient in Room 544. Now! Code 11. I'm on my way up."

Alex redrew his gun and handed the phone back to the guard. He waited impatiently as the elevator moved smoothly and effortlessly down from the third floor. It was almost there.

When it arrived, he and the guard stood astride the doors as they opened pointing their weapons toward the inside. A couple of young staffers were finishing an embrace when the doors slid open. They found themselves staring down the barrels of two ebony lethal weapons.

"Christ. It was only a kiss, the youthful looking orderly uttered as he and his girlfriend backed awkwardly out of the elevator cage. "There's no hospital policy against that is there?"

Alex motioned them out of the elevator with a quick gesture of his Beretta and the pair blurred past him and out of the way.

"C'mon, for Christ sake," Alex complained as the doors to the big elevator glided slowly shut. He pressed 4 then 6 in sequence.

Secret of Ekaterinburg: The Hour-Glass

"Didn't you mean the fifth floor?" the guard asked.

"No. Whoever's up there will be expecting us. You get off at four and plant yourself in the stairwell. I'll bypass five and go up to six and get down to five another way. Whatever you do, if someone with a gun, tries to get past you and he doesn't look like me, shoot him."

"Jesus. Right."

The elevator stopped at four and the guard got off cautiously with gun drawn.

"Stop anyone attempting to come down the stairwell," Alex reminded him. He didn't need to. The man was scared stiff.

He disappeared from Alex's view around the corner, right where Alex told him to position himself. Fear had a way of making you pay attention to a lot more detail.

Alex knew there had to be another way up and down the terrorists wouldn't know about. He had to find someone who did.

He readied himself to exit the elevator on the sixth floor as the machine slowly moved past the fifth floor without stopping. He had been lucky. No one wanted on there.

Then, it stopped abruptly on the sixth, and he waited for the doors to open, his gun pointed outward.

Secret of Ekaterinburg: The Hour-Glass

Standing there was a doctor and a nurse. When they saw him, they backed away the instant they saw the black-barreled 9mm and the CIA badge held out in front of Alex. He motioned them aside, and moved quickly to the nurse's station. The security alert was already flashing at the nursing station and throughout the other hospital floors. Medical staff were posted on the outside of all rooms.

God, he hoped Artie was still alive. He had promised his wife. He motioned to a staff nurse and spoke to her quietly not wanting to alarm the rest.

"I've got to find another way down to the fifth floor other than the stairwell. Is there another way?"

The nurse gave him a quick once-over.

"Yes. If you're in great shape."

"How?"

Not used to having a gun waved in front of her, she pushed the gun aside pointing it toward a linen room door. Even though he had already asked the hospital guards that same question, hospital staff knew novel shortcuts through the maze of hallways and tunnels.

The nurse responded. "Well, occasionally, a few young interns have curled up in the laundry chute and crawled down to the floors above or

Secret of Ekaterinburg: The Hour-Glass

below to scare the hell out of their friends. Know what I mean?"

"No. What do you mean?"

"What I mean is that there are some interns who don't mature at an early age, and they play practical jokes on each other. So they scuttle down the chute, and sneak up on another intern catnapping in the laundry room or a buddy making out with a nurse and peep in on both of them."

Alex rolled his eyes toward the ceiling.

"Good, God. At Johns Hopkins?"

"Especially at Johns Hopkins."

She looked at him then added, "Why should it be any different here?"

"O.K. How do I get down there?"

"Over here."

"Where does it come out?"

"Inside the linen room off the main nursing station exactly like you see here only one floor below. They're all the same."

Exactly what he needed. A position from where he could emerge, unobserved, and not be detected by anyone.

"What's the name of the head nurse down there, the cute blonde?" Alex remembered flirting with her briefly on the way out.

"Sarah, but that's not her. She's off today.

Secret of Ekaterinburg: The Hour-Glass

Sarah's a brunette. I don't know the blonde you're talking about."

"What do you mean you don't know her?"

"Look, this is a big place with a lot of damned people. I don't know everyone in this mausoleum," she deadpanned. "Even the live ones."

A frightening thought entered his head, too frightening to think about for long. Instead he told her to show him the chute. They went inside the linen room and Alex prepared to make his assault down to the fifth floor.

"Any special way to do this," he asked her while positioning himself inside the square opening where hospital workers emptied laundry to the basement seven floors below. "I mean, is it dangerous. Anything I ought to know about before I start? I know you've probably done this yourself."

She grinned.

"Yeah. I guess I have as a nursing student, just a short while back," she kidded. "You can hold onto the side brackets where the cable wheels go in the track. They make pretty good hand-holds. Whatever you do. Don't let go. It's a long way down - nonstop. Put the inside of your heels along the corners of the track to act like a brake. When you feel the door, push on

Secret of Ekaterinburg: The Hour-Glass

it slowly with your toes and haul yourself in. Just don't let go."

"Yeah, I'll try and remember that especially," he grimaced. "Piece of cake."

He grabbed onto the outer door and started his descent into hell feeling with his fingertips for the track. He grabbed onto it and lowered himself feet-first into the dark scuttle-hole until his head disappeared from the nurse's view. She quietly closed the door shook her head and listened for any thuds. His descent was agonizingly slow, even though it was a mere 15 feet below. He looked down, but couldn't see anything, but he could feel the cool rush of air rising up from the basement, like a chimney draft. It was a long way down to the bottom. No mistakes, he thought.

Alex lowered himself through the crawl space hoping nobody dropped anything down the chute from the floor above him. Certainly, he didn't have to worry about anything coming up.

Inching down, he felt his way along the track by planting the insides of his heels in the corners of the track. The nurse was right. It worked. Suddenly, he felt something give as he pushed forward with his right foot, careful not to pat too hard. He didn't want anybody to

Secret of Ekaterinburg: The Hour-Glass

hear him coming in.

This must be it. Down he went, farther into the darkness. A few more feet. He groaned as he pushed with his left foot and the laundry room door swung freely as he applied more pressure to it. He gingerly lowered himself toward it both feet now inside the cubby-hole and reached down the track to lower his upper body into position to exit the chute.

His legs were draped inside the room with his waist covered by the door. He scooted himself into the linen room.

"Piece of cake," he said looking up toward the sixth floor.

He quickly surmised where he was. Now, where was that blonde nurse? He opened the door slightly to get a partial view of the nurse's station. Everyone was talking quietly but the head nurse was nowhere in sight. The station was isolated from the other field agents down the hall and Alex could see the guard outside Artie's room. But, no head nurse. She could be making rounds with the doctors. He had to act quickly.

Alex opened the door a bit more enough to slide through, gun-first and moved silently toward the nurse's station. Two hospital workers saw him and froze in their tracks.

Secret of Ekaterinburg: The Hour-Glass

He put a finger to his lips. One of the field agents recognized Alex, and quickly motioned to the others that he was onboard. He lowered his gun at an angle and flicked the safety off.

An agent approached.

"Where the hell did you come from?"

"I just sort of dropped in. How's Artie doing?"

"O.K. No sign of trouble."

"Where's the other guys?"

"They're scattered throughout the floor three of them and me."

"Good. I just killed two terrorists in the parking lot. I don't know what the third terrorist looks like."

The agent nodded.

"You sure Artie's alright?" Alex asked again to reassure himself.

"Yeah, the head nurse's with him, now. She's giving him an injection."

The bit of information registered like a bass hitting a fishing lure.

"Jesus! She already gave him his medication a half-hour ago. I watched her do it. It's the fucking nurse."

Alex reacted bolting toward Artie's room. He pushed opened the door with his foot and held his 9mm straight-out in front of him. The

Secret of Ekaterinburg: The Hour-Glass

startled nurse stopped what she was doing and put her hand on Artie's I.V. bag.

"Good heavens, you startled me. What are you doing with that gun?" she started. "What the heck is going on?"

"You tell me, nurse Cratchet," Alex intoned. "Put the needle down. And, step away from the patient. Do it now."

The other field agent thought Alex had gone crazy. It couldn't be the head nurse?

She didn't budge. Instead, she calmly and nonchalantly continued to do what the nursing manual instructed, insert the hypodermic needle into the opening of the I.V. valve, and readied herself to administer the medication.

"I said put the needle down and back away from the patient or so help me I'll kill you right here and now," Alex ordered.

Astonished, the nurse glared at what she thought was a crazed field agent carried away with all this terrorist business.

The other agent chimed in.

"Do as he says, ma'am. Alex, you'd better be right. How do you know it's her?"

"Pure instinct, Jim. Pure instinct. After so many years, you get this way."

The other agent gave him a funny look.

"Don't do it nurse. Don't do it God-damn it

Secret of Ekaterinburg: The Hour-Glass

or you'll never see the inside of an operating room again."

He pointed the gun directly at her chest.

The young nurse stopped what she was doing and reassured Alex, but he wasn't buying it.

"Put the needle down on the tray and step away from him. Easy now," Alex prodded her gently.

She was too young to be a head nurse. She appeared to be in her early twenties. Nope, Alex thought, too young. Not this one.

"Are you a crazy person?" she questioned him. "Or is this just my imagination running wild."

"I'm not asking you again. Put the needle down, now!"

"It's just medication. Look, I'll show you."

She lifted the needle away from the I.V. tubing and held it up in the air.

Alex ordered the other agent, "Get a doctor in here fast to check the syringe."

The agent moved immediately.

"What kind of medication?" Alex asked her.

"Coumadin. A blood thinner. It prevents the blood from coagulating, from clotting. He needs it or he could throw a clot that could hit his heart or lungs."

Secret of Ekaterinburg: The Hour-Glass

"O.K. But, let's let the doctor give it to him. Step away from him."

The nurse shrugged her shoulders and let out a nervous sigh, then stepped back a bit.

Alex moved a step closer and looked down at the chart. The hieroglyphics meant nothing to him. But, he could clearly read the word Coumadin written in on the chart.

Suddenly, the nurse moved forward with the needle, toward Artie. She grabbed the I.V. tube inserted the needle while Alex's attention was focused on the chart.

Alex saw her out of the corner of his eye and responded instinctively by bringing the gun up to firing position pointing it directly at her.

"Don't do it," he yelled at her.

"Nonsense," she answered professionally. "He needs this medication. Now."

"I said we'll wait for the doctor. If you so as much move one more inch, I'll blow you and your nursing degree to hell and back," Alex said pointing the 9mm at her point blank.

She was determined and his final warning didn't stop her as she pulled back the injection mechanism to administer the medication. Alex reacted with deadly force.

He fired twice.

Secret of Ekaterinburg: The Hour-Glass

"Blam. Blam."

Two shots exploded in quick succession, the noise thundering across the room and out into the hallway.

Alex couldn't afford to wait. The other agents came running in with guns drawn.

Sarah fell away from the bed, two hits to the chest, the needle dropping away from Artie's I.V. tubing and onto the hard floor.

She just couldn't wait for the doctor. She was the killer all right. Pretty, efficient and well-trained, not only as a nurse, but as a professional killer as well.

"Christ, Alex. Why the hell did you do that?" one of the agents rapid-fired at him as he came through the door with his gun drawn. "What the hell have you done?"

"I just killed a killer."

The doctor came in and knelt over the dead nurse. He picked up the needle. "900cc's of Demeral. It's supposed to be Coumadin. That's enough Demeral to kill a horse. She didn't even disguise it. But, how did you know for sure?" he asked Alex.

"I didn't. Except, I know that Coumadin is clear,
Demeral is yellow. That's all I knew. And, her eyes. She wouldn't look at me. She just kept

Secret of Ekaterinburg: The Hour-Glass

looking at Artie, knowing her assignment was to kill him. It's something you feel from experience. You learn to look inside a terrorist's heart through his eyes. Find out just exactly who she is, will you?"

"Some replacement nurse. We get them all the time. We don't get to know all of them very well," the doctor said. "The injection would have killed him for sure."

"Well, I guarantee you that we'll find out who she is. We'll send you a copy of her resume. You were probably overstaffed anyhow?"

Artie was still unconscious. Alex spoke to him, but doubted he could hear him.

"Everything's all right, Artie. Nothing to worry about. Just something routine. Sorry about the noise. Sleep tight."

The doctor and the others in the room were in disbelief as they left the room and quietly reposted the guards.

Room 544. It was a good room number.

The integers added up to 13, Alex's lucky number.

It was Artie's lucky number this time.

Secret of Ekaterinburg: The Hour-Glass

CHAPTER 25

Baltimore, June 25, 1950

The middle-aged woman with streaks of gray at her temples entered the turnstile and slipped past the crowded gate to get on the 4th Street bus.

Looking younger than her age of fifty, she managed a charming smile when she came into contact with everyone, especially the young slender bus driver, of dark skin tone everyone called "Spence." She deposited her bus token into the glass-and-metal change box and strolled the aisle quickly to find her seat before Spence accelerated into the city's traffic.

"Da, good morning, everyone," she exclaimed. She was known by fellow bus patrons as Ana and she quickly stepped to her favorite seat at the rear.

She smiled contentedly at those who met her gaze. That was her hallmark. It was the way she had become familiar to everyone who knew her. Her smile always revealed she was glad to be alive on any given day.

Secret of Ekaterinburg: The Hour-Glass

Ana took her seat next to a gentleman in the right corner of the bus and efficiently spread out her newspaper on the empty seat to her right placing a purse and a small bag of daily belongings on top of it. It was a daily ritual. She had already read the morning paper at her kitchen table in her small efficiency apartment which had been set up for her by an unknown patron.

She was on the way to her flower-lady job where she would stand for eight hours on a street corner near the old downtown main wharf and sell her tulips, roses and carnations all handpicked and delivered from the wholesale growers in the nearby Maryland countryside. She didn't make much money, but at least whatever she made was hers to do with as she pleased; no one would ever again tell her how to live for that matter.

* * *   * * *

She had come to America twelve years after the 1947 takeover of Czechoslovakia by the Russian communists, living with a family near Prague in a small farming town nearby the cultural city. When the host family learned of the impending communist takeover from local authorities, they made arrangements for Ana to

Secret of Ekaterinburg: The Hour-Glass

leave by way the country via Germany obtaining a special permit for her entry into the United States. Ana never could know how the Prachek family could obtain such influential services on an emergency basis, but they had seemed to work miracles for her throughout her life.

She remembered very little about her past except that she had been a Russian immigrant who had escaped the throes of World War I and the communist takeover in her country before she was smuggled out of Russia for her own safety. No one had ever told her who her parents were, or where she had come from, except the only mother she ever knew who strangely would refer to her as "little princess."

"Princess Ana" she would call to her at night after dinner. She would quietly whisper to her among close family friends as a very special young lady and that someday she would become very special to all those who needed her help.

She knew she had been adopted by these caring people who raised her with their own last name. She had grown up in Russia but had received a superior post-high school education from the University of Prague in the fine arts and writing. She had graduated with honors,

Secret of Ekaterinburg: The Hour-Glass

but had no idea where her life would lead? Her mother explain to her again and again that everyone was equal in the eyes of God, but that every person had to make his or her own personal choices in order to reach personal goals in life. Indeed, Ana was Mrs. Prachek's chance to shine before God.

And, Ana was about to make her choice very quickly when she was presented one morning with the shocking news that the Nazi's were planning to invade the Sudetenland. It meant war to all nearby countries and eventually to all of Europe. They all understood the ramifications of that calculated move by Adolf Hitler. They had all been through it during the first world war which had begun with the assassination of Austrian Archduke Francis Ferdinand in Sarajevo, Serbia.

It had all started quickly. Austria-Hungary declared war on Serbia and those responsible for the act, then directed against Russia and Italy. And, before it was all over, Europe was in total chaos. Alliances among countries were violated and the war didn't end until 1918. Now, this new truce between England and Germany at Munich in 1938, would eventually erode and be violated by the Germans who were bent on revenge. That's how all the wars

Secret of Ekaterinburg: The Hour-Glass

had started in Europe because of power and domination over another.

Ana tried to remember an earlier, happier time, but her mind would not let her breach those memories. She could not remember anything between the age of four and seventeen and didn't understand why? She couldn't remember anything except for what various doctors had told her about her condition – deep traumatic shock had erased her memory. Her mother and father had told her some details of her ordeal background but only tidbits and clues as to her real identity. They would occasionally say that they had known her real mother and father, that they had been kind and decent people who loved their country and the Russian people.

* * *   * * *

The bus swayed from side-to-side as a young man leaned over to her and whispered, "They are coming for you today? You must not go to the corner today? Do you understand?"

Ana's face turned white with fear.

He put a hand to her mouth.

"What do you mean?" she managed to whisper.

Secret of Ekaterinburg: The Hour-Glass

The well-dressed gentleman, in a gray wool suit, leaned toward her, pulled up a newspaper to his face pretending he was reading, and replied, "They mean to kill you, today. Do you understand? You must not go to the flower stand today. It is important that you not go. Get off the bus two stops early. I will get off one stop later and meet you where you are. Do not move from that spot. Is that clear?"

"Da," Ana answered, the smile gone from her face.

With that, the man relaxed his grip on the newspaper and lowered it slightly to peer over the top of it to make certain that nobody was paying too much attention to them.

Satisfied, he motioned to her that her stop was next. Ana reached for the cord that would alert Spence and gave it a yank. A "ding" rang out for him to prepare to brake for the next stop. Nobody else but Ana rose from her seat except the man in the wool suit, but he would get off later. If someone suspicious had risen with her, he would have gotten off to guarantee her safety.

Spence looked up in his rearview mirror from the front of the bus and curiously watched Ana gather up her parcels and prepare to disembark. She hurried past those standing on

Secret of Ekaterinburg: The Hour-Glass

the full bus and waited for the vehicle to stop. When the bus stopped smoothly without a noticeable jerking-motion, Spence signaled to her that it was safe to step off. She liked Spence. Everyone did. He had always been one of the kindest drivers on the Main Avenue run. She smiled and waved to the others as she stepped off and onto the sidewalk.

She stood there now not knowing what to do except wait like the man in the wool suit and sunglasses had instructed.

Alone in the snarl of downtown traffic and the midst of hundreds of passersby jostling their way to work, she waited. Five minutes. Then ten minutes, before she spotted the same young man making his way to her from the next stop as he had promised.

He approached her almost casually scanning the crowd for KGB agents then pulled her gently by the arm toward a nearby building where they sat down at a sidewalk coffee shop. They talked for a few minutes, then he patted her on the arm, leaned over and handed her a written note with instructions on it with money attached before he departed.

She read the note, folded the money into her purse, hurriedly got up and left melting into the boil-pot of people on the streets.

Secret of Ekaterinburg: The Hour-Glass

She would walk to a new location. She was never to return to her apartment. Everything she owned would be moved for her to a new undisclosed location where she would again set up a household for herself.

It was a hard life for her. The note warned her that the Communists had only days ago assassinated an accomplice of Leon Trotsky in Mexico City. They had killed Trotsky in Coyocan, Mexico, in 1940. And, they would come after others, including her, if they knew she was alive. She was a White Russian democrat and they would kill anyone like her who could prove the that the communists had ordered the killing of the royal family of Russia.

She had been through this before. The United States Office of Strategic Services, the forerunner of the Central Intelligence Agency, had protected her before, and had come to her rescue several times before when something like this had occurred. They had changed her identity and location to guarantee she remain alive until the eventual overthrow of the communist system.

After all, she was Ana, still the little princess to everyone who loved and venerated her legacy.

Secret of Ekaterinburg: The Hour-Glass

But, only a few, including Ana herself, really knew that she alone was the living legacy and final direct blood-link to Czar Nicholas II and the Romanov's – the Russian Royal Family. Only a precious few in her proud country of Czechs and Slovaks knew the true significance of the woman who had lived more than a decade with the Prachek family. And, the Prachek's as a family, had held her destiny in their hands for years before she came to the U.S.

Indeed, she was Anastasia Nikolaevna Romanov, the daughter of the great Czar Nicholas II of Russia.

And she had to be protected for all time.

Secret of Ekaterinburg: The Hour-Glass

CHAPTER 26

Danzig, Germany. Nov. 27, 1919

The weather was brutally cold. Fourteen inches of snow had clogged the city's outskirts where a family of four huddled beneath piles of straw lay shivering and swaying to the back-and-forth motion of a rickety, wooden wagon.

Inside, they bobbed about like sailors on a sea-going vessel their bodies adjusting to its uneven rhythm. They had traveled a long way from the port of Bremen on the Baltic Sea to this quiet town. In the distance, they could hear it slowly awakening while their horses stubbornly found sure footing on the rutted, frozen road near the city limits.

It was a crossroads of sorts, where city-dwellers, farmers, and peasants crossed paths, staring blankly past each other and going on with their purposeless lives.

They were stark columns of refugees - young boys and old men evacuating this once glorious city where a proud German army had defended its citizens from the western armies of

Secret of Ekaterinburg: The Hour-Glass

the French, British and Yanks. These same allies had stormed the battlefield positions to rip away the last remnants of whatever dignity was left of the great German empire.

How could these refugees who were marching in a search for work in the coal fields possibly know that in less than twenty years they would again be marching off, this time in new clean German uniforms, brazenly invading the same territories they had just retreated from only a few months ago.

They spoke to each other infrequently and never to strangers. They were starving. Their families were also starving. It seemed the entirety of Germany was starving.

Their once-great country was now in the throes of a mighty threat to its own existence. The allies had exacted war reparations of such magnitude that there was very little material substance left for anyone to live on.

The Treaty of Versailles had seen to that.

And, it would prove to be Europe's undoing twenty years into the future. Like a sword, the unfair and unsound peace cut both ways. This sword of peace would soon exact a punishment upon the punishers and revenge upon the revenge-seekers that would be unfathomable.

The Prachek's, one of hundreds of thousands

Secret of Ekaterinburg: The Hour-Glass

of refugee families pouring out of Russia, knew the signs all too well. They, themselves had witnessed a dethroned Czar, had observed passively the takeover of a huge Russian empire, and witnessed the final destruction of a once-proud Moscow monarchy society and the installation of a new, brutal regime under comrades Lenin and Trotsky that would mark the beginning of a hell-on-earth existence for nearly a century. This new culture would be a demonstration of rigidity and repression that few civilizations had experienced since the great Roman Empire. The wagon lurched ahead hitting ruts coaxing those aboard to move closer to each other to keep warm.

"Auntie, where are we going?" Ana, now eighteen, asked over the grinding of the wagon wheels and disordered tramping of the workers boot steps trudging through the heavy snow.

"Be still, my dear. You must save your energy for the long trip to our new home."

"And, where is that, Auntie?" she asked.

"We must travel across Germany, through dark thick forests and over large impossible mountains then down into a place called the Sudetenland. That is where the new country of Czechoslovakia is being created. It will be a land of freedom and prosperity. It is a place

Secret of Ekaterinburg: The Hour-Glass

where we have friends who have found us a small farm. It will be a good life there. It was once called Bohemia. And, it means freedom. And, Czechoslovakia will be free. It will become a great country soon."

"Auntie, I miss papa. Will I ever see him again?"

"No, my dear. You shall not see him again as long as you live. But, you must always remember him in your heart and in your prayers. He is with God. And, your brother and sisters and mother Alexandra Czarina, too. They are all gone. You must face that my child. And, you must never speak of them again? Or, the men from the NKVD, the angels of death, will come for you if they know you are alive. Do you know what that means?"

"I don't understand, Auntie," she replied.

"It is important, very important. We must not speak to anyone about such matters anymore. The communists are everywhere and they have murdered Nicholas and the others. If they were to know that an heir to the throne was still alive they would hunt you down mercilessly. They would make short work of all of us, especially you, Ana. Now, do you understand?"

"Da. They would send us to God? But, I

Secret of Ekaterinburg: The Hour-Glass

have escaped death before, auntie. I am not afraid. I remember all the shooting. I cried when Yakov spared me. I had pretended to be dead. Then, you came and took me from him."

The old woman hugged her niece more closely and prayed to herself.

"You are like your father."

She was protecting the last direct descendent of the Russian throne, the crown jewel of Czar Nicholas II. Ana was the last living heir to the Romanov legacy. Anastasia was a direct threat to all the madmen who had killed thousands in the name of Lenin and communism. These same murderers had orchestrated the great Marxist revolution which declared that everyone should be the same.

Ana cried. She knew the significance of what Mrs. Prachek had told her.

"It is all right my child. It is all right to want to live."

"Yes, Mrs. Prachek. Everyone wants to live. Why should I be any different?"

"But, you are different, my child. Very different. And, you must remember that always. It will protect you. It will remain our family secret, forever?"

"All right, Mrs. Prachek. I will do as you say."

Secret of Ekaterinburg: The Hour-Glass

The travel was tedious, but they had been lucky to contract the services of an obscure man they knew very little about. But, he, on condition of anonymity and money, had agreed to arrange for safe passage to their destination.

The trip would last four weeks and after that, they would be safe forever.

"Forever," the old woman said to herself stroking Anastasia's dark brown hair.

"Forever."

The wagon moved slowly past the snowy ruts of Danzig's outskirts but before dawn, the Prachek's had bypassed the main arteries of the city and were heading deeper into the heartland of Germany, east toward the Czech border and up through the perilous Bavarian Alps where secret political factions inside Germany were already at work on major schemes to wrest power away from the Weimar Republic.

Secret of Ekaterinburg: The Hour-Glass

CHAPTER 27

Langley, Va., Nov. 2, 1989

Alex was mesmerized behind a thick glass that soundproofed his office from everyone else's. He didn't like being alone at his desk in this labyrinth of the Company, but then again he was not used to being in his office this early in the morning. No one was around yet and wouldn't be until around seven o'clock.

It would be an important meeting. They would want to know exactly what he and Artie had uncovered but he was still somewhat stymied. No real progress had been made since Artie was wounded.

There was one man at the CIA who might be able to impact the puzzle a bit. Alex hadn't wanted to use him unless he absolutely had to. It was an analyst's prerogative to ask the advice of another analyst if he was stumped, but none of them liked to do it. It was tantamount to admitting defeat. It had to do with professional ego. But, he didn't have much choice at this point in the investigation. He just had to cave

Secret of Ekaterinburg: The Hour-Glass

on this one; he needed help, from someone outside the loop.

He could bring in Vladimir. He could handle his concerns professionally without compromising security. Vladimir was indeed unique. He had defected from the Soviet Union some thirteen years earlier just three years before the collapse of the Berlin Wall. The event sent millions of Germans rushing toward the Brandenburg Gate. But, he had come from inside the KGB, and was extremely knowledgeable of their habits and work practices including the idiosyncrasies of the Kremlin bosses and the newest ones like Boris Yeltsin.

Vladimir had become an integral part of the system which coveted valuable information on which to make important decisions involving the spread of communism worldwide. He knew how the Soviets operated and he knew it was a dangerous game. If you were wrong about something, it could have a direct corollary on the lives of millions of citizens. The KGB itself would take care of your mistake, then they would take care of you. Not much had changed in that regard about the KGB since its earliest days of Beria and Stalin. You could suddenly cease to exist if you

Secret of Ekaterinburg: The Hour-Glass

wronged a high official without any detailed explanation to your family or friends. The KGB not only protected the Soviet Union's hierarchy of leaders from mistakes and its inbred political cronies, but more importantly it protected itself from outside influences which could threaten it. It also protected the officers of the Red Army.

Staring blankly, Alex was interrupted by something on the other side of his office wall. He adjusted the horizontal blinds sandwiched between his glass partition and opened them a bit to peek.

To his shock, Vladimir was peering back at him from the other side.

His head snapped back.

Vladimir grinned at him.

"Good, God!" he yelled through the glass. "Do you have to do that?"

Of course, Vladimir could not hear a word he said, but he could read his lips and was laughing hilariously.

"Da. I have to do that once in a while," he said entering the room. "Do you realize I could have been a spy? A real Russian spy? A double, a triple or even a quadruple agent? You Americans are worse than the KGB."

Alex was used to his humor. At times

Secret of Ekaterinburg: The Hour-Glass

Vladimir could be downright hilarious, but he wasn't in the mood for it this morning, and Vladimir finally saw that as Alex refused to smile at his prank. Clearly, such talk was not a joke anymore with all the double-agent talk going around capitol hill these days. They had already caught two Russian spies in the heart of D.C. Nothing new would surprise him now. But, he knew and trusted Vladimir completely. He had been with him a long time and he had proved his reliability and trustworthiness time-after-time in real world crises involving the Soviets. If he was a double-agent working for the Ruskies then so was his own mother.

"What's up, Sir Alex?" Vladimir asked strolling in the office door carefully shutting it behind him.

"Glad you're here so early. I was about to give you a call," he lied through his teeth. I need your help on something as long as you're asking."

"Wait a minute. Did I hear you correctly? Are you begging me for help or am I hearing a Rasputin-like incantation totally meaningless to this poor Russian Pushkin?"

"Very funny. Knock off the crap, Vladimir. I'm damn serious. Can you help me?"

"Well, it depends. I don't know what it is

Secret of Ekaterinburg: The Hour-Glass

yet, do I? So I can't answer that until I know what it is you're asking?"

"Fair enough. We've only been working on this for about three weeks . . . Artie and me . . . but, so far we've come up with a big fat nothing, built around some tantalizing information and intelligence photos we've never seen before. Here are the facts so far . . . listen up . . . and tell me what you make of it."

Vladimir was all ears between sips of coffee and a piece of pumpernickel bread he had purchased from the CIA cafeteria deep in the bowels of the secret building. It was as close to Russian black bread as he could get at Langley. There were no Russian bakeries there.

Alex recounted the entire sequence of events beginning with the assassination of the field agent three weeks ago, the main gate murder, and the assassination attempt of Artie and him at the Potomac boathouse. He also filled him in on the events which took place at the hospital afterwards detailing the information he had received from Artie on the intelligence photos on Krazcoff.

"Mother of God. Whatever it is they are planning with that equipment cannot be good," Vladimir ascertained. He knew that the Russians didn't have the resources to waste on

Secret of Ekaterinburg: The Hour-Glass

meaningless projects which were not related to changing something in the world balance-of-power either involving the United States or some other country. He had come up through the ranks of the old KGB guard and had won-over several friends during that piece of his own personal history becoming a trustworthy colleague to the grand secrets in the inner-sanctum of the main politburo body and subsequent successor unit - often acting as an inside advisor on anything that involved the western world. He had been a close advisor to the dictator Stalin and subsequently all the other communist leaders who assumed power including Premiers Brezhnev and Gorbachev.

When Vladimir grew disenchanted with the slow progress of change inside the Soviet Union, he had decided and defected to the west. Once safely inside Great Britain, he subsequently offered his talents to the United States CIA in return for freedom, a new identity and a large sum of money to secure him financially.

But, his chief goal was to bring about a dramatic change in the way the world perceived Russia - his beloved mother Russia, even though he was no longer a part of it anymore. He was one of the bright, few who might be

Secret of Ekaterinburg: The Hour-Glass

able to bring about these changes peacefully, given the right opportunity. Now, he was being given that chance by the Americans. Perhaps someday he could return as a free citizen without fear of anyone. Or maybe he just wouldn't want to return.

"Who else knows about these photos?" Vladimir asked.

"Just you, Artie and myself. Not even Nelson knows - not yet. The old bastard will shit when we show him these photos without anything else to tell him."

"Sometimes, you cannot shit until it is time to shit. You have to have time to figure it out first."

"Uh . . . right. Do you want a few days to think about it? I can stall the director that long if necessary?"

"Thank you, Alex. You are very generous with my time."

Alex was looking for more even though Vladimir had only just heard the information for the first time. Vladimir was quick. One of the quickest minds he had worked with and he had expected much of him in the past. Was he expecting too much of him? More than just humor? It was a serious matter.

Vladimir immediately grasped that fact and

Secret of Ekaterinburg: The Hour-Glass

focused on it.

"Well . . . I can say that it's definitely going to hold our interest for a while. They don't do anything on a scale like this without consequence to the United States or to someone else. You can, as you Americans say, take that to the bank. But, what exactly it means, I don't know, except to say that whenever the Russians mount a major world threat it usually involves their merchant fleet or navy or both because it's the one thing they can support the best without land-based military platforms. They can sail those fishing trawlers all over God's earth and back. Everyone knows they're not just fishing out there, too many antennas and everyone knows that everyone knows, but they expect that. It's the unexpected that worries me and what should worry you. What you've got here is something that no one knows about, yet? Right? That really makes it dangerous for us. And, equally as dangerous to them. Oh, you can bet they realize that. What bothers me, though, is why they would station it at Krazcoff where all eyes from the sky are trained on it. Krazcoff. Vladivostok. Kamchatka nearby. Krazcoff is not their main naval base. Murmansk is, up north above Sweden, in the Arctic Circle. Something this top secret

Secret of Ekaterinburg: The Hour-Glass

wouldn't necessarily be sitting out there in the open. There is a big sub base at Krazcoff, but it's designated only for attack configurations against the U.S.'s big missile-launching subs. They don't launch their big stuff from there. The only thing I can figure quickly is that maybe . . . and this is an extreme low probability . . . just maybe someone's doing something inside Russia that nobody knows about . . . not even the Kremlin? What do you think?" Vladimir analyzed.

Vladimir's reply rocked Alex like he had been hit by a hard, right hand to the jaw.

"For Christ's sake. Are you serious? Somebody or some rogue dissident group inside Russia, could do that? Some military faction inside Russia, a radical element, perhaps military, could actually get away with something that big without anyone else knowing?"

"Yes. It's a remote possibility. One we ought to consider."

"What kind of risks are we talking about here?"

"Possibly a risk level of four. If the Kremlin knows, I would reduce that to a risk level of two. Five means big trouble."

Alex couldn't believe what he was hearing,

Secret of Ekaterinburg: The Hour-Glass

but instinctively he knew Vladimir could be right. He had been many times before.

"Have you any idea what they could be doing with all that equipment?"

"I must be taking a very close look at it, along with the rest of the other information you've given me. Can I take the photos with me over the weekend. Trust me. I'll be on it all weekend."

Alex knew he would. Vladimir's interest had really been tweaked. He had hooked him in good. He could see it in those sharp, steely, blue-white, Cossack eyes and flared nostrils when he spoke. His eyebrows were raised, and Alex could see that it challenged him to get to the bottom of this newest secret.

"All right. Report back in on Monday, and I'll buy you the best cup of coffee and black bread that you've ever had in your entire American life. Don't worry, I'll find a Russian bakery somewhere."

Vladimir smiled. "But, first you must learn how to brew coffee the Russian way. Strong and scalding hot."

"I said I'd buy you a cup of coffee."

"Nas dravia."

"Nas dravia," Alex answered. "Tell no one about this. This is top level. Understand?"

Secret of Ekaterinburg: The Hour-Glass

Alex reminded him though he didn't need to. "We'll compare notes first thing Monday morning here in my office."

"Da. Enjoy the weekend."

"Das Vidonya," Alex replied.

As Vladimir left his office and headed toward the main elevator, Alex reached underneath his desk, and flipped a small black switch unnoticeable unless you were a flea crawling up the inside center drawer. It was connected to a microphone which had just recorded their entire conversation. He hated to do this, but it was CIA policy for insiders to record conversations of anything top secret, whenever someone new was coming in on a case and being briefed or brought up to date. It was a precaution, a necessary precaution to provide detailed accounts of who knew what and when they knew certain key information. The tape would go into a centralized file for later retrieval if necessary to prove reliability. Only five persons in the CIA had such taping equipment known only to themselves and one other person - President Ned Nelson of the United States. If and when the prez found out the content of the recordings, a national crisis was usually at hand. Vladimir certainly could be trusted by now, and he would take no

Secret of Ekaterinburg: The Hour-Glass

offense to it if and when he found out that Alex had taped him. It was a professional thing. He had always understood that. No one had to read him the policy or the specific rule, and besides, it was the same thing he would have assumed when he worked for the KGB. They taped everyone there, too. Everyone was taping everyone. They had even video-taped Vladimir having sex with his secretary one night. It was no embarrassment. It happened regularly to nearly all KGB agents at one time or another. But, Alex still felt slightly guilty none-the-same. Vladimir was a trusted friend. He just God-damned-well hated to do it. If something went wrong, his ass and Vladimir's would be in the same sling.

Protection. Security. Need to know. Secrecy. It was all bullshit, but that's the way the system worked when it worked. When it didn't work you lost valuable information to the other side. And lives could be lost. That made it worse. Everyone counted on each other to make sure the rules worked. Because, everyone benefitted from the same protection. And, if that protection broke down you never knew if you were next in line for a bullet to the head. It's something they all got used to living with.

Secret of Ekaterinburg: The Hour-Glass

He sipped at his coffee and leaned back in his brown leather chair and turned on the computer monitor to look at a satellite image of Krazcoff.

"Good, God," he wondered out loud. "What in hell's name are they planning to do?"

Secret of Ekaterinburg: The Hour-Glass

CHAPTER 28

Krazcoff, Nov. 18, 1989

Andre picked up the telephone and dialed the secret number he had written on a slip of paper a month ago and had slipped to Sergei at the sub pens where they had rendezvoused.

It was time to give him the message he had waited for so long. Sergei was due back in Moscow any day, and what he had accomplished on this trip was to guarantee his usefulness to Kremlin leaders and "party dogs" who were left to oversee what was left of the once- sacrosanct politburo. Sergei had become one of the most trusted friends of new Russian president suddenly in the throes of a political threat from the extreme left socialist camp.

The communists were again trying to restore power in old Russia and they not only wanted it restored to the way it was before Glasnost, but they wanted the entire Iron Curtain to be lowered once again over their once-powerful domain of former central Warsaw Pact states. The Czech Republic, Poland, Slovakia and others were not willing to rejoin the Warsaw

Secret of Ekaterinburg: The Hour-Glass

Pact, so they were desperately seeking admittance to NATO. The new Russian president also desperately wanted Russia inside NATO because it would be a guarantee to the west that Russia would stand good on its promises to further democracy and to encourage future economic reforms.

On the other hand, the old Bolsheviks wanted no part of NATO; indeed, they wanted to thumb their noses at the western powers and undo all that had been done up to that point.

In the midst of this political turmoil, a lone figure waited in the wings to wrest back power to the communists still burrowed deep inside the Kremlin. He stood waiting for his opportunity to grasp control once again to move the Russians back toward communism. He had understood the philosophy of a "go slow approach" from the very beginning, but few had the same wisdom to apply the brakes gently to make sure that the reforms and transitional economy would take place at a low cost in human terms. Now, this lack of wisdom was costing the Russian people dearly.

Czechoslovakia, a former sister communist state, had managed it deftly, and had installed the partition of Slovakia and the Czech Republic. Not only was it done successfully,

Secret of Ekaterinburg: The Hour-Glass

but they showed the other countries in the Warsaw bloc how to accomplish it peacefully. Few other countries were as wise. The split-up by the Czech Republic and Slovakia became known as "the velvet divorce." It was something which both countries were proud of and they could still do business with each other on the basis of mutual national respect. It was an extension of the old Bohemian spirit which was had been traditional and prevalent in the region for hundreds of years. This common spirit had been bred into Slovakia and the Czech Republic for generations.

Historically, they managed to discuss their differences in a mutually respectful way. Those issues they couldn't agree upon, they ignored by putting them off until absolutely necessary, and only attempted to negotiate them again when enough time had passed and progress was made to logically discuss them once again. During the time interval, new light could be shed from a different perspective on the remaining problems. Usually a compromise could be reached.

Andre listened as the phone ring three times, then four. On the fifth ring, Sergei answered and upon hearing Andre's voice, he uttered the phrase.

Secret of Ekaterinburg: The Hour-Glass

"The swallow has returned."

"With or without its mate?" Andre answered.

"With," Sergei intoned into the mouthpiece and hung up.

Sergei now knew that everything was set in motion to begin in two more days. He knew Andre had planned everything in detail down to the precise minute. The crews of the ships would be standing-by under strict military blackout ready to depart at moment's notice.

He put on his winter jacket and stepped into the miserable Siberian cold. It was another frigid day, and he didn't relish trudging down to the officer's motor pool to pick up a staff car. Since, he wasn't a senior officer, he had to do this chore on his own. The other important naval officers all had drivers waiting to transport them anywhere they wished.

Halfway to the motor pool, he looked back over his shoulder to make sure nobody was following him. He knew from his old KGB days that he must trust no one except Andre.

It was an important meeting. No one in Moscow knew anything about it. Not the army, the navy, the air force, nor any of the Spetznatz paramilitary unit commanders. All were in the dark on it even though they were curious about

Secret of Ekaterinburg: The Hour-Glass

all those specially rigged boats parked in the bay. They knew better than to ask questions of the base commander. They figured he had special orders for a special project. They didn't realize how wrong they were?

* * *   * * *

Across the base, Andre put on his winter uniform of woolen grays and his officer's cap. He casually strolled through his comfortable office and out into the Russian winter. The wind had reached thirty knots and was building quickly. He knew it meant a major winter storm forming. All ships would be put ashore on an emergency notice if it continued and Kamchatka Bay would be filled to capacity, exactly what they needed to hide what they would be up to. The Holy Mother was with them.

But, could they actually pull this off? Could it really be done? Without the risk of another bloody revolution?

That's not what the world needed right now. It was not what Russia needed at this very moment.

A second revolution.

He hoped they could do it. He hoped they were both right. They had come so far when

Secret of Ekaterinburg: The Hour-Glass

they had dreams of a free Russia.

Now, it was time to act forcefully and decisively. When freedom was restored, the world would be astounded. At first, everyone would fail to believe it? And, who could blame them. It was hard for themselves to fathom the possibilities. Yet, it was going to be done all within two or three days. And, it would astonish the entire world.

Andre smiled and reached into his coat pocket for his smoking pipe.

His pipe would relax him while he drove to his meeting with Sergei at the sub pens. Unknown to Sergei, there would be three very special guests who had arrived in secret who would also be there for the rendezvous. With Andre was a guest of unquestionable importance both to Russia and to the United States.

He was Alex Ayers, the highest ranking CIA analyst and agent in Washington; representing Russia, Georgi Soltinoff, the current top FSB officer in Moscow; a third guest had also arrived with Alex from the United States traveling with Ayers at the request of the President of the United States and the President of Russia. Each side would be delivering a very special "gift" to each other.

Secret of Ekaterinburg: The Hour-Glass

Georgi would deliver a former American spy who had been held captive for thirty years whose very existence was denied for the last 15 years - by both sides. The Soviet KGB had claimed the American was dead rather than admit having him under arrest and imprisoned all these years. He had simply disappeared one night on a secret mission deep inside the Soviet Union and had not been seen since.

In exchange, Alex was delivering a former Soviet citizen, an old woman with graying hair, now in her nineties and in deteriorating health. But, to those who knew her, she was one of the most important humans alive on the face of the earth.

Each side knew the significance of the meeting, and the historic importance of it, including the ramifications it held for all of Russia and the remainder of the free world.

Alex was delivering a special woman named "Ana" to Russia returning her to where she was born. And to where she would be returned as the legal and rightful heir to Russia's aristocracy.

She was "Anastasia Nicholaevna Romanov", the last princess of Russia.

It had been an enormous undertaking because only a precious few knew she had

Secret of Ekaterinburg: The Hour-Glass

survived the murders of 1918. The communists thought they had murdered them all and buried the secrets with them for all time in a forest outside of Ekaterinburg. They had believed that Anastasia had ceased to exist forever. Now, she was being resurrected and would become the new figurehead of a newer, more modern Russia under a bold plan worked out between the two governments and their intelligence units. When the Russian people learn about the true story and escape of Anastasia, and that the precious daughter of Nicholas II was still alive, they would demand for her return to the Holy Throne.

Secretly, the CIA had contacted their Russian KGB counterparts of her existence, they had sent special agents in secret to the U.S. to prove the fact beyond a shadow-of-a-doubt. They performed countless blood and DNA analyses, tissue matches, genetic coding and imprinting, and questioned her over and over again until they were satisfied. Above, all, the most important piece of evidence proving that Ana was indeed the legendary Anastasia was a set of antiquated dental and medical records by one of the first dentists to use such techniques for identification. It was these dental and physician's records of the Czar's

Secret of Ekaterinburg: The Hour-Glass

entire family smuggled out of Russia and into safekeeping by members of the royal cousins who had escaped from Russia years earlier.

Finally, on Anastasia's torso were three scars left by the bullets which tore through her body. Two were deflected from vital organs by the specially fitted jeweled-laden corset. But, the third round had lodged beneath her rib cage and was still there, undisturbed for more than eighty years. She had been examined, x-rayed, and a holographic image was taken of the cartridge identifying it as the exact type used to execute the Romanov family - a Berdan II round, 10.66mm. The words had come from Yakov Grachev's own words in a newspaper interview by Pravda years after the assassination in 1930. He had recounted the entire story for the world to hear during an "show" inquest of the episode. The Bolsheviks basked in the fact that they had murdered them all, but they refused to acknowledge that Lenin has actually ordered the executions. The world held its collective breath in revulsion as the endless denials reached epic proportions that such a grotesque incident could have occurred in a modern, civilized society.

But, Yakov was a living, immovable testament to the braggardly confession that he

Secret of Ekaterinburg: The Hour-Glass

had led the execution squad and had indeed accomplished the deed.

Physicians at the Bethesda Naval Center in Maryland, at the request of the Romanov family, left the bullet inside Anastasia's body to be left there forever so that no one could ever disprove the fact that she was who she said she was. No surgeon would be allowed to extract the "Holy Bullet" which failed to take her life. It would take God to do that.

After all, she was Anastasia Romanov.

And, that bullet would now become part of her legacy, her final proof of birthright to the Russian Crown.

She was the living legend of Romanov sovereignty. She was the last living royal of Russia. And, these men would reunite her with Russia for all to be in awe.

For sure, the old line communists would despise the whole affair, but such denials would guarantee their defeat in future elections. Democracy would prevail in a land where once it had been forbidden.

* * *   * * *

Andre regained his thoughts as he stepped from the staff car. His driver saluted crisply and opened the door to the Krazcoff Command

Secret of Ekaterinburg: The Hour-Glass

Headquarters. The others had already greeted each other inside and awaited the arrival of Sergei. He was late but it would not matter this day.

"Alex, do you understand the importance of what we are doing here today?"

"Yes. It is something I have thought about all my life but never thought possible. Today will mark the beginning of a new relationship with the Russian people toward their own government and toward the United States of America."

"It is true. For all these years, citizens of Russia and the entire world believed that she was dead. Murdered with Nicholas, Alexandria, and their unfortunate children, Olga, Maria, Tatiana, and Alexis. Even, as intelligence operatives we believed that no one had escaped the brutal massacre. But, now we have come to learn the inevitable truth my friends?"

"You cannot imagine the reaction that Sergei will experience when he realizes he is being introduced to Anastasia. He will be speechless. And, that is saying something for a former politburo member and member of the NKVD."

At that very moment, Sergei arrived accompanied by two Russian naval guards.

Secret of Ekaterinburg: The Hour-Glass

They saluted him, turned one-hundred eighty degrees, and left the building.

"Dobroe utro, Sergei," Andre greeted him with a stone like expression not wishing to reveal his secret.

"Standing beside me is the top agent of the American Central Intelligence Agency, Mr. Alex Ayers. You two have not met but I know you know everything about each other."

The pair shook hands.

"And, of course, Sergei, you already know, Mr. Alexander from our own FSB in Moscow."

Sergei glanced at the woman standing beside Alex. She seemed somehow familiar to him.

Sergei and Alex both respected each other's capabilities coupled with years of mistrust and miscalculations by both sides.

"How do you do, Sergei," Alex spoke first. "I hope your family is well. And, Natasha? She is married for nearly fifteen years now?"

Sergei returned the polite question with a friendly smile and nod.

"She is a fine doctor in Moscow. She obviously does not take after her father. And, how is your family, Alex? Your wife, Sally? And, little Heather. Let's see, she is sixteen now. Am I correct?"

Secret of Ekaterinburg: The Hour-Glass

Alex didn't have to correct him. He was appropriately right.

"Yes. Sergei, as usual you know more about them than I probably do myself. But, don't tell me anything I don't want to know about her. People must have some confidentialities to themselves, right?"

"You are quite right, Alex. Andre and I have formulated a lifelong relationship built on that premise."

Andre interrupted, "And, now, Sergei, I can keep this secret from you or from the rest of Russia no longer."

"Yes, my dear brother; what is that?" Sergei anxiously awaited.

"This woman standing here beside me . . . you had better brace yourself . . . she has been brought here by the American CIA, by Mr. Ayers and by an agreement between our two governments that she should be returned to Russia as soon as possible. Do you know her, Sergei?"

Sergei studied her face closely before speaking to the 88-year-old silvery haired woman. She struck a familiar pose to him but he didn't wish to venture a guess.

"I am sorry. I don't know you. I apologize for it, especially if you are someone I should

Secret of Ekaterinburg: The Hour-Glass

recognize," Sergei positioned his Air Force cap under his arm and moved forward with his hand extended, eyes cast downward. It was a gesture of deep respect for this important person, whoever she might be. He knew she was someone special, to be delivered from America by the CIA's top special agent. She, indeed, was someone important to everyone in that room and Russia.

Then, suddenly, like a bolt of lightning, he recognized her when she spoke. It was Ana. His Ana.

"Dear God," he blurted out. "Ana, is it really you? My beloved Ana?"

He moved toward her.

"Yes," Alex said. "It is Ana. But, it is also someone else you did not know existed."

Sergei kissed her on the cheek and embraced her. He looked into her eyes.

"It is all right, Sergei," Andre called to his old boyhood friend. "You could not possibly know who she really is unless you were told because no one else in Russia, except myself and the Russian president know her secret. But, I will give you a clue. Czar Nicholas II and his family."

Sergei stared at her and suddenly his eyes widened in disbelief. No, it was impossible. It

Secret of Ekaterinburg: The Hour-Glass

had been over eighty years ago, in a dark, dingy basement of the Ipatiev House. Could it really be?

"My God, those eyes, they are the eyes of the Romanov's. The eyebrows they are his. Dear God you cannot be the Princess . . . but if you are indeed a Romanov, then you must be, dear God . . . of all persons . . . you must be Anastasia?"

Anastasia stepped forward and offered Sergei her hand. Sergei gently kissed the top of it and bowed.

"Yes, Sergei. I am Anastasia. Princess of Mother Russia," she said in perfect Russian. She then repeated it in perfect English. "An older and wiser princess, now."

Andre interrupted, "She is to be returned to the throne to the Czar's throne. It has been agreed to by the Orthodox Church and by Boris Yeltsin, the President of Russia. It will be a figurehead arrangement but her return will mean much to the people of our land. I cannot even imagine their reaction to such an event," Andre described.

"People will need proof and we have arranged that with the American government and CIA. We have direct proof that it is one-hundred percent accurate and true. She has recorded a written diary."

"Besides that, what kind of proof?" Sergei asked.

"We have all the necessary papers of birth even Czar Nicholas' many gifts to her after she was spirited out of Russia, and another piece of evidence beyond reproach - a bullet calcified inside her bearing the special ammunition used to kill the entire the family. The bullet will never be removed, because if that were to be done, no one would believe the truth of the matter."

"With all due respect, how can you be totally sure of such a claim?" Sergei again intervened.

Alex recounted how Anastasia was hidden after the assassination when she was found still alive at the mass burial site by the communist executioner assigned to the grisly task of disposing of the bodies.

"He thought he saw a small movement. A tiny hand protruding from the pile of bodies. He uncovered her and saw that she was still breathing. His first instinct was to finish her with a single shot to the head but he had remembered this innocent child from an encounter he had with her as a palace groundskeeper. The communists had spies

Secret of Ekaterinburg: The Hour-Glass

everywhere, in-and-around the palace, and he remembered her being kind to him in a way that cannot be explained. It had been an especially hot day and he was miserable from performing work among the flower beds when he accidentally stumbled upon her playing. She was full of boundless energy and he, exhausted. At first, he wouldn't talk to her, in the accompaniment of her governess but she persisted in asking him all kinds of questions about his work. She obviously liked him, and she intuitively knew he was not like the others. They subsequently talked about many things, when she asked him if he knew about the story of the "hour-glass." His reaction was one of bewilderment at first, until she explained what the Czar had told her as a child. He came to admire her as truly one of the innocents. She would visit with him often after that and he would remember her with a life-saving gift. He would scoop her up from the burial site, place her into a burlap bag, cover the mass grave, and then take her to a trusted uncle - the Prachek's.

That's how she survived that horrible night. No one ever knew except for the Prachek family who took her out of Russia."

Alex continued.

"You see the Prachek's became her mother

Secret of Ekaterinburg: The Hour-Glass

and father. They were the Russian scientists who were supposedly murdered by the NKVD. Indeed, they were marked for death because of their involvement as loyalists among the White Russians defending the Czar's return from exile. However, when their efforts were lost to the Bolsheviks, they and others fled into the countryside to disappear forever. A few returned to their village when the war started and worked for Stalin government attempting to develop a nuclear bomb. Stalin knew the Germans were after the long-sought after secret, and the Americans and British were in a feverish race to beat them to it. Your mother and father contributed much knowledge to the Soviet effort but it was to no avail. When Stalin's anger boiled over at the scientific ineptness on the part of the Russian program, in his paranoid state, he singled out key scientists for death - your mother and father – not because they were uninspired but because Stalin had discovered through NKVD Cheka operatives that they had once been loyal to the Czar. He marked them, along with two hundred scientists who also had been loyal to the Czar, for execution by Beria's death squads. Hundreds perished. Scores fled. They were those who successfully escaped to

Secret of Ekaterinburg: The Hour-Glass

Czechoslovakia. Others were not as fortunate. They are buried in secret graves in the Poluchna Forest, near Moscow. Thousands of lives were affected because of a paranoid leader who believed, in his own mind, that everyone was against him.   It is a historical fact. We have the authoritative proof of all of this.

Sergei was dumfounded.

"I have heard these rumors before. Everyone has heard them; that she was still alive somewhere, but I would have never imagined that she was living inside the United States of America.   And, the rumors were always followed by the suggestion that the story was a made-up lie by the American CIA. That's what I always remembered."

Alex laughed nervously. The American and Czech intelligence teams that delivered her to Baltimore after World War II aboard a cargo ship carrying coffee products from South America had on board in Baltimore's Chesapeake Bay where it docked a cargo so valuable that kingdoms and world peace hung in the balance of her guaranteed safety.

Anastasia arrived in Baltimore on the 17th of October, 1945, the 28th anniversary of the Bolshevik takeover of Russia.

Today, was another anniversary, Alex

Secret of Ekaterinburg: The Hour-Glass

observed. It was the first day that Anastasia had set foot on Russian soil in nearly 80 years. And, she would be placed back on the Russian throne on the same anniversary date that Czar Nicholas was first coroneted.

It would be a unique day in Russian history and a unique day in the lives of millions of Russians who always somehow believed that this could be possible – the restoration of the throne.

Russia was a religious country by its very history. Religion, no matter how long it had been banned from the people, had never been removed from the hearts and minds of the Russian people. And, because the throne answered only to the guidance of divine intervention, the people believed in the holiness of the throne and the divine right of the Czar's family to be the head of state of Russia.

It would be a wonderful day.

It would be a day that no one would quite believe. And, it would be a day that would live forever in the soul of writers and artists who had long described the secrets locked forever in the deaths of the Romanov family.

Anastasia could now unlock some of those secrets. Anastasia Nicholaevna Romanov.

"I still cannot believe it?" Sergei responded

Secret of Ekaterinburg: The Hour-Glass

once more. "Truly, Andre, if you have brought me here to witness a miracle, then I have done so."

They all sat down at a table in the headquarters and sipped coffee and ate black bread.

What better way to celebrate life but with something substantial from Russia on its very own soil?

Anastasia and Russian black bread.

A hush Fell over everyone at the secret meeting at the Krazcoff Naval Headquarters.

Everything had changed, but in truth, nothing had.

Secret of Ekaterinburg: The Hour-Glass

CHAPTER 29

The Oval Office, Nov. 3, 1989

"Mr. President, we have no choice but to acquiesce to the demands of the terrorists including the possibility that we may never obtain enough explicit evidence to prove who or what they are," President Nelson's CIA chief informed him with all the respect he could muster.

Nodding, the President said, "Bullshit, Ben. You're just a bit politically naive to believe that anyone who sends a message with this kind of intent doesn't really know what the stakes are worldwide?"

"Well, Ned . . . I'm sure they have their own political agenda as far as that goes, but I'm not so sure from the intelligence briefings I received that they are aware of just how crucial other world leaders and other countries will perceive their actions."

"Again, Ben . . . . if you'll pardon my digression . . . bullshit. These demands are being made at a time when Russia has broken

Secret of Ekaterinburg: The Hour-Glass

away from a political system and embarked on an ambitious plan to open the way for them to democratize whatever's left of the old Soviet Union. I realize there are some of them who want to turn back the clock to 1987, but, we can't let that happen. There is no other choice for us or for Russia. This is going to happen unless we intervene and stop it. And, I'll be damned, even if I am a lame duck president, if I'm going to stand by and let it happen. The United States has always been a shaper of world events and outcomes and it's not going to be any damned different this time around."

"O.K. At least, I understand where you're coming from," Ben reiterated. "Then, you'd better let me call in the National Security Agency on this. So everyone will be on the same page."

"That's right, you do that, and do it pronto, because I don't want anyone out of the loop on this one except who I say. Believe me, my political ass is on the line here because it involves national security. I don't want some God-damned neophyte reporter busting my balls on this just so he can be the first in line for next year's Pulitzer. Absolute secrecy is a must. Nobody says anything to anybody unless they have a need to know. That includes the

Secret of Ekaterinburg: The Hour-Glass

Secretary of State and the Pentagon brass until we're ready to tell them, and of course, especially that bumbling vice president of mine. He doesn't need to know anything until we're ready. Got it?"

With that the CIA chief left the Oval Office, signaling to the President's secretary that he needed to use the white telephone. She handed it to him and he dialed-in the security code which connected him to the NSA via encryption technology. He pressed the glowing, red light on the dial pad and started a high-pitched frequency which destroyed any rogue micro-sound waves emanating from the phone set just in case any foreign agents were trying to listen in. Such counter-espionage techniques were commonplace in the Oval Office and had been throughout the White House since the Nixon years. Nothing had changed any. Every president, including Nixon, still wanted to protect himself for posterity.

Ned talked into the Oval Office telephone . . . "Jeter, this is Kasim. Look, we need to set up a big meeting on this for everyone. Keep in tight within the loop. In two weeks. The timeline has already been set by the President to begin unveiling it to the public and the rest of the world. As far as you're concerned

Secret of Ekaterinburg: The Hour-Glass

though, if anybody gets a whiff of it, it's news to you. For Christ's sake, of course, the CIA has been notified, you're the last fuckers to be let in, even though you're usually the first," he grimaced at the lie and rolled his eyes at Kathryn, the President's secretary, a former CIA agent. She could hardly contain herself at the remark.

"Now, be certain that none of your gay reporter friends hear about this. This is an absolute top priority and security is at the highest government level - a Tag 4.

A smile confirmed that Jeter had clearly gotten the message on the other end of the line and Ben hung up abruptly.

He walked over to the outer office, a door already electronically controlled for his departure; he turned and winked at Kathryn. God, she was a beautiful creature. Too bad the President was still fucking her. She crossed her legs high to tease him. It provoked a reaction in him. He had fucked her too, only once, but that was enough to remember for a lifetime. He'd of liked to do it again, but she was preoccupied with her career. And, besides, it was the president, she was still fucking, and he couldn't cross him. Better to remember the good times ebb into his past. The French say it

Secret of Ekaterinburg: The Hour-Glass

best, "C'est la vie". Kathryn did like Ben, but she couldn't fuck them both at the same time or could she? Her swept-back, long blonde revealed a lot about her at thirty-five. She was still good to please most men and bright as hell. Too bad, she had ended up in the Oval Office. She had much more capability than most top female corporate executives and could out-think most men, but her job for the National Security Agency was far more important than that. Anybody in the general populace who thought Rosemary Woods was just a mere, secretary for Nixon when she erased the Watergate tapes, didn't know how the higher administrative levels of government worked. Rosemary Woods was no naïve individual. She knew exactly what she had to do to without asking the president and Nixon knew it, too. Hell, that's why they paid her so much. They all knew, but they wouldn't admit it publicly even to close intimates and insiders.

Neither was Kathryn a fool. She got the job because of her loyalty to the government no matter who sat in the Oval Office. Her duty was to the President of the United States not the man in the office. She knew that instinctively, if not implicitly, she would do whatever it took to protect the President, his life or his

Secret of Ekaterinburg: The Hour-Glass

reputation. She was sworn to it. And, yet, nobody, not even the press had figured it that way.

He hurried into the elevator that would take him to the lower level parking lot and picked up the White House staff escort to insure his safety upon exiting the White House grounds. He instinctively pressed his fingers to his left suit-jacket pocket to make sure his priority security badge was still there. Most of them nervously fidgeted with it all the time, unconsciously making sure it was still there because the CIA director's office at Langley had become a virtual turnstile for would-be nominees and appointees over the past few years. And, it wasn't getting any better.

The badge was still there.

It's presence reassured him for the moment.

But, that could change quickly.

Secret of Ekaterinburg: The Hour-Glass

CHAPTER 30

Peregrebnoye, Nov. 13, 1949

The cold Siberian air penetrated the weave of his ankle-length black overcoat as he stepped onto the back porch of the dacha where he was taken from five years earlier.

Sergei was careful not to tread heavily on the rotting boards beneath his feet.

He surveyed the extensive damage to the farmhouse which had occurred during the bombing raids by the Germans. It had been badly damaged but not enough to make the place uninhabitable especially if those living there were making a supreme effort to stay alive.

Sergei stopped just outside the kitchen entry and looked in.

He called out, "Who is there?"

After a moment, a voice answered, "It is Valerya. Our mother and papa are dead. Leave us alone. What do you want?"

"It is Sergei. I have returned."

"Sergei!" came back a sudden shriek.

Secret of Ekaterinburg: The Hour-Glass

Valerya appeared at the doorway and leapt into his arms. "Andre is still in Moscow. Helenka and I are left here. I have managed to hunt a few rabbits, and I go into the village and beg for sparse gatherings here and there," she rattled on.

"Of course, of course. I understand. I am grateful and relieved to see you alive after all this time."

He stepped forward and into the semi-darkness of the kitchen. It was still the same as he had last seen it except for some light coming through several holes in the roof where bombs had separated it.

He looked at the old, oak table still exactly in place where it had been when he had last eaten there. He surveyed the huge porcelain sink, yellowed with age because there were no cleaning agents available to keep it spotless the way mother used to; he eyed the cabinets, its shelves lined with oil cloth, and the thin beads of paint worn off the window frames where moisture from the rain had eroded and peeled it bare in places.

"My God, I have missed you both."

He practically clung to them in his eagerness to hold onto something familiar to him. They looked weak from the lack of an

Secret of Ekaterinburg: The Hour-Glass

ample diet. But, they still managed enough energy to muster the gentle smiles they had worn their whole lives. Their dark brown hair was pulled up with neckerchiefs and tied-up behind their heads in the typical Russian babushka style, and they wore the bright patterns of homemade dresses made by their mother.

They jumped for joy around Sergei.

"Sergei. Sergei! You have returned. We thought you must be dead. But, you're here at last. You have survived."

"True. I have come home at last.

"Have you found Andre?"

"Yes. He has a very important job in Moscow now that the war is over. He belongs to them now," Sergei said.

"He writes to us often, at least once a month, to tell us news, and he sends us money so that we may exist," Valerya said. "Thank God for that."

"What has become of Ana?"

"She is gone."

"Gone? Where?" Sergei, clearly bothered, pressed her.

"She was taken from us near the end of the war by a family who traveled to Germany and then who knows where? We don't know what's

Secret of Ekaterinburg: The Hour-Glass

become of her, and we have not heard anything from her since," they told Sergei. "What is this about Andre, who has he become one of?"

"He is a member of the Communist Party in Moscow. He works for Comrade Stalin," Sergei told.

"What?" they stepped back in dismay.

"I'm afraid it's true. He is working for that butcher.

"You cannot be serious?" Valerya screamed.

"He is secretary to the Politburo Chief Counsel and he is as close to Stalin as anyone."

"As close to Stalin as anyone? Sergei, it is dangerous to be too close. And if that is so, why cannot he do better for us here?"

"Ah, being well-positioned in Moscow does not automatically allow you into the privileged class unless there are favors to be courted in secrecy. Andre would have none of that. And, besides, it is extremely dangerous. He could be killed at a moment's notice if he were to say the wrong thing to any of the powerful. No, he is better off the way he is, and so are we."

"Yes. You are probably right on that count," Valerya said. "Please come in and relax, and we will fix you some hot tea and some poppy rolls. We don't have much but you are welcome to it."

Secret of Ekaterinburg: The Hour-Glass

Sergei hugged them again. The years had taken their toll. They were now in their thirties but they already had deep lines etched in their faces, once healthy cheeks now swollen from the endless hours of working in the fields where they managed to unearth a meager supply of potatoes from the frozen ground in an attempt to stave off hunger for yet another year.

"What more do you know about, Ana? Who took her?" Sergei wanted to know.

"I don't know the name of the family who transported her," Valerya said. "Father only told us that she was in extreme danger if she stayed in Russia any longer. That's why he sent her away?"

"But, why?"

"I don't know why. Except, one day, the same man who took you away to Kiev arrived here, and he and papa stood talking near the barn for a good hour before he left. When papa came back into the house, he whispered something to mother. All we were told was that Ana must leave as soon as possible for her own safety. She was gone within a few hours. She left by train from Peregrebnoye."

"Grachev!" Sergei mustered angrily in a fit of recognition.

"Yes, it was him," Valerya answered

Secret of Ekaterinburg: The Hour-Glass

without hesitation.

"What else did mother and father tell you?"

"Only that she was being taken away."

"Did he say if she would ever return."

"He said we would never see her again and to make our kisses our final ones . . . which we did. I pray I may see her again someday."

"As do I," Sergei stroked their heads pressed to his shoulders. "As do I."

"I must find out the name of this family, it will be the only way I can possibly find her and I may need the help of Andre. I will travel to Moscow as soon as possible to do this and I will write to you explaining what I am doing."

"No, you must not go there. And, don't write. They open our mail these days. Besides, Andre says it is extremely dangerous. They are arresting anyone suspicious in Moscow. You will put yourself and Andre in grave danger."

"Do not worry little ones. I will be careful not to involve him for personal and political reasons. If Ana is in danger, then we are all in danger. I must find out why. I'm afraid when I do, we, too, may be forced to leave the Soviet Union. Be prepared to travel if necessary, whenever I inform you. I will send money but you must not speak of this to anyone. Is this understood?"

Secret of Ekaterinburg: The Hour-Glass

They nodded and busied themselves pouring the hot tea from the kettle. Then, they sequestered themselves around the oak table and remembered the yesterdays and wondered if there would be any more of them.

Outside, the wind from the Urals thrashed the tree branches against the roof of the old house breaking the solemnity of the occasion.

Kasha, the shy one who had hardly spoken throughout the entire meal, suddenly let out a shriek.

"Prachek! That was the name of the family, Sergei! Prachek! I have kept it inside all this time. That is the family who took her. Do not forget it, Sergei!"

Valerya gasped.

Sergei knew the name instantly. It was the boy he had escaped with from Kiev.

"Josef. Josef Prachek. His family!" Sergei repeated out loud.

He would remember it all right.

He would only forget it if the communist bastards were too nosy or if they asked what this name meant.

Then, of course, his mind would go blank.

Secret of Ekaterinburg: The Hour-Glass

CHAPTER 31

Bardejov, Slovakia, April 25, 1949

The Prachek family had made the preparations earlier than usual for their Saturday morning stroll through the village streets.

It was a cool but gloomy day, an acceptable diversion to prepare Ana for her departure to Bremen by train.

Ana had become one of the most beautiful women in the village. She was an accomplished seamstress and worked at a local village shop, her beautiful, long auburn hair had grown considerably since she left Peregrebnoye and she lingered on her thoughts one last time before she would depart for America.

"Josef," she interrupted at breakfast, "what is it really like in America? I know you have told me all these wonderful stories and what I will do there when I arrive. All my life I have wanted to go there and now my dream will come true. Is it possible?"

Secret of Ekaterinburg: The Hour-Glass

"Dobry. It is possible my pet," the elder Prachek spoke gruffly but with the wisdom of a real father. "For people like myself it would be only a useful existence, but for you. . . well, you will not have any financial worries, and certainly, one free from the shackles of these communists bastards, you will breathe new air and perhaps develop the wisdom to endure any tribulations that may come."

Ana smiled at Mr. Prachek for she knew deep in her heart that he was a solid but devout man who had a special genius for figuring out sensitive moves politically. He had an impeccable timing that had enabled them to escape their Mother Russia long before the NKVD death squads had closed-in on them. He knew very well whom he could trust and whom he couldn't for he had become the master of deception during World War II in dealing with the Wehrmacht, the Gestapo and even Stalin's lead henchman, Laventry Beria.

He cautioned, "We will leave on our usual Saturday outing at around nine o'clock, but we will proceed to the train depot where you, Ana, will remain on the pretense that you are leaving for a three-month study in Bremen. We have secretly bought your passage to America. Be very careful and speak to know one of your

Secret of Ekaterinburg: The Hour-Glass

destination. Once you reach Berlin you will then travel secretly to the Port of Bremen. There, a special key and a new passport will be waiting for you in the main terminal. The locker number is 2-3-6. You must remember it. It is your life and your survival. If you are approached by strangers, more importantly, by East German authorities, you must tell them that you are waiting for a friend's arrival aboard one of the trains, any train you can memorize on the arrival schedule. Then, you must get away from them and board your own ship. This is very important. The NKVD agents may be searching for you. They are crawling all over Europe, especially in Germany. That is why I have chosen it because they will not expect anyone as important as you leaving from there. Speak in the Slovak tongue. It is your best disguise. And, once you are aboard, you may socialize a bit but under no circumstances, should you give out your name freely to anyone who asks, except of course, to maritime officials. In Bremen your ship's name is the S.S. Linsk; it is a modern vessel complete with the amenities of the wealthy. Do not become overindulged?"

Ana laughed but quickly recomposed herself upon observing the serious expression written

Secret of Ekaterinburg: The Hour-Glass

on Mr. Prachek's face.

"From there, you will travel to the Port of Baltimore, and there you will be contacted by the American Office of Strategic Services. They will protect you. Trust them. But, during your voyage, you must protect yourself. Is that understood? There will be no one aboard to protect you from the KGB. It is very important that you play the role of an older research student traveling to an American university."

Ana listened carefully, stroking her long hair in her usual manner while the others ate. She had become nearly reclusive in her will to survive. But, this would be an entirely new and different adventure for her.

She remembered an earlier time. Back at the dacha with her beloved Sergei. Her earlier memories of him had nearly faded, yet she had not married because of the spoken vow they had made to each other.

"Mr. Prachek, will I ever see him again?"

"Perhaps . . . someday . . . but, if and when you do, it will be at your moment and at no other's."

"What do you mean?"

"Simply that Sergei, wherever he is has close ties to members of the Communist Party. If you were to be found out by your connection

Secret of Ekaterinburg: The Hour-Glass

to him or if he has by now become one of them, he may have forgotten his deep feelings for you after all these years, and even possibly, he may have married. Then, of course, your life would be in extreme danger if he ever spoke to others about you."

"You are wrong on that count. Sergei has always loved me and he will always protect me. We are sworn to each other for now and forever. We promised each other that we would someday be reunited in our love."

"Perhaps . . . but love is one thing . . . and life is another . . . I caution you that you are worth more dead than alive to the Bolsheviks. That is not by your choice, it is by theirs."

"I will make you this promise," Ana spoke with a reverence reserved for only those she fully loved and trusted. If I am able to make this journey successfully, I will enlist the help of the Americans to help me find him."

"Hush, my daughter. Do not tempt the fate that has brought you to us. Do not speak of this anymore. Come, it is nearly half-past eight and we must embark. Priscilla, my dear, will you carry an umbrella in case the rain comes? We must look and act normally on this very important morning. We must not fail our Ana today."

Secret of Ekaterinburg: The Hour-Glass

The breakfast done with, the Prachek family gathered a picnic basket, and a few meager scrapings from the table and left their home. Mr. Prachek made sure he closed the door behind him after putting on his walking coat. He heard the familiar click of the latch that told him everything was secure. For a brief moment, his eyes focused on the decorative door with no outside handle. In Slovakia there was no need for doorknobs on the outside. Carpenters never installed them anymore because no one could be trusted not even the neighbors. Safely inside, a family could go out, but once outside everyone had to knock to get in. Or, you had to break the door down. If that happened, there would be ample warning to the family to hide something or stop discussing confidential matters behind closed doors. Having no doorknobs gave every Slovak a reason to remind himself that they had very limited freedoms. On every block was stationed a communist party member who was the eyes and ears of the neighborhood, who could make decisions affecting everyone's daily lives. But, the one decision they couldn't make was to invite themselves in.

Secret of Ekaterinburg: The Hour-Glass

CHAPTER 32

Bardejov, Slovakia, April 25, 1949

Ana and her family had been walking for fifteen minutes to the train station at the village's outskirts. Bardejov was a quiet quaint town of Burger style assortment of buildings exhibiting old-world architecture where kings and queens once made their travel connections in this tiny domain of Moravia.

The sun slid behind the clouds and soon the day became overcast, the kind of morning citizens often failed to appreciate. So many of their compatriots had not survived the onslaught of the Nazis and the subsequent invasion of the communists, that they often had to remind themselves of the minor miracles of life such as the scrounging for food to put on their family dinner tables.

Josef Prachek walked only quickly enough to attract just the right amount of attention from the villagers while he quietly gave instructions to the others to follow quietly behind.

On such occasions, the head-of-household

Secret of Ekaterinburg: The Hour-Glass

took the lead and the younger family members lagged behind paying closer attention to each other.

"Come, come, already. Cannot you three walk any faster," Josef pleaded.

"Of course, we could walk a bit faster, but what's the use?" the mother retorted making sure that everyone could hear her.

"Katrina. Please. I beg of you. Stop your constant dawdling and keep up."

"No one could keep up with you today, Josef," his wife complained just loud enough to irritate him. The others giggled as did Ana. This aroused no suspicion as to what they were actually about that morning. Waving to others with his walking stick, Josef was the essence of the unheralded Slovak patriarch who had been set-upon with an unrelenting admonishment by his family members at his own doing but to their obvious delight. He endured the constant punishment of their jokes instead of the other way around now that they were older. It had become a weekend ritual where the children had become the critics instead of their parents.

They passed within sight of the neighborhood communist regulator, Nina Eransko, an old spinster who one day had tried to indoctrinate everyone at a recent block

Secret of Ekaterinburg: The Hour-Glass

meeting. The men would have no part of it, and exasperated, finally walked out stating they had to return to the coal mines earlier than usual the next morning. That was, of course, if she wanted to continue to heat her communist apartment with an ample supply of communist coal. She relented failing to obtain their signatures as full-fledged party members. In reality, she had done an adequate job, enlisting more than half of the village as members and that was the reason why Josef could not trust anyone anymore. Not even his closest relatives could be told of Ana's escape plans until after it had materialized. And, then the story had to be carefully crafted so as not to point the finger to some sort of plan. Someone always knew someone who knew someone else which could lead to disaster. When Ana boarded the train, they would tell the ticket master that she was off to Berlin for individual advanced study. That would please Nina, the all-knowing communist apparatchik, and it would arouse no suspicion. Once gone, they would explain that she had run off with a lover at school. That would raise more than a few eyebrows among their friends, but it would protect them from the local KGB because everyone would simply want to believe it as a scandal. At forty- eight,

Secret of Ekaterinburg: The Hour-Glass

it would look as though Ana could not afford to be choosy anymore.

"Ana, what will you do in Berlin with your extra time?" Josef asked her vociferously.

"I will study, father. It will be very difficult but reading is my great strength."

"You mean I could be wasting all my money on an education when you could be reading at home?"

"I will have the very best professors at the school and they have already written to me stating that they will pay very special attention to me."

"I am sure that they will, my dear," Josef responded raising an eyebrow and winking at his wife. "I am sure they will be paying very close attention to you. That will be the problem."

Ana giggled at whatever thoughts Josef had planted in everyone's minds.

She waved unenthusiastically to the Nina as she sat on the swing of her front porch listening and scrutinizing their every move. Each of them gave a quick wave, an almost mechanical gesture lacking any sincerity as they strolled by.

She sat stoically immobile on the swing without as much a smile as the family moved

Secret of Ekaterinburg: The Hour-Glass

past her. Finally, out of shame, she managed a returning grunt, like a snorting hog. Nina Eransko didn't like the Prachek's, especially Josef, because of his indifference toward the communists but everything about the Prachek's that morning appeared normal, and for now they aroused no suspicion. Nina was suspicious of everyone and everything. It was her job to be that way.

As she watched them disappear around the corner, she already knew their destination while pretending not to be interested. Her informers had made sure of that. Josef had been quite correct in not trusting anyone near him. So everything went smoothly except for the two men walking toward them as they neared the station. Josef spotted them first, then Katrina, then Ana and Priscilla.

"Father, who are those men ahead of us?"

"Silence, Ana. Leave this to me."

The men approached and signaled Josef that they wished to speak with him.

"Remain here. Be prepared to run for your life if you must. If they challenge me, I must kill them," Josef said, lifting his sweater slightly to show them the handle of a pistol stuffed into the front of his belted trousers.

Ana's eyes widened, but from experience,

Secret of Ekaterinburg: The Hour-Glass

she showed no sign of alarm. She must continue the charade.

Josef closed his sweater and sent them along their way, waving good-bye to them then turned and walked toward the trench coated men. Moisture stained the brims of their black hats.

He approached in a friendly manner, slightly turning his head to make sure the others were safely ahead of him.

"Hello, and good morning to you," Josef engaged them.

Both men tipped their hats. Even the communists had perfected the manners of the local populace.

"How may I be of service to you this day?" Josef asked.

The taller one spoke first.

"Spare me the pleasantries, Josef. Where are you going this dreadful morning?"

"We are taking a short stroll to the train station to see my daughter Ana off on her excursion to Berlin. Will you wish her well?"

"We wish her well because party comrade Eransko asked us to insure your safe return?"

"Yes, I am sure of that. Comrade Nina so worries about everyone these days. It is too bad that no one worries about her?" Josef

Secret of Ekaterinburg: The Hour-Glass

replied with a derisive quality he reserved for only those he despised.

But, these two men were different as he eyed them more carefully. These two were indeed not local party officials. They were KGB. He sensed it and he instinctively knew that they held much trouble for him and his family if they even suspected anything out of the ordinary. Josef felt his anger rise up inside as he objected to the direct questioning, but he held it in check because he did not want to jeopardize his family if he had to shoot them.

"What business is it of yours that we see our daughter off on the train? Why do you object to that? Do you take away that privilege, too?"

"Careful, comrade Josef. Do not try to intimidate us. It will serve no useful purpose to you or your family. We only ask that you verify the purpose of your outing."

"But you already have that information and from where you got it, I have no idea?"

Josef had played the part deftly enough to anger them. Now he would acquiesce to their questions and apologize profusely.

"I am sorry. Perhaps, it was the stale coffee I drank this morning. Yes, you are quite right. I am escorting my family to the train station as you can see. Ana is leaving this morning, then

Secret of Ekaterinburg: The Hour-Glass

we will stroll to our church to pray for a short time, then return home for a noon meal. You may attend with us, if you wish, but I am afraid we don't have enough food to invite you to lunch. Perhaps, if only one of you could stay?"

"Nyet. Don't let us deny you the eagerness of enjoying your family on this fine day," the KGB agent said.

"Oh, so now it has become a fine day? It was dreadful a moment ago."

"Comrade Josef. Do not push the limits of my tolerance. We decline the invitation to attend your so-called church. As for lunch, that is another matter completely out of our hands. The party is working very hard on the food shortage. It is a temporary situation, I assure you."

"You have been assuring us of that for the past four years, comrade."

"Silence, you fool. You are fortunate we are in good moods today, comrade. We may even let you continue on your way."

"Thank you, gentlemen comrades. I bid you both a pleasant morning."

Indeed, Josef knew the communists were always working hard on the food shortages. They were, in fact, creating them by sending most of it back to the motherland to feed the

Secret of Ekaterinburg: The Hour-Glass

starving masses. It was that kind of lying that everyone loathed. They were ruining Slovakia. What the Germans had taken, the communists duplicated and stripped the land.

Josef saluted with his cane like an obedient soldier then hurried to catch-up to the rest.

From a distance, the watchdog Nina eyed him carefully. The two KGB agents nodded to her. She and they were quite satisfied that Josef was a harmless, diminutive with nothing more to hide than his deep embarrassment that he was no longer able to provide for his family. But, no one in Slovakia could do that any longer because of the lost opportunities to be free.

"What did they say?" his wife asked.

"The usual shit. They wanted the usual. More information. There is nothing to fear because there is no more information to give them. You will soon be on your way to Berlin. Enjoy your trip Ana, it will be our last opportunity to see you forevermore."

The statement made Ana gasp with surprise. She had nearly forgotten in the frantic moment why she was there. To escape to America. Dear God, she would never see them again and began to cry when the reality hit her. She embraced them all as the train steamed into the

Secret of Ekaterinburg: The Hour-Glass

station.

"Katrina, please take care of your family," Ana cried.

"You can be sure of that. Our love goes with you," Katrina replied releasing her grip on Ana's waist.

Josef whispered, "Be happy. Live a long life. Perhaps someday, we will see each other again. Marry and raise children before it is too late."

"Yes. But, you know who it is I have loved all my life? Perhaps, I will find him again. Perhaps, the Americans can help me find him," she whispered in Josef's ear.

Josef let her keep the impossible fantasy.

Ana reached for her small valise and carried it to the landing of the passenger car as the conductor collected the boarding passes.

"Good-bye, Josef. Thank you for all you have done. Thank you for everything. Thank you for my life."

Josef was moved to tears.

"Ana. Trust no one."

The train began moving away from the platform as Ana jumped onto the passenger car grabbing the handrail tightly. The conductor snapped-up her suitcase and held onto her as she leaned over the steps.

Secret of Ekaterinburg: The Hour-Glass

"Remember me. Remember the story of the hourglass."

"I will," Josef shouted. "God be with you!"

The train chugged away and into the haze disappearing from view. The smiles vanished as they watched the train fade into the distance. There was a long silence, except for the sounds of the horse-carts rumbling through the cobblestone streets.

For the Prachek's, life would slowly return to normal.

But, for Ana things would change quickly and her life was about to become something far more remarkable.

Secret of Ekaterinburg: The Hour-Glass

CHAPTER 33

Moscow, Oct. 20, 1947

Andre poured the coffee into the pot to be reboiled. It tasted better that way and it was the way the politburo members liked it. Brewed twice for strength.

Coffee was in short supply in Russia because the usual shipments from Brazil were always late. Most of it was spirited away by black marketers as it entered the country through Vladivostok then shipped overland through the Western frontier of the Soviet Union, then entering the central part above Mongolia, and finally over the Urals and into Moscow. By the time two hundred tons of shipment had arrived, forty tons had been stolen. It was a problem for all products crisscrossing the country especially involving those goods which weren't produced in the Soviet Union.

Andre picked up the coffee pot after it had brewed and poured it into a separate serving carafe placed it onto a tray, and carried it into

Secret of Ekaterinburg: The Hour-Glass

the meeting room filled with thirty-five politburo members and the premier of the Soviet Union - Josef Stalin.

Andre was nervous. He approached Stalin hesitantly because he had never done this before. He had been ordered to do it but he couldn't shake the intense fear surging inside him as he put the tray down beside Stalin.

Stalin appeared thin and waxy his hair fully grayed. The war had taken its toll on him and the deep lines in his face were pronounced even in the poor lighting. There, in front of his very eyes, Andre could see the dictator in person making decisions that affected millions of eastern bloc citizens trapped in the socialist quagmire called the Iron Curtain, sealed inside the eastern border by a standing army of three million. None of them was getting a taste of the promises that communism had made more than thirty years earlier. Perhaps the lucky ones were the ones Stalin had purged on his rise to power if they were lucky to be alive.

The live ones, however, were not quite dead but they might as well have been. At least, in death they couldn't feel any more physical pain. For those who survived, the mental anguish could make their lives intolerable until God himself ended the life of this murdering despot.

Secret of Ekaterinburg: The Hour-Glass

Unfortunately, like Hitler, those who had plotted Stalin's death had met their own sooner failing in their plans to assassinate them years earlier. And now, they cowered even more and began to think of Stalin as invincible by God's own design. Certainly, God was the only one who could now dare strike him down. Those few who had tried or who had even harbored the thought were "liquidated" dutifully by Beria's Cheka agents.

Andre had hidden his thoughts well. He had come a long way from his humble dacha beginnings after he, Sergei, and the older brothers had left the farm and gone their own separate paths.

He dared not ever speak of such things aloud, nor even let on any suspicious nature of such hideous thoughts toward the fiend he now worked for. Stalin's time would come later, he contemplated.

"Comrade Stalin, sir, would you care for coffee this afternoon?" Andre asked not too firmly yet not too timidly.

Stalin motioned him to fill his cup placed to the right of him, but in order to do this, Andre had to pour cross behind him to the other side and pour across his writing tablet. Nobody dared cross directly behind Stalin. To do this

Secret of Ekaterinburg: The Hour-Glass

could be a fatal mistake and Andre knew that. Stalin's paranoia had nearly paralyzed his thinking and his mood was so unstable that any slight provocation could bring about a disastrous result for any would-be offender.

"Comrade Stalin, may I bring the boiling pot over your writing space?" Andre asked.

"Of course. How else can you pour it? If you spill it, the consequence to the table will be little, but the consequence to you could be immense."

The politburo members froze as Andre picked up the boiling carafe and carefully lifted it above the paperwork. He dared not spill a drop. His hand slightly trembling, he steadied the pot with his other hand carefully pointing it away from Stalin.

Cautiously, he poured the black rich liquid into the cup when the unthinkable happened; the handle slipping away from his grasp as if by some wretched curse.

The pot fell onto the table with a sharp crack. Andre reacted swiftly catching it with his other hand before it could spill over the table, perhaps even burning Stalin. It was a near disaster.

"Good, God, you madman, you have nearly burned me with your carelessness," Stalin

Secret of Ekaterinburg: The Hour-Glass

screamed.

Stalin stood at once while his aides brushed at his uniform.

"You clumsy fool, I should have you shot for your incompetence."

"Yes, comrade leader. You should order me shot as soon as possible but that would not cure the mistake in me."

Stalin was stunned, as were the politburo members, at Andre's sudden reply. Sitting in their neatly arranged seats, they realized it was an oft-handed remark but a fatal one. After a long pause, Stalin eyeing Andre up and down, said, "You are quite correct, comrade. It would not cure you. Only close attention to detail and nerves of steel will cure you. You will pour me another cup."

Andre grimaced as he picked up the carafe and poured another for the dictator. This time it went flawlessly. Not a drop was spilled and this time his hand was steady.

"You see, comrade. Only those with nerves of steel can carry out orders under pressure. It takes practice and discipline. Did you feel any pressure, Comrade Andre?"

"Da, comrade Stalin. But, it was better the second pour."

"Then the next time they send for you to

Secret of Ekaterinburg: The Hour-Glass

bring coffee, act like a man and not a boy. I respect only this kind of behavior. You have learned a valuable lesson from me, yes?"

Andre snapped, "Yes, thank you chairman Stalin," and held his breath waiting to be dismissed.

Members of the politburo in the room were dead silent.

"You may leave us," Stalin commanded.

Without another word, Andre quickly withdrew from the meeting room.

"Comrade, Andre," Stalin called before he got to the doorway. "Exactly, what did you learn?"

"Comrade leader. I learned never to be afraid even in the face of certain death."

Stalin howled and doubled over with laughter.

"Ha! That is good. That is very good comrade Andre. You are much smarter than anyone gives you credit for," Stalin roared with a gusto not seen by anyone since the end of the war.

"Politburo members, take a lesson. Someday, Andre may be leading all of Russia."

The politburo members rose to their feet and began applauding the chairman. They stood for a full minute before retaking their seats.

Secret of Ekaterinburg: The Hour-Glass

And, Andre slipped quietly from the room. With everyone now reseated and in a better mood, Stalin surveyed the room and spoke first to his deputy premier, Alexi.

"What is the least important item on the agenda today, and what is the most important?"

"Comrade Stalin, the most important item is that of the East German federation keeping up the blockade of goods into Berlin as ordered. Nothing is getting through and the Americans can do nothing about it at the present time. Berlin will collapse in only a few days. The least important item is that the KGB has again discovered a new rumor that one of the Czar's family is still alive, although there is never any evidence to prove or confirm it."

"What is this?" he demanded. "What is this?"

"Comrade leader, I apologize. This can wait and we can discuss it later if you wish?"

"I wish to talk about it now. What information is there that exists, that a member of the Czar's family could possibly still be alive after nearly 31 years. Comrade Lenin personally ordered them all to be put to death before anyone escaped from the Ipatiev House. I remember it well, comrades, because in case any of you have forgotten, I was there by

Secret of Ekaterinburg: The Hour-Glass

Lenin's side when the order was given to execute them. What chance is there that any of them escaped alive?" Stalin shouted back at Alexi.

"Comrade Stalin, the man who carried out the execution made a statement to another member of the firing squad that he knew of some kind of information, that one of the princesses had somehow survived the execution. His name was Yakov."

"But, that would be impossible. The reports from the NKVD itself and in Beria's own words to me, were that each was shot several times at close range, many of them stabbed repeatedly with bayonets, then shot in the head to make sure they were finished. How could this possibly be?"

"Comrade Stalin," Alexi continued. "The bodies were moved to a mass grave site, then moved again farther away from Ekaterinburg. They were thrown into an abandoned mine and covered with sulfuric acid and lime to augment the decomposition according to the witnesses who were there. They returned several weeks later to move the bodies to another site because villagers had learned of the burial location and when they retrieved the bodies from the mine, they could not find one of the daughters? No

Secret of Ekaterinburg: The Hour-Glass

one knows what happened to that body, comrade."

"What kind of incompetence is this," he roared. "Thirty years ago, and we are finding this out only now. Who is this Yakov?"

"His name is Grachev, sir. Yakov Grachev. A local party official and postmaster in the Ural city of Peregrebnoye. He has long since disappeared from there, and we can no longer locate him or his family. They seemed to have disappeared from the face of the earth. We only know that he served in the war and served commendably under Field Marshall Georgi Zhukov, but has since disappeared and was last seen alive during the counterattack at the Dnepr River."

"If one of the Czar's family is still alive, and this Yakov has any information about it, then you can be sure he will want to remain erased from the face of the earth forever," Stalin replied.

"It was said that a certain Yakov, the leader of the 1918 execution squad, died in 1933."

"How did you come to learn of this, Alexi?"

"From old Cheka files given to me by Beria. What do you wish me to do about this matter?"

"I want you to pursue it further. Not as a priority, but still, pursue it. I, myself, find this

Secret of Ekaterinburg: The Hour-Glass

very difficult to believe. It would have taken a miracle to escape the deadly onslaught of bullets that night. Even I know that. And, I, gentlemen, don't believe in God anymore. Still, it would take a miracle by the Mother of God herself whom we don't believe in. The only miracles that have happened recently have been by our own doing including the victories of the Soviet Supreme Red Army over the Wermacht. That is the only thing we know for a fact, comrades.

"But, if one of them did survive after all these years, we will find her. She is too important a creature. She is a threat to the very existence of the Soviet Union. In effect, comrades, she is a direct threat to not only me but to you as well. If you do not think so then you are all bigger fools than the believers. And, all of Russia whether we like it or not are all believers. Do you know what they still believe in. God. And, if a Romanov is still alive, then they will believe in her, too."

Alexi sat down at the table and scribbled on his writing pad.

"Take care of it. Now, let's be on with the Berlin issue. Tighten the grip. Do not let anything in or out of the corridor supplying them. The Americans want everything in

Berlin. They have forgotten that the Russian people paid for it with twenty-two million dead. Germany will never be reunited while I remain alive. I will never allow it. Ever!"

Secret of Ekaterinburg: The Hour-Glass

CHAPTER 34

Aboard The Train, Austria, Oct., 27, 1949

The train rumbled effortlessly under the pull of its huge engines with twenty cars in tow, all passenger coaches designed to afford a minimum of comfort to those venturing across the border into Austria.

The passengers were a mixture of many from all over Europe on their return from Prague, long considered the cultural capital of Europe, a major center of theater, music and the arts.

Many were going home to East Germany. Others were traveling elsewhere; some to Belgium, a few to France and some even as far away as Spain. They had come to Prague because even now it was still the symbolic center of free expression despite its being entrenched behind a new barrier, the iron curtain. Ana was seated in the last car from the engine. She had made it to the train with only moments to spare. She clutched her return ticket and unfolded her briefcase deftly tucking

Secret of Ekaterinburg: The Hour-Glass

the return ticket inside a secret compartment in the bottom. It would be safe there. She must not lose the briefcase or she would lose the most important piece of her disguise – the return trip to Czechoslovakia. The ticket would guarantee her safe passage through East Germany, then onto Bremen where she could safely leave Europe. But, if she had the misfortune to encounter the KGB, the return ticket would convince them of her travel plans for return.

Ana was now alone for the first time since she had left Russia. Josef had taught her independence like he had his own daughters because Ana was something special to him and he had come to love her as one of his own.

At four, Czar Nicholas, had instilled in her, a ferocious passion for competitiveness that surprised even the Czarina. When she played with the other children at school or on the palace grounds, she played with a tenacity to win. She could be so unnervingly intent on her objective that the other children often simply gave in letting her have her way. Her treatment, by Josef, however, had been far different. He gave her an education coupled with a remarkable sense of creativity. She developed amazing talents from playing the

Secret of Ekaterinburg: The Hour-Glass

piano to writing poetry and mastering a seamstress competency in addition to other fine arts. She, had indeed, become a prize worth winning by all the men in the village who sought her continuously. Her intellectual abilities were fabled in Bardejov, but nobody really knew who she really was. And, she remained true to her belief that someday she would be reunited with Sergei, and refused all the advances of her suitors, in part to find out what had happened to him.

That, coupled with the fact that she was in extreme danger made her trip all the more adventurous.

The communists had made life extremely hard in the days immediately following the war. Even as things were improving, they still made it difficult for relatives to trace lost siblings, aunts, uncles and parents. They trusted no one, and who could blame them for they had lost more than 25 million in the war by some counts and they wanted to guarantee it could never happen again.

Ana's thoughts drifted back to the present as she observed the ticket master collecting fares. She clutched hers at the ready. Crossing the border would not be a problem, but getting into Berlin, especially into the neutral sector would

Secret of Ekaterinburg: The Hour-Glass

be a challenge as Josef had warned. There would be NKVD at every important gate and even where she would least expect them.

"Madam, your ticket please," the ticket master asked politely.

Ana handed him the ticket with a steady hand and with a simple click, punched it and returned it to her. Austria. She breathed a sigh of relief.

Secret of Ekaterinburg: The Hour-Glass

CHAPTER 35

Moscow, Nov. 4, 1989

Solotzin was already in his Kremlin office. He fidgeted in his red, satin chair embroidered in gold threads and perched upon a deep red carpet. A beautiful hand-woven tapestry hung behind his chair. The circular walls were ornate and had been hand decorated for a Czar Nicholas II. Solotzin nearly was such a man but Russia wanted and craved a real Czar, and Solotzin knew that. Whether or not the people referred to him as President or by some other title, it didn't much matter. He was a virtual Czar in his own right. Certainly, he had the power of one and soon he would be handing back that part of Russian heritage missing for nearly eighty years.

Solotzin studied the pages of a report handed to him by his top aide, Andre Kirov. Andre had survived more than 40 years of hardship at the hands of those who didn't trust him. So, in the end, and at the last possible moment, he had bolted from the communist

Secret of Ekaterinburg: The Hour-Glass

party in an effort to save his country and himself. He was the consummate Kremlin worker and more importantly, the closest aide to all of the former Soviet premiers He had finally reached the zenith of his political insider career at the age of seventy-seven. He was too old to continue much longer and they would force him to retire soon. But, because he could not survive comfortably on his government pension he would fight the bureaucrats to the bitter end. Pensioners they called themselves in Russia. They were called retirees in other countries but they were all the same. Survivors in a world-wide political war. Solotzin read the reports from the Federal Security Service.

Andre still thought of them as the NKVD because he still remembered the terrible days when Stalin and Solotzin had used its power to murder not only the guilty who tried to betray him but the innocent as well.

He approached Solotzin who was deeply absorbed in his reading. Solotzin motioned him to be seated in a nearby chair.

"Andre what do you think of these reports? I know you have already seen them, so what do you think?" the president asked him pointedly.

Andre shifted in the red-cushioned chair, still somewhat uncomfortable at what his leader

Secret of Ekaterinburg: The Hour-Glass

had just asked him then he put his hand on the papers, palm down, and said, "It is probably the best solution we can offer our people. It will cause us no security threat, it will bring in hard currency; and it will stir the patriotism of every Russian man, woman and child including those who have gone to live elsewhere.

"Da, Andre. I would tend to agree with you on all counts. But, when it is discovered that we have negotiated with the American government for all this, for dollars, for gold, and for other things, including our own national security, what will the people think then?"

"Mr. President . . . the euphoria will be so great they will not remember so much the reason how it was done, they will remember only the reason why it was done. The people have endured untold hardships over the past 80 years, more than anyone can possibly imagine. A few more years of transitional struggle will barely affect them. Mr. President, you will be regarded as a hero of Russia."

Solotzin murmured with pride. Rumbling in a low, short burst of air, was a cultural idiosyncrasy, a gesture of respect to the opposition, or in this case, a colleague who could be trusted to give an honest opinion and a direct answer.

Secret of Ekaterinburg: The Hour-Glass

Andre watched the president closely and laid his hand on the report. Solotzin placed his hand on top of Andre's fist, and gently pressed down on it. Andre was an old and trusted friend.

"Yes. You are correct. We must do this, Andre. But, I am not looking forward to becoming a hero. There are many dead heroes buried in the Kremlin Wall close to the high position from where I watch the parades. They all stood there at one time, too. Being a hero can be dangerous. However, I will accept that precarious status in exchange for what is coming in the next few days. If what you say is true in this report then the people of Russia have much to be thankful for. And more. The resemblance to the Czar is uncanny. It is Anastasia, is it not?"

"Yes. Without any doubt."

"And, how long have you known her?"
"My entire life and I have missed her for that long as I have missed my brother. You know she was always in love with Sergei."

Solotzin gestured lightly with his hand and reflected.

"I once was in love, too. It was a love that took the strength from me if you can believe that, and then she was killed in the war. I

Secret of Ekaterinburg: The Hour-Glass

eventually married Sophie, but, you know, it was never quite the same. They say it never is. Do not misunderstand me, Andre, I have always loved my wife, but I have always wondered at what might have been? So, we have all probably had these experiences somewhere, haven't we. We understand the situation perfectly. We comprehend that the other person knows what it is like? And, that gives us compassion."

Andre nodded and removed his hand from the desk. He could only gaze at the report. Dear God, what were they about to do?

"Andre, notify the military commanders that all units are to be placed on alert, but do not give them any reasons for it until we make the announcement. Also, notify the Presidium for a meeting this afternoon, and then we will address the Duma in full session tomorrow. I want national and worldwide television coverage of the event so that everyone in the world will be focused on Russia and Russia alone."

"Absolutely. And, what about the currency and gold shipments? When will they begin?"

"The currency will be transferred via the international wire from the IMF and deposited into the vaults at the Bank of Russia. As for

Secret of Ekaterinburg: The Hour-Glass

the gold, put into effect the plan that you have devised with Sergei, to begin the shipments across the Bering Strait. Imagine it, sixty billion dollars in gold bullion being transported from their Fort Knox to Russia in exchange for this. I don't suppose we thought forty years ago, Andre that the price of Russian democracy would become this expensive did we nor the Americans?"

"There is an American expression that says that money cannot buy happiness. But, still there are a lot of other things it can buy, Mr. President."

Solotzin grunted from his chair again.

"Yes, but one of the things it cannot possibly buy is the security of my re-election, can it?"

"We shall see, Mr. President. At the very least, you will leave your mark upon Russia as no other leader has since Lenin or perhaps Peter the Great."

"Perhaps. But, once you are dead, your memories go with you and the money does not." Solotzin quipped.

He took a deep breath and dismissed Andre. He wanted to be alone in his thoughts. Andre excused himself and promptly left the room.

Solotzin, still staring at the report, wondered

Secret of Ekaterinburg: The Hour-Glass

what Lenin, Trotsky, Stalin, Khrushchev, Brezhnev, and all of them would have thought. There could be no answer. Only he, Yeltsin and Gorbachev were the ones left alive to change Russia.

Perhaps, in his own mind he had already departed this earth.

Even he knew it didn't matter now.

A new beginning for future generations was at hand.

Secret of Ekaterinburg: The Hour-Glass

CHAPTER 36

THE Oval Office, Washington, Nov. 6, 1989

The president leaned over his desk. Five aides were next to him while he nervously flipped his tie back-and- forth wondering how he should solve the problem. He had listened to his advisers dispense their advice on all the feasible solutions and which one they had singled out as a preference. But, he wasn't sure if it was right. He thought for a moment, then began.

"Ben, why do you think this scenario is in the best interests of Russia and why do you think it's in the best interests of the United States?" the president asked the CIA chief point blank.

Point blank was his usual way of conducting meetings with his advisers, straight forward and to the point.

Ben cleared his throat, looked at President Nelson, and commenced. . . "because by their cultural standards, and I'm talking about 900

Secret of Ekaterinburg: The Hour-Glass

years of cultural standards, they have always coveted a dynamic, unrivaled leader, and their economic system has always centered around him, in most cases, a czar. It is in their best interests to once again carry on that relationship with their people. It's like saying the President of the United States is no longer relevant to the country. Maybe he is. Maybe he isn't. But, it's what the American people are used to. It's like a security blanket. Once you've had it, you don't want to give it up. As for the United States' best interests, anything that improves their chances to succeed at democracy improves our chances to succeed with our relationship with them in the long run."

"Good, Ben. Very strong case. Just what I might expect to hear from you," the President spoke with a slight tone of sarcasm without arousing Ben's suspicion that he didn't think much of the analysis.

The president got up from his chair. He wanted to hear more but from someone outside his staff.

"Kathryn, send in Alex, now," he instructed pressing the blue button on his intercom-phone.

"Yes, Mr. President, right away," Kathryn responded instantly.

The president moved to the right, turned

Secret of Ekaterinburg: The Hour-Glass

facing the large bullet-proof windows, and looked out toward Pennsylvania Avenue. Good God, is this damned plan really do-able? For Christ's sake, someone had to give him a more conclusive answer than what he had just heard. He needed the right rationale, the right moral reason.

Alex entered the room and made eye contact with the men present. They all knew each other, and there were no preliminaries necessary.

"Alex, you can stand or take a seat. You already know what we've been discussing and before I ask you this, I want you to take all the time you need, not that you wouldn't anyway, and think over what I have just asked you. And, before you respond, I'll have Kathryn take everything down just to make sure we get it right the first time, straight off the cuff. You know, those are the best words when it really comes right down to it."

He pressed the blue button.

"Kathryn, you ready?"

"Ready to go, sir."

The President locked the intercom button into place with a click and leaned back in his padded chair. He looked squarely at Alex, still standing, pointed a finger at him, and asked.

Secret of Ekaterinburg: The Hour-Glass

"Why do you think this is so important to the Russian people and why do you think it is important to the American people?"

Alex hesitated for a moment, but he had already practiced his answer while he was waiting yet he didn't want to look too prepared; he wanted to look near brilliant.

The President knew him like a good book. He could tell Alex was ready but the other advisers didn't have a clue. And, so he let them wait without saying anything to prompt Alex's response faster than normal. He could afford to wait. It would be worth it - for the rest of them. The others would learn something about critical thinking. Alex sat down in the empty chair placed directly in front of the President who had also taken his seat behind the massive Lincoln desk.

"Mr. President. It's what the Russians expect. It's not so much what they want. They want a lot of things they can't have. But, you have to understand where they are coming from. They have been repressed for the last 81 years under communist rule which allows them almost nothing. Generations sacrificed not only their possessions but even their lives for a corrupt system without getting anything in return, except for one thing."

Secret of Ekaterinburg: The Hour-Glass

"And, what is that one thing, Alex?" the President asked playing his game and drawing him out on the question.

"Uhh. . . sir . . . that would be security. Under communism, they at least, had the security of knowing that a huge standing army supported by a huge standing government would protect them from another Germany or some other aggressor. That is worth a lot to them. And, there is a difference in terms of wanting something and expecting something. When you want something, it's something that either doesn't exist or it's something you don't possess. The Russian people always possessed individual freedoms, in the sense that it is natural for them in their expressions of speech, art, religion, theater, music, and especially in their poetry. It's the one thing out of life that they could control. The expectation of expressing their feelings from the depths of their souls. The communists could not take that away from them no matter how hard they tried. In fact, they quietly condoned most of it, although the official policy of the state was that no official religion was allowed to exist in the Soviet Union. For instance, Mr. President, the Russians practiced it on a regular basis everywhere they could. They prayed at home,

Secret of Ekaterinburg: The Hour-Glass

in catacomb-like churches set up on a moment's notice; hell they even prayed in Red Square, two blocks away from the Kremlin. And, the whole time, the official state policy was a huge lie and nobody ever believed the Russian government would ever kill their own people over it. It was something very basic and individual to them. It was an expected right. And, when you have an expected right, it is far different from something that you just want. An expectation is already set. And, you have a natural jurisdiction over it."

The President interjected.

"And, as far as the United States is concerned?"

"Sir, it's already spelled out in our Constitution. The right to pursue, freedom, life, liberty, and happiness. And that includes security. If the arrangement between Russia and the United States permits the furtherance of liberty and all of the above then how can we argue otherwise. That is our security. Their security is our security."

Good God, the President thought. He was a fucking genius. How could he always be so right? It was precisely what he needed to make his decision and the others just sat there staring at Alex knowing that he had provided that truth

Secret of Ekaterinburg: The Hour-Glass

the others had missed. That truth was now in the President's mind. You could almost see it embedded there.

The Oval Office was iced with silence. It was as though everyone had gone to church.

"Yes. Alex. I concur," the President chimed in quickly so as not to appear off-guard in his thoughts. The silence disappeared in an instant.

"Alex, don't ever quit the CIA," he added in a low voice and with the motion of his hand indicating that Alex could leave the Oval Office when he wanted.

"Thank you, Mr. President. My wife probably wouldn't allow it anyhow. At least not for a few more years. Is that all, sir."

"Uh,. yes, Alex . . . " the President said. "As usual a fine analysis of the situation. Please stay in touch and give my regards to your family."

Alex smiled and left thanking everyone for listening to an old warrior. He closed the door behind him and winked to Kathryn on the way out.

Back inside the Oval Office, the President issued several orders to his aides to make all the necessary plans to meet with the Russian President at some near date, to set up the news media, and alert the military as a usual standby precaution, just so they were ready in case anything . . .anything . . . went wrong. But, the President didn't see how anything could.

Ben, somewhat embarrassed, offered. "Sir, isn't it great to be an American president?"

President Nelson didn't look at him.

"Sometimes it is . . . sometimes it isn't. This is one of those times that it is."

Secret of Ekaterinburg: The Hour-Glass

CHAPTER 37

Krazcoff, Nov. 13, 1989

Andre had flown from Moscow to the secret submarine base on short notice after he had been contacted by Sergei.

It would be now or never.

They would meet together in the presence of the KGB chief and the special CIA agent assigned to the case – Alex Ayers.

Russia's president had already approved the plan, and the President of the United States was in agreement. The plan would begin as soon as the monetary arrangements were in place.

Andre approached the sub pens where they had met before. Everything was quiet at this late hour in the evening. Military personnel were scattered all over the base because of the weekend with only light duty personnel on active station.

He went inside the small shanty and waited for Sergei.

He didn't have to wait long. Sergei arrived within minutes. The two shook hands, hugged and got down to business.

Secret of Ekaterinburg: The Hour-Glass

"Sergei, what have you got?" Andre asked immediately.

"Dobro pozhalovat," Sergei answered and motioned to Andre to take a chair. Sergei once again laid a portable transmitter on the table and turned it on. The scrambler's red light came on indicating it was functioning properly.

"We put the plan into operation beginning tomorrow at 0600 hours," he said tersely.

"What about Ana?" Andre said. "Is she in harm's way?"

"Nyet. Not for now but there will be great resistance to the plan from certain elements especially from those communist dogs. They will never accept it for what it is. But, we both know that it must be."

"How is she? I cannot wait to see her. It has been more than five years since we last saw each other," Sergei spoke while looking away from Andre.

Andre smiled. He always suspected that they had been in love even back when they were children at the dacha. They would always be in love and it was something they both deserved. They at least deserved that much from life. They could never be married for if that were to happen it would put Ana in extreme danger perhaps the both of them.

Secret of Ekaterinburg: The Hour-Glass

"Da. You saw her last during a secret visit to the United States on behalf of the great motherland – is that not true?" Andre asked.

"Yes, it was during the last Russian-American summit six months ago. The American CIA took me to see her at a secret Maryland location near Baltimore. She has had a good life there, and . . . . " Sergei's words fell away from his lips.

"But what . . . " Andre asked.

"But, we could only be together for a few days, before I finished my official business on behalf of the party. The party. The damnable party. Lenin's great folly to all of mankind. His gift to the masses," Sergei mocked disturbed at what had happened her.

"Was she freely willing to do this?" Andre pressed him.

"Da. But, it took some convincing. She has a decent life in America; she is not known there and she has never been recognized by anyone except by those of us who really know who she is."

"What is it like there for her?"

"She has taught history Russian history, at the University of Maryland for more than 20 years, before she finally retired. Her physical health is satisfactory but her mental health, they

Secret of Ekaterinburg: The Hour-Glass

say, is in question. I would never agree to that diagnosis because they do not know her as I know her. And, they will never know her or what a terrible price she had to pay for all the physical and mental pain throughout the years. She is a person without a country. Thank God, I have known and loved her as family during those years."

"Sergei, does she really understand what is being asked of her and what she must do once she returns?"

"Yes. We discussed it at great length."

"Perhaps she has changed her mind."

"Andre, you know Ana better than most, and I know her even still better than you. She has accepted it. She will not change her mind any more than you and I will change our minds about this mission."

"It is true, Sergei. She will go through with it because she still believes like you and I, like the millions of Russians who still believe in the truth."

"And, what of the rest of the plan? How long will it take and how much time do we have to carry it out?"

"There are 4000 metric tons of gold to transport from Point Barrow, Alaska to Kamchatka in only two days. It must be all

Secret of Ekaterinburg: The Hour-Glass

transferred before the anniversary of the Bolshevik Revolution, on March 6."

"And, why is that timeline so important," Andre pressed him again.

"It must be so to give the event the highest significance that can possibly be attained. Lenin will roll over in his Kremlin grave, if he is still there, and the rest of the communists will probably have heart attacks," Sergei laughed.

"It will be a day I will celebrate for the rest of my life," Andre agreed nervously checking to see if anyone was outside the shanty. He moved the curtain aside from a small window and peered out toward the sub pens.

"And, how about the missiles and their warheads?" Andre wanted to know. "That was part of the plan. Twelve hundred medium-range missiles with more than 10,000 warheads. Is that correct?"

"Da. That is correct," Sergei reaffirmed. "They have already been loaded onto ships for delivery."

"That is good, Sergei. The world will be a much safer place because of this and because of us. Can you imagine if they were in the hands of one of the dissident republics or in the hands of Iran? Better they will be in American

Secret of Ekaterinburg: The Hour-Glass

hands."

"As for the gold. It has come from their Fort Knox, Kentucky, and after it is delivered to Kamchatka, it will be transported by airlift to Moscow where it will be deposited into our national coffers. God only knows, we need this to continue on as a nation, don't we? It is the right thing to do, isn't it? Or did we pay too high a price with our souls?"

"Nyet," Sergei responded to the doubt raised by Andre. "Unfortunately, as the communists under-estimated in their ruinous plan of our country, it takes capital in the form of hard currency to enable an economy to function, to grow, to prosper, and to encourage private businesses. They never understood that. And, because the fool-bastards tried to equalize everything and every person in the Soviet Union, they equalized nothing but a lower class. They became the new bourgeois. They became the upper class in a supposedly classless society. Well, we all know the truth of that, don't we, Andre?"

"Four-thousand metric tons of gold. Can you imagine how much that is?" Andre spoke excitedly. "Can you imagine?"

"Yes. Fifty-one billion. In American dollars."

Secret of Ekaterinburg: The Hour-Glass

"Your math has improved," Andre joked.

"That takes care of all the details, except a minor one," Sergei countered. "How will the remaining communist threat be dealt with."

"We have a special plan for those opposing the President. It will be similar to the one that Vladimir Ilich Lenin imposed upon his own friends in the early days. Exile by execution," Sergei said. "That is what he offered the Czar and his family, and others, and that will be our offer."

He shrugged his shoulders.

Andre sat transfixed at what they were discussing and let the silence continue for a moment.

"Then let us drink one final toast to each other and pray that all goes well. I will see you in Moscow in three days. Nas dravia." Andre raised his glass to Sergei's pursing his lips.

"Da. You will see me in Moscow, Andre," dead panned. "Or, you will see me in hell."

Sergei grinned.

Indeed, Andre would see Sergei in three days if all went well.

But, in the new Russia things could change in an instant no less a lifetime.

Andre, Sergei and Ana didn't have any more lifetimes left.

Secret of Ekaterinburg: The Hour-Glass

And neither did the people of Russia.

Secret of Ekaterinburg: The Hour-Glass

CHAPTER 38

Moscow, Nov. 23, 1989

The assassin squad had cleverly set up in an apartment on Red Square across the street about one-half kilometer directly across from the Kremlin Wall where President Yakov Grachev Solotzin of Russia and the American CIA representative would deliver Anastasia to the Russian people.

Karl looked out the window from the dingy apartment and surveyed the location. Blonde, blue-eyed, and built muscular on a short physique, his square jaw reminded his companion of the prototypical Red Army officer. But, he wasn't. Karl had a new assignment in the Russian government. He was a member of the new Federal Security Service, but it was filled with elements of the same old KGB with a new name still loaded with unreformed communists.

The new government under Solotzin had done well, but they had missed these dogmatists. Karl and Friedrich were bought and paid for by the Leninists - those few who

Secret of Ekaterinburg: The Hour-Glass

still believed that a communist system should prevail in Russia. They believed they had been betrayed by Gorbachev who accused him of working for the CIA who had ultimately delivered Russia to the United States.

"It will be a difficult shot. But, this is the best angle I could get on such short notice," he remarked to Friedrich.

"No matter. With my skill and your intellect we will perform the deed without error," Friedrich responded coldly looking out the apartment window which opened to transform the living area to an open air balcony.

Both knew they would soon become traitors to the new Russia but the assassination had to be performed if Russia was to survive and return to its glory days under communism.

"What will you use?"

Friedrich opened the suitcase with callous routine and began to assemble the weapon. A special AKM M43 Kalashnikov 7.62mm x 39mm, the type used by the Russian Spetznatz troops arrayed against NATO across Europe. He had fitted it with a 20x power Manhauser scope capable of hitting a nail head at 400 yards. Even though it was an automatic weapon, it had been converted with special weights to offset the lighter stock and the barrel

Secret of Ekaterinburg: The Hour-Glass

made heavier to keep it steadier in the capable hands of a sniper. It could be fired and re-fired in less than one-half second. And again, if needed at that speed without the shooter missing a beat. It could be quickly broken down and tucked inside a small briefcase and dropped off almost anywhere without traceable links.

Friedrich smiled to himself and turned. "Karl, you over-estimate my abilities with this formidable weapon, yes?"

"Nyet. I have seen you shoot before at the Kiev training center two years ago. No one could compete with your accuracy. Not even myself. And, I regard myself as extremely skillful."

"Even so, there is always the possibility that something could go wrong," he toyed with Karl.

"Look. We must do this in two days. Nothing must go wrong," Karl said letting Friedrich get his ire. "We are doing it for the party. For us, it is a matter of survival."

"Is the escape plan set?" Friedrich interrupted.

"Da. It is a perfect plan designed to let everyone think that the shot came from within the crowd. Only the professionals will know

Secret of Ekaterinburg: The Hour-Glass

otherwise. They would not believe that such a chance shot from a mad shoving crowd could hit its target. So, they will quickly seal off the square and all the surrounding buildings with us still inside. We want to move quickly but not too quickly so that is why I have devised a plan that will allow us to exit in a casual, cautious manner without raising anyone's suspicion."

Friedrich knew that Karl was a master at planning such escapes. He had done it in Istanbul five years ago in the assassination of a Turkish ambassador with the same rifle. He literally put his weapon away and walked to a bus stop and boarded it to the airport. He was out of the country within hours letting the original owners of the apartment be arrested and interrogated by Turkish authorities.

It was actually rather simple.

Find an apartment which was already rented but where the tenants would be out of the city.

Then, after the assassination had been completed, leave the apartment immediately, putting the suitcase with the rifle inside, then pass it off to an innocent dupe they had already set up outside the apartment on the pretense that they wanted it delivered immediately to a destination for 25 rubles. Any schoolboy

Secret of Ekaterinburg: The Hour-Glass

would do it for the money. And, they had already set up the plan. A Moscow schoolboy had been checked out to be dishonest but reliable enough to do the job.

"Who is this hapless lad we have hired?" Friedrich asked.

"He is the son of a local police officer within the current government. His father will be suspected immediately and that is the beauty of the plan. It will allow us time to disappear from Moscow and into Siberia."

"How will the party reward us for our heroic deed?" Friedrich quizzed.

"Perhaps with a promotion or an important position inside the new government," Karl shrugged. "Who knows how the party really works on such matters. But, we will be paid in American currency for it."

"Yes." Friedrich answered automatically. "Who really knows?"

He finished assembling the weapon and held it out for Karl to inspect. It was a beautiful piece of craftsmanship that could kill an adversary at 1200 meters without varying a quarter of an inch in repeated attempts at the target. In the hands of an expert shooter, it would not fail the person who squeezed the trigger.

Secret of Ekaterinburg: The Hour-Glass

"I test fired it only yesterday," Friedrich boasted. "It is sighted-in for 500 meters. It is about 300 meters to the wall from the window. We will draw the curtains and I will mount the weapon on a table for stability; then I will wait for the crowd to roar before I shoot. No one will hear the shot. She will just fall as if in a faint. It will be hot, and they will think that she has fainted from the excitement. But, she will be dead. We will know that, but no one else will suspect it for a few precious minutes."

Karl sat down in front of the window, opened it, and let the fresh air fill the humid apartment. He opened the doors leading to the balcony and walked outside into the fresh Moscow air. It actually was cleaner than most western cities he had often visited while performing KGB work. Stockholm. Amsterdam. London. Washington. They were all dirtier than Moscow but what they lacked in the way of clean air they made up for in the novelties and niceties of life.

"How many people do they expect in the square for the ceremonies?" Karl asked.

"If it's as usual, I would estimate about a million citizens will be jammed into expanse wishing to see a piece of history in the making."

Secret of Ekaterinburg: The Hour-Glass

"Then, we must not disappoint them, eh, Friedrich?"

"Indeed, we must not disappoint them." Friedrich retorted and walked over to the television to catch the latest Moscow news report.

"The important thing is to remember that the plan is designed to place blame and cause an unstable government. That is the real objective. She will be our instrument to achieve it. She never was of any real value to us anyway. Even Lenin recognized that when he had the entire family massacred," Karl argued.

He would receive no quarrel from Friedrich. They agreed on most everything including this cowardly act.

And, he knew they would carry it out with precision. The news announcer came on the air and began the newscast.

The top story was about the very event they had just been discussing.

The newscaster said officials expected an overflow crowd of some million-and-a-half Russians at Red Square.

Karl and Friedrich nodded to each other.

The trap was set.

Secret of Ekaterinburg: The Hour-Glass

CHAPTER 39

CIA Headquarters, Langley, Nov. 20, 1989

Alex slipped unnoticed into the meeting room sipping his usual cup of morning coffee.

He was perplexed. He hadn't quite figured out what Artie was getting at with all those Russian ships lined up at Krazcoff. Everyone at the CIA knew it was a major, secret submarine base the Russians didn't like to talk about located a scant one hundred twenty-five miles from Kamchatka Peninsula where the Russians launched secret missions into space and performed mysterious experiments relating to the development of new weapons systems.

What he couldn't figure out was why the Russians would assemble and leave these ships out in the open for anyone to see. Did they think others might confuse them for fishing vessels? He didn't know what to think. Artie must have something more he forgot to tell him as he drank his coffee and relaxing in one of the many high-backed textured leather chairs.

Secret of Ekaterinburg: The Hour-Glass

Two CIA agents had been killed in the past eight weeks. Somebody had tried to kill him at the CIA main gate, the Potomac boathouse, and then tried it a third time at the hospital. If they were contracted to kill him, he knew his luck couldn't last much longer. The agency had to come up with some answers in a hurry. He knew the guys in the counter-intelligence units had their hands full trying to get the live one to talk. He wasn't convinced they were Arab or that their reasons for the assassination attempt were Middle East in origin.

He thought about it for a minute and decided to pay a visit to the interrogation room, off-limits to field agents, but what the hell. It was challenging enough to involve yourself in undercover work but when you were personally involved, it sometimes got a little too emotional to be present while they were working someone over. The agency needed specialists to take care of the cross-examinations, personnel who weren't involved personally. They could control things better that way. Alex knew the rules. That's the way it had been set up purposely; it's the way the CIA worked best. What the hell could they do, bust-out their best agent?

He walked down the hallway and into the

Secret of Ekaterinburg: The Hour-Glass

main reception area then through a set of double glass doors. He got in his car and drove to the other side of the CIA compound, normally a fifteen-minute walk but he wanted to go directly from there and to the hospital and see Artie again before the meeting with Kasim and the security staff. He could see interrogation building a half-mile away. He hadn't been there for some time and only a few things had changed slightly. Newer parking facilities, a few buildings had been added, and more shrubbery had been placed in the area to dress it up. He could figure out why?

Hidden cameras were placed inside these and on rooftops and he couldn't resist the urge to wave to one of them. Not only were they constantly monitored by live security personnel but continuous tapes were made so they could be reviewed if necessary. Once inside, he asked to see the agent in charge. Wearing his identification badge, Sarah not only knew immediately that he was Company, but more importantly, she also recognized Alex by sight. There weren't many at the agency who didn't know him. Alex had been at the CIA for more than 30 years and his record and reputation read like a spy-novel. Everyone liked him, and the women; well, they would have all been

Secret of Ekaterinburg: The Hour-Glass

eager to crawl into bed if he wanted. There were a lot more men around at the Company than women so they could have their pick of the lot. They all knew Alex was off limits, however, but who knows, maybe on a bad day, he just might go after it. The female agents knew it would be strictly a longshot. His wife was a real looker, and Alex was a hopeless romantic. He didn't give a damn about extra-marital affairs. He just cared about getting the job done.

"Excuse me, Sarah, who's in charge this morning?" Alex asked glimpsing his watch.

"Hi, Alex. Brian Adams is. He's in his office. Down the hall, first room to the right."

"Thanks," he said and parted company quickly not stopping to talk.

"You guys keep changing these rooms. I know, I know, for security reasons. You can flip the safety on your weapon back on now, Sarah."

Sarah, a receptionist, but not really a receptionist, was a trained killer. She laughed. Alex knew the system all right. Hell, he helped design it. Whenever the public came into contact with the system, they hardly realized they were not dealing with ordinary secretaries or receptionists, they were dealing with live,

Secret of Ekaterinburg: The Hour-Glass

honest-to-God undercover agents who worked full-time for the CIA complete with weapons at their disposal in case of trouble.

It had been that way since a couple of agents had been gunned down outside the CIA grounds in a park-like area five years earlier. That wasn't going to happen again he thought as he walked down the brightly lit corridor entering the first room. Inside, another woman agent stood and met him before he reached her desk.

"Is Brian busy? I'd like to see him?"

"Wait a minute, Alex, I'll see,," she picked up the telephone and pressed a button. "Brian. Alex Ayers is here. You busy? O.K. I'll send him back."

He winked at her and walked through the electronic doorway which would have detected his weapon but she had quickly neutralized it with a switch beneath her desk. No false alarms this time.

"Hi Brian," Alex greeted him.

The two shook hands and sat down at his desk.

"Look, the reason I'm here and I usually don't interfere with your interrogations, but this is something you know I'm personally interested in because that bastard Vladimir

Secret of Ekaterinburg: The Hour-Glass

almost killed Artie and me. I can't tell you what I'm working on, but you're supposed to feed us any information you've got from him. What's the latest?"

Brian sized up Alex quickly and knew he wanted something but he didn't know what particular piece of information he was looking for.

"There's not much so far. We've run through the whole sequence twice. He's tough and he's good. He's not Russian. He's Arab."

"Arab," Alex replied to that bit of information.

"Yeah, but his name is Russian, at least that's the name he's using. The Arabs do that a lot. They've been trained in Russia for five years before they're sent out on assignment. He's a real cool type. He can do many things that most agents can't including speak seven different languages, depending on his assignment. His English is flawless and very convincing. Hell, it even fooled me, and I'm an expert on dialects."

"What else did you find out?"

"Not much, except he denies the fact that he's FSS. We know better, because we've already showed him his own file, but he keeps denying it. He says it's not him . . . that he's

Secret of Ekaterinburg: The Hour-Glass

more handsome than the man in the file photo. Can you believe that? He's a tough bastard all right."

"Is there a chance I can see him?"

"Alex, you know the rules. I really can't let you."

"Yeah, I know the rules all right. I helped write them. But, this case is different. Just let me have a talk with him for five minutes. Maybe I can get something out of him you guys haven't already."

"Please, Alex, my ass will be on the line if I get caught," the agent begged-off.

"Look, I'll take full responsibility for it. You know I mean it if I say so. Hell, I've been around here too long to double-cross anyone."

Brian thought it over for a few seconds and knew he'd cave in. Hell, if you can't trust an agent like Alex, who in the fuck could you trust. Even if this was a test of some kind, hell it was worth the risk just to have Alex owing you a favor. With his pull, he could get just about anything done at the CIA; he might even get a career enhanced.

"O.K. But, if anybody asks, you weren't inside the interrogation room. Just the observation room." Alex agreed quickly.

They entered the room catching the two

Secret of Ekaterinburg: The Hour-Glass

other agents inside questioning the prisoner by surprise. The captive looked tired, unshaven and dirty. But, otherwise, it looked as though they hadn't roughed him up too badly. They had followed the new rules. Alex remembered the old rules and what a lot of agents did to a guy if one of their own guys got killed. Sometimes they beat the prisoner into unconsciousness. He hadn't personally seen it done or taken part in it but he had heard about it. Things like that could happen when thousands of lives were at stake. Especially, if an enemy agent held the secret to whether those innocent lives would be lost. There wasn't much they didn't try to do and pry the information out. And, one time they overdid it, and killed the prisoner. It was an unusual occurrence, but it could happen. It was an ugly business where something occasionally went wrong. He didn't relish being part of that aspect, but he lived with it, because in the end, it made the country safer, and it was part of his job to make sure the country was protected at any cost. The liberals in congress would bitch-and-moan whenever they heard of something like that but when the chips were down and lives were on the line and when they had to start sending their own sons and daughters to

Secret of Ekaterinburg: The Hour-Glass

faraway places to fight and die, suddenly it wasn't dirty work anymore, but a patriotic gesture. The simple remaining fact was that good intelligence, however, brutal on the face of it, saved countless lives. And, good intelligence might save their own kids skin on any given day. The stakes could get very high, very quickly on a personal level. They all knew that deep inside. Hell, the whole damned espionage business was dirty, tough and unreliable at times. And, it didn't matter which country you were working for. All intelligence agencies operated the same way. Information was valuable and it had to be obtained. Sometimes the price was higher than you wanted to pay for it, but you eventually paid it if you thought it was important enough.

Alex motioned for the other agents to leave the room. Brian nodded his approval and they left.

"What's the chance you could leave me alone with guy? Just for a few moments?"

"Jesus H. Christ, Alex. It's one thing to let you in here, but now you're asking me to leave you alone with him. What the fuck are you going to do, ask him to dance? Christ, I'm already bending the rules."

"Look. I'll never ask you for this favor

Secret of Ekaterinburg: The Hour-Glass

again. Maybe, someday I can do something for you."

Now, there was an offer he couldn't refuse, Brian thought.

"O.K. But, God-damn-it, I just might hold you to that."

"Agreed. I owe you one."

"Five minutes. No more."

"Ten."

"O.K. Don't push it. When you're through come into the outer office."

"Right."

Brian breathed a sigh and left the room closing the door behind him with it locking automatically.

The prisoner had kept his head down the whole time not wanting to look at Alex, but he pursed his lips. He knew who he was. Hell, he had tried to kill him twice.

"Well. Vladimir you tired old bastard. You look like shit. Why hasn't anybody killed you, yet?"

The remark caught him by surprise because Alex knew his real name not just his covert name. He raised his head but showed only a little emotion.

"There's something I want. And, you have it. It's that simple, Vladimir. That something is

Secret of Ekaterinburg: The Hour-Glass

the reason you were sent here to kill me?"

"Nyet. No one sent me here to kill you. If they had you would be dead by now."

"Perhaps, but even experts miss occasionally."

"I have heard of you. I have seen pictures of you. And, I have heard of your many accomplishments, but I have never met you until now. Alex Ayers. Married, two children, both college educated. Very nice intimate American family."

"Very good, Vladimir. But, if you don't give me what I want, I'm going to kill you in spite of what I have just told the other man. He's a nice young, man, but he's not a skilled killer like I am. You know me. You know I'm telling the truth. You have read and learned all about me. And, you know what I have done in this area. Am I right?"

Vladimir, the experienced KGB agent, knew he was talking to Alex the experienced CIA agent.

"Don't even attempt to cry out. If you do, I'll kill you before the scream leaves your throat. It makes no difference to me, it will just take me a little longer to get the information I need, but I will still get it. I always do," he told him and reached inside his jacket and pulled

Secret of Ekaterinburg: The Hour-Glass

out the Beretta from his shoulder holster.

"Right now, I've decided to take early retirement. One more dead KGB agent won't make much difference in my pension benefit. You know, it's just like yours, only maybe mine's worth something because it's paid to me in American dollars, not rubles."

Alex gathered his thoughts for a second while studying the man. What would it take to crack him quickly. He knew the answer before the thought left him.

"Why don't you come over and work for us. You've been working for those communist bastards for too long, anyhow. What kind of life have they given you?"

Vladimir flashed a crafty smile that let Alex know he knew what he was up to. Alex was smooth. Especially when brandishing a 9mm. There was something about a gun in his hand that made him speak more succinctly. It cleared his head and it was a confidence builder. At any rate, it enabled him to articulate much clearer.

"What if I did make a deal and came to work for the American CIA," Vladimir blurted. "Would the protection and new identity hold up?"

"As long as you wanted it to."

Secret of Ekaterinburg: The Hour-Glass

"And, if I refuse?"

"Well, you'll be poorer all the way around, Vladimir. No money and no life."

"Either I or one of our guys will kill you in the end if you don't help us. Better help us now and live for a long time. We know we could never fully trust you but we would trust you enough to give you a comfortable life here in the United States. Say, $70,000 American dollars a year. You have no family. You could live pretty nicely on that. Let's face it you've paid your dues for the communists. Their era is coming to an end."

Vladimir knew Alex was right. He was almost 40 and had nothing to show for it but the ideological satisfaction of seeing a Soviet system crumble before his very own eyes.

"Vladimir, everyone is afraid of everyone else. It took Russia longer to collapse because everyone was propping up everyone else to keep the system going."

"Put your gun away, Mr. American CIA agent. Your points are well taken," Vladimir repeated and shrugged his shoulders with ambivalence. "Of course you are right. The American point-of-view is always right."

He had caved in sooner than Alex thought he would because no one had made Vladimir

Secret of Ekaterinburg: The Hour-Glass

an offer like that. He didn't even have to cock his weapon.

"It's not much of a life back there anyway. It's better here. It will take another 20 years for us to catch up to you economically. But, if the communists get back in power it will take us a hundred."

Alex relaxed and put his gun back in his shoulder holster. The two shook hands.

"They tell me you are a pretty tough character," Alex complimented him. "I already knew that before they did. And, I knew they wouldn't break you. Unless, of course, it was in your best interests. Believe me, Vladimir, this is in your best interests."

Vladimir nodded in a sigh of relief. It had been a long, drawn-out career, going all the way back as a volunteer in the Russian youth camps. That's the way all dictatorships hooked them. Brainwash them while they were young. But, it had to end sooner or later. Better this way than some other way. At least there was a future now.

"Vladimir, I need to know exactly what is going on? What the hell are you guys doing with all those ships?"

"Gold, Alex. Gold. Straight from your Fort Knox."

Secret of Ekaterinburg: The Hour-Glass

"What the hell are you talking about?"

"You're going to give us gold. Four thousand metric tons of it? And, it's going to be shipped from Alaska to Kamchatka Peninsula using Russian naval vessels."

"For what reason, Vladimir? For what reason would we give you that much gold?"

"For missiles, Alex. RDS-7, 500 kiloton nuclear bombs and SS-18 Satan missiles."

"God, are you serious."

"Not only am I serious but your Mr. Kasim knows all about them. And, your president and our president know it, too. They approved it. But, unfortunately the communists know about it, too. That's why they are trying to regain power. They want to stop it."

"If what you say is true, of what value is it to them that they stop the shipments. It would still make everyone safer, even the communists. The missiles would be dismantled and the warheads converted into harmless uranium by-products."

"Yes, you're right about all that, except for one thing, Mr. Ayers. All the missiles aren't going to your country for dismantling. A few hundred are being sent to . . . a country called . . . you know it well . . . Iran."

"What?"

Secret of Ekaterinburg: The Hour-Glass

"That is quite correct, my friend. They will be shipped to Iran with the full knowledge of your American government. And, if you don't believe me, why don't you ask your Mr. Kasim when you meet with him again?"

"Lenin would be rolling over in his grave if he could hear this," Alex mused out loud. "Vladimir, why in the hell would we be sending nuclear missiles to Iran, a sworn enemy for God's sake?"

"It is an attempt to balance the power in the middle east region and besides it makes things a little more equal for everyone's safety, Israel's included."

"That doesn't make any sense?" Alex retorted.

"Well, even though we came close to nuclear war between our two countries over Cuba, in the end it seemed to keep us from going to war for more than 40 years, didn't it? And, now the wisdom of such a policy can be seen. Am I correct?"

Alex knew damned-well that he was although he hated to admit it.

"Uh . . . it's one thing though for two countries like ourselves to monitor the nuclear situation but in the hands of the middle east, I'm not so sure it can be made fool-proof."

Secret of Ekaterinburg: The Hour-Glass

"Oh, there is something else, which will finish the deal."

"What is it?"

"That I cannot tell you because you will never believe me. But, I will give you a clue and your CIA director will have to tell you the rest."

"What is this clue, Vladimir?"

"She lives."

"Who lives?" Alex responded with a reflex question.

"She lives. That is all I will tell you. Believe me, you have already got your $70,000 worth. The rest your director Kasim will brief you on. But, it's worth more than I already have told you and if you think this bit of information has astounded you, what he will tell you will stun you even more."

His ten minutes were up. Alex, nodded to him, shook hands and left the room. In the outer office, he told Brian he had got what he had come for and that they could treat him as a converted Russian agent."

"Are you shitting me?" Brian said sharply.

"How in the hell did you do that?"

"Oh, just a few tricks you guys hadn't thought of. You know, we analyst-agents may not be as physically tough, but mentally, Christ, we've outdistanced your intellect many times over."

"What's the deal?"

"He's made a deal with us. Don't worry, I'll sign for everything. Put him on cooperative status and upgrade the security arrangements we use to quarter him. We'll start an indoctrination program immediately. He's a tough one all right. Never underestimate him."

Brian would have loved to have been inside that room, but whatever Vladimir told Alex would never be known until much later. Maybe, someday he would become like Alex, a well-experienced field agent, an analyst who was the best and the brightest in the spy business.

He watched Alex leave the building and walk to his car to begin his drive to Johns Hopkins.

Secret of Ekaterinburg: The Hour-Glass

CHAPTER 40

CIA Headquarters, Nov. 20, 1989

The CIA director stood up and walked over to her without any formality . . .

"Everything is ready for you. Will you be able to do it, Ana?"

She looked at him without a shred of anxiety. Over the years she had got used to men like him holding important positions always telling her what to do. She regarded them all with a bit of discernible disdain; certainly, she was not afraid of them. She reserved that emotion for her creator. At the same time she knew that only because of them was she still alive.

"If I am not able to do it then who can?" she answered smoothing the light, blue, silk dress she was wearing.

Ana, now at eighty-eight had lived a remarkable life and was still a remarkable woman despite a remarkable past. Anyone who knew her would have known that. But, they had all thought she was dead for more than four

Secret of Ekaterinburg: The Hour-Glass

generations. Now, this long journey which had brought her to the United States was nearly at an end. She had lived for more than 50 years in exile in America under the protection of the CIA and the National Security Agency and only a handful, only a few chosen presidents who were able to keep a secret, knew of her existence. It had to be that way because the Soviets had spies everywhere in Washington and in the surrounding Virginia outskirts. To even suggest or give a hint that one of the original Romanov's had survived the murders would have brought about a massive manhunt by the KGB inside the U.S. in an attempt to kill her. Ana was protected because in 1949 deep inside the American CIA someone knew this day would come and the Soviet system would collapse. The only question was would Ana still be alive when it did?

"Your presence in the United States has been an honor for me. I hope you realize that," CIA Director Kasim told her. "I have only one regret after all these years."

"And, what regret is that, Mr. Kasim."

"It's that the American people never knew you existed."

"Well, it is much too late for that. But, I pray the Russian people will appreciate and

Secret of Ekaterinburg: The Hour-Glass

accept me. I speak their language, you know," she said satirically. Her humor did not go unappreciated by Kasim and he viewed it as a good omen. At eighty-eight, she was still quick and sure of mind.

"Believe me, Ana, once they know you are alive they will revere you as no other Romanov."

"We shall see. We shall see," she said continuing to smooth her silk dress with her legs crossed at the ankles in a royal-like pose. "They revered my father once. But, in the end, they murdered him."

The two were interrupted by Alex as he barged into the director's office.

"Ben, you asked to see me right away?"

"Yes. It's rather important, and by the way you don't know anything about this meeting, right?"

Alex knew the drill.

"Right, sir."

"Alex, I'd like you to meet someone," the director said positioning himself between Anastasia and Alex.

Alex studied her features carefully. Dark hair. Medium-boned. The woman's hair was silver and piled up high into a bun at the back of her head. She was wearing a pearl necklace

Secret of Ekaterinburg: The Hour-Glass

with a simple high collar dress. Nothing fancy, in fact, rather simplistic but elegant. Well put, together he thought. A woman of breeding and character. But, her lined and hollowed face had a familiarity to it that bothered him, still he couldn't quite recognize her.

"Not off-hand, if you'll pardon my being direct, sir . . . ma'am," Alex graciously extended his hand in a return gesture to hers.

"Alex, look carefully and think. The name Romanov. What does it mean?"

"Romanov . . . it's Russian. Very Russian."

"And, this lady is very Russian, too," the director continued. "Think back. What does the name Anastasia mean to you?"

Alex immediately remembered the Czarist family members who were murdered at the hands of the communists in 1918. He was a student of history, but anyone with a knowledge of contemporary world history would know the answer. Then, a sudden, foreboding remembrance hit him. She looked like . . . could it be . . . impossible?

"My God. Could it possibly be? Are you a Romanov? One of the immediate family. It can't. It's impossible, isn't it?" Alex said stumbling his way through the introduction.

"Not only is she a Romanov, but she is **THE**

Secret of Ekaterinburg: The Hour-Glass

Romanov. . . Anastasia Nicholaevna Romanov," the director instructed.

Anastasia interrupted.

"It is quite true. But, do not be so shocked. No one besides, Mr. Kasim, your president, yourself and a handful of others in Russia know that I am still alive and no one has known that for more than 70 years."

Words failed Alex. The pronouncement was having the predictable effect on him.

"Holy! Pardon me, ma'am. I mean, you are supposed to be dead. In fact, you're supposed to have been dead for 77 years."

"Yes, the communist government tried to make sure of that when they sent a contingent of men to murder my entire family that night. I am fortunate to be alive. Mr. Kasim will explain to you how I managed to do that and how I came to be living in the United States."

"Living in the United States?" Alex shot back. "But, where? How?"

The director interceded in Anastasia's behalf. Now was not the time to discuss the minute details of the past, because they had another job to do with utmost speed.

"Alex, I'll fill you in later. Only a handful of people know of her existence. The two agents who were killed, the president, and

Secret of Ekaterinburg: The Hour-Glass

myself. We are the only ones who knew through four generations. They were trying to stop what we are about to do. The assassins were sent by communist elements inside the old KGB in an attempt to stop an important announcement that we're going to make very soon. They want to murder Anastasia. The attempt on your life was a mistake by them. They thought both you and Artie knew about her."

"Excuse me, Ben. They failed to kill her the first time so they are trying again? Why? What importance is Anastasia to them now? What announcement are you talking about?" Alex rapid-fired at Kasim.

"The plan to restore Anastasia to the Royal Throne of Russia," he told Alex.

When he said that, Alex's mouth gaped open and he froze in disbelief.

"Someone inside Russia wants to stop it from happening."

"Jesus," Alex added. "It's like changing history."

"It is changing history. There's a lot more to know. Her personal story is utterly amazing. She's got a lot to tell people, a story that could read like a novel. A lot more than you or anyone could possibly know, Alex. Her secrets

Secret of Ekaterinburg: The Hour-Glass

will unlock the mystery of that tragic night and more things that have happened and why they have happened since. You and Artie managed to figure out a few things on your own but you didn't have enough time to guess the part which involved her. It was a case of you knowing more than we wanted you to know, but we couldn't tell you just yet."

"Do you mean the satellite photos?"

"Yes, and there's more."

"I'll explain the details to you at a special meeting we'll be holding tomorrow without Anastasia's presence. It'll take some convincing the committee that's why you're here. I want you to prepare everything for the meeting – the history of Anastasia's background, point-of-view, etc. . . . everything we'll need to get this thing done. The President has signed off on the plan along with his Russian counterpart. It's top secret on both ends and the fewer people who know about it including the press for the time being, the better off we'll be from a security standpoint when we deliver her."

"God, this is going to blow the lid off the free world."

"How do you like perestroika now, Alex?"

"I knew Gorbachev was on the right track, but this?"

Secret of Ekaterinburg: The Hour-Glass

"But even he didn't know the secret. So, we're going to announce it for maximum emotional output for the Russian people. We're working together or this you know, together."

Alex leaned back in his chair, then stood up to catch his breath.

"I'll get right on it, sir. I'll take care of all the details - everything."

"I know you will, Alex. We'll see you tomorrow at the meeting. Nine o'clock sharp."

"Right. Your majesty, it has been a pleasure meeting you. I sincerely hope we meet again, very soon."

"Oh, you will, Alex. You see, you'll be the one escorting her back to Russia."

Alex's mouth gaped again. He hardly knew how to approach her. Should he kiss her hand. Should he bow. Shake hands. He felt awkward. He hadn't felt that way for a long time. Only one other time, when he first met his wife.

Alex walked to the doorway.

"Sir. You don't happen to have any Excedrin in your desk, do you. It seems I've come up with a slight headache."

Director Kasim looked at Anastasia, laughed and shook his head.

"Without a doubt, Alex. It's the same kind of headache I got when I first learned of her

Secret of Ekaterinburg: The Hour-Glass

existence," he said and reached inside his desk and tossed Alex the bottle of capsules.

Alex caught it on the fly.

"Take four. Two won't work," Kasim grinned.

Secret of Ekaterinburg: The Hour-Glass

CHAPTER 41

Johns Hopkins Hospital, Baltimore, Nov. 20, 1989

Alex pressed the accelerator to the floor and watched the speedometer inch its way toward 85 as he sped down the freeway from Langley then onto the beltway and finally onto Interstate 95 which would take him to Johns Hopkins.

Traffic was unusually heavy. But, he managed to maneuver his way through the six lanes approaching the city from the north. He quickly branched-off northward toward Baltimore's maze of streets. He flicked on the radio and tuned to the news.

Nothing much happening there he thought and pressed the search button. The stations clicked-by every three seconds until he caught WVAB giving headline news.

It was a twenty-minute drive to the hospital and he had to see Artie once more before the 2 o'clock meeting called by Director Kasim. Christ, he thought, there must be something else Artie didn't tell him. Something he must

Secret of Ekaterinburg: The Hour-Glass

know but was hesitant to tell. Maybe, it wasn't a hard fact, but something - maybe a hunch - connected to what Vladimir had told him in interrogation.

Great God, missiles from the Russians sent to the United States then redirected to Iran.

What the hell was going on?

Did the President understand what he was doing?

What in-the-hell could be the reason he would trade for that?

He needed answers fast and he had to verify who in-the-hell inside the CIA was lying and why they were covering this up.

There had been rumors for a long time that the communist-KGB had a mole deep inside the CIA at the highest levels. Now, what everyone needed to know was if the same KGB mole was still in place now working for the new FSS. But, everyone had been thoroughly checked out by FBI, internal security, defense intelligence teams, even the IRS. It just didn't make any sense to him. We had been at odds with Iran for too many years now to do them any favors and things weren't changing for the better. In fact, they were much worse.

"What in the hell is it?" Alex said out loud to himself. "Why would it be in the best

Secret of Ekaterinburg: The Hour-Glass

interests of the United States to suddenly turn over two hundred missiles to Iran especially when things were heating up in the middle east again?"

He had to think about it some more. It was probably something simple but not obvious if you didn't understand what was going on over there. He hadn't a clue yet as to what he was missing. He had to come up with it. That's what he was good at. That's what the CIA paid him to do. And, that's why he was still there.

Alex was almost at the hospital now. He downshifted the Reatta into third, then second as he approached the off-ramp, and slowed to about 35 mph, turning left onto Orleans Street. A few more hundred yards, he thought, and he would be there. Take your time, he contemplated, it's early and he still had plenty of time to get back for the meeting.

He turned the Reatta into the familiar parking lot, took the ticket from the attendant, and drove toward the front entrance so he could be in close. Vandals could do a number on a car if he parked out too far. Spray paint was hard to remove. They roamed even that section of Baltimore in broad daylight performing their random acts. He got out of the car and entered the building, up the elevator, past the security

Secret of Ekaterinburg: The Hour-Glass

guards and to the fifth floor where Artie was.

There was a new head nurse, but Alex had met her before and knew she was legitimate. He flashed his CIA identification to the guards at the desk who waved him quickly through upon recognizing him.

He entered Artie's room. He was awake, the blinds were open, and the sunlight was diffusing into the room. Artie looked good. Real good.

"Boy, you are a sight for sore eyes," Alex began. "How're you feeling? Sorry, if I've been a little remiss on visiting but you wouldn't believe what is happening back at the Company?"

"Oh, I'd believe it, if you'd tell me but I know better," Artie replied while propping himself up to talk.

"So are you allowed to walk around. You look too damned good to be still laid up."

"Yeah, they let me walk around the hallways now. My shoulder still hurts a lot, though. And, my side, where the other slugs went through. They want me to begin physical therapy tomorrow, for the shoulder. It's a bitch, the human body. It's wonderful at the same time but when it isn't working right, it's a real son-of-a-bitch."

Secret of Ekaterinburg: The Hour-Glass

"Yeah, tell me. I've never been shot, but it's this damned age creeping up on me that's starting to cause me problems. Hell, I don't need to get shot to feel the pain."

Artie chuckled.

"Look, I came all the way over here for a really good reason, not that I didn't want to see you anyhow . . . but . . . "

"I know, I know.. . it's God-damned business, right? You want to pick my brains again."

"Whatever's left," Alex remarked.

"O.K. Pour me some coffee and have some yourself. It's free. It comes with the Medicare. They give you all you want. Compliments of Johns Hopkins."

Alex poured two cups and handed one to Artie.

"Usually, I don't talk about the internal parts of my assignments to guys the likes of you but I'm going to have to tell you something I want you to keep secret, until death do we part. Understand?" Alex winked.

"Understand," Artie raised his good arm and feigned an oath-like gesture.

"O.K. Here it is. You won't believe this but the U.S. government is going to supply missiles

Secret of Ekaterinburg: The Hour-Glass

from Russia to Iran. Two fucking hundred of them."

"What!!? Are they fucking crazy?"

"Yeah, that's right. They're fucking nuts all right. That was my reaction was too."

"They can't be serious, can they?"

"They're dead serious. The president's already made the decision with Kasim and the timeline has already been set."

"How are they going to deliver them?"

"You already know that, Artie."

"I do?"

"Take a wild guess?"

Artie thought for a second, then quickly countered.

"The satellite photos?"

"Yep."

"Jesus Christ. So, that's what they're for. Two hundred ships carrying the cargo. Boy, that's a big job, almost certain to be noticed by someone."

"That's just it. That someone would have been us during a cold war situation but since we have agreed to it who in the hell else is going to care?"

"Yeah, who else?"

"I'll get to that in a moment. But, there's something else you need to know. In exchange

Secret of Ekaterinburg: The Hour-Glass

for this, the U.S. is paying the Russians some 60 billion dollars for the missiles and nuclear warheads."

"Why don't they just simply destroy them and neutralize the threat? Everyone wins that way."

"That's what I was thinking, everyone wins except one of the key players in the middle east."

"Who's that?" Artie asked knowing that Alex would have the correct answer.

"Israel."

"Israel," Artie intoned. "Yeah. You hit it right on the head. Israel. Would they stand for that?"

"Are you serious. Would any country worth its salt stand for that?"

"Do you think the Israelis know?"

"If they don't, it won't take `em long, once they see the cabinet being assembled in the war room. We're going to announce this to the world in only a week. Only we aren't going to tell everyone about the missile part of it."

"Which part am I missing? Which other part are we going to tell the world?" Artie wanted to know.

Alex hesitated a moment and readied his thoughts so he could make Artie believe it as

Secret of Ekaterinburg: The Hour-Glass

fact the first time he said it. There was no short concise way to explain all of it, so he just came straight out with it.

"Anastasia Romanov, daughter of Czar Nicholas II, is alive . . . and well . . . at the age of 88 . . . and she's been living right here in Baltimore, right under our very noses for the past 45 years. The United States and Russian presidents are going to announce her existence and then they're going to re-store the "Holy Throne" of Russia back to its people."

Artie's head snapped back and he stared at Alex in disbelief.

"That's one helluva piece of information, Alex. Do you want me to make an appointment for you with your psychiatrist? Christ, I knew the pressure was getting intense over there for you guys to produce, but this . . . this isn't reality, is it, Alex? I mean, the Romanov's were executed by the Bolshevik's, let's see now, some 70 years ago? How in the hell could that be true? And, if it is, how in the hell did this person you call, Anastasia, escape?"

"It's true, Artie," Alex said giving him the most serious look he could muster. You can bet she'll be explaining that to the entire world, soon. They'll have her on every fucking talk show over here and over there and they'll all be

Secret of Ekaterinburg: The Hour-Glass

so damned distracted by her that they'll miss what is really going on?"

"Now, that's one helluva diversion, huh?" Artie said in wonderment of what Alex had just told him.

"Who in the hell came up with this fucking scenario anyway?"

"Well, it's not a scenario anymore. It's true. Right down to the fact that only a month ago, the CIA informed the President for the first time that Anastasia had survived after all these years. I didn't think he'd turn it into a scheme to re-balance the power in the middle east for his own posterity. But, he did, God-damn-it. You know, every fucking president I ever knew has his own personal, political agenda."

"Yeah, but isn't the real agenda supposed to be the security of the United States?" Artie chimed in.

"Yeah, that's what they say. I mean, that's why I go to work every morning and that's the reason the boys show up at NORAD every day, isn't it?" Alex intoned, his ilk higher.

He got up from the edge of Artie's bed and walked over to the windows. God, it was a beautiful day. Nothing like living near the ocean. He could see out To Fells Point into the Chesapeake about two miles away.

Secret of Ekaterinburg: The Hour-Glass

"Artie. Ever do any fishing? Any serious fishing?"

"Yeah, but what's that got to do with this?"

"Well, I need you to go fishing for me. I'm missing something terribly important in all of this. There must be something else that I'm just not seeing. I've got to leave now, but keep thinking about it for me. And, if you come up with anything give me a call. Pronto."

"You mean something I might have seen in the photographs?"

"Possibly or something we just haven't thought of."

Artie looked at Alex like he was asking him the impossible. Christ, he wasn't the intelligence analyst. Alex was.

"I haven't the foggiest notion of what you're getting at, but I'll give it a try. I'll probably have to sleep on it, though."

"Thanks, Art. Don't sleep too long. Look, I've got to attend a special 2 o'clock back at the agency. You don't think you could come with it by then, do you?" he left with a big grin. "I'll see you later. Give my best to Pat and the kids."

"Yeah, I'll tell `em," Artie said propping his head up on the pillow. "I'm sure I'll come up with it by then."

He leaned back and closed his eyes feigning

Secret of Ekaterinburg: The Hour-Glass

sleep.

Alex was out into the hall past the nurses and into the elevator with cat-like efficiency. He knew his way around the hospital pretty well by now having visited wounded agents before.

When he got to the car, he drove off thinking about what they had just discussed.

He knew the truth couldn't elude him forever. But, in the meantime, he had to pay that price with patience and worry.

Missiles for Iran.

Christ! The thought of it scared the hell out of him!

Secret of Ekaterinburg: The Hour-Glass

CHAPTER 42

Baltimore, April 21, 1950

Sergei swept Ana up into his arms and kissed her. They could now be together for a week of uninterrupted togetherness. Sergei had obtained permission from the Kremlin to stay in the United States on official business at the Soviet Embassy and visit with friends in the Maryland countryside.

What the KGB didn't know was that Sergei would spend it not with friends but with Ana through a cleverly concocted story set up through the agency and the FBI.

"Sergei, Sergei, put me down, you are making me lose my breath," she teased him.

Sergei was carrying her around the small apartment like a new bride.

"You are my bride even though we are not yet married," he twirled her around.

"Sergei. Put me down! I swear I'm going to faint!"

Sergei gently let her feet touch the carpet and held her for a moment until she regained

Secret of Ekaterinburg: The Hour-Glass

her balance not letting her go just easing the pressure on her waist.

He kissed her again this time harder. She returned the kisses with a feminine ardor which meant only one thing. She was ready to make love. And, Sergei did not mistake it for playful affection. He picked her up again, this time more urgently and carried her to a nearby bed and laid her upon it.

He unfastened his trousers kicking off his shoes while Ana reached up and unbuttoned his shirt helping him slip it off.

Then, she started to unbutton her blouse while he removed her skirt to reveal her long, slender legs. She pulled away her blouse and flung it off to the side of the bed. Her breathing increased as he bent down to kiss her neck and reached up to caress her inner thigh. Her breath caught in her throat and quickened biting her lip as his fingers tugged at her undergarment pulling it loose.

She was wet with desire and she spread her legs so that he could caress her where she desired. He kissed her on the lips then moved to her neck then gently to her breasts. He reached around her back with one hand unhooking her bra, pulling it from her in one smooth and quick motion. She was now in a

Secret of Ekaterinburg: The Hour-Glass

full state of arousal, her nipples taught with desire. His mouth was on them at once for he could no longer control himself. There would be no stopping now for either of them. After what seemed like an eternity they were about to make love and they could devote themselves to each other if only for this night and the remainder of the week. If that was all life offered them, they would be fools not to take these moments alone.

"Oh, Sergei. Please . . . harder . . . now . . . " she whispered in his ear as he penetrated her deeper over and over again. "Oh, Sergei, I have waited for you so long. You must never leave me."

Sergei whispered that he loved her while not stopping but giving her the pleasure that a man half his age would give to a schoolgirl. Their lovemaking went on for hours before they finally fell asleep late into the afternoon.

Outside the cottage, a solitary guard nonchalantly read a newspaper account of an atomic bomb blast that the Soviets had just detonated.

It was on the front page and it was a startling announcement, one that would change things forever. The successful test would neutralize the nuclear advantage that the United

Secret of Ekaterinburg: The Hour-Glass

States held over the Soviet Union.

Somewhere, someday, the rookie CIA guard, Alex Ayers, knew that nuclear parity would be used as a threat against America and its allies across Europe or elsewhere.

Inside, Ana and Sergei's world was coming together.

Outside, their world was about to fall apart.

Secret of Ekaterinburg: The Hour-Glass

CHAPTER 43

In The Maryland Countryside, A Year Later

Ana trembled as she awakened inside her darkened tiny row house apartment and carefully felt her way to the bathroom. She was not yet used to her surroundings having only moved into the new townhouse a few days earlier when the CIA suddenly decided to change her location outside of inner Baltimore.

It was quite different to be living in the suburbs in a more rural setting. Two years in one place had kept her urban bound and at the mercy of traffic and noise everyday even if she wasn't working. The countryside and its natural surroundings had its advantages and it brought much pleasure to her.

And, now at fifty-one years of age and at her peak of vitality, she still had the fresh look of a strong Russian woman who once had the privilege of luxury with servants meeting her everyday needs including the drawing of her daily bath or the preparation of her breakfast.

Secret of Ekaterinburg: The Hour-Glass

She could still remember the time, at an early age, when all these things were done for her by obedient and faithful attendants who would dress her meticulously. They had even been willing to die for her. Those days were gone forever. She was to meet for only the second time in ten years, the man she was in love with - the man she hadn't seen for most of that interval and for whose romance she longed for.

In secret words he had written her so often, his letters protested about the complexities of their lives. And, when he traveled to the United States as an ambassador, he was able to visit her in secret with the help of the U. S. government.

It was Sergei.

And, it had always been Sergei.

The same Sergei she played hide-and-seek with in the hay loft at the dacha; the same Sergei she had chased in the wheat fields near the Urals; the same Sergei who had kissed and caressed her near the small pond where he had spotted the horse and rider that fateful day which separated them both.

She would meet him again today at a small restaurant near where she lived. They would spend the entire day together. One day every

Secret of Ekaterinburg: The Hour-Glass

few months was all that could be arranged by the American government. A few hours to do with as they pleased in exchange for a wealth of Soviet information that Sergei had managed to furnish the Central Intelligence Agency about the Soviet regime and its plans.

If there was a price for love, Sergei was paying it now. It was his obligation to deliver the information in her behalf. That was the deal he had made for her protection. That was part of the secret pact he had made with the devil, his own personal devil, that enabled them to survive.

Sergei had established himself as a chief diplomat with the Soviet embassy and had now become a trusted, integral part of the Russian politburo.

His days as an air force officer had served him well and he had worked his way up into the hierarchy of the Soviet State Central Committee by showing them his creative forces, his intuitive mind and his original ideas about how Soviet life should be changed.

Better still, he had now worked himself into a position where he could travel to the United States often and visit her.

They had found each other after an exhaustive search initiated by Ana through the

Secret of Ekaterinburg: The Hour-Glass

Central Intelligence Agency. The CIA kept tabs on everyone important in the Soviet Union and Ana "knew" that Sergei would be one of those persons who would become important. Andre would become another important person.

But, she already knew that having read about Andre's achievements and influence in the Soviet Union and what some of his policies could mean.

After an exhausting effort, Sergei's own search for her, performed in secret through family and friends who had known them both, had finally produced the desired result.

She was alive and he knew where she was. The main problem was getting to her. Because security within the party levels was so strict, he had at last resort turned to an old enemy who would give him the clue that would eventually lead him to the Prachek family in Slovakia.

When they first were reunited in 1949, at a small public park in Georgetown, the reunion was charged with excitement and wild embraces. They were long and intense, and the emotional meeting was like the end of a love story.

"Ana," he had called to her a short distance away as she sat waiting for him at a park bench. "Do you recognize me?"

Secret of Ekaterinburg: The Hour-Glass

She leapt to her feet and hugged him until neither could breathe.

"Sergei, my love. Is it really you? It is a miracle."

"No, Ana. You are the miracle. The miracle of Ana. You are alive. Thanks dear God."

During that first reunion, they talked endlessly until late in the afternoon before retiring to her apartment where they would enjoy intimacy.

"It was an evening well-spent," Ana mused aloud as she busied herself and got dressed for her new meeting with Sergei.

Her reflection in the mirror satisfied her. She was still a young woman able to attract any man, especially her Sergei. He would always appeal to her. She wondered if she would forever appeal to him.

"It is written by the Divine Hand," she prayed answering her own question. "It cannot be changed by anyone except God."

Whether or not her prayer was true didn't matter. She believed it and that fact alone gave her a sense of security.

She recalled Sergei's pledge before they had last parted.

"Ana, my soul is yours. My love is forever

Secret of Ekaterinburg: The Hour-Glass

in your heart."

She had replied, "And mine in yours."

Ana finished putting on her makeup, and gently brushed her light brown hair below her shoulders.

She locked the apartment door and signaled to her bodyguard that she was ready for the brief journey to the secret location.

Getting into the unmarked car which looked like the hundreds of others passing-by in the streets, she spoke to no one while she descended the steps.

The bodyguard opened the car door for her and she got into the front seat.

Their presence on the street was unnoticeable except for those neighbors who recognized her. They smiled as she departed with a good morning.

The short drive took them to a small nondescript restaurant located at the edge of one of the many inlets on the Chesapeake Bay near a stretch of untraveled highway. Nobody was in sight except a few fishermen who frequented the place.

As Ana entered the cafe, she immediately spotted Sergei sitting near a window booth, a favorite spot. She had gone inside alone. The CIA had already checked out the facilities

Secret of Ekaterinburg: The Hour-Glass

satisfied that everything was safe for them.

The agency had used this spot before for other rendezvous, but Sergei and Ana were their favorite subjects because in helping them they somehow satisfied that spark of fantasy devoid in their own lives.

"Sergei," Ana spoke and embraced him. "Have you been well? Are you in any danger?"

"No, my love. I am well. And, most importantly, I see you are well, also. I wish we could be together always and not separated by our pasts."

Both sat down near the window and held hands. There were now only a few other patrons inside.

In actuality, the restaurant was owned and operated by the Central Intelligence Agency itself, using it on a regular basis for such meetings and operating the business at a loss.

But, it was one of those necessary expenses where things could be controlled to a preciseness required when such tight security was needed. This was the way things were done in the spy business. They could set up things to look real because, in essence, they became real.

"Sergei, I've got some important news for you," she said leaning over to him at the table

Secret of Ekaterinburg: The Hour-Glass

in a whisper.

His reaction was a moment of gentleness punctuated by a long smooth kiss on her cheek. The gesture made her cry as he reached inside his pocket to daub the tears streaming down her face. She regained her composure and returned the kiss.

They talked in secret for hours before having to part company. The bodyguard interrupted them only after they had finished their meal, completely unnoticed by the few others remaining.

"Be safe, my love. God is always with you and I am always with you," she said as she prepared to leave him.

He leaned over and kissed her on the neck promising to visit her again, soon.

"Next time, we will spend the weekend together. I will plan it well."

Their fingertips reached out one more time then she was into the black car driven to another location before she would be dropped off at her apartment.

It was wonderful to be alive but terrible to remain apart.

Would her life ever be normal? Would there ever be a sense of normalcy?

Even the CIA had no answer for her.

Secret of Ekaterinburg: The Hour-Glass

"What's that ma'am?" the driver said to her.

"Time," she repeated.

"What about it?" he asked.

"Time has a way of making you forget the bad things but at a terrible price."

"What price is that, ma'am?"

"It makes you remember all the promises you must keep."

He could only nod his head in agreement.

He didn't make the rules.

He just carried them out.

Sergei and Ana had made their own rules in this game - and their game was just beginning.

Alone at the restaurant, Sergei sat contemplating his future and looked far out into the Chesapeake.

Ana was already far from his mind.

Something else was now fixated in his thoughts.

Something far more critical.

Something far more important to both their futures.

Something that would become remarkable and regrettable to their beautiful country . . . the USSR.

That something else was the defection by Sergei to the United States of America.

And, more importantly, the defection of his

Secret of Ekaterinburg: The Hour-Glass

soul to the Central Intelligence Agency - the untouchable spy organization of the free world.

Secret of Ekaterinburg: The Hour-Glass

CHAPTER 44

Moscow, Nov. 27, 1989

Ana stood at the podium with the new president of Russia, Solotzin, whose own father, a White Russian, was killed in the 1918 battle with the Red brigades in the fighting near Ekaterinburg to rescue the Czar. He had been on the opposite side. Unlike his father, Solotzin had been a Red Bolshevik, and he had been bitter toward the Czar. He couldn't figure out why his father had joined the White brigade and fought his way toward the Royal Family only to hear they were too late to save them. His father paid for the effort with his life after he was captured by the Reds. Perhaps, that's why he had changed his mind during the brutal execution. Perhaps his father's ghost was in the basement of the Ipatiev House that night that directed him to save Anastasia's life.

The noise of the crowd jolted him back to the present.

"There must be two million citizens jammed into Red Square to witness this today, eh?" he

Secret of Ekaterinburg: The Hour-Glass

exclaimed pointing to them assembled in Red Square. The CIA station chief in Moscow grinned at Solotzin and placed his hand upon the shoulder of Anastasia's.

"It will be spectacular," he whispered to Ana. "Television crews from around the world will bring this event to some two billion people around the globe. They will be watching by satellite in tiny African huts, from rice fields in China and India, from mountain homes in Switzerland and South America, in the Australian outback, the rice paddies of Japan, and in the millions of homes inside the United States."

"Yes, it is an amazing sight, a day I thought I would never live to see," Ana repeated. "We have come a long way, haven't we?"

The CIA chief nodded and waved at the crowd undulating like a gigantic sea-serpent winding in-and-around the avenues and kiosks.

Solotzin and Ana were waiting for the excitement to subside and they delayed approaching the microphones for a good twenty minutes. In a moment, the newly installed president would explain to the Russian people what was about to occur. They had waited patiently for so many years, a little longer would not matter, Solotzin reckoned.

Secret of Ekaterinburg: The Hour-Glass

If only Sergei could be there, too, Ana felt.

There was no hurry. It only meant a little more sand would fall through the hourglass, the same hourglass that Czar Nicholas had philosophized to her as a child.

Not far from that same hourglass; however, across from Red Square in the small apartment the two assassins set up their equipment and gave silent hand signals to each other because of the din of the crowd as they prepared for their final assault upon Ana.

"It will be an easy shot from here," Friedrich said comfortably while he fastened the telescopic sight in place atop the high-powered rifle. The rifle weighed exactly fourteen pounds and was outfitted with a special sling and tripod to steady the aim of the shooter.

"It will not be a problem," Karl agreed.

Friedrich set the AKM M43 rifle atop the small table near the large window overlooking an adjacent balcony. He moved the table approximately three feet back from the window so that no one outside looking up could see the gun barrel.

"Yes. This is a perfect location. The angle is slightly downward and the sun is behind us. Anyone looking toward us will be looking into the afternoon sun. There will be glare for the

Secret of Ekaterinburg: The Hour-Glass

KGB agents on the rooftops. It will be impossible to see except for the muzzle flash. But, I will take care of that now."

Friedrich pulled out a black metallic cylinder from the same suitcase and handed it to Karl.

"It's what we call an eliminator. It will silence the explosion of the rifle at the same time conceal the muzzle flash, plus it will eliminate the infrared signature when I fire the shot. Special FSS agents are on the rooftops with equipment that can trace the origin of any gunshot. But, if they cannot hear or see it and there is no infrared signature, there is nothing to trace, eh?"

Karl nodded in agreement.

In fact, Karl seldom disagreed with Friedrich on anything. Indeed, he was still an apprentice learning the assassin trade and he had much yet to learn. And, there were only a few communist KGB left who could do this job. And, only a few in the old politburo who could order the deed to be carried out. Friedrich was one who would follow such orders.

If they were to succeed in this eleventh-hour attempt to overthrow the present Russian government and put back in place the old

Secret of Ekaterinburg: The Hour-Glass

communist guard, then agents like Karl and Friedrich were the ones to perform this horrible task. In return, they would be given preferences inside the new government as a reward.

Friedrich skillfully calibrated the telescopic sight bringing the crosshairs slightly to the right and into precise alignment with the special laser mechanism mounted beneath the gun barrel. He put on a headset and listened for a special frequency while he made minor micro-click adjustments to the delicate sight.

He smiled when he heard the shrill tone and let his fingers instantly lock the button down on the side of the tiny lock button. The sniper's weapon was now sighted-in and operational. When he squeezed the trigger, a special 7.62mm laser guided bullet would speed to its target instantly destroying its intended victim as long as he kept the red dot precisely on the spot he was aiming to within a quarter-of-an-inch. He had done this many times before in previous assassinations and had not missed. He would not miss this time either. Maximum effective accuracy within was 1000 yards. Anything less improved the odds twofold. The distance to Anastasia atop the Kremlin Wall was a mere 500 yards. With a laser sight and

Secret of Ekaterinburg: The Hour-Glass

laser-guided bullet, it would hardly be a challenge for a skilled marksman such as Friedrich.

After the shot was fired, he would quickly wipe the weapon down, lay it on the floor, and both would quickly leave the apartment.

"I am ready now. Let this travesty begin," he said to his accomplice. "I am tired of waiting. We have been here for two days."

They both stepped out onto the balcony to observe the throngs massing in celebration of today's events.

They focused on the Kremlin Wall where Ana and the premier were waving to their well-wishers. Were all of them below White Russians, now? Or, were some of them still red?

Friedrich and Karl were about to do something that would make Lenin stir in his grave. Nor would Stalin be unmoved.

It was a truly historic moment even for the assassins. They could not help but be amazed at the simple facts before them. Communism had been erased after seventy-two years.

And, the highlight of the day, Anastasia would be announced as heir to the Russian Throne, unoccupied since the reign of Czar Nicholas II. Glimmering in her resplendent

Secret of Ekaterinburg: The Hour-Glass

dress, Anastasia was the shining symbol of life, the birthright of the complete Russian woman, and there she stood before the precipice of history in front of two million of her people who had believed she was dead.

Solotzin moved forward and addressed the crowd. He introduced and explained the appearance of this woman by his side and who she was. The crowd roared their approval upon learning of her identity - that Anastasia had somehow survived the murders at Ekaterinburg and that she had miraculously returned to Russia. The stunning announcement sent shock waves through the crowd, and to the world capitals as television cameras recorded the events live. The emotion was tremendous and instantly, congratulations started pouring into Washington and Moscow and the event was explained by the Russian President. The reaction was so astounding that the Kremlin and White House phone lines were jammed as fast as the news was received worldwide.

And, when the special announcement that the surviving daughter of slain Czar Nicholas II would return to the throne, the people were delirious with wonderment. Anastasia was alive and living proof that miracles were possible.

Secret of Ekaterinburg: The Hour-Glass

Anastasia.

Ana.

The flower woman of Baltimore and Ekaterinburg.

The connection to the Prachek's.

The young farm girl from the Urals.

And, like the third prophecy foretold by the Blessed Mother to three Portuguese children at Fatima, Russia would be reconverted to the church.

So, Anastasia stood waiting alone in the shadow of history as principal to a contemporary miracle for modern Russia. Indeed, she would ascend to the throne representing the official conversion of Russia back to its orthodox roots.

There she was for all to see in grandeur. And, there she was in the crosshairs of Friedrich the assassin.

Karl handed him the laser cartridge.

History and the prophecy were right on schedule.

But, it was a schedule that no one really understood.

Secret of Ekaterinburg: The Hour-Glass

CHAPTER 45

The Kremlin, Moscow, Nov. 29, 1989

Andre walked briskly to Solotzin's office struggling to hold onto the stack of papers left over from an earlier meeting at the Duma Ruling Council.

He entered the first doorway through an electronic security gate and motioned to the secretary to let him pass without setting off the alarm, an elaborate device that would detect whether or not he was caring an excessive amount of metal. They were similar to the anti-terrorist gates at an airport terminal. He stopped just short of a second vestibule door, and waited for another secretary armed with a firearm to motion him forward. The man pressed a button and Andre stepped inside the small enclosure. In a wide sweeping motion, the guard swept the hand-held scanner from the top of Andre's forehead to his feet searching for any hint or trace of bomb materials, plastic explosives or a gun he might be carrying. The device contained an element analyzer more

Secret of Ekaterinburg: The Hour-Glass

powerful than the best bomb-sniffing dogs. The device was technology given to the Russian FSS by the U.S. Secret Service. A green light flashed on after a few seconds signaling the guard that he was clear to pass into the President's Kremlin office.

Andre acknowledged the clearance and stepped through the unlocked door.

"Good morning, Mr. President," Andre uttered in his usual manner. "And, what is so pressing at this hour that cannot wait until a decent lunch can be served to us?"

Solotzin motioned him to be seated and to halt the idle chat.

"You know what this is about. We are ready to start our plan."

Abruptly, Andre assumed a look of self-preservation. He cast his eyes nervously around the room, an ominous response from a man who had served the Russian government for so long. After a sigh of relief and a deep revelation of thought, Andre acknowledged that they were about to put into motion the adventuresome plan they had formulated with Sergei two years earlier. The plan was ready, the military was ready, but would the world be ready?

Ana would be delivered to the Kremlin Wall

Secret of Ekaterinburg: The Hour-Glass

to be installed to the Russian throne. In return, Russian nuclear tipped missiles would be exchanged for her and a king's ransom in American gold deposited in Russia's treasury. The deal was to be financed by the International Monetary Fund, with the U.S. treasury at Fort Knox the sole contributor. In return, for this nuclear exchange and the destruction of most of the old Soviet Union's warheads, which would be shipped by 200 of Russia's specially created fleet of naval vessels from Krazcoff across the Bering Strait to Alaska, then overland from there through Canada, into Washington State, then through the interior of the United States, to their final destination - the Oak Ridge Nuclear Facility in Tennessee. There the warheads would be dismantled, disarmed, rendered harmless, and the nuclear material stored in secret facilities throughout the country. It was a powerful moment in the history of both countries. For, the United States would become the stand-alone supreme nuclear power in the world. It was the security America had sought since its creation nearly 250 years ago, and it was the security that the Czars of Russia had once promised its citizens nearly 75 years ago, and 150 years before that.

Secret of Ekaterinburg: The Hour-Glass

Andre was stopped by Solotzin.

"You are having doubts, my friend?"

"Nyet, my president," Andre answered dutifully. "But, I could not help but wonder what Premier Stalin would be thinking at this moment."

The president chuckled and poured Andre a glass of vodka from a flask near his desk. The two men raised their glasses and drank.

"To the success of a mission that will complete the restoration of Russia, its proud heritage, its re-joining of the league of nations of democracies and to a capitalistic society that every Russian man, woman and child so badly needs."

The Russian president drank the entire glass in one gulp and cleared his throat.

"Now, let us get down, as the Americans say, to the brass tacks. When "our" Anastasia is installed as the rightful religious monarch of the throne of Russia our ships will be already sailing with the deadly materials, Andre?"

"That is quite correct my President. It will take two weeks to complete the deliveries, and it will take the U.S. government more than a year to dismantle and render the warheads useless."

"And, after that?"

Secret of Ekaterinburg: The Hour-Glass

"During the entire episode, the gold will be transferred to our ships via the same ports in Anchorage and into the coffers of the Russian Treasury traveling overland through the interior of our country from Krazcoff. And, of course, all this will be kept a secret, Andre."

"No one from either the Russian or American press will know of the most important trade since the beginning of mankind."

"Yes. It's one I thought would be impossible in our day, Andre. But, thanks to the likes of Brezhnev, Stalin, Beria and Lenin and the countless numbers they murdered during their communist reign, it's the least we can do to make their afterlives in hell even more miserable."

Solotzin sounded a lot like Sergei.

Andre studied him closely; he knew the man quite well. He knew his endurance; he knew the amount of patience he could tolerate; and he knew that Solotzin was capable of extracting the maximum amount of revenge from someone if pressed, especially if he hated him. And, God forbid, if that person was an enemy. The revenge would be even worse. He was that type of man. He was a proud man once dedicated to the ideology of communism but

Secret of Ekaterinburg: The Hour-Glass

that dedication had waned suddenly when as a young soldier in the Red Army he was ordered by a Russian general to kill a protestor at a political rally during the 1968 Prague Spring in Wenceslaus Square. The hapless protestor had gotten in the way of a T-54 Russian tank commander and would not budge. The tank commander ordered Solotzin, the young gunner, to shoot him without a warning shot. It was a direct order and he did it. What the young gunner did not know until years later that the protestor was the very father who had raised Anastasia in Slovakia and had protected her throughout her years of hiding. He had been the one who killed Joseph Prachek. And, Prachek had become the martyr of the Czech people for eternity.

After that, Solotzin vowed he would never kill another human being again and that he would do everything in his power to destroy a communist system that had taught him think this way to think.

Now, Andre and he would re-design the Russian system so that it would offer its citizens an economic security they had never achieved under the Bolsheviks.

And, who was this brave man who had become a household name in the world of

Secret of Ekaterinburg: The Hour-Glass

international politics? Who was this beloved person who had once held a gun on a hero martyr of Czechoslovakia, and who had killed scores of Nazis during the Great War and who had hundreds murdered in the secret purges of Beria's NKVD, and who at one time had even pointed a gun at Andre's father threatening to kill him if he refused to let him take his son from that far away dacha?

He had been an old nemesis, a very old nemesis to Andre. But, he had changed since that time. He was wiser. More disciplined and rededicated to a new cause that could save Russia.

He was Yakov Solotzin Grachev.

Grachev.

The man who would at one time have killed Andre on the same orders from the communist party.

Andre smiled to himself staring into the empty vodka glass resting on the table in front of him.

Grachev stood up and issued a toast to Andre, then whirled around and spontaneously picked up the whiskey glasses and sent them hurtling across the room crashing into a thousand pieces onto the white bricks of the fireplace some fifty feet away.

Secret of Ekaterinburg: The Hour-Glass

"Nas dravia," Grachev yelled. "The communists were fools all these years. We were even bigger fools."

"Final victory to the people," Andre chimed-in.

"This time, the right people," Grachev repeated oath like.

"God-willing," Andre said grasping the right hand of Grachev. "May the Holy Mother always protect Russia."

"And, dear Anastasia, also," Grachev declared, "for she now is the future of the Russian people."

Secret of Ekaterinburg: The Hour-Glass

CHAPTER 46

The Oval Office, Nov. 30, 1989

The President got up from his desk, put down his morning cup of coffee near the table-stand near the huge window overlooking 1600 Pennsylvania Avenue and contemplated the ramifications of what he was doing.

The damned thing didn't make much sense to him, but he had authorized the go-ahead for the covert operation anyway. If anything went wrong, he could trust the CIA to cover his tracks to the "nth" degree. He didn't want the Oval Office directly implicated as far as the press was concerned if things went badly.

That had always been a problem of his - the press-be-damned. The public didn't have a right to know everything that was going on in the world especially when it came to national security. Sometimes, the people really didn't want to know. Most Americans just wanted to live their lives with some degree of certainty, comfort and security. Too bad, the rulers in other parts of the world didn't share the same

Secret of Ekaterinburg: The Hour-Glass

concern or that the press couldn't respect that same degree of responsibility when it came to secrecy when it applied to national security. You just couldn't tell them anything when lives were at stake. It was their job not to keep anything secret.

He looked through the bullet-proof glass and gazed in the direction of the gathering crowd of walkers near the black wrought iron gate that encircled the White House grounds. He forgot himself and waved to them. But, he realized they couldn't see him since the Secret Service had installed holograph glass so that any would-be assassin would never be sure of exactly where the President was at any given particular time. The holograph produced a visual image of the President which looked normal to observers wishing to see inside, but the image wasn't real. What they were actually seeing was a 3-D holograph of the President projected onto a special glass window showing him moving around the Oval Office, a brief apparition to make those outside think they had really seen the President that day.

President Nelson pushed a button and called to Kathryn, "Get me the CIA chief on the phone. Tell him to stand by for a moment or two. I want to make a quick personal call, then

Secret of Ekaterinburg: The Hour-Glass

I'll be right with him."

"Yes, Mr. President," came the instant response.

Ned picked up the special private telephone that would connect him to anyone without having to go through the special scrambler lines set up by counter-intelligence. His phone voice would still be scrambled, but he insisted on having the personal line because it would not be monitored by any of the special intelligence agencies used to monitor calls in and out of the White House.

He dialed 5567, waited a few seconds, heard the familiar gentle electronic click, then pressed 3 and #. The telephone came to life. He listened for the messages, made a mental note of just one and pressed another numerical digit. His last action erased the messages.

As he hung up, his other line rang. He didn't pick up the handset but instead pushed the speaker phone button. He liked talking to the CIA chief in this manner, where he could move about the room to facilitate his thoughts, keeping him slightly in the dark as to who else, if anyone, might be present. The CIA was a paranoid bunch anyway and he liked to keep it that way. Seldom was anyone actually in the Oval Office during these times, but it was a

Secret of Ekaterinburg: The Hour-Glass

habit the former President had developed and it probably did some good. It kept the conversations more secure.

"Well, Ben, you're up to your ass in it now. We just received word from Andre that the operation has begun. They're on their way now," the President told him. "Want to know how many?"

"Well, Christ yes . . . right?" Kasim asked.

"Even better. Seventy-five missile-systems complete with RDS-7 warheads. Some 400 nuclear warheads heading to Alaska as we speak."

"I hate to piss you off, Ned. But, I could have told you that an hour ago."

"Well, why didn't you?"

"Oh, I know you like to get the jump on us guys over here at CIA and you have your own arrangements to get that done through the NSC boys, but sometimes the old fashioned intelligence loop gets it done a lot better than the high falutin electronic way."

Ned and Kasim were old Yale classmates and they liked the gamesmanship they played with each other sometimes inventing grandiose schemes to beat each other to the punch. Their families had political ties going back to the American Revolution. Maybe that wasn't

Secret of Ekaterinburg: The Hour-Glass

saying much but both men were proud of their heritage even though they rarely talked about it. Nonetheless, they were proud of their families' tradition of keeping America secure and free.

"By the way, when are you going to get over here so I can give you a decent intelligence briefing? There are some things you don't even know about in your own agency," the President cajoled.

"I'll take you up on it tomorrow at noon sharp. One more question though, and you won't like it one damned bit. I know your man Andre inside the Kremlin. I've known about him for a few years. Didn't have to be the one to tell you, best friend and all. But, God-damn it Ned, you've got to quit hiding this fucking crap from me. I mean, after all, that's why you appointed me CIA chief in the first place, to keep you informed, not the other way around. Now, how in the hell can I keep you informed, when you're better informed than I am."

Ned countered, "You really are pissed-off."

"Not really. But, look, if the press ever got wind of the fact that the CIA chief isn't always on top of things that would be a scandal in-and-of-itself. What's worse than a CIA chief performing a cover-up? A CIA chief who doesn't know what the fuck to cover up. Now,

Secret of Ekaterinburg: The Hour-Glass

I'm not saying that's what's actually happening, but hell Ned, quit trying to keep me in the dark. For the love of Christ, you may as well call in one of those bastard liberal newspaper editors and put a collar and leash on him. Am I making myself clear on this?"

"Uh. . . yes, Ben, . . . I didn't mean for you to take it personally. . . "

"Personally, has nothing to do with it. I mean whose reputation is it anyway?"

"All right. Calm down. We'll talk about it at lunch tomorrow. I'll meet you at the racquet club in Arlington. It's on my schedule already. Just take it easy . . . Lighten up a little. Look, we've been close friends for too long to let this get out of control. From now on, you'll know everything I know. That's a promise from one family to another."

Kasim knew the President would be true to his word. Whenever he got angry and had to make a point, the President usually listened-up. That's the kind of President he was. He could be trusted when the chips were down.

Kasim knew which ones couldn't.

He ascertained that from the many CIA recordings of conversations he listened to in his spare time. It was useful information. Information he could sink his teeth into and

Secret of Ekaterinburg: The Hour-Glass

make it pay off at a later date.

Kasim hung up the telephone.

The President pressed the off button of his speaker phone, and stood by the window facing the avenue again. The same people were still there waving at him at the wrong window.

It's a good thing the Secret Service had installed the holographic device.

Because, hell, how much white paint could they look at?

Secret of Ekaterinburg: The Hour-Glass

CHAPTER 47

The Oval Office, Dec. 1, 1989

The CIA chief arrived earlier than Ned had expected.

The president hoped that Kasim wasn't still angry about his remarks the day before.

"Where are the missiles now?"

"Well, according to your people they've already been loaded and left Krazcoff at 0400 two days ago, twelve hundred of them to be exact," the president said.

"Good God, Grachev sure moves quickly when he does," the CIA chief retorted.

"Those newly-designed trawler look-alikes used to ferry them across the strait thoroughly fooled everyone," the President quipped. "They are bigger and better than anything we've ever seen before. Plus, they have the ability to secure nuclear warheads without refueling stops and they include a special shielding which prevents spy satellites, including our own, from detecting even infinitesimal traces of radioactivity leaking

Secret of Ekaterinburg: The Hour-Glass

from the warheads. They're virtually untrackable."

"Good thing, Solotzin has his act together, huh? The British and French are going to be surprised when we tell them about this, eh what, Ned?"

"Uh . . . I suppose so, except for one thing, Kase. We aren't telling them . . . at least, not yet."

"Jesus . . . we're not going to tell them anything? How long do you think it'll take to find out. I mean nothing is secret around here . . . two, three months, max, maybe?"

"Yeah, that's the way we figure it. But, by that time, everything will be over with. Except for one thing. The missiles will have to be readied and on-line within thirty days of delivery . . . and when that happens, if they don't already know what happened . . . good, God almighty, they sure as hell will when France's spy satellites fly over Iran for the first time. Can you see the Brits at ICE sitting around chatting, tapped into the Frenchies spy networks on their computers, and all of a sudden every fucking alarm goes off. It'll make Big Ben sound like an alarm clock."

Kasim belted-out a chuckle as he poured himself another cup of coffee.

Secret of Ekaterinburg: The Hour-Glass

"It's a damned good thing the Prime Minister has a good sense of humor. He'll fucking need it."

"Christ who would have thought? Missiles to the United States in exchange for the delivery of Anastasia. Missiles to be deactivated, with several hundred being diverted to Iran in order to change the balance of power in the Middle East for the explicit purpose of getting both sides to negotiate a peace treaty in the middle east now rather than later."

The CIA chief let out the whoosh of air caught in his lungs.

"Damn. You don't have to be a genius to appreciate what impact this will have on world events."

"Let's face it, Kase. If we don't give them the missiles, the Chinese will and anyway we'll have the capability to track them because of special technical precautions we've worked out with the Ruskies and, ready for this part - the warheads are dummies. They don't work. Can you imagine the dirty ones they'd get from the Chinese? Plus, we have the ability to sabotage them if they ever modify them and to decide to launch them. We have a self-destruct mechanism built into the computerized launch

Secret of Ekaterinburg: The Hour-Glass

system. And, if they launch them against Israel or us, **Ka-booom**! They'll nuke themselves into the afterlife with their forty virgins ."

"Wow, if the technology works as advertised it will save the Middle East from a horrible nuclear war and maybe us, too. This way, if necessary, we can render them simply useless at the press of a button from NORAD or from Air Force One.

"Sounds good in theory but what about the Israelis?"

"They've got spies everywhere, so we leaked it to the Mossad early, but not the info I just gave you. Besides, the Israeli Prime Minister needs to know as a safeguard. They'll want to track those radioactive signatures just in case they have to destroy them if for some reason we can't."

"Well, that's it Kase. That covers everything you need to know and all you wanted to know about the middle east. You know, I don't have to tell you to keep it to yourself. If this gets out into the press or leaked to any news agency in Washington, it'll be our political asses and you can start planning your retirement on some offshore island somewhere in the Caribbean."

Kasim grimaced . . . he wasn't being funny . . . but, then he wasn't trying to be. He put on

Secret of Ekaterinburg: The Hour-Glass

a quick smile, anyway.

"Don't worry about me. Worry about your sniveling little aides running around the White House ordering everybody around. With those carping little bastards around you all the time, who needs political enemies. Christ, they'd trade you for a nickel."

"Do you really think so, Kase? After all I appointed most of them to where they are?"

"Yeah, and Caesar appointed everyone, too, and look what happened to him?"

"Point well taken. Let's get to lunch. Kathryn order the limousine. We're going to Blakley's on the Potomac", he said over the intercom.

"Yes sir," came the usual response. "It'll be a few minutes."

"We'll wait at the portico. Tell the secret service we're hungry and I'm buying."

Kasim laughed as they left the Oval Office, hurried past Kathryn out into the hallway where other staffers were hoping to get some time with the President. But, when they saw him with his CIA chief, they immediately began dispersing to other parts of the White House. They knew better than to interrupt him now. It usually meant they were discussing something important and it would be none of their

Secret of Ekaterinburg: The Hour-Glass

business.

Adrienne, a White House staff reporter, happened to be outside the Oval Office when she noticed the President and the CIA chief hurrying to the Portico entrance. She stepped aside and let the pair pass with a "Good morning, Mr. President, Mr. Kasim."

Both men acknowledged her but walked quickly past without engaging her in any conversation.

She wondered what was up? She always wondered what was happening in some part of the world that she didn't know about. As usual, it was none of her business. Except this time, they had taken an unusually long time to discuss whatever they were discussing and Kasim looked more uneasy than usual.

She left the reception area of the Oval Office and walked swiftly to her office located in the basement of the White House, skipping the elevator and instead opting for the staircase. It was faster. And, more reliable when she was in a hurry not wanting to engage anyone in idle talk.

She turned down the first hallway at the bottom of the stairs and stopped at her office, second door on the right. She fumbled for the key, found it, then quickly unlocked the door

Secret of Ekaterinburg: The Hour-Glass

and carefully set the bolt behind her. She opened her desk drawer and reached underneath it for another key, a smaller one that fit a small briefcase stashed inside her tiny office. She walked over to the high bureau and reached behind it to a special hook, and carefully brought out a small leather pouch which contained a tiny transmitter. She laid it on her desk, and reached inside her pocket for a tiny headset with earplugs. She turned the transmitter on, dialed in the right frequency and plugged in the earphones. She was now listening to a digital transcript of what had just taken place inside the Oval Office. The recording device had got the first five minutes of the conversation and then would re-loop, so the full conversation wasn't there, but she didn't know that. She listened for a few minutes, then her facial expression froze.

"Good, God," she spoke unable to control her emotions. "Have they gone crazy?"

She pulled out the digital recording from the transmitter and placed it inside her purse. She had to get this to Rick who was still in Stockholm. He'd know what to do with it. If she got caught with it, she'd spend the next fifty years in prison for espionage against the United States. As a foreign journalist, they wouldn't

Secret of Ekaterinburg: The Hour-Glass

just toss Adrienne out of the country. She'd spend a hell-of-a- lot of time in prison first. Then, maybe with a little luck, and pressure from Great Britain, she might get leniency . . . but that could be after 20 years. Christ, she had to get the hell out of their without arousing suspicion. She opened up her eye shadow case, and slid the tiny microcassette inside a special slot behind the blue eye shadow. She knew it was a tacky color, her colleagues criticized her all the time, but it worked as a ploy for them to leave her alone most of the time. And, certainly nobody ever wanted to borrow her eye shadow. But, now she had to get inside the Oval Office, retrieve the bug and get the hell out of there. It would be risky but she'd done it before. This time it had to work in a hurry. Adrienne left the office, latched the door behind her and heard the self-locking mechanism click into place and hurriedly climbed the stairs . . . nothing unusual she thought. Let them think that I'm conducting business as usual. Set the normal pace. Talk nonchalantly. Don't get excited. Just the business-as-usual White House bullshit.

But, what Adrienne didn't know as she closed her office door was that it had automatically shut-off a secret camera hidden

Secret of Ekaterinburg: The Hour-Glass

in the wall clock placed there by the CIA as part of their routine surveillance of all the press corps. It was something they did to monitor national security, and no one, not even the vice president ever knew anything about it. Only the President and the CIA chief knew. And, they were careful never to engage in sex with any of the White House female staffers. Others, who didn't know, weren't so careful as plenty of tapes revealed that when they were reviewed by CIA technicians.

She entered the reception area and casually reached inside her jacket pocket holding a silver, pearl earring in her right hand but didn't reveal it. She nervously fingered it and saw Kathryn reaching for a file.

"Oh, Kathryn, could you do me a big favor. I think I lost an earring yesterday in the President's Office. Do you think I could go inside, escorted of course, to take a look around the carpet? I swear, I'm going to quit wearing these silly things. Have you ever tried talking on the phone with these on? God, they hurt like hell."

She knew Kathryn was a stickler for being well-attired, and the one thing she knew for certain was that Kathryn hated wearing those damned earrings all the time, too. She had

Secret of Ekaterinburg: The Hour-Glass

complained about it out loud several times to her. It was the one thing she could count on to work, and it did.

"You, too. I'm always taking mine off, setting them down somewhere. They could be on the floor. The White House guards will wonder what the heck we're both doing on the floor at the same time in the Oval Office if they see us," Kathryn laughed.

"Remember, President Hinton and his girlfriends? Two of them on the floor at the same time. We'd better leave the door open," Adrienne wisecracked.

Secret of Ekaterinburg: The Hour-Glass

CHAPTER 48

Stockholm, Sweden, Dec. 1, 1989

Rick Waite took the phone call in his bureau while folding a hard copy of his story in half, stuffing it into his leather notebook.

He always made a backup copy; he had learned his lesson the tough way, losing important information via the technology "black hole" also known as the corrupted file disk or crashed hard drive.

"Hello . . . Rick here."

"Hello . . . Adrienne here."

God, he hated when she did that, mimicking him.

"Where in the hell are you calling from?"

"Washington. Where in the hell have you been?"

"I just got in from Moscow." Rick countered.

"Well, you'd better get back there in a hurry."

"Why what's up?"

"Well . . . I just can't figure out what Iran is

Secret of Ekaterinburg: The Hour-Glass

going to do with 200 or so SS-18 missiles and RDS-7 nuclear warheads to go with them?"

"Jesus, you're kidding aren't you."

"Afraid not. You know, I don't make these calls because I love my cell phone."

"Where are you going to be?"

"I'll join you sometime tomorrow depending on my flight. Look, I've got something else, something the U.S. President is going to announce to the world on Saturday. Only, we're going to beat him to it with the help of Pete."

"Does Pete know anything?" Rick asked.

"Nope. I've just found out myself. But, I'll call him when I change planes in London on the way to Moscow. I'll tell him what I've got. I'm sure he'll be interested as hell. You know, Pete, he doesn't like to miss anything," Adrienne remarked.

"Jesus. Never a dull moment. Just like Beirut, huh?" Rick said.

"God, but it was nice, though, in case you forgot," Adrienne admonished.

"Yeah, I haven't forgot. You saved my life. . . twice. Sex, love and danger! What a combination?" Rick expressed.

"Twice?" Adrienne questioned.

"Yeah, the first time you saved me from

Secret of Ekaterinburg: The Hour-Glass

Fasi. The second, when you agreed to marry me."

Adrienne laughed through the mouthpiece, but her eyes welled-up in tears when she heard him say it. They had married in a whirlwind, but the circumstances back then had necessitated it. They were lucky to be alive working independently, even if it was for the London Times.

"Look, I'll see you soon, she said. Love, you."

"Love, you back," his response was quick.

Now, he was mimicking her.

He hung up the phone and resumed what he was doing trying not to think about what Adrienne had just told him. He would call the airlines from his apartment. Adrienne clicked off the cell phone and listened for the telltale electronic signature. She didn't hear it. She was safe.

At a nearby CIA listening post at Fort Meade, a digital device switched off. The NSA technician picked up the telephone.

"Chief. They know. Just as planned. Looks as though they took the bait."

"Great," Kasim answered casually. "Everything should be public by Saturday afternoon. God, it's great to be part of the

Secret of Ekaterinburg: The Hour-Glass

United States, isn't it?"

"Is everything set with the Russians?"

"Everything's a **GO**. Anastasia is already in Moscow," the CIA chief noted then disconnected.

Secret of Ekaterinburg: The Hour-Glass

CHAPTER 49

Red Square, Moscow, Dec. 20, 1989

The Russians jammed into the square some two million of them waving and roaring their approval at the twelve shapes moving into position atop the Kremlin Wall like small puppets bobbing around in unrecognizable silhouettes shaking hands with each other and returning the frantic waves of the masses below.

It reminded Grachev of the way it used to be. The way the Soviet citizens would mass throughout Red Square to hail their leaders while the tanks and armies that rolled and marched past, missiles anchored onto flatbed trucks and jet fighters screaming overhead in flyby maneuvers which had always delighted the celebrating thousands below and the millions watching the carefully orchestrated extravaganzas on Soviet state-controlled television. It was the same in the U.S. at the air shows. People everywhere liked the same thing, military power.

Secret of Ekaterinburg: The Hour-Glass

It reminded Grachev of when Lenin had first come to power in 1917, and when Czar Nicholas was forced to relinquish the throne in exasperation and then prepared to leave with his family in exile. It reminded him of the old days, when all communists were young and when they all believed their own propaganda.

Today, there were only a few hundred diehards who still believed their own lies, but they were more realistic than to still think they could still take over the world.

"Throw off the chains and the shackles of the bourgeoisie. Fight for your freedoms. Overthrow the decadent governments of democracy. Power to the proletariat."

These were the slogans of days gone by, far different from the chants they were hearing now after the tempest subsided and the Berlin Wall came apart. Grachev grasped the hand of Anastasia firmly. The others, standing on the platform alongside him, heightened with pride at the celebration below. Grachev knew how to orchestrate such gatherings with perfection.

Only a trusted few, including Anastasia and Sergei, knew Grachev's real role in the communist party a half century ago. Beria had already been dead since 1953, but Grachev was still very much alive and kicking.

Secret of Ekaterinburg: The Hour-Glass

A handful of old KGB and CIA old timers knew that it was Grachev who had ordered the execution of the Czar and his family members that night; and of course, Anastasia. Why Grachev had changed his mind and saved her had been a long and closely held mystery. And, in a quirk of historical consequence, he would bring her to the very throne of her father he had murdered.

As Grachev approached the microphone, he gestured to Anastasia in a tribute of her well-being. The crowd roared their approval. The news was out by the State media. They had been informed of her survival the day before and it was broadcast to every Russian citizen in the nation.

In the apartment only five hundred yards away, the two assassins worked feverishly to finish setting up their lethal equipment.

The rifle was poised and already aimed toward the podium. The curtains were half-drawn and Friedrich positioned himself several feet back from the window so no one would be able to detect him. He turned on the laser sight and reached into his jacket pocket and pulled out two 10.66mm x .42in gas-powered cartridges and loaded them into the clip. He moved the bolt up and to the left and back, then

Secret of Ekaterinburg: The Hour-Glass

forward, slamming it shut again. The round entered the chamber with a precision a German craftsman had designed into the rifle. The smooth action of the mechanism reassured Friedrich that everything was set, the weapon ready to do its job.

He knew he had only time for two shots at the most, if the first one missed. The FSS security forces would be on top of her in an instant. But, he hadn't ever missed. Still, the second round was there just in case he had to get another shot off.

Friedrich nestled his face into the eyepiece and focused the scope. Everything was perfect. He quickly found his target in the crosshairs on the podium to the left of Grachev. In the communists eyes, Grachev had become the consummate traitor, but his orders were not to kill him . . . they might need him later . . . only Anastasia . . . the rightful successor to the Czarist throne. He peered through the scope while tightening his grip on the rifle, steadying it on the table in front of him. He felt the slack of the sling tighten around his wrist minimizing the side-sway. He pushed the rifle butt into his shoulder with a steady pressure, stopping the vertical movement on his target.

His right hand lightly touched the laser sight

Secret of Ekaterinburg: The Hour-Glass

and he switched it off until he was ready. Friedrich would now wait until Grachev was halfway through his speech, about ten minutes, before he would commence his deadly assault upon Anastasia.

"Karl. Come here. Look through the telescope and tell me what you see?" Friedrich said.

Karl moved quickly to the table and peered through the 20X scope.

"Yes. I see him. The CIA agent, Alex Ayers. He is standing right next to her. You have two bullets. Perhaps you could shoot twice?"

"Believe me, I would like to, but those are not my orders. It would send the wrong message to our benevolent friends in the communist party. Since, he has done so much harm to the KGB over the years, it would be nice to send him into permanent retirement. But, know this, Karl, you don't disobey orders, especially when it involves the CIA."

"It is all I can do to concentrate on one target, not that it would be impossible. But, I am in no mood to risk fouling up my primary target."

"Then do whatever you must and do it well. Communism will make a triumphant return this

Secret of Ekaterinburg: The Hour-Glass

day to Russia. Today, will mark the beginning of a new struggle," Karl repeated without taking his eyes off Anastasia.

Grachev had nearly spoken for the required ten minutes, and now Friedrich realized what he must do.

He signaled Karl to draw the curtains closer together. He would have only seconds to aim and shoot. The laser sight could not be operational too long because special federal agents assigned to the rooftops had special equipment to detect the use of such gun sights. Ten seconds at most, then he would have to turn off the scope. Any longer would risk giving away his position. Friedrich moved carefully to the wooden table letting the breeze gently lift the curtains while Karl slowly adjusted them to within six inches of the gun barrel. He pulled at the rope slowly so that no one would detect any sudden movement from below.

Federal security agents were positioned everywhere for the occasion and they were themselves subject to random searches by Moscow police searching for would-be assassins. Even though they had dead-bolted the lock behind them, the agents would break the door down if they suspected something

Secret of Ekaterinburg: The Hour-Glass

wrong inside.

Friedrich steadied the rifle and motioned Karl to step away. He clicked-on the laser sight and picked up his target approximately four-hundred ninety yards away lighted on the range estimator inside the scope. Four-hundred forty-eight meters diagonally across Red Square. Anastasia was not moving at all. She stood there smiling, motionless, waiting for her introduction to the masses below. She was ready to accept God's miracle. It would be a moment to fulfill her destiny. For those who loved her, she was the remembrance of countless parables of the Czar and his family who had lived a fairy tale existence until the revolution. For those who still hated her, they were present to watch the ceremonies out of a morbid curiosity. Nonetheless, whether they despised her or loved her, Anastasia represented a historical moment that would be witnessed by the entire world.

It was the beginning of a new era for Russia. One that would renew the spirit of its traditions, its glorious days of the past, and restore its pre-eminent position in world politics as a world leader among great nations.

The thousands applauded as the magical moment drew near. Grachev had nearly ended

Secret of Ekaterinburg: The Hour-Glass

his speech and was making the final introductions . . . Friedrich was late . . . "And, because the people of Great Russia who make up the ultimate fabric of our society have prayed and demanded that once again this great and historical daughter of Czar Nicholas, who was indeed very much alive in the United States . . . that she must without hesitation or without any doubts by any citizens present and those watching via television . . . be restored as the rightful heir to the Holy Throne of Russia. Long live Anastasia . . .Nicholaevna . . . Romanov. Long live the new Czarina of Russia. Long live the rightful holder of the Holy Throne."

Friedrich took great aim, the crosshairs centered directly on her chest, upper left quadrant, precisely at the heart. It would be a fatal shot, killing her instantly. There would be no second shot. He pressed a button with his left hand, refreshing the laser sight and instantly saw a tiny red dot appear on the just a few millimeters to the left-center of the crosshairs. The crosshairs self-adjusted in a millisecond to the exact spot so that they were congruent. Five seconds elapsed. Friedrich was firing late. He gently squeezed his hand and felt his fingers tighten on the pistol stock of the

Secret of Ekaterinburg: The Hour-Glass

rifle. Carefully, tightening, one-by-one, squeezing the trigger slowly so that there would be no movement when the firing pin struck the bullet.

Suddenly, the rifle jerked backward.

There was almost no sound when the rifle recoiled and Friedrich watched in the scope as the cyanide-tipped bullet struck her exactly where he had aimed. The gas-powered bullet had found its exact mark and struck her with full force pitching her rearward toward the others on the reviewing stand. The crowd was stunned into abrupt silence as Grachev spun around and grabbed her. Alex leaned forward to catch her while others screamed to get down behind a partition at the wall.

Below, thousands frantically trying to catch a glimpse of Anastasia and others to see what had happened, surged toward the podium while some looked up into the many apartment windows facing Red Square. There had been no muzzle flash seen and no loud report to direct their senses.

Friedrich calmly put down the rifle on the table, first replacing the second round in the clip with another, unmatched round. He dared not attempt to disassemble it, there was no time. When the security forces would find it,

Secret of Ekaterinburg: The Hour-Glass

they would know it was a professional assassin anyway. No use being caught with it.

Karl unlocked the door to the apartment. They would be gone in less than 30 seconds. Agents would be swarming all over the place in minutes. But, both of them heard the blast at the same time, the door being kicked open by Russian security agents. They were already there. Someone had tipped them off Friedrich knew from instinct. They had been double-crossed by their own KGB.

"Mother of God," Friedrich yelled to Karl guarding the doorway. "They have come to kill us. We have been betrayed."

Karl pulled a pistol from beneath his jacket. Friedrich jerked out a hand gun from his jacket pocket.

"We are dead. Kill as many of them as you can. There is no choice now but to end it this way. God forgive us for what we have done."

Karl swore as he glimpsed the first agent round the corner of the hallway and focused on the doorway.

He stuck the gun through the doorway and opened fire at him, hitting the first of three. Behind them, more agents barged into the apartment. They were trapped. Friedrich slammed the door shut but there were too many

Secret of Ekaterinburg: The Hour-Glass

of them. The door slammed back, knocked off its hinges by a battering ram. Before they could get more shots off, five men pinned them to the floor kicking at their heads. Karl screamed in agony as the butt of a rifle came smashing down on his skull.

Friedrich's gun was wrestled away as they bent his wrist until it broke with a disquieting "crack."

He screamed in pain until a rifle butt smashed into his jaw knocking him into unconsciousness.

An agent went to the balcony, opened the curtain, and signaled to the others on nearby rooftops that they had apprehended the assassins. He reached inside his pocket and transmitted an order to his commander.

Below, and still on top of the giant Kremlin Wall, others helped attend to Anastasia. She was in severe pain but still conscious. Unbelievably, they sat her up and loosened the chest-protector inside her coat which had saved her life, stopping the bullet just inches from her heart. She was alive. Anastasia was alive.

She had survived a second assassination attempt on her in one lifetime.

She truly was the holy one. She truly was the rightful successor to the Holy Throne.

Secret of Ekaterinburg: The Hour-Glass

The crowd saw her movement and cheered.

Even those who had been against her, stood and applauded as she stood up before the millions packed into the square. She signaled to them that she had survived a murderous moment.

Alex had made sure of that. He had taken the precaution to make sure she wore a Teflon jacket beneath her blouse.

The chest-protector wasn't made of diamonds or rubies this time; it wasn't fancy or precious, but the military-style garment had done its job.

And, so had Andre and Sergei.

Secret of Ekaterinburg: The Hour-Glass

CHAPTER 50

The Oval Office, Dec. 20, 1989

One of the ivory telephones on the President's desk rang three times before he walked over from the far side of the Oval Office to pick it up.

"Yes," he spoke crisply into the mouthpiece.

"Mr. President, I have President Grachev Solotzin on the line. It's an urgent call. He asks you to take it on the secure line. Shall I put him through?"

"Immediately," the President ordered.

After a series of clicks and the familiar wail of the toner set into operation the line went dead, except for the voice of Grachev beginning to communicate on the other end.

"Yakov, how have you been? Isn't it late for you to be away from your dacha? I thought you would be still busy making the announcement at Red Square.?"

"Da, Mr. President. It's rather unique for me, but after the events which occurred a half-hour ago, believe me, I am fortunate just to be

Secret of Ekaterinburg: The Hour-Glass

able to talk with you now. They could have gone after me. Has your CIA informed you as to what has happened here?"

The president turned to Ben standing in front of the window facing Pennsylvania Avenue. He had . . . they had both watched it on television . . . and they were expecting Grachev's call.

"Ahhhh. . . . yes. We saw it a few minutes ago. How is Anastasia?"

"Thanks be to God, just some minor bruising to the chest, but she has been properly stunned by the experience. You know this kind of thing is new to her. It is not at all like what she has been used to, guards here, guards there, secret service prowling about like Halloween cats, Mr. President."

"Yes . . . and I'm afraid that routine now will be a way of life for her. It is a deadly business."

Ned turned to Kasim and motioned for him to listen closely.

"Solotzin, I've got Kasim here, you know him. He and your KGB man talked a few hours ago. I know you already know that, I'm just trying to be upfront like we've always been with each other. Look, I'm worried, and he's worried as to how the world is going to react to

Secret of Ekaterinburg: The Hour-Glass

all this. I know we anticipated just about everything there was to on this, except a possible assassination attempt on her or you. What surprised us both, was that the attempt was made by someone inside the FSS itself."

"Yes," Grachev replied. "You are quite correct in your assessment. We caught the culprits in a matter of minutes. One of them was pounded to death, the other we have captured alive and we want to keep him that way for the moment."

"Is he clean?"

"Yes. There is no one else involved, but there are others deep inside the KGB who have attempted this, and in the process, they were hoping for a quick kill, and then an attempt to take over the government. It reminds me of the old days, Ned. It reminds me of 1918."

"But, you won't let that happen again, will you Yakov? Tell me you are able to resist all attempts at an overthrow of your system?"

"We are investigating furiously. And, those who are caught will be shot for attempted murder of a state official. She is more than a state official. She is considered holy by Russian believers."

"What happens next, Yakov?"

"It is now a matter of performing the

Secret of Ekaterinburg: The Hour-Glass

ceremony when she feels up to it. Perhaps in a few days."

"Yes. That would be good my friend. That would be quite good. Now, that we have the entire world's attention focused on Russia, it would be a good time to complete the other part of our bargain, yes, Grachev?"

"That part is going smoothly, Ned. It is about half-way completed and the missiles will be delivered to you in exchange for the gold in three or four days. The balance of the missiles and their components will be diverted to Iran as promised."

"That is what we agreed to, Yakov, in exchange for gold and in exchange for a stable middle east."

"Yes, even though we were at odds with each other at one point in our history, it is apparent now, that this must be the case in order to stabilize the region since the return of the Ayatollah ten years ago. The Ayatollah was a scourge upon his own people and a threat to Israel; but worse, he became a threat to the entire middle east region," Grachev said.

"You are absolutely right, President Grachev. The leaders in power now are far more dangerous in their wishes to keep the middle east region in turmoil. And, when it

Secret of Ekaterinburg: The Hour-Glass

comes down to Israel's right to exist, they might not have any restraint to attack them. This will keep Iran in check and its neighbors from going too far in either direction if they think the missiles guarantee nuclear parity with the Jewish State," the American President declared crisply.

"One more thing," Ned interjected before letting Solotzin think the conversation was finished. "There is the matter of Turkey, Afghanistan and Pakistan. The whole region is Islamic. If Turkey breaks from NATO and closes the Straits of the Dardanelles at Istanbul, then we will automatically go to war as an ally with you against these Islamic regimes. Is that how you and your security council feel?"

"Da. That is correct, Ned. We feel strongly that if Turkey breaks with NATO and becomes a renegade nation aligning itself with the other Islamic states fueling the fires in the middle east, then we will have no choice but to declare war against Turkey and whoever joins them on their side. If they close the Dardanelles, a crucial chokepoint where the flow of oil travels from the Black Sea to the Mediterranean, and if Iran closes the Strait of Hormuz, that would be a total of 60% of the world's oil supply at risk.

Secret of Ekaterinburg: The Hour-Glass

It would bring Eastern and Central Europe to its knees, bring you to your knees and us along with you. We would join you in fighting these evil forces, Ned. You have our oath on that."

"That is very good, Yakov. I will meet with my security and military chiefs to discuss that dreadful possibility within hours. We will share our intelligence information with you including satellite positioning so that you can follow troop movements in that region. We will hook up directly to you and feed the information through mutually established military channels. Is this all right?"

"Da. That is very good, Ned. Only ten years ago, this would have been unthinkable and not possible, eh?"

"Unthinkable, yes. And, impossible with the distrust that used to exist between our two nations. But, that is no longer the case and no longer will it be the case in the future."

"Is good, Ned. Is very good for both countries."

"Before I let you go. I am asking you and the other Russian Republics to become full-fledged members of the NATO alliance. Do you think you can persuade your military and political people that we have more in common than any differences?"

Secret of Ekaterinburg: The Hour-Glass

"I will personally oversee it, myself," Grachev replied. "Good-bye and good luck. I will be thinking of you as Anastasia reclaims the throne of Russia."

"Yes. I will be watching on television as will all the American people," Ned answered.

"Dos vidaniya, Ned."

"Dos vidaniya, Yakov."

The President hung up the special telephone and stood at his desk a moment before walking over to his favorite spot at one of the Oval Office windows.

It was starting to rain outside. Kasim watched but kept silent.

Nelson wondered if it was raining in Moscow.

He presumed the CIA chief already knew if it was.

Secret of Ekaterinburg: The Hour-Glass

CHAPTER 51

Stockholm, Dec. 20, 1989

The telephone rang at Rick's desk.

It was business as usual. Unmanned phones didn't get answered in a newsroom. It's not that anybody wasn't paying attention to it as the ring reverberated through the newsroom again and again. It was just that nobody cared, and even worse, nobody wanted to answer anybody else's phone.

It was an ego thing. Most reporters learned to ignore the sound when they were on deadline. One of the them looked over toward the phone in exasperation hoping that somebody would answer it or wishing it would self-destruct. But, it didn't. It just kept ringing until the person on the other end gave up.

It was 10:53 a.m. and most of the big news of the day had already crossed the news wires in Europe.

Anastasia of Ekaterinburg had been restored to the throne of the largest country in the world.

Russia was resuming its place among royal

Secret of Ekaterinburg: The Hour-Glass

families despite a dwindling number of countries that kept the monarchies alive. The world had changed a lot since 1918.

Rick entered the newsroom in a huff.

"God-damn-it, Rick. Answer that fucking telephone or take the damned thing off the hook when you leave for a cup of coffee."

"Yeah . . . yeah . . .yeah . . . dash-thirty-dash," he yelled back while hurrying to the phone knowing that it was probably Adrienne calling him.

He was right when he heard the familiar pause over the handset.

"Hello . . . Adrienne. It's me. What the hell is going on over there? It's awfully early for you to call me."

She blithered, "I know, but this couldn't wait any longer. I've got something for you, but I can't give it to you over this line. Can you call me at a pay phone. You know, the usual one, plus one."

"Plus one, Rick repeated into the mouthpiece."

He had memorized the code they had put into place before they separated. Plus one meant she would be calling from a cell phone, not a phone booth, but she would be inside the phone booth when she placed the call so that

Secret of Ekaterinburg: The Hour-Glass

anyone watching or intercepting the call would try to intercept a line signal when they beamed-in on her. She had only a few minutes to accomplish this, and the information she passed to Rick would have to be spoken quickly.

"O.K." Rick responded. "I'm hanging up now. Give me three minutes, O.K.?"

"O.K." Adrienne replied and hung up.

Rick moved from his desk almost at a jog and rounded the hallway which led to an obscure stairwell near the top floor of the building. He sprinted to the roof exit and stood atop the flat roof surrounded by an assortment of complex-looking antennae.

He reached into his jacket pocket, pulled out a small cellphone and extended the antenna. He turned it on and waited.

The cellphone came alive.

He answered it on the first ring and activated a micro-cassette tape recorder to record the conversation for later reference if he needed it.

"Yeah, go ahead."

"A shipment of 1,200 SS-18 missiles from Kazakhstan, tipped with MIRV RDS-7 warheads are being delivered to the United States as we speak. They will cross the Bering Strait bound for Alaska then be flown to Oak

Secret of Ekaterinburg: The Hour-Glass

Ridge, Tennessee, for deactivation. In order to accomplish this the United States and Russia entered into a secret deal. First, to restore Anastasia of Ekaterinburg to the Royal Throne of Russia, pay for the deactivation of those missiles and then take them out of active service in exchange for sixty billion dollars in gold. Guess where the gold is coming from?"

Rick understood immediately. "Fort Knox," he answered.

"You got it."

"Actually, that's not a bad deal for both parties. It's a safer world, Russia regains part of her past glory, and she's sixty billion dollars richer able to pay off her debts and expand capitalism in exchange for world security."

"But, there's one hitch," Adrienne complained on the other end.

"What?"

"The Russians have perfected the art of the double cross and some 200 missiles are being diverted to another country - an Islamic country."

"Which country - Iraq?" came Rick's response.

"No worse. Iran."

"Iran, Holy Christ," Rick's voice exploded.

"Look, we're coming up on two minutes. I

Secret of Ekaterinburg: The Hour-Glass

don't know if I'm under surveillance, but, if I am, they'll realize they're looking for the wrong frequency with their scanner, so I'm ending this now. Get this information to Pete as soon as possible. See you in Stockholm in a few days," Adrienne confirmed.

"Gotcha."

Rick retracted the cellphone antenna and stood there for a minute letting the information sink in.

Good God! Two hundred missiles equipped with MIRV warheads from Kazakhstan to the Iranian military. Were the Russians mad? They had to be. It meant nuclear annihilation for Israel and God only knows for who else in the region."

It had to be stopped.

But, he had to reach Pete first.

Knowing Adrienne's precision for accuracy, he knew she was onto something real big.

He leaned against the edge of the roof wall and contemplated his next move. Adrienne would be back in two days, on Saturday, that would give them the entire weekend to plan their announcement of the breaking story through the Times. He would arrange the news carefully, so as not to antagonize events in the middle east any more dangerously than they

Secret of Ekaterinburg: The Hour-Glass

already were. If Israel got wind of this first, they would bomb the hell out of Iran, maybe even before the missiles arrived. No, it would have to be planned and managed extra carefully."

He sat there puffing on an unfinished cigarette in the cool rooftop breeze.

A short distance away, on another rooftop, 500 yards to his south, stood a different rooftop gazer pointing a micro-gun at him from behind a chimney. The man, a mossad agent named Ariel, had recorded the entire conversation, simultaneously transmitting the output to Israeli intelligence via American satellite.

The Mossad was something else. U.S. intelligence didn't even know their equipment was being used by the Mossad. U.S. intelligence technicians only knew that the satellite channel had been activated by one of their own codes. So, it went unnoticed. The wily Ariel smiled and casually lit a cigarette. He was an unlikely-looking spy lurking alone in the shadows perched feeding his pigeons. Some thirty of them flocked around while he fed them bird seed in a swirling arm motion.

Startled by the cigarette smoke, they erupted from their roost flapping their way into the sky. Rick looked over toward the sound and

Secret of Ekaterinburg: The Hour-Glass

wondered what had scared them? But, he couldn't see Ariel tucked in the shadow of the chimney and went back down the stairwell into the newsroom.

Secret of Ekaterinburg: The Hour-Glass

CHAPTER 52

NORAD, Colorado Springs, Dec. 21, 1989

NORAD Air Force Brigadier General G.T. Williamson picked up the phone and nonchalantly dialed the OD's phone number over a secure line. The red and green lights flickered to life as he activated the scrambler and codified the numbers into a series of complicated sequences designed to block any interception by satellites beaming in overhead by a foreign country.

God knows who else had satellites up there besides Russia, Great Britain, France, and Japan. Even Iran had launched a small satellite into orbit a few years ago. Anybody could be listening in as the technology gap narrowed around the world.

"Hello, Jake. This is Gordon over at CFO. The president will be calling me in five minutes regarding new orders on the interdiction of those Russian ships in the Bering Strait. We want to make sure everything goes damned smooth. Is that understood? If there's anything

Secret of Ekaterinburg: The Hour-Glass

new, I'll make sure you get it first. Otherwise, continue naval operations as planned. The Air Force will take care of its end. We'll be flying round-the-clock on this with surveillance and protection. No interdictions will be made without authorization from the president. Understand?" Gordon shook his head as the other party obviously agreed with what was said. He hung up and walked over to the computer where others were already assessing the situation.

The giant screens were lit up with green dots marking the long miles of Russian ships strung out across the Bering Strait. There were no other ships in the area except for the U.S. 3rd Fleet moving into position just ahead of them and slightly below the Aleutian Islands. No other passenger or civilian cargo ships were anywhere nearby or within a 1,000-mile radius having been warned by U.S. and Russian navies to keep out of the area because of maneuvers.

"How does it look, Jake."

"Everything looks good. Naval operations are in sync with us and our F-16s are sortieing near Alaska to intercept anything moving across those interdiction lines. If necessary, we'll chase anyone from the area. If we have

Secret of Ekaterinburg: The Hour-Glass

to, we'll blow anyone out of the sky or out of the water, wherever the perceived threat is. Dan, give me an on-station fly-by time?"

"Check-in time two minutes. Those F-16's coming in low at one-hundred feet off the water will absolutely impress the Russians."

"Hell, Jake, that'd impress me," Gen. Williamson retorted.

"The president is due. I'll wait for the call here. I wouldn't leave this to chance if my life depended on it."

"Once we get the go ahead, how many missiles are we transferring?" Jake asked.

"About one thousand. Two hundred are being withheld for another destination."

"Good, God, that's going to take a couple of days. Will the weather hold?"

"According to the weather guys upstairs, a high is expected to hover over the area for four to five days. If things go well, we can do it in less than that."

"Why not just send the Ruskie ships to Iran?"

"Good question, Jake. I can't answer that until the President says I can. You know, it's the same old need-to-know crap. But, it works."

Gordon eased away from the briefing officer

Secret of Ekaterinburg: The Hour-Glass

to the front of the console to get a better look at the ship alignment of the Russians and Americans. There was a hell of a lot of everything out there . . . so many of them. Some 250 of them strung out like a pearl necklace from Kamchatka to St. Matthew and St. Lawrence islands in U.S. territory to Kotzebue on Seward's Peninsula.

"Jesus," he muttered to himself. "If anyone knew what the hell was going on. Two hundred missiles being sent to Iran to equalize the balance of power in the middle east. What the hell was the world coming to."

Gordon knew the reason the President didn't want to send the Ruskies to Iran via the Persian Gulf was because everyone would notice it. The British would know immediately, then we'd have to tell the French and besides, our ships were already in the Persian Gulf. It would be business as usual for us. The other way was too risky. This was better. Transferring them to U.S. naval vessels, they would go undetected and offloaded into any one of the myriad Iranian port cities along their coast, and nobody would be suspicious of the U.S. 5th Fleet operating in or around the Hormuz Strait. Or, if the President wished, the actual transfer of missiles could be done using

Secret of Ekaterinburg: The Hour-Glass

Iranian ships in international waters. That was the choice he favored.

Suddenly, Jake turned to Gordon and signaled him that a call was coming in from the White House.

"I'll take it," he turned quickly and walked a few steps to a glass-enclosed structure adjacent to the watch room. From there he could monitor the ships and see exactly what was going on in the air."

"Hello, Mr. President," Gordon responded picking up the telephone. "On time as usual. What have you got for me?"

The president talked for a few minutes giving Gordon the information he needed to proceed with the next step of the operation.

"Yes, sir. The interceptors are already above the navy guys. The F-18s are scrambling now from the deck of the carrier. Let's hope the Russians don't forget themselves and get trigger happy. They're usually steady. Anyway, none of our flyboys have their weapons turned on. No need is there? This is a joint mission, isn't it?"

Suddenly, out of the corner of his eye, Gordon saw everybody react to a blue blip flashing on the screen, identifying an intruder in the water.

Secret of Ekaterinburg: The Hour-Glass

"Good, God, hold on Mr. President! What the hell is that, Jake!?"

The entire room of eighty technicians and intelligence processors froze in their seats. "Where in the hell did that come from? What the hell is that!?" Gordon shouted.

Jake ran over to the screen and punched in key numbers that would identify the vessel. It was sea-going, alright.

"Mr. President. It looks like a sub is surfacing in the area. Not one of ours and not Russian. Who the hell is it, Jake?"

Nelson hung on the other end, "Gordon, what the hell is going on?"

"I don't know, Mr. President. It looks like a bogy submarine has just surfaced near our battle group from what I'm getting from our technical people here. We don't know whose it is yet?

"What the hell is it doing there?"

"Don't know that either. But, judging from our satellite view, our navy guys are already reacting to it. I'm calling off the flybys just to make sure they don't sink any Russian sub accidentally."

"Confirmation coming in now. It's a diesel-powered, standard French-class attack sub. Flying the Iranian flag. I repeat identified as

Secret of Ekaterinburg: The Hour-Glass

Iranian. They aren't supposed to have subs operating out here. They don't have the supply ships to refuel those old diesels. But, God-damnit they're here."

Jake studied the display from the spy satellite. It was a French sub all right. A Class 2, the type that was sold to the Iranians five years ago. What in the hell were they doing out of the Indian Ocean? What in the hell was going on? They were supposed to wait for the missiles. A sudden silence engulfed the room.

"We've intercepted their communications, General. Tell the President he isn't going to believe this. The sub is in direct radio contact with Tel Aviv. They are not Iranian. I repeat, they are not Iranian . . . sir . . . they are Israeli."

"Good God, Mr. President. You aren't going to believe this. It's not an Iranian sub, it's Israeli operating under an Iranian flag. It surfaced ten miles south of the fleet and is closing at flank speed toward our carrier. Our navy guys are going out to assess him with two destroyers. If he dives, we'll know they're trying to avoid us. If he doesn't, it's anybody's guess what they're up to. But, I'll bet a dime-to-a-dollar it's the cargo they're interested in."

"God-damn-it. Can't we keep anything from the Israelis? I don't understand how they do it,"

Secret of Ekaterinburg: The Hour-Glass

the President answered testily. "Keep me informed. I've got an important meeting going on here in the Oval Office. Call me back immediately if they threaten our ships or the Ruskies. Find out what the fuck they want?"

"Yes, sir," the general answered and hung up.

In the NORAD operations room, all eyes were glued to the giant screen. The sub maintained its heading toward the carrier. Christ were the Israelis crazy. Our navy boys wouldn't fuck around with them. They'd sink them in a minute if they moved to within striking distance, only a few more miles. Gordon heard the battle station horn blare over his headset from the lead USS Theodore Roosevelt, Nimitz class supercarrier.

"Shit, they won't fuck around with these guys this time," Gordon said to Jake. "The last time the Israelis tried something like that the U.S. lost 34 sailors dead and 174 wounded involving the USS Liberty during the Six-Day War in 1967. You can bet that isn't ever going to happen again. They'll destroy anybody that fucks around with the United States Navy this time."

The U.S. wouldn't be taking any chances with a $2 billion piece of equipment floating

Secret of Ekaterinburg: The Hour-Glass

around in the Atlantic carrying 6,000 American sailors and more than two hundred warplanes. They'd sink the son-of-a-bitch outright, Gordon figured.

"Jake, get me 3rd Fleet commander on the hotline pronto," Gordon ordered.

"Right away," came the matter-of-fact response.

"Jake, it's Gordon over at NORAD. What the fuck is going on up there?"

"Don't know yet, we're trying to raise the sub on military frequencies but they haven't responded yet. What do you want me to do?"

"Don't know yet. The president was on the hotline when the silly bastard surfaced "

"Look, Gordon. Our standard naval operating procedure dictates that we sink him if he moves in a threatening manner to within five miles of us. Does the President know that?"

"Yes, he does. He's been briefed on it before. When you raise that sub and get a response, let me know immediately. I'll contact the president for authorization and agreement on the procedure. Do not fire unless ordered. Do you understand? Let the Ruskies know what's going on if they don't already know. No use surprising them, too."

"Affirmative. We'll be standing by unless

Secret of Ekaterinburg: The Hour-Glass

the stupid bastards make a move or launch a torpedo or missile at us."

Gordon pressed the keypad twice. It automatically dialed the Oval Office hotline. After one ring, the President answered.

"Sorry to interrupt, Mr. President, but our navy guys tell me the sub hasn't changed course and is still closing toward the carrier. They are trying to raise the sub captain, but so far no luck."

"All right. On this end NSC is already in contact with the Israeli government and we're in communication with Tel Aviv at this very second trying to assess the situation. One thing you can count on. We're not going to fuck around with the Israelis this time. They're on notice. Those are American sailors out there and they're going to remain alive. We've dropped everything here waiting for an explanation from their prime minister. We'll have a handle on it soon."

"Affirmative, Mr. President. Call me when you get the information I need to react appropriately. You know the navy boys will destroy him if they threaten?"

"Don't worry, Gordon. This is not the U.S.S. Liberty. You'll know when we know. Keep trying to raise that sub and find out what

Secret of Ekaterinburg: The Hour-Glass

she's up to?"

"Affirmative, sir."

Gordon hung up the phone and looked at Jake. Had the whole world gone crazy?

"Anything, yet?"

Jake, waved him-off with a motion indicating there was a message coming through from CINCPAC.

"What have you got?" Jake said to the 3rd Fleet commander.

Admiral Hamilton chimed in on the line, "We've raised the sub on military frequency 7533 Mghz. They are definitely Israeli. No doubt about it. I repeat, the sub is Israeli. They are in direct contact with . . . are you sitting down for this one?"

"Yes . . . go ahead with your transmission."

"They are in direct communication with Tel Aviv."

"Jesus, God. . . Holy man . . . wait till the president hears this one?"

"He already knows, we picked up the intercept just a minute ago by NSA. They're loading it to the 3rd right now," Gordon yelled back to Jake.

At that moment the computer screens flickered with an emergency transmission from that agency.

Secret of Ekaterinburg: The Hour-Glass

"Yes. . . you're right. It's coming through now. From Fort Meade. Wait, there goes the hotline again. It's the President. Hold on, I'm going to patch you in on the conversation."

Gordon pressed a button on the red phone and switched-in Hamilton on the President's line.

"Mr. President. I've got Admiral Hamilton from the third patched into the conversation. He's identified the sub as an Israeli command."

"I can affirm that Gordy. Admiral, we've identified it through NSA."

"Right, we got your intercept of the last transmission to Tel Aviv. What the hell are the Israelis doing in on this?"

"Well, we figured to tell them eventually, but they must have got it through their own intelligence. They're damned good. Best in the world, huh?" the President said.

"Yeah, don't even say it," the admiral responded.

"Why do you think they're closing in on our carrier?" the President asked.

"Don't know, except there is precedent for it when they feel threatened," Gordy responded.

"You mean the USS Liberty attack?" the admiral mentioned.

"I mean exactly that," the president

Secret of Ekaterinburg: The Hour-Glass

answered.

"LBJ had all the intelligence to launch a counter-attack when we identified the attackers as Israeli, but he backed down and recalled the planes. You know the rest," the admiral repeated.

"Yeah, I know. And, so did the 294 men aboard. Thirty-four were killed defending an American intelligence vessel from attack because the Israelis didn't want us monitoring their military frequencies," Gordy intoned.

"What do we do this time, Mr. President." he continued.

"This time, if they get too close, we'll assume it's an attack and if they continue, we'll sink that sub no ifs-ands-or-buts. In the meantime, before they get that close, we're contacting Tel Aviv at this very second, and I'm telling the Prime Minister to back off. In fact, I'm giving him an ultimatum."

Gordon and Adm. Hamilton listened for the President's next command. Three minutes went by. Nothing. The longest three minutes of dead air they'd ever heard on the hotline. Adm. Hamilton crackled onto the line.

"Gordon, our tracking at 3rd indicates they are not backing off. They are within six miles of the carrier and we've begun defensive

Secret of Ekaterinburg: The Hour-Glass

procedures as a fleet. The Hornets are in the air with instructions to attack on my order if he makes a threatening move, dives, or launches any weapons."

"Affirmative, admiral. But, **do not** launch any countermeasures until you get a direct order from the president. Understood."

The admiral knew the president was on the line.

"Can't guarantee that, Mr. President. The procedure is to defend our carrier if a torpedo or a missile is fired toward us. I've got 6,000 men and women on board here. I'm sorry, but even you can't override the order to defend ourselves."

The president heard the explanation and there was no need to relay it him again. He knew Navy defense rules to defend at all costs. "Well, if the Israelis are stupid enough to try something like that, then God help all of them in that sub," the president said. "But, make sure you give them every chance. Just be damned sure it's a threatening situation before any retaliation takes place. I want to be able to justify anything that happens out there, the president barked into the phone. I don't want any bullshit on this. Everyone understand?"

They all did.

Secret of Ekaterinburg: The Hour-Glass

"Got NSA on the other line now Gordy. Wait. Wait. . . . . Tel Aviv has instructed their men in the sub to turn around. Do you copy that, Jake? Jake . . . did you copy that?"

"Uh . . . yes, sir . . . roger . . . copy that."

"Mr. President, we're observing the sub now. Yes. . . . he's turning away. He's coming about and starting to move away. It looked as though he was ready to fire a missile on his run at the carrier, but he's turned around. He's diving hard and fast now. Our hunter subs will track him to make sure."

"Good job, Jake. Tell your men good job from the President."

"I will. Thanks, Mr. President."

"I've got the Israeli prime minister on the other line. I've got to go. I'll find out what the fuck was going on. You'll be briefed later. My heartfelt thanks."

The three men hung up and breathed a sigh of relief. The missile transfer would take place uninterrupted.

But, what in the hell were the Israelis up to and what would Nelson tell the Israeli Prime Minister about the missiles. Surely they knew what was going on now. And, the United States got a glimpse of their reaction to it. God, that was a close one, Gordon thought. A

Secret of Ekaterinburg: The Hour-Glass

fucking war with Israel. No one in his right mind wanted that.

Not your average Jew. Not your average American-Jew. Not your average American. Nobody.

What the hell would you say to each other?

We'd always been on the same side.

Except once.

Secret of Ekaterinburg: The Hour-Glass

CHAPTER 53

London Times, Dec. 15, 1989

Rick hurried into Pete's office with his micro-cassette tape recorder firmly in hand. Barging through the door and slamming it behind him, he handed the copy to Pete who was busy editing another story on his computer. Rick wasn't used to pencil editing by hand any more. Those days were long gone since the technology age came into being, but he could manage it in a pinch and sometimes it was downright refreshing. With no time to get it into the system, he was lucky to talk the story into his recorder while waiting for his flight to London.

"What do you have for me this time," Pete said looking up from his computer screen. Rick tossed him the audio tape.

"I told you over the phone, you weren't going to believe this, but I've corroborated it with three sources."

"And, just who are your sources," Pete growled adjusting his headset.

Secret of Ekaterinburg: The Hour-Glass

"Adrienne, for one. She tipped me to the entire thing. She's in D. C., but she's on her way here first, then to Moscow."

"She doesn't count. Who else have you got?

"How about a digital recording from inside the Oval Office? And, how about a KGB contact inside the Kremlin?"

"Christ, " Pete said unbelievingly. "You guys really uncover the big ones don't you? What about the fucking president. Did anybody ask him? You broke national security laws. That's foreign espionage. Let me listen to the tape before I pass judgment."

Pete listened for the sensational phrases he anticipated would be there. They were. His editor's eyes nearly glazed over about halfway through the tape. He jerked his head back suddenly.

"You're telling me that 200 Russian missiles with nuclear warheads are being transported to Iran by the United States at this very moment with the help of the FSS? And, that Anastasia, the youngest daughter of Czar Nicholas II has been discovered alive? Are you fucking crazy? I mean, I know the Pulitzer Prize means a lot to you and it's hard finding a follow-up after breaking the story-of-the-century about nuclear missiles in Palestine nine years ago, but you

Secret of Ekaterinburg: The Hour-Glass

just can't start making this shit up? Christ, if the intelligence spooks don't kill you, I will."

"I'm telling you Pete," Rick interrupted him. "Everything you heard on that tape is true. We both grew up believing, like the Russians and the entire world, that Anastasia was dead. We thought nobody survived the assassinations of the Czar's family. But, there it is. She is about to be installed to the throne of Russia in a matter of days. The President and the Russians are going to announce it together. It's unbelievable if not impossible, but it's going to happen. And, the CIA and FSS are going to make it happen."

"What's the purpose?" Pete interjected. He was a smart editor who knew the right questions and he wanted to know.

"Don't worry, it's all covered in there. Pete fast-forwarded and found it.

"Christ they're going to restore old Russia back to the days of the Czar."

"Yes, but there's a catch. It's being done in exchange for the stability they think the throne will bring them and to fend-off a possible takeover by the communists trying to regain power. The United States has agreed to purchase some 1,200 missiles transported from Kamchatka by a fleet of new Russian ships to

Secret of Ekaterinburg: The Hour-Glass

the U.S. for deactivation. Once in the U.S., the warheads will be destroyed guaranteeing they can't get into the hands of a rogue country hell-bent on the destruction of one of its neighbors or the United States."

"What's the other catch," Pete asked knowing there had to be more.

"Well, the real hook is that we're paying nearly sixty billion dollars in hard currency and gold for all this, and we're going to divert 200 missiles to Iran, which could pose a threat to Israel. The very threat they're trying to eliminate. Does that make sense to you?"

"Christ, no. But, why doesn't it?" Pete asked him.

"The reason it doesn't is that Russia wants its influence to remain strong in the middle east, and the U.S. has acquiesced to the deal rationalizing that Iran once was the foremost U.S. puppet in the middle east region providing a strong security umbrella against the threat of the Soviet Empire and at the same time, making sure that Israel didn't get out of hand. Since, the Shah's overthrow, there has been a power vacuum in the region for 15 years. Also, an Iran armed with nuclear weapons is dangerous to the entire region including the Asian continent, especially preventing Pakistan and

Secret of Ekaterinburg: The Hour-Glass

India from getting into a shooting war. Both have nuclear capabilities now. But, if Iran were drawn into it with its arsenal, India would be no match for Pakistan, and India will understand that."

"Christ," Pete said rubbing the back of his neck. "That's one big fucking assumption - that India won't turn those missiles on Pakistan anyway."

"You're right, Pete. But, I'll let the President of the United States explain that one to the Pakistanis."

"So that's it?"

"That's it," Rick said.

"When is the president going to announce what's going on?"

"According to Adrienne, in eight days."

"That doesn't give us much time to get ready. Look, how soon can you get this onto the computer?"

"I can digitalize it in a few minutes. "Why?" Rick responded.

"Because I'm going to put it out over the news wires from here then contact the CNN guys and coordinate a hookup from here. Call Adrienne and tell her to get here as soon as possible and we'll do a live remote as we're breaking the story. It'll look sensational, not

Secret of Ekaterinburg: The Hour-Glass

that I'm trying for that, but shit, this is one fucking, sensational piece that will stand the world on its ear. It's a once-in-a-lifetime deal, and I want to be in on it from the start. But, we don't know yet where this is all going to take place. I would bet it's somewhere in the Persian Gulf, but our guys haven't noticed anything building fleet-wise over there, yet. We're watching and waiting?"

"What about the CIA, British SAS or the FSS?" Rick asked. "Have we tried to contact them? Pete asked.

"No, we've lost contact with them. Usually, they come to us with something they want in the news. We haven't seen them in days. So, to hell with them. Do they consult us on everything? We're going to have to find them on our own."

Pete had a point.

Maybe they needed each other some time. But, they didn't much like to do it that way. It took something away from the thrill of the chase; the quarry eluding the hunter, the secret agent eluding the pursuer, all of it.

"O.K. If we find them, we can do all of it on the same day. That way they can't stop the transfer, and CNN crews can shoot it with their cameras when the whole deal takes place.

Secret of Ekaterinburg: The Hour-Glass

Pretty hard to cancel a fleet of some 250 ships and the U.S. 3rd fleet in action, huh? But, where are they?"

"That's a damned good question, Rick. God-damnit, so we're now in the dark as to just exactly where is this going to happen? How in the fuck are we going to film it if we can't find it. Did anyone tell you about your great sense of timing?" Pete said sarcastically.

"Please, let's try to get this done." Pete said. "Rick answered by grabbing for Pete's handshake. A rare moment they realized. The last time they shook hands, albeit reluctantly, was when Pete fired him five years ago. Both remembered it at the same time and quirky grins slid across their faces, sheepish for remembering the incident.

Pete shrugged. Rick shrugged. They were over it.

Rick spun around and took off from Pete's office to the nearest phone. Adrienne should have landed in London by now, and should be at their flat. He dialed the phone, got no answer. He left a message for her to turn around and meet him at the airport for the next plane to Moscow.

Secret of Ekaterinburg: The Hour-Glass

Secret of Ekaterinburg: The Hour-Glass

CHAPTER 54

Tel Aviv, Israel, Dec. 22, 1989

The Israeli ambassador to the United States plied his way through the morning satellite messages from Washington.

On top of his batch was one from American President Ned Nelson.

That one would receive his immediate attention.

Israeli Prime Minister Yitzak Nethanyu was already at his desk planning major moves with his top military advisors garrisoned in his office with him.

Moshe remained in the outer waiting room for his announced entry into the meeting.

He knew it would be a long, tiring and miserable meeting. That was always the case when the meetings involved national security. This time, it not only involved national security, but national policy as well and a representative from the Mossad would be sitting-in on the meeting.

He wasn't worried about that because he

Secret of Ekaterinburg: The Hour-Glass

knew Yentl very well. He had met him at his son's bar mitzvah a year earlier when he had been appointed to his high office. They had checked out Yentl's background thoroughly and given the prime minister a dossier on his personal background, education, family and personal idiosyncrasies.

"Benjamin, come in immediately," the prime minister spoke from behind the door of his well-secured office, motioning with a quick jerk of the arm.

"Would you like some coffee? There is always plenty of that around here. Especially when the meetings go late into the night."

"Yes, of course, Mr. Prime Minister. Shalom, everyone."

"Shalom, Benjamin."

"How can I be of service to you Mr. Prime Minister?"

"You know by now what has occurred, do you not, Ben?"

"Yes. The security council informed me about the submarine incident a few hours ago. It is a terrible thing for Israel, is it not?"

"I'm not so sure, exactly, Ben, that is why I need your opinion on the matter. The U.S. president will be calling on the hotline in about an hour and I need your assessment on what

Secret of Ekaterinburg: The Hour-Glass

you think of the situation."

"Well, it is a difficult thing to assess, Mr. Prime Minister. After all, I wasn't privy to the operation initially and I didn't know anything about it beforehand; therefore, that will cloud my judgment somewhat as to the advisability of such an event, or to the wisdom of undertaking such an operation. What was the purpose of the mission? Were we really going to attack a United States aircraft carrier? Certainly, now that it has failed, it is easy to dismiss the operation as insane. Did anybody here think that we could possibly defeat the U.S. Navy?"

The prime minister was taken aback by the directness of his response but appreciated it anyway.

Benjamin moved further inside the office as the secretary closed the outer doors.

"Let's look at it this way," the prime minister said. "Perhaps I was a bit too aggressive in my dealings with the more conservative factions inside the Israeli government, especially the Likud factions which offer a more militant stance toward anyone that interferes with Israeli national interests or security. We weren't sure we could trust the U.S. government that they and the Russians were giving the Iranians sabotaged

Secret of Ekaterinburg: The Hour-Glass

nuclear equipment or that such a system would actually work if they tried to launch them."

"But, Mr. Prime Minister, the United States government funds our defense budget and makes needed equipment available to us so that we can defend ourselves from the Arab states who wish to drive us into the sea. That is why we receive fourteen billion dollars from the United States. And, that is where all the donations flow from American Jews. That is where another secret $5 billion flows to connect with American defense contractors in the U.S., giving us the ability to manufacture our own arms. Now, you're telling me our government seriously considered an attack on a United States aircraft carrier?"

"It had been done before," the prime minister answered curtly.

"It had indeed. But, not against an aircraft carrier. The USS Liberty, an electronics eavesdropping ship, was nearly sunk after a brutal 5-hour air and sea assault during the Six-Day War, with some thirty-four American seamen killed. It was a chapter in U.S.-Israeli history that nobody to this day cares to talk about, especially the politicians who had an implicit interest in good, American-Israeli relations in the United States. it was

Secret of Ekaterinburg: The Hour-Glass

unnecessary," Benjamin told the prime minister directly and braced himself for the response.

"Our military intelligence felt we didn't have any choice. It was an electronic monitoring ship and it was eavesdropping on our secret military frequencies uncovering all our secret codes for counter-attack. Even a friend can know too much, Benjamin?"

"Yes, perhaps that could be so, but to kill thirty four American seamen in such an operation and today to threaten some 5,000 on a U.S. carrier - do you want the United States government to annihilate Israel? We wouldn't have to wait for the Arabs to do it."

"You're saying it was madness?"

"No I'm not saying that, Mr. Prime Minister. You're saying it. Only one thing is certain. There is a certain amount of madness in the world that even the Israelis have captured."

"Yes . . . on the surface, you may be quite correct, Benjamin. I value your opinion. Now I need to know how we apologize, how we correct what we did, and how do we explain it to the Americans? Anyway, the orders were not to really attack the American carrier; it was a diversion to make them think the Iranians were going to attack and to get the U.S. to counter-attack Iran for the threat. Who knows

Secret of Ekaterinburg: The Hour-Glass

if it would have worked? We'll never know. "

Benjamin paused for a moment walking around the office looking for the cup of coffee he was promised and poured himself one after a few minutes of tinkering with the coffee pot placed on a side-stand at the back of Nethanyu's office.

"There is one possible explanation the President will accept. But, it has to be on behalf of the people of Israel - directed to the American public. One they can fully appreciate and understand."

"Mr. Prime Minister, having grown up and been raised in America, there is one thing Americans understand better than anything else, and that corollary is that you never, I mean, never double-cross a friend. Never surprise a friend. And, never launch any kind of a surprise attack against the United States. In short, never blind-side them. It is an unwritten and unspoken truth of American tradition and fair play. If it is ever breached, you can be sure it will never be forgotten. Their entire American history is littered with such catch-phrases as "Remember the Alamo?" "Remember San Juan Hill? "Remember the Maine?" And, "Remember the USS Liberty?"

Nethanyu knew immediately the impact of

Secret of Ekaterinburg: The Hour-Glass

Ben's statement. It was indeed true. How could he have disregarded it?

That very argument could have been used against the Likud faction that had advocated retaliation. My God, it was a close call.

But, now he had to apologize to the American people and a U.S. President. How would he do it.

Ben could see what Nethanyu was thinking.

"Just apologize. Keep it simple. Promise never to perform such an act again against the United States, and to prove it, fire the top military advisors who suggested and formulated the response in the first place."

Everyone in the room, including the Mossad's top intelligence officer cringed. Fire military heroes? Who would then defend Israel?

"Schhhlleeppps." he quipped. "Israel isn't used to apologizing to anybody?"

"Well," Benjamin continued. "There must be a first time. And, I can't think of a more important time than now. Unless, of course, you want to risk losing the entire friendship of the United States, Great Britain and France, and . . . ."

"Enough. Enough, Benjamin. You already convinced me I was wrong. I just needed to

Secret of Ekaterinburg: The Hour-Glass

hear you say it like that. Moshe will agree, won't you?"

Moshe reluctantly nodded his approval. There were only so many things a small nation like Israel could take on. The United States wasn't or shouldn't be one of them.

"Then, consider it done. I will talk to the U.S. President in an hour. Do you want to be here for the phone call?"

"No, sir. I'll leave that up to you. It is going to be difficult as it is, isn't it?"

"Yes, it will."

With that Nethanyu dismissed Benjamin, and the others present except for the Mossad officer. He retained Yentl to discuss other pressing business.

"I know what you are thinking, Moshe. But, I must do it anyway. To risk losing the support of the United States could pose an even bigger risk to us. We could risk losing every American Jew to a restart of hatred toward them. There is enough anti-Semitism in the U.S. as it is. We don't need to add anymore, do we?"

Moshe shook his head in agreement.

"Look, I will have to make direct amends to the President. I will have to go on Israeli television and talk directly to the American

Secret of Ekaterinburg: The Hour-Glass

people and apologize for what we have done. But, it is better to humiliate myself than to risk the friendship of even one American who has supported us throughout all these years."

Moshe walked to the window over-looking Tel Aviv.

"We owe them this apology. If it weren't for the Americans in the Persian Gulf wars, we would have lost more Israeli lives than we did."

"Yes, Mr. Prime Minister, in the end, you are right. We owe them for every American life that has been lost."

Secret of Ekaterinburg: The Hour-Glass

CHAPTER 55

Moscow, Dec., 1989

Anastasia struggled to regain her feet helped by Grachev and Alex who had been standing beside her when the assassin's bullet knocked her backward.

The two million jammed into Red Square and surrounding openings in nearby buildings from rooftop perches to theater-like balconies sighed a collective sound of relief which moved like a huge audible wave sweeping past the dignitaries to the Kremlin Wall. They maintained a rapt composure having been shocked into a rare and sudden silence. Suddenly, they saw her move, disturbing their evident anxiety wondering if Anastasia had been hit or if she was still alive? Cautiously, the men lifted Anastasia to her feet, blood oozing from the left side of her chest. They slowly turned her to face the crowd.

Suddenly, a gigantic roar swept across Red Square from front to back as she stood facing them, still composed, yet clasping her wound in

Secret of Ekaterinburg: The Hour-Glass

obvious discomfort.

She had been saved by a Zefron bullet-proof garment worn underneath her blouse and she had been lucky that only an instant before, Alex had said something to her that had made her move from a full upright position to a slightly bent stance.

That slight movement had decidedly preserved her life.

But, Alex knew the attempt on her life meant that there were others opposed to this transition of power. They had to be dealt with and the new FSS would have to be the ones to do it. Pausing for a moment, Anastasia moved deliberately to address the crowd. Two bodyguards flanking her assisted holding her steady.

"My friends, my people, my family of Russia," she spoke into the microphones assembled before her, "It is a day that you will long remember, as long as you live, and as long as I live. The throne of Mother Russia is restored today, here, now, and for all time. I must confess, there is significant resentment to my returning to the throne and I have only agreed to it under two conditions."

A murmur rose from the throngs assembled at Red Square.

Secret of Ekaterinburg: The Hour-Glass

She hesitated.

"Not to be alarmed. I am not abandoning my position as rightful heir to the Holy Throne of modern Russia, but I am remembered by some of you through my father, Czar Nicholas II and especially by those who rejected him. With that in mind and because there can be no forgiveness by some of you toward me, there can be no real peace among Russians as long as I am alive. That is why a few have tried to assassinate me today."

Anastasia spoke the words from her heart for she knew the truth of the matter. And, so did the gathering. They listened with guilt; they listened with the innocence of lost youth; then with patience and the understanding of wisdom as Anastasia finished her explanation to them.

"My two conditions are these, which I hope you will all accept," she went on. "First, to those who are still trying to kill me after all these years, this is the second assassination attempt that I have survived. It is enough for two lifetimes, let alone one. Whether you like it or not, I will not fail the Russian people - and to guarantee that - I will hold the throne for one year only - one holy and prayerful year - to be dedicated to all of Russia so that it may heal,

Secret of Ekaterinburg: The Hour-Glass

prosper and grow.

"The holy mother has told us in her prayers that Russia must be converted and when that event occurs, the end will be near for all of us on this earth as we know it. However, that time is now for many who are near death; they will not have to wait much longer. For them, there will be life after death, eternally with our mother and with God. To that end, I will be seated on the throne for one year. Then, I will relinquish it to a successor that none of you know exists, except, the Holy Mother, myself and God. That person is . . . it is . . . my living daughter, Anastasia II, who was born to me thirty-five years ago, and now living in St. Petersburg. Only now, am I able to announce this secret and deliver it to you. Only now, can I show her to you," she gestured pointing to her left where a mysterious but beautiful young woman was now standing beside President Yakov Grachev Solotzin.

Her resemblance to Anastasia was uncanny. It was as though someone had tipped the hourglass of time over and started it over again. The mysterious woman moved forward under the protection of the Russian FSS. Her long auburn hair floated in the breeze and the sunlight caught the glint of her deep blue eyes,

Secret of Ekaterinburg: The Hour-Glass

bluer than any Siberian sky. She was the absolute reincarnation of the much-remembered Princess Anastasia of 1918.

"Her name is Anastasia Nicholaevna Romanov Boscov - daughter of Sergei Boscov, a former Russian Air Force Commander. She is the main reason for taking on this fundamental responsibility and she is here beside me, my heir and your heir to the throne. I introduce to you and the entire world . . . Anastasia Nicholaevna Romanov II."

The crowd nearly rushed toward the wall nearly out-of-control. Anastasia not only was alive, but she had given birth to a daughter, a direct bloodline heir to the throne.

Surely, for those who still hated her and what she might have stood for nearly eighty years ago, they surely could not hate an innocent, Anastasia II.

It was truly a historical moment for all Russians. Beside her, was the man most responsible for this, the man to whom she had confided most in all these years, the man who had rescued her from the death heap of bodies outside Ekaterinburg, the man who for most of those eighty years had hidden her and had given her the means and the ability to be moved from country-to-country, and finally to the

Secret of Ekaterinburg: The Hour-Glass

United States where no one would suspect she survived.

That man was Yakov Solotzin Grachev, both her would-be murderer and her final savior.

Alex knew him well. He was the secret man the CIA had long-held in abeyance in the inner circles of the Kremlin with Andre. He and Andre had reported everything to the Central Intelligence Agency throughout the cold war. They were the ones who had provided the most accurate information to them. They were the most trusted double-agents of all time, ones the CIA could not have recruited on their own, but rather they would be willing accomplices on their own passing along secrets of a menacing Soviet Union to the Americans.

Thank God, the U.S. had someone like them in place during the many crises over the years including the Berlin Blockade, Korea, the Cuban Missile Crisis and the Bay of Pigs.

Grachev, Andre and Sergei.

Alex knew in an instant, the final secret that Artie and he could not figure out. The three were the troika that Jenkins had spoken about.

The perfect Troika. Like Russia herself, they were the riddle wrapped in an enigma just as Winston Churchill described some forty-five

Secret of Ekaterinburg: The Hour-Glass

earlier.

Now, the three were together again standing atop the Kremlin Wall waving to the millions assembled to honor them.

Anastasia stood silent for a moment and let her daughter take it all in. She was so beautiful and important . . . as was her mother in her youth.

She motioned to Alex, her trusted CIA friend, that she was in much pain, and needed to be helped from the podium.

Both, he and a Russian FSS officer carefully removed her from the podium and laid her upon a stretcher. They would take her to a nearby hospital for treatment but before they could lift her, Anastasia called out to Alex.

He was old enough to remember most of the myths written about her. Anastasia had been a symbol throughout the cold war years, a mysterious symbol whose legend had been told-and-retold countless times about her possible survival. That somehow miraculously, she had escaped the death squad on that fateful morning in the basement of the Ipatiev House. The rumors had refused to die. And, Anastasia had also refused to die.

Grachev had guaranteed that. He had come to her final rescue and that was a miracle in

Secret of Ekaterinburg: The Hour-Glass

itself.

It was he who had talked with her as a small child in the gardens of the St. Petersburg Palace. Yakov, the young gardener had grown to know her and, finally, in the end, protect her at that moment of destiny at his own hands. When she had been four, he had told her always to believe in the future, her faith, and that the Mother of God, would never let her down. Grachev, who had become the consummate communist ideologue, was the one who had instructed the servants to dress the princesses in their jeweled corsets and bed clothing that ultimately had saved her.

Anastasia whispered something to Alex. He leaned closer to the stretcher.

"Protect my daughter and Our Mother will protect you and all of mankind," she whispered placing her hand on his.

"Yes. You have my promise," Alex answered quietly. "And, you have the gratitude of the United States. I tell you that from the President of the United States. And, there is something else you need to know. I, too, am a believer. What the KGB didn't fathom was that there were many believers in the CIA, too. And, now there are many believers in the new FSS, yes?"

Secret of Ekaterinburg: The Hour-Glass

Anastasia gripped his hand tightly and smiled.

She closed her eyes.

Secret of Ekaterinburg: The Hour-Glass

CHAPTER 56

The White House, Dec., 1989

The President marched into the Oval Office with his aides in hot pursuit.

"Christ, Dan did you see that on world news?" the President snapped to his top aide and the others scrambling to join him. "Did you see the reaction of the Russian people? And, the reaction of our people to Anastasia including our involvement with the FSS?"

"Uhhh . . . . yeah, it was great wasn't it? To think that you had a hand in shaping Russia and the history of the world . . . that's something fantastic, isn't it?"

"It sure as hell is. Get me Alex on the Moscow line. I want to speak to him directly over a secure phone. If he's not at OPS, try to get him on a secure cell phone, right away. There's something I need to tell him."

The aide rushed from the room and returned within a minute with a cell phone in tow and one of the Oval Office secretaries hurrying behind connecting him to the main speaker

Secret of Ekaterinburg: The Hour-Glass

phone so everyone would be able to hear.

The phone rang at Alex's apartment in Moscow.

There was no answer after four rings and the president motioned the secretary to disconnect. With another motion, she spontaneously dialed the cell phone that Alex carried on him at all times.

The call rang twice and Alex's voice could be heard on the other end of a hissy connection, but overall, the connection was good. Those U.S. communications satellites were indeed a marvel of science.

"Alex, the whole world was watching. The people's reaction here has been incredible. Our phone banks have been jammed all day long. You did one hell-of-a-job over there. How's Anastasia? Is she going to be all right?"

"Yes, Mr. President. She is going to be all right thanks to CIA technology. But, it was a close call. She's going to remain in the hospital for a few days, then Sergei and she are going off someplace to collect themselves, and present themselves to the Russian people in a few weeks."

Alex's voice began to garble as the communications satellite coasted over the horizon and another one loomed up in its place

Secret of Ekaterinburg: The Hour-Glass

to take over the uplink-relay to the White House.

"Alex, I'm losing you. . . wait a minute, you're back.
Go ahead. What about Anastasia's daughter? How do you think they accepted her? No one even knew Anastasia was alive, no less her daughter who will take the throne after her?"

"They are taking it quite joyously. . . I'd say overwhelmingly . . . I mean, you had to be here to believe it. The Russians are delirious. It's like the last piece of a long-forgotten puzzle has fallen into place for them."

"You should be proud of the hand you had in all this, Alex. When you get back, they'll be an apt reward for your part."

"Thank you Mr. President. But, you know I'm awfully close to retirement and Rita will probably not want anything too extravagant, if you know what I mean. We've got two kids to finish educating though. I hope what you have in mind for me doesn't interfere with that."

Alex could have some balls every now and then to challenge the President like that in front of everybody, but that's the way he was. That's who he was, and the President didn't mind as long as he got the job done.

The President motioned for the others to

Secret of Ekaterinburg: The Hour-Glass

leave the room. He wanted to say this in private.

"Look, Alex. I owe my political career to you. You've made the difference in terms of me going down in history a winner instead of a loser in foreign affairs. But, even larger than that, you've performed an invaluable service to America herself. By moving Russia toward a democratic government, they and we will forever be grateful that we can now live in peace and harmony with each other and with other partners in the world. A safe, solid, secure Russia means a safe, solid secure United States in what we can still call the Free World. It means fewer nuclear weapons for everyone concerned and someday, perhaps, the elimination of them all. We owe it to future generations, don't we? Isn't that what Ronald Reagan meant?"

"Yessir," came the quick reply. "That's why I've been working all my life in the military and intelligence circles. Everyone needs to be secure, don't they?"

"Yes," the President responded.

"It will take more time to get the other, smaller nations who are developing nuclear weapons to go along with us but it can be done. It will take some time, but there is no

Secret of Ekaterinburg: The Hour-Glass

alternative if the world is to survive as we know it in the future, is there?"

"No, Mr. President. There isn't." Alex replied.

The president reached over to his desk and pressed a button on his telephone which connected him to the secure hotline at the Kremlin.

At that very moment in Moscow, Russian President Solotzin was standing in the Kremlin equivalent of the Oval Office - the White Circle - and picked up the phone.

Solotzin recognized the president's voice immediately.

"Tell Sergei and Andre that the United States and all the people of Russia are indebted to their heroism over the years and that the United States will never forget they are not only Russian heroes but American heroes as well."

"Yes, Ned, he is listening to you speak right now."

The President was glad Andre was present. He would share that with Sergei.

"Look, I cannot stay on. This phone is to be used for emergency conversations and when both our intelligence services know the line is being used, they get a little "frantic," Yakov. We can appreciate that, right? Remember, no

Secret of Ekaterinburg: The Hour-Glass

matter how it looks on the news to you over there, I'm trying not to take too much credit for all of this, but it's difficult not to. The damned news media is relentless on picking out their heroes, and I guess I'll be one of them. But, I'll direct enough attention to you. We're in this together? I suppose it's the same over there."

"Indeed, Mr. President. The Russian press has been all over us these past few days," Solotzin remarked. "Good-bye, and good luck, Alex. See you in Moscow sometime, eh?"

"Thank you, Yakov."

The president clicked off the line and turned to Alex still on the other line.

"I've got to call Rita and tell her I'm on my way back. She's been wondering where I've been for the past month," Alex quipped.

"Well, she's probably seen you on television."

"Yeah, but she's never sure how long I am in one place."

"Right. See you when you return."

Alex dialed his cell-phone and waited for Sergei to answer on the other end. Sergei answered it at his desk.

"Sergei, there's one thing I don't understand about all this. How did you learn about Anastasia being alive during all those years

Secret of Ekaterinburg: The Hour-Glass

everyone believed she had been murdered?"

Sergei propped his feet up on his desk.

"It was Yakov Grachev Solotzin who told me. I hunted him down after the war. I discovered he had been in Kiev. Back then Grachev was a designated liquidator for Beria's communist NKVD and he had murdered his share of fellow Russians for the people's cause - always for the people's cause. But, before that, he knew Anastasia as a tiny child long before at St. Petersburg Palace. He was there in the Palatial gardens where he talked to her about her father. He was the one in the garden who used to console her whenever she got tired of playing. And, Grachev was the one who came to regard himself as a protector of her even though he despised the Czar. He knew what Lenin had planned for the entire family. But, he could not see any reason for the children to die at the hands of the Cheka death squads.

He somehow had to protect her and the others from that terrifying morning. If he could not smuggle them out alive, then he had to make them think they were dead.

Unfortunately, it didn't work, and Anastasia was the only one who was saved in the end. It was not totally his fault. He was given the

Secret of Ekaterinburg: The Hour-Glass

orders and he obeyed them, but tried to figure out a way to save a few of the children. But, because he had betrayed Beria and Lenin, he hid for decades in the Crimea, to escape Stalin's purges. He changed his identity and his appearance, and when it was safe to come out, he embarked on his ascent through the party ranks.

"That night, before the morning execution, Grachev instructed the governesses to dress the children in their jewel-ladened corsets and sleep-wear. Grachev felt that if he could save even one of them, then he might be able to redeem himself in the eyes of God," Sergei confessed.

"When the shooting started and execution squad panicked, the plan disintegrated into utter chaos ending up with them bayonetting the victims and bashing in heads with their rifle butts. Only Anastasia managed to live through all that. It truly was a miracle. But, when she lived with us on the dacha in the Urals, I didn't know her real identity. To me she was simply Ana, the adopted child like myself whom I later fell in love with. And, of course, you know the remaining details, Alex. That's the complete truth."

Alex knew it was the truth.

Secret of Ekaterinburg: The Hour-Glass

"Yes. We have proved this brutality beyond the shadow of a doubt and to the satisfaction of the entire international community that Anastasia did survive those awful murders. And, she has survived again. In fact, we have all survived in a way because of her, Sergei. We can be proud of that if nothing else."

"Agreed, my friend. Agreed."

Alex hung up the telephone with a sincere good-bye.

"Dos vyazee," Alex said in Russian.

"See you later," Sergei replied in American.

Secret of Ekaterinburg: The Hour-Glass

CHAPTER 57

Ekaterinburg, July 17, 1918

In the darkness of the early morning hours, Grachev motioned to the grave diggers to leave the bodies of the Czar's family where they had been dumped and lay mangled in a shallow pit. Blood still oozed from the gaping wounds on the bodies only a short distance away from the mining town. Impatient to be done with it, he barked orders for the others to leave the scene, except for a chosen few who would pour lime and acid over the bodies in an attempt to destroy any and all traces of the family. The men would then cover the mass grave with freshly dug earth which had been piled to one side of a thick tree line obscuring it from passersby.

Grachev studied them in detail, especially the one he had come to know as the beautiful Anastasia Nicholaevna.

He knew her well. Extremely well and had guided her throughout her excursions through the palace gardens where he had worked as a

Secret of Ekaterinburg: The Hour-Glass

gardener. It was there he used to read to her and discuss things at idle hours of play or at lunch.

"Ana" he used to call to her and she would always come running to him. She had grown to trust him. And her governess had also grown to trust the man she knew only as "Yakov", the thick stocky man wearing a heavy black mustache that twisted downward at the corners of the mouth. His dark brooding eyes trusted no one in return. He was unlike the other Bolsheviks who stood guard outside the Ipatiev House in the event the family had tried to flee into the night.

Yakov knew deep inside there would be no secret escape from that place. Only death awaited the Czar's family at the hands of Vladimir Ilyich Lenin - the kind of death that had been administered to thousands of others who tried to resist his iron rule. The black limousines, which transported the Cheka execution squads into the dreaded night, crept silently into the neighborhood of a known collaborator, and swiftly took the victim away to be dealt with in the only form of vengeance the communists knew - execution by firing squad, hatcheted to death or liquidated by strangulation. Thousands like this were taken,

Secret of Ekaterinburg: The Hour-Glass

never again to be seen by their families. Even their burial sites would remain undiscovered forever.

The Czar and his family would be executed in the same, secretive manner and no different than the rest of the traitors to the communist effort.

"Sas chvatchen," he commanded. "Hurry from here. All of you. I will personally take care of this myself with only the others I have assigned."

Grachev waited until he and only two guards were left.

But, as he waited for them to depart, he spotted something moving. Beneath Nicholas' body, arms spread out atop one of the children, Grachev detected a small movement. Tucked underneath was the body of Anastasia, the little princess he had cared for so much.

He knelt down by the Czar's body and with a great effort, pulled her from underneath it. He leaned closer to her auburn hair and felt a slight breath of air exit from her mouth. He placed his ear against her chest and heard a faint heartbeat.

"My God, she is alive," he said quietly to himself.

The two other guards moved toward

Secret of Ekaterinburg: The Hour-Glass

Grachev to help him position the bodies for burial, but he abruptly stopped them. He held up his hand.

"You will bury the others immediately. I will bury this one, myself. She died quickly in the arms of her father. It is fitting that she not be buried like the rest of them. She was his favorite. I will bury her myself. God will take no pity upon us unless she is buried properly."

The two Bolshevik guards did not question his authority. Their orders were to do whatever Grachev said and obey him as their unit commander in that area. He was one of Laventry Beria's hand-picked leaders and they knew better than to challenge anyone who was under his direct command.

"Yes, comrade sir," they replied obediently and picked up their shovels to begin covering the bodies with lime.

"When you are finished, carefully leave no trace of the dig. Report back to party headquarters for further orders. Speak to no one of this. Believe me, if you do, your lives will be shortened significantly. Revenge has a strange way of catching up with you and even though we are winning the fight today, who knows what tomorrow will bring. Repercussions can come from any direction.

Secret of Ekaterinburg: The Hour-Glass

Lenin will not live forever and neither will we. Do not doubt that for a moment. As far as you are concerned, you had no part in this and you do not remember any of it. Do you understand?"

The men began digging furiously immediately after Yakov finished his sentence. It was a macabre chore, but the ground was soft and they dug quickly.

Grachev picked up Anastasia and carried her swiftly to his car parked in the nearby muddy road.

He must get her to a doctor - a White Russian doctor who could be trusted. He knew of just such a doctor locally. Anastasia was bleeding from a shoulder wound, a gaping hole on her right where at least one bullet had entered, and another which had creased her right temple rendering her unconscious. But, she was still alive. Her governess had dressed Anastasia like Yakov had instructed, in the heaviest of all her bejeweled clothing, rubies, diamonds, and pearls, forming a full protective garment which encircled her vital organs. The clothing had helped save her from the fusillade of bullets. The jewels had caused the bullets to ricochet off the garments, deflecting away from her vital organs. The impact of the exploding

Secret of Ekaterinburg: The Hour-Glass

projectiles had knocked her from the arms of her mother, and thrown her to the floor before the others could fire at her. Like the other family members who fell, the execution squad thought she was already dead. But, she had been lucky. Nicholas had fallen on top of her trying to protect her. That accident of fate had saved her life. Beneath his body weight, she dared not move as she regained consciousness. She closed her eyes and waited for the fatal bayonet strike to come. But, it didn't. The next thing she heard was the comforting voice of Comrade Grachev, then she slid into unconsciousness.

Grachev knew the doctor who might be able to save her, but he had to get her away from there. He would devise a plan to smuggle her to safety, somewhere far away, perhaps a mountainous region. He could trust this doctor. He knew him. And, he owed him a favor. Many owed him favors.

Grachev knew of a perfect hiding place. It was where he had grown up - the consummate hiding place. A dacha. A small farm in the Urals where families toiled alongside other families and where the revolution had failed to take root. Sergei's family.

He would take her there to safety far away

Secret of Ekaterinburg: The Hour-Glass

from the murders and where she could begin a new life.

In time, she would remember nothing about her own family. Only he and this new family would know who she was and where she would be.

He took this risk so Anastasia might live. A risk of his life for her life. He had never intended Anastasia to die.

He remembered the story that Anastasia had taught him years ago as he carried her to the black vehicle. It would be his turn to turn over the hour-glass. Anastasia was a mere grain of precious Russian sand which had to be saved to become a link to the past forever.

And, it didn't matter what the others would think of his actions if caught. His own spirit was already lifeless at having served so well in Lenin's cause.

No matter. They might all be dead in a short while anyway?

Grachev knew well the treachery of revolutions and what unpromising futures heralded their originators.

Secret of Ekaterinburg: The Hour-Glass

CHAPTER 58

The Oval Office, Christmas Eve, two years later, 1991.

Ned asked Kathryn to send in Alex and Kasim from the outer waiting room.

Both had been highly instrumental in seeing that Anastasia was returned safely to Russia. Yakov and the Russian people had been grateful for that.

The president was also deeply indebted to them for their exemplary efforts to maximize the security of the United States including the deliverance of the RDS-7 weapon systems for destruction.

Russia had been stabilized. The Middle East had been stabilized. And, in turn, the security of the United States, Israel and all of Europe had been preserved.

Everything seemed too good to be true.

But, no one could hold permanent sway over the future. So, now there wasn't much left to do but tie-up some loose ends on the international front letting the diplomats do the rest.

Secret of Ekaterinburg: The Hour-Glass

If Ned had learned anything as President during the past four years, it was better to let "them" attend to the diplomatic language and protocol.

"Come in fellows and have a drink," the President said getting up from his chair reaching for a hidden canister of Scotch-whiskey. Ned knew they were both Scotch drinkers, and he didn't have to coax them. They were both relaxed and comfortable on the huge couch the President had just installed near the Lincoln desk that had been a fixture in the Oval Office for more than a century-and-a-third.

Besides, it was tradition, CIA tradition after things had been wrapped up, to have a drink in the Oval Office after the successful completion of one of the most bizarre, but complex missions ever undertaken to influence world events.

Not only had the CIA program been one hundred percent successful, it had been performed with the unprecedented cooperation of the Russian Federal Security Service.

It proved that with a lot of ingenuity, American and Russian foreign policy could successfully transform nations and bring them into "a new world alignment" - the alignment

Secret of Ekaterinburg: The Hour-Glass

his predecessor's had talked about prior to the Persian Gulf War.

And, not a moment too soon.

"Alex? Anastasia's final moments? How were they?"

"Peaceful and serene, sir."

"I'm glad she didn't suffer."

"Same here, sir. I was with her during the last few moments she spent on earth . . . along with Sergei. It was a sad moment . . . especially for him . . . and a very sad moment in Russian history."

"I'm sure it was terrible for him . . . he had a great love for her . . . you, of course, delivered my condolences to Andre as well. They managed to carry out their end of the bargain supremely well, didn't they?"

"Yes, sir, they did," the CIA chief spoke up. The President continued, "They spent over fifty years in the hierarchy of the Kremlin working for the Central Intelligence Agency. Sometimes, what people don't know won't hurt them?" Kasim remarked.

"Sometimes. That was Andre's favorite expression only he applied it to the Soviet people. It clearly applied to both sides," Alex said.

"He was right," said the president. "None of

Secret of Ekaterinburg: The Hour-Glass

the Kremlin leaders ever realized she was alive and hidden in the United States. Oh, the rumors persisted, didn't they? From time-to-time, news agencies would follow those rumors to numerous well-planned dead-ends, attempting to verify them or even find her, but the counter-intelligence campaigns were more than enough to throw them-off - like the Anna Anderson campaign, just some crazy woman with a mental illness, an unlikely imposter, just a grandiose, strange attempt by a lost soul from Poland who had spent time in a German insane asylum who liked to fantasize about herself being the fabled Princess Anastasia. Not only was she fantasizing, she didn't know how right she was? Nobody ever knew about the second Ana, the real Anastasia" the CIA chief went on.

"Anyway, Anna Anderson died on Feb. 12, 1984, of pneumonia nearly penniless and forgotten, almost like they had found her in Berlin. Her real name was Franziska Schanzkowska, born in West Prussia . . . Poland . . . in 1896. A shame in a way. Her unique masquerade made our job easier."

"Alex, exactly when did the CIA learn about Anastasia's existence?"

"It was shortly after the war, when thousands of refugees were fleeing central

Secret of Ekaterinburg: The Hour-Glass

Europe into Germany. Back then, we were called the OSS assigned to Berlin, cleaning up the mess left behind by the Nazis. One night, an army intelligence officer came barging into headquarters with a tale so bizarre that it made my hair stand on end. He told us that a Czechoslovakian girl and a young Russian man had contacted them in an attempt to reach the western lines. They confided to us that she was an important person that the communists were searching for to execute because of her activities in the Czech underground. They brought her to Berlin and my boss's superiors completely unwrapped that phase of her identity. I mean, to say they completely fell-off their intelligence-stools would be a dramatic understatement. To say they had the intelligence coup of the century was closer to the truth. With all the Nazis being rounded up, the likes of Goering, the hunt for Martin Bormann, and all the rest of them; it was easy to hide a lost, lonely, refugee named Ana. No one had a clue to her existence, nor had they even suspected it. Everyone during the previous thirty years had believed she was dead. And, she was, along with her family, as far as all mankind was concerned. But, I and a few precious others knew, that Anastasia had

Secret of Ekaterinburg: The Hour-Glass

survived her own personal holocaust."

The president interrupted.

"Yes, and every subsequent president of the United States, except me, had never known about the existence of Ana, Sergei and Andre. And, to really make it all both plausible and believable, Andre became a member of the inner-circle of the politburo, a close aide to six Russian premiers and helped lead his country's march toward democracy while in the employ of the CIA. Quite a thrilling moment in the history of intelligence work, wouldn't you say, Alex?"

"Yes. By the way," the President interjected, "whatever happened to those two London Times reporters in Stockholm – Rick and Adrienne Waite? How close did they get to figuring out what was going on?"

"Well, we got them to take the bait here at the White House and over there, but they kind of got lost in the shuffle, if you know what I mean," Alex said. "They only got enough information from us to throw them off track over there. Once, they met in Stockholm, we made sure the trail went cold for them. They never got the story on the Israelis sub attack and we sure as hell ain't going to tell 'em."

"Oh, well. That's the way the intelligence

Secret of Ekaterinburg: The Hour-Glass

game goes. I guess you could say they missed that part of the story?" the President chimed in. All-in-all, you use them when you need them. This time we didn't need them."

Choked with passion, Alex could hardly get the words out. "Yes, Mr. President. Can you imagine, a top Kremlin leader - a spy for the United States CIA? It is an unbelievable account, isn't it?"

"Only a trusted handful knew about it. A Siberian family from the Urals and an impoverished Czechoslovakian family who conspired to take care of Anastasia Nichoalaevna Romanov. It truly was a miracle. And, it finally closes a chapter in a book that nobody ever knew existed. Yakov was a trusted friend of the Russian royal family until the communists got hold of him. He really didn't want to carry out the execution; he was forced to do it. His real name was Yakov Grachev. He later changed his name to Yakov Solotzin and the party over time forgot who he was; they didn't recognize him after he returned from 10 years of exile in the Crimea. Knowing this, he worked his way back into the communist hierarchy. History is a funny thing. It's a thing that is created by individuals. Yakov created a new history for himself and Anastasia."

Secret of Ekaterinburg: The Hour-Glass

"Isn't it ironic that after what she had been through, that in the end, it was a stroke that finally killed her? That's what Lenin died from, too. An odd coincidence. What were her final words?"

"She spoke to Sergei from her deathbed and told him that she loved him . . . that life had been unfair to the both of them . . . but in the end they were finally together again . . . . thankfully, death came peacefully to her. Sergei held her until she drew her last breath. Her dream to reunite was fulfilled like some prophecy. She also told Sergei that the hour-glass was full again. Do you know what she meant, Mr. President?"

"Yes, I think so. It's her legacy . . . the story of Anastasia, Czar Nicholas II, Yakov Grachev Solotzin, Sergei and Andre . . . and now her daughter Anastasia II will reign for decades to come. Most importantly, it's the continuation of life for those in Russia who want to live it. They are the grains of sand that sift through the hour-glass and those grains of sand represent people and time and they must never run out."

The president was still for a moment.

"Tell, me Alex. You're our top analyst here. What happens when we need you again?"

"Please tell me you won't. My wife and I

Secret of Ekaterinburg: The Hour-Glass

would like to spend some quiet time together, someplace where we won't be bothered for a long while."

"Yes, I'm sure. And, quite frankly, you both deserve that. We'll promise to leave you alone for a while – at least until the next crisis comes along. See you in a few months?"

The three laughed and shared a final toast.

Alex and Kasim had been loyal men to the president during the past four years and even more loyal to the United States for a longer time before that.

"By the way Mr. President, what happens if Iran tries to use those defective nukes we transferred to them?" Alex asked without warning.

The President paused, then countered, "Well, if they do, they'll nuke themselves into oblivion . . . it'll be one great big glass parking lot, if you know what I mean?"

Alex did.

He knew there was precedent for such covert actions by the United States. It had been done before in the Reagan Administration – the Iran Contra arms deal for hostages with money funneled to the Contras; and the Bay of Pigs Invasion botched by Kennedy – all performed under the auspices of the CIA's explanation of

Secret of Ekaterinburg: The Hour-Glass

"plausible deniability."

But, Alex also knew that America needed men like these. They were no different than Samuel Adams and the tea party activists against the British in the American Revolution. You do what you have to do for your country.

And, besides, these men needed America.

What's more, Russia needed them, too.

The President raised his glass with a twinkle in his eye.

"Merry Christmas to the United States of America, Russia and Israel."

"To Anastasia and the hour-glass," they replied.

THE END

Secret of Ekaterinburg: The Hour-Glass

Map of the Bering Sea and Bering Strait

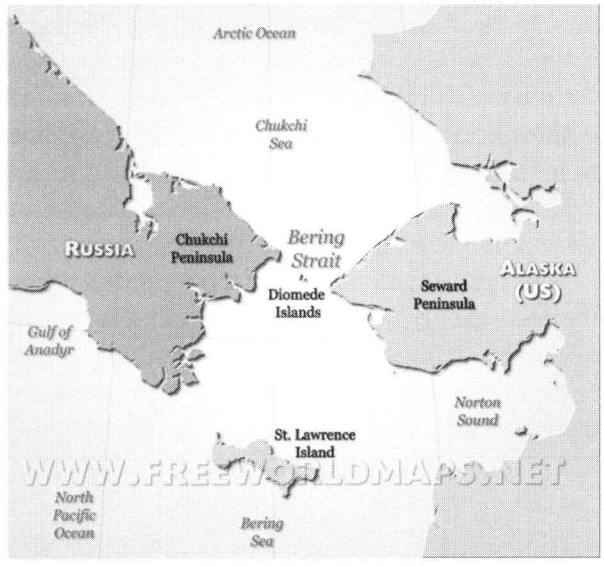

Photo Courtesy of Free World Maps.Net

Secret of Ekaterinburg: The Hour-Glass

About The Author

Robert Spirko is a graduate of the Kent State University School of Journalism and studied for his MBA at the same school. Now, a full time author, he was previously a Middle East analyst and owned his own investment advisory firm near Cleveland, Ohio, predicting the wars in the Middle East including the recent Libyan intervention.

His remarkable ability to forecast events before they occur has been described as truly uncanny by his friends and acquaintances. His predictions about a coming war with Iran are dire unless steps are taken to neutralize Iran's drive for nuclear weapons and missiles that can threaten Israel and the United States, as well as Russia, Great Britain, all of Europe, and the Middle East region as a whole.

"The nuclear option for Iran must be stopped. Iran's leadership must understand the continuing march toward weapons of mass destruction and terrorism against nations who wish to live in peace will end in the complete destruction of that nation and others like it."

Time is running out in the hour-glass.

Secret of Ekaterinburg: The Hour-Glass

REVIEWS

"A riveting, suspenseful tale of what happened to Anastasia, the lost Russian princess, wrapped in an intriguing saga of intelligence-espionage, engaging elements of Russia, the United States and the Middle East." - A FORMER CIA AGENT.

"A spine-chilling tale about Russia and the internal workings of early Leninists and Stalinists and how they came to the realization that the Soviet system was doomed from the very beginning." - A FORMER KGB OFFICER.

"A scintillating spy-thriller in the style of John LeCarre destined to become one of the best spy tales of the 21st Century." - A NEW YORK BOOK SELLER.

Secret of Ekaterinburg: The Hour-Glass

"An extraordinary analysis of what's coming in relation to Iran, Russia, the United States and Israel. If war proves inevitable, then we are all aboard the doomsday bus." - OLIVE GROVE BOOKS

Secret of Ekaterinburg: The Hour-Glass

An exciting masterpiece of epic proportions!

An inside peek at the secret workings of the White House! A superb, first-rate spy-thriller

A taste of the exotic covert operations that only the CIA and NSA could pull-off working with Russian Intelligence!

An inside look into the minds of secret agents before the world knew there were secret agents.